FORGOTTEN REALMS®

THE ELMINSTER SERIES

Elminster
in Hell

ED GREENWOOD

ELMINSTER IN HELL
©2001 Wizards of the Coast, Inc.

Cover art by Matt Stawicki
Interior art by Sam Wood
First Printing: August 2001
Library of Congress Catalog Card Number: 00-190893

9 8 7 6 5 4 3 2 1

ISBN: 0-7869-1875-6
UK ISBN: 0-7869-2627-9
620-T21875

U.S., CANADA,
ASIA, PACIFIC, & LATIN AMERICA
Wizards of the Coast, Inc.
P.O. Box 707
Renton, WA 98057-0707
+1-800-324-6496

EUROPEAN HEADQUARTERS
Wizards of the Coast, Belgium
P.B. 2031
2600 Berchem
Belgium
+32-70-23-32-77

Visit our website at **www.wizards.com/forgottenrealms**

FORGOTTEN REALMS®

Novels by Ed Greenwood

To Page and Mike
Because the most glorious adventures are those shared.
Let yours be one of the long and wondrous ones.

Let it be known: The wisdom and skill of Rob King
made this tale far brighter and better
than it could otherwise have been.

REALMS LORE

Is there not Hell enough awaiting you, that you must go seeking it in books and spells and consorting with strange wizards?

Resaugiir Ravendarr, a rich
mechant of Amn,
speaking to his daughter Daluthra in the play
Bold Hearts Broken *by Nargustarus Grithym*
(playwright of Athkatla)

confutatis maledictus, flammis acribus addictus

etiam sanato vulnere cicatrix manet

Students of the history of the Realms should know that this tale of Elminster's torment befalls in 1372 DR, the Year of Wild Magic, and that the memories seen in these pages depict events that took place, so far as can be determined, as follows:

• "The Day the Magic Died" (and the associated memories preceding it, in Chapter 2, except for Khelben's flying over Waterdeep, which befell in 1351 DR) in mid-Kythorn of 1358 DR, the Year of Shadows.

- "The Reaching Hand" (the memory in Chapter 4) on 17 Marpenoth in 1357 DR, the Year of the Prince.
- "Here Be Wizards" (the memory in Chapter 5) in Alturiak of 1365 DR, the Year of the Sword.
- "One Night in Waterdeep" (the memory of Mirt in Chapter 6) on 6 Eleint in 1321 DR, the Year of Chains.
- "Night Comes to Tamaeril" (the first memory in Chapter 7), "Resengar, Too" (the second memory in Chapter 7), and "A Daughter's Duty" (the memory in Chapter 9) in early Flamerule of 1355 DR, the Year of the Harp.
- "A Surprise for Laurlaethee" (the memory in the midst of Chapter 8) in the afternoon of 4 Tarsakh in 261 DR, the Year of Soaring Stars.
- "A Touch of Heartsteel" (the memory in Chapter 11) in early Mirtul of 1369 DR, the Year of the Gauntlet.
- "The Harper Without" on the night of 12 Uktar in 778 DR, the Year of Awaiting Webs.
- "When Sembians Stop for Tea" (the memory in Chapter 13) on the afternoon of the 4th of Elesias in 1364 DR, the Year of the Wave (it should be noted that Nouméa Fairbright is no relation to Nouméa Drathchuld, who was then Magister).
- "A Small Sort of Dragon" (the memory in Chapter 14) on 16 Ches in 1356 DR, the Year of the Worm.
- "The Wisdom of Our Sages" (the memory in Chapter 15) in late Mirtul of 1360 DR, the Year of the Turret.
- "Sit Not Alone on Thalon's Cold Throne" (the memories of Laeral at the end of Chapter 16 and the beginning of Chapter 17) in mid-Kythorn of 1357 DR, the Year of the Prince (it should be remembered that this Laeral is Laeral Rythkyn, called by some "Laeral of Loudwater," a Harper mage who is the namesake—not related—of Laeral Arunsun Silverhand of the Seven).
- "The Tears of a Goddess" (the memory at the end of Chapter 19) in late Eleint of 1371 DR, the Year of the Unstrung Harp.
- "The Srinshee Plays With Fire" (the first Srinshee memory in Chapter 20) on the morning of 9 Nightal in 241 DR, the Year of the Hippogriff's Folly.

- "Kisses and Damnations" (the second Srinshee memory in Chapter 20) in the early evening of Midsummer 30th in 666 DR, the Year of Stern Judgment.
- "One Fool Deserves Another" (the third Srinshee memory in Chapter 20) on 14 Hammer in 907 DR, the Year of Waiting.
- "The Coming of the Shadow" (the memory at the end of Chapter 21) on 6 Flamerule in 1294 DR, the Year of the Deep Moon.
- "Fools as Her Champions" (the memory in Chapter 22) on 21 Eleint in 1246 DR, the Year of Burning Steel.

BEGINNINGS

Memories are wonderful things.

Yet they can burn like the hottest fire, raging and consuming their bearers, or cut like cruel blades. I can trap one in a gem and hold it in my hand to give to another and yet keep it also in my mind, fading slowly over time, like paths to favorite places that have become overgrown and lost.

What is a human but a bundle of memories?

What better treasure can the aged keep to warm and delight them whenever they rummage through the sack of their own stored remembrances?

And what more hideous crime can there be than to snatch away memories from a man?

Only my kisses should be able to do that to him—and then only when Mystra deems it needful. Yet a *thing* called Nergal dared to do this to my man. I, Alassra, made Nergal pay a fitting price and was damned in that doing—and care not and would do it again.

I dare anything and will die doing so. Fools of Thay and other places know me for my slaying spells and my fury. Often it masters me, and men call me "mad," when they should use the words "reckless" or "lost in bloodlust." I *do* enjoy destruction, I admit—yet I also nurture and defend and treat with kindness.

Here I've done both, showing all who read of the kindnesses I so love, the reason I'd lay down my life as freely as I do my body before this man called Elminster, even if he had no more magic than a village idiot. Some will say I've set down secrets that common eyes should never have seen, and to them I say two things: "Have I truly?" and "I care not!" Some have said holy Mystra and others of the divine will smite me for this doing—yet here I still stand, unrepentant.

So come, and read secrets. Heed this tale I have gathered, and learn—or care not, and turn away, to walk defenseless the rest of your undoubtedly short days. Choose freely.

I am the Storm Queen, and I never threaten. I merely promise.

One

ROCKS AND A WARM PLACE

There is no greater blasphemy than this.

This is the thing forbidden, for all gods and men, for every living being of this or any world—to shred asunder the stuff of which we are all made, leaving rents of crawling nothingness in Toril. Roiling, weeping wounds for all the Realms to spill out through, and all the cold and gnawing void to rush in. . . .

With all the selfish and headstrong and uncaring fools who'd hurled magic about for all these centuries, it was a wonder this didn't happen more often. This thought offered little comfort.

The worlds roared. White-hot and all-devouring, the torrents of force spilling from the Weave snarled all around the tumbling man, tugging at his robes and old limbs and beard alike as he spun along in a roaring rush of air. What might have been the green trees of Shadowdale turned crazily above his head. Beneath—or was it above?—his booted feet stretched a blood-red, sunless sky. He'd seen it a time or two before and had no desire ever to see again.

Streamers of noxious gas streaked that crimson dome like dirty clouds. They whirled to form what looked like giant eyes staring down, eyes that were swept away before they could focus, only to form anew, again and again. Beneath the ruby glow lay a dark night-mare land of bare rock and flumes of sparks and gouting flame, where things slithered and scrambled half-seen in the shadows. Mountains clawed the ruby sky. The Land of Teeth, Azuth had once aptly called it, surveying the endless jagged rocks. This was the Greeting Ground, the realm of horror that had claimed the lives of countless mortals. He was whirling along above Avernus, uppermost of the Nine Hells.

"Mystra," the tumbling man groaned. He called to life all the magics on his body, bringing them to tingling readiness in his fingertips.

Whether the Lady of the Weave heard and assisted him or not, life ahead was not going to be pleasant for Elminster Aumar. He was going to have to spend all of his magic healing this rift, for the love of Toril that so seldom loved him, be burned and blasted in the doing, per-haps fail and be torn apart—and if he succeeded, plunge at the last down into Avernus, bereft of spells and defenseless.

Yet his duty was clear.

Dark, bat-winged shapes were already soaring aloft, beating their menacing way toward him, seeking to plunge through the rift or tear it open farther, ere he could close it. The rift could be closed only from this side, not from the more pleasant skies of Toril—and if he were to do it at all, he would spend his magic so swiftly that he could not help making himself a bright beacon to all infernal eyes.

Those eyes were watching. Oh, yes.

Elminster saw something huge and dark and dragon-winged rise from a distant mountain, spreading leathery wings and trailing a long, long scaly tail as it rose ponderously into the sky of blood. Rose, and turned his way . . .

Nearer at hand, lightning cracked and stabbed out of the edges of the rift. Glistening black devils struggled to pluck it farther open . . . struggling, no doubt, under orders from unseen devils below.

The hurtling wizard saw the blue sky of Toril one last time. A mighty crash of lightning thrust blinding-bright talons through devils. Sleek obsidian and crimson bodies twisted in pain as they burned, their blood blazing up in red flames even as their scorched ashes fell to the uncaring rocks below.

"To Hell with ye all," Elminster murmured sardonically. He closed his hands into fists and drew forth the silver fire within him, as small and precise an unleashing of it as he could manage. When the rift closed, he'd almost certainly lose touch with the Weave and Mystra and be unable to regain magical power. Silver fire consumed the rings and bracers and even the vestments he wore.

Strange singings and snarlings filled his ears as enchantments dissolved, flowing through him to spin in glowing blue-white flames around his hands. The racing fires of his magics hummed with comforting power as they crackled, spat, and grew stronger. The Old Mage's clothes became tatters. Ancient metal bands around his fingers fell away in dust and were gone. His hat burst into a blue flame that sank down into his long tresses. He called in its power. A dagger in one boot crumbled, then the boot itself. He said a fond mental farewell to his favorite pipe ere it fell into ash. In its last tumbling moments El spent tiny bolts of his precious magic to guide his fall, turning in the air to swoop back to the rift.

The scar was growing, spitting vicious lightning in all directions across the dark sky of Avernus. Bolts arced across the bloody vault like so many angry stars streaking to fading falls. Far below, many red, glistening eyes looked upward at the deadly splendor.

Lightning clawed the air nearby, and the gaunt old wizard sent forth blue fire from his fingertips to snare it, or some part of it, to turn that raging energy to his task.

The bolt plucked him from the sky like a gnat caught in a gale, whirling him away. His teeth chattered, his hair quivered on end, and the hoarse beginnings of a scream froze in his throat. Caught in its grip, Elminster of Shadowdale could not have moved even a finger. Fires charred him black. Surging, searing force flung his arms and legs rigid into a scorched star, and then threw him across the sky.

When he could see again, tiny lightnings streamed from his nose. The rift was a bright, distant fire in the red sky. Its flames were suddenly blotted out by a black and grinning form, horn-headed and bright-eyed, racing through the air with claws outstretched to rend stricken wizards.

"Tharguth," Elminster murmured, recalling an old grimoire's name for such devils—abishai, these were, for he saw a second and third swooping along in the wake of the first.

Then there was no more time to think; the abishai rushed at him like a striking hammer.

It tore at the air eagerly with its claws as it came, its poisonous tail curled up beneath it to stab if need be. Elminster looked into the devil's exulting eyes. He felt a rush of warmth and the vinegarlike tang of its hide as its jaws gaped wide. Its head turned on an angle to bite out his throat. He fed it fire, searing claws and head alike to nothingness in an instant and letting it tumble away into the rocky darkness below.

The second abishai was coming too fast to veer; El twisted away from one sky-raking claw and sent a tiny blue-white bolt of his magic into the howling mouth of the third winged devil. Its head exploded. Its racing body arched back and clawed the air in silent, spasmodic agony as it rushed past.

A flight spell was one of the few left to the Old Mage; fearful the magic roiling within him might twist and shatter it, he cast it with infinite care. Another tiny tithe of power gave him greater speed than the spell alone could furnish. He needed to get back to the rift, swiftly.

He did not need to look back or hear the snarls of rage to know that the second abishai had turned to come after him. The sky was full of tharguth now—black and green and even the larger, more cruel red abishai. Their eyes blazed like pairs of ruby flames as they rose to hunt him. Their cries of rage and glee rose into a roar that overtopped the thunder of the rent. It grew larger . . . and larger. . . .

Elminster Aumar was not the least of Mystra's Chosen, but neither was he a great and vigorous creature of battle. Like a tiny blue-white star, he raced across the sky of Avernus.

Dark red dragons glided now among the devils, biting and pouncing like great cats, preying hungrily on this flock of flying food. Little spike-studded gargoyle-devils, spinagons, were in the sky, too, darting and ducking aside from the tharguth. Looking back, El saw the abishai that pursued him gutted from belly to throat by something winged and hungry. It flew away almost faster than he could turn his head.

His gaze fell for a moment to the land below and its twisting ribbon of red that could only be a river of blood. His attention flicked up again to the swift beat of those elusive wings. The flying slayer was slowing to a halt, standing on air to watch him. Their eyes met.

El found himself looking into the eyes of a lone devil beating feathered wings in the sky. She was sleek and graceful and deadly, dusky-hued and more beautiful than any mortal woman: an erinyes, doubtless a spy for a greater devil dwelling deeper in the Nine Hells.

My, but he was popular. Avernus must furnish poor entertainment, for a lone human wizard to attract such interest.

Well, no. He set aside proud thoughts. It was undoubtedly the rift that was drawing the devils aloft.

El saw more bat wings tumbling helplessly across the sky, caught by more lightning bolts from the torrents of force where world met world and clawed at each other.

Another bolt rushed at him, and Elminster was ready. Spreading his hands, with magics crawling between them in a blue-white chain, he plunged into its raging heart. With a wordless shout, he drank in power until it rose hot and choking within him. He was forced to rear up out of its flow and into the ruby sky again, gasping and trembling.

He'd been driven back only a little way this time, and his limbs were blazing bright with energies. In the distance, winged devils tried to drink in the power of the bolt as he had done but plunged to their dooms as the bolts consumed them in brief gouts of red flame.

A dragon saw him and wheeled from its sport of tearing apart tharguth and devouring them. It came thundering down at him like a great wall of scaled flesh. It spat fire, the ravening flames that did so little to devils but could cook and doom a mortal man.

Elminster swooped and drank in that dragon fire, setting his teeth and grimly riding out the fierce but brief pain, quelling its heat with his own gathered magic.

Gasping, he prevailed. The Old Mage was full almost to bursting now. His body trembled with the effort of holding such force. He was no longer its vessel but its heart, wrestling with its surges and flows merely to move as he desired to and not be torn apart by its raging.

Or by draconic jaws. The great red dragon, thrice the size of any he'd seen on Toril—even old Larauthtor, who'd filled the sky like a moving mountain—swooped, fangs gaping.

Elminster threw his hands behind him and let tiny jets of flame spurt from his fingers, hurling him up, forward, and away—beyond the reach of even a frantically twisting wyrm.

It clawed wildly at the air in its haste to turn. Snapping its jaws vainly at him, the dragon flapped its great wings so hard that the air cracked like thunder. Caught in a trio of rift bolts, the wyrm stiffened, scales melting into smoke. It was too racked with pain even to scream as it died. Its eyes burst into flame and smoke that trailed from dark sockets and loosely flapping jaws. The wyrm fell away into the jagged darkness below.

None of this was getting Elminster back to the task of healing the widening rift, looming like a weeping eye in the sky of Avernus. Elminster called up a half-remembered snatch of a bawdy song as he banked on wings of his own spell flames. He raced, singing merrily but badly, to meet his doom.

Bolts stabbed out to meet him. He spun chains of snarling magic around them and dragged them around in roaring, sky-shaking arcs. They plunged back toward their source—a racing flood in which he joined. Falling headlong into the blinding brightness, he thrust his hands out before him.

All sound died away in the echoing roar. Elminster became a racing dart among mighty flows of force. They rolled ponderously past him, a great chaos of surges that battered and tore at him, threatening to whirl him away into bone-shattered, bloody pulp.

When searing force burnt away his fingertips, he sent forth spell-fire to cleave it and master it, plunging on to the roiling edge where Toril began. He plucked and swooped and wove, surfing surging torrents of force to knit the blue sky together again.

Devils screamed as they were torn apart or blasted to shreds somewhere behind him. Elminster scarcely heard them. He gazed hungrily at the world he must wall himself away from to save. He looked longingly down at Shadowdale, a little green gem far below, ere he flung himself across the sky, stitching its ragged edge in his wake with teeth-jarring, surging force.

"The bards could never find words for this," he gasped. Red sky and blue slipped and slid and battled for supremacy overhead. He raced along the raging line. Sickening force slammed through him like the sword that had once plunged down his throat and out his backside in one icy moment. . . .

Long ago, that had been, and with rather less hanging in the balance. A memory among far too many, always beckoning him for a wander among their shadows. The offers were more enticing as Elminster grew ever more tired—and weariness rode his shoulders like a heavy, clinging cloak these days. . . .

Suddenly he was done. Energies veered away to complete what he'd begun, reshaping what had been shattered and cloaking bright Toril from his view. The roar of the sky died, and he was falling, a dwindling star, into the deep ruby gloom of Avernus.

He'd done it. Dazed and exhausted, he knew that much. Toril was saved and his own doom sealed.

"Have my thanks, Great Elminster," he told himself with dark humor, toasting himself with an imaginary goblet as black fangs of rock rushed up to meet him. "Fair Faerûn has seen thy greatest victory—though none know it, or care. Welcome to the waiting dunghill."

With the last of his weary will, Elminster made himself into a lump of stone and hurled to one side, so that his fall would become a plunge deep into what was probably the Lake of Blood. Let its warm and fetid waters take his fall. The rotting flesh that cloaked its bed would hide him. Perhaps he could lie unnoticed there, until he had strength enough again to—

After such a fall, even a stone hits water as hard as a smith's hammer. His brutal shattering of the surface would have made Elminster gasp—if he'd had anything to gasp with. Warmth bubbled past as he sank, tumbling in the warm, wet depths, slowing now as . . .

Something dark and snakelike coiled out of the red depths and snatched him. The tentacle lashed around him with the searing bite of a drover's whip . . . and then he was being dragged back up again.

Well, in the Hells it was hardly to be expected that there'd be any rest for the wicked. So—let the torment begin. Mystra preserve and forfend. Please.

He was up out of the blood-water now, dripping. Unfamiliar magic raged around him, darting into him in little numbing jabs. He was changing, forced under its goads, flowing and unfolding and becoming . . . himself again, a human with arms and legs and—eyes.

Eyes that swam even as grunts and rending groans and a shrieking symphony of squeals told him he was growing ears. Then all at once, the world spun and shook and came to a halt, amid shocking clarity.

Elminster was standing on warm, sharp rock, and his feet were bare. He had feet, and legs . . . and his own old, gaunt body, even to the beard. He was standing in a little hollow in a great waste of rock, with foul streams of gas curling around him, burning his legs as they sighed past. Atop the rocks, bare, thorny branches of stunted trees stabbed like despairing fingers up into the blood-red sky. The ground trembled. From somewhere near at hand a flame shot up, raged briefly amid scorched rocks, and fell away out of sight again.

El became aware that something was standing in the deep shadow at the far end of the cleft. It strode forward, stepping around many teeth of rock. Flame-yellow eyes met his with the force of a striking serpent and held him in thrall as their owner advanced leisurely, giving Elminster a smile that was a long way from pleasant—and at the same time promised many things.

An eyebrow lifted, mirroring curving horns above, and a softly hissing voice asked almost gently, "Don't know me, little cringing wizard? I favor a more splendid shape, these days!"

Magic curled around Elminster's throat, choking any answer he might have wanted to make, and the devil's smile widened. "Like my gentle talons spell? Nothing to touch the great and mighty magics you're wont to hurl, of course, but it serves me . . . aye, it serves."

The horn-headed devil turned its head and smiled, those flame-yellow eyes still transfixing Elminster like the tines of a gigantic fork. "Still know me not, Old Mage? You *must* be tired."

Elminster gazed at the burly devil, wondering just when he'd become, in this unholy creature's eyes at least, any sort of expert on the diabolical.

His captor was a naked humanoid whose skin was seal-smooth and mottled gray, shot through with hues of brown and darker gray . . . very like the shadowed stones of Avernus that rose around them both.

A few scales glinted on the fiend's neck and ankles. Its humanlike head sported two curving horns. What had seemed at first glance to be a cloak drawn around the devil could now be clearly seen as a necklace of tentacles. One shot forth to curl around Elminster's bare shoulders, thrusting like a vengeful eel through tatters of drifting vapor—a good thirty feet or more—as the eyes that held Elminster's became a little redder.

"Know, then," the devil said with grotesque formality, sketching a little bow—and forcing, with his tentacle, the dazed and exhausted Old Mage to match it—"that you are the guest of Nergal, most mighty of the outcast lords of Hell." His smile broadened, and his eyes were now as red as old coals. "You may greet me."

El struggled to speak, finding his throat dry and stiff. Nergal's smile became a smug, crooked thing. "Body a mite rebellious, great wizard? How sad. You will already have noted that my poor and paltry magics have served to return you to your true shape, and you've already felt my gentle talons. They ensure that any magic you cast or unleash is drained to strengthen my bonds upon you—oh, you may see them not, but bound you are, and shall be for as long as it's my pleasure to keep you so. You're wrapped in spell bindings linked to my mind; you'll never escape me unnoticed."

Nergal's lips curled in a sneer as he added, "None have broken my mind yet, Elminster, though you're welcome to try. Attaining freedom is a laudable goal for any sentient being."

The ground trembled again, and a flame shot up over their heads, searing a squalling imp. Nergal's smile broadened as he withdrew his tentacle—and the shuddering of the rocks beneath Elminster's baking feet made him stagger and almost fall.

"Laudable," the devil added gloatingly, "but nigh impossible. You see, I've spent much time observing your exploits, Old Weirdbeard— and I have uses for you. Oh, yes."

The archdevil's tentacles were suddenly writhing above his shoulders, like the limbs of an excited and gigantic spider.

"You will, of course, attempt to escape, perhaps even to harm me. Such failures will make little difference to your torment—and they *will be* failures."

Tentacles stretched forth almost lazily, and a diabolical smile widened.

"You see: You're in *my* cozy little dale now, wizard."

And wearing that same welcoming smile, Nergal reached out with a tentacle and tore Elminster's right arm off.

Two

A DEVIL'S WARM MERCY

Nothing is more important than pain. Nothing. It sears and gnaws life itself, commanding all attention, thrusting even archmages into moaning despair.

This particular archmage was only dimly aware of anything more than his pain. Elminster knew he was staggering, trying vainly to clutch at his torn and burning shoulder as tentacles slapped and spun him with lazy glee. Gradually, he became aware of more. The tortured rocks of Avernus stood on all sides, stabbing up into the blood-red sky like the black fingers of corpses. Someone nearby was screaming—a raw, hoarse, and endless cry, a siren of agony amid Nergal's gusty laughter.

Sharp stones laid open El's feet. He barely felt that pain through the agony stabbing through him, leaving him sick and weak. Slowly, he realized something more. The screaming was coming from him.

"Sanity," the archdevil remarked casually, "lasts longer when some vocalization is permitted. It may be an overvalued condition in most expendable slaves, but I need yours to persist awhile longer. Sing, then."

Tentacles wriggled and plowed under human skin, burrowing. . . .

El stiffened, trying somehow to scream even harder as talons of pain transfixed him. His cry died as he choked and strangled on the blood that an outraged stomach spat forth.

"Not even a dagger drawn in defiance?" Nergal mocked. "Not one cantrip, cast to try to make me belch? *Such* great magecraft!"

El sagged to his knees, only to find that the tentacles around his legs kept him half-upright, sprawled limp and broken in midair well above the rocks. Tentacles tightened anew, and El's remaining arm snapped in three places.

Jagged bones jutted forth as El's arm was twisted crazily— bones that came at the Old Mage's swimming eyes like blood-drenched daggers as his captor forced El's limbs this way and that, playfully.

"Not even one feeble, flailing spell? Not a ring awakened against me?" The devil's taunt was accompanied by more sickening pain as the rings on El's remaining hand were wrenched off—along with the fingers that bore them. "You disappoint me, famous wizard. I expected more. Much more."

Retching, El never saw the tentacle that smashed his nose into bloody shards, or the one that slid across his chest, slicing open the skin like a razor. Suckers latched onto certain winking things of magic that Mystra had left in his flesh, centuries ago. They flared blindingly and made the devil hiss in pain and fear ere the tentacles hurled them away.

A blast shook the rocks under El's feet, and then another. Nergal laughed with something that might have been relief.

"Trinkets under your skin—my, what a valued slave you've been. I should be flattered, entertaining such importance. Even if it is old and feeble, and knock-naked, scarcely worth the effort of tormenting. Quivering like a lemure—and about as much sport."

Tentacles shook Elminster, and red eyes blazed. "*Look* at me, human—and heed!" Nergal bellowed. "I'm your doom, and worse. You're going to be my claw to tear open Faerûn, once I've prepared you properly. There're just a few more things to do first. I'll tear out all but a tuft of that beard, to leave me something to haul you around by, and tear away that which makes you a man—"

El screamed higher and harder, helplessly.

"Nergal am I, old fool, and a rightful Prince of Hell. So heed my words. I've few enough visitors who can appreciate proud speeches, so you're going to listen to my every word. My spells will keep you aware, no matter how much pain besets you—and I've had enough of your keening, faster than I'd thought I would. Wherefore, be still."

Elminster suddenly found himself silent, though his throat still rippled in midshriek, and his body trembled with its aching effort to spew forth blood.

Nergal gave him a merry smile. "*That's* better," the archdevil cooed, as if addressing a favorite child. He drew himself up, tentacles rising above him in a soaring, peacock flourish, and spoke like a king declaiming proudly from his throne:

"Outcast and exiled here, I am yet the mightiest of all—aye, o'ermatching even Tiamat the Many-Mawed—who call Avernus home. Too proud and too accomplished to serve the Reigning Serpent, but too mighty to be slain. Dispater is no greater than I, nor Baalzebul . . . and therefore I am useful. Some day, Asmodeus might have need of me."

Tentacles caressingly lifted their broken burden. Human skin fell away in strips as Nergal drew what was left of Elminster close, so their eyes stared into each other across a very small distance.

"And on that day," the gleeful outcast devil added in lower tones, "it will be my distinct pleasure to defy the lord of Nessus in his hour of need. Defy him with power enough to shatter his throne, and over his shrieking bones bring war to Hell. And you, little cringing human, shall be my way to some of the weapons I'll need."

Tentacles tightened, and El spat blood involuntarily.

"I—ugh! Uh! Aagh!" was all he managed to say, struggling for breath through the blood choking him. Then the moments allowed him were over. Silence settled icily over his throat again.

"I'm glad you agree so eagerly," Nergal purred. "Hearken and learn, little tool. I'm but one of those, both great and wretched, who lurk in the shadows of Avernus awaiting the day we all know will come. Archdevils may be slain, but it's not easy to destroy us forever. The lord of Nessus must burn away some of his power to bring about such a doom. He's done it, yes—but only in punishment for the most deadly doing that could be launched against him: archdevil lying with archdevil to have offspring they hide from Asmodeus, to bring to Hell an archdevil the Lord Below knew not."

Tentacles thrust Elminster down firmly on a spine of rock. Unyielding sharpness jabbed into raw flesh. Staring at the blood-drenched sky, El arched and writhed in silently screaming agony. A tentacle thoughtfully lifted his head so that he could look along his body . . . and see the bloody spire of rock standing amid a glistening welter of his organs. He stared at it, too racked with pain to cling to his frayed memory of Mystra's face.

Nergal loomed over his captive and explained almost merrily, as if telling a fancy tale to a child reluctant to drift off to sleep, "Lucifuge was but a puling thing when Asmodeus devoured him—literally, growing his teeth into fangs to do it. I saw."

Slithering tentacles plucked the Old Mage from the rock—gods, the tearing *pain!*—and held him aloft in front of Nergal's face once more. The archdevil's eyes were a bright flame-red now.

"He gave Lucifer and Batna the final doom for having that child," Nergal added excitedly, "executing them as Baalzebul, fiercest of Lucifer's foes, watched. Baalzebul he plucked from his palace and snatched across the Hells to hold in thrall—just to show us all that he could burn a prince and princess of Hell to nothing whilst he racked another prince, despite their struggles, all three. He gave Malbolge to Baalzebul purely to torment Lucifer in his last moments—and tore it away again later, to elevate another to the greatness that should have been *mine!*"

Nergal's voice rose into a roar, and brutal tentacles shook Elminster like a rag doll. "That *will* be mine, and only a small part of what's mine, in time to come." The archdevil's voice lost its rage as he added, "Sooner, now, than before you fell into my hands."

A many-toothed smile broadened. "I should thank Mystra. Years she meddled with you, shaping you into a meddler in turn . . . all to make you useful to me. You see, old Elminster, you're going to be important after all. What do you say to that?"

Thickly, around the blood, El managed to shape the trembling words, "My usefulness lessens . . . the more ye . . . ruin my body."

Nergal threw back his head and guffawed, even as tentacles lengthened into deft darts of slimy flesh and surged forward.

El clenched his teeth and shook his head in a vain effort to keep them at bay. The archdevil merely thrust them in through El's nostrils instead, down and in. There was a clawing, a horrible wrenching—and more blood. The archdevil tossed aside the bloody gobbet that had been Elminster's tongue, dealt El a slap that spun his head around, and stanched the welling, choking blood in his mouth at the same time.

"Ruin it? Why, what need have you for a tongue when we can converse in your mind? I can gouge out your eyes and tear out your every organ—even dine on your liver, say, with sauce and salt—and then restore you with my magic. You think small, man! This is Hell, and here archdevils can do anything!"

El struggled—successfully—to raise a disbelieving eyebrow.

The eyes looking into his blazed up in fury, and tentacles rose in a menacing array. Rose, surged forward, and sank back again.

Nergal gave his captive a nod of rueful agreement and a wintry smile. "Well, then, let us say 'anything another archdevil does not manage to prevent,' hmm?" The tentacles set Elminster down against a rock as sharp as jagged glass. The Old Mage slid a little, wincing despite all his other raging pains, and fetched up in a sitting position.

Nergal paced back and forth, something catlike and yet serpentine in his stalking. "There are a dozen of us outcasts, eight among us with power enough to challenge, say, Mammon, if the battle were between two, alone, without armies to call on. We are not friends, one with the other, and Asmodeus sees that our regard for each other remains fierce. As rivals, we lurk in the caverns and mountain rifts of Avernus, pursuing our individual plots against the ruling devils—and avoiding the patrols, for even stinging insects have the power to weaken and annoy."

The tentacled archdevil came to a halt close by his slumped captive, looming up dark and tall. Barbs and claws rose out of his flesh like the fins of cruising sharks and ran down his tentacles in a hungry cycle. Teeth that seemed long enough, now, to be called fangs flashed in a less-than-pretty smile.

"Men and devils are not so different that you'll be unaware of what we outcasts hunger after: power. We are always seeking it, armed with our magic. Devils with minds of their own can grasp and work magic as readily as men breathe. We have one other weapon that the Lords of the Nine can never have: time to spare. With my time and magic, I watch your magic-rich Toril."

Nergal crossed arms that swam with a glistening array of small, blinking, human-seeming eyeballs, and bent their manifold gazes on Elminster.

"Beings of power interest me, from the puny masters of your thieving guilds to the dragons and lich lords of Faerûn who wield almost a tenth of the spell-might they think they do." With a grin too wide for human jaws, the archdevil began to pace again. "So I use my spells to spy on Faerûnians of might who may prove useful. I've been watching *you* for a long time, Elminster Aumar. You are the key, I've long thought. Not because you're half so mighty as you think you are, or even a match for a spinagon in a fair battle, but because you are my road to gaining Mystra's power over magecraft. She works through you very strongly, and what she has, when suitably modified, could thunder just as strongly in Hell . . . giving me control over all magic, and in some measure those who work it!"

Nergal laughed again. "This tumult over Shade captured my attention at just the right time and has delivered you to me. Now all I need do, to gain the powers of the lady you serve, or at least the ways of calling on and controlling it, is master your mind."

Tentacles plucked Elminster from the rocks again and held him with casual tenderness. Another tentacle stabbed down, bursting the Old Mage's left eye like a raw egg. After a momentary chaos of swimming brightness, Elminster could see once more—albeit dimly, through a blood-red haze.

"See? You can't even die on me," Nergal purred into Elminster's face, as tenderly as a lover. "Understanding your wits will deliver to me control of the silver fire, all your other little powers and favorite spells, and your storehouse of memories. That last alone is the key to ruling Toril with magic and making it my own realm. A Hell away from Hell, as it were."

Fingers as hot as fire irons took hold of Elminster's cheeks. The archdevil's forked tongue undulated hungrily forth as he bent his head to kiss the helpless wizard, tentacles tightening suddenly into chains that held Elminster immobile.

Nergal's lips were like ice—a searing cold that raged through Elminster's ruined mouth and nose. He tried to murmur, tried to pull away . . . but could do nothing until the archdevil released him with a gloating smile.

"Taste my mindworm, mage. A magic of my own invention, devised to take your memories, to learn how you call on and control Mystra's power and what you know of things and beings of power in Faerûn that I can snatch and use myself. Of course, each memory I gain will be lost to wise old Elminster. In the end, there'll be naught left of you but a lurching, drooling half-wit, remembering only that you were once mighty . . . once, before you met Nergal."

The archdevil roared with laughter, and darting tentacles touched Elminster here and there, sending smaller spells through him until the naked, exhausted man could stand once more. In a shuffling stagger that made him gasp in wordless pain, he struggled away. Tentacles whipped his still-raw flesh, goading him into movement.

Leaving a bloody trail, Elminster tried to hasten beyond the reach of those cruel tentacles.

Go, Nergal's mocking voice said, deep in his mind. *THE GLORIES OF AVERNUS AWAIT. I SHALL RIDE WITH YOU, SEEING WHAT WOULD FLEE OR HIDE FROM ME . . . AND LYING WITHIN YOU, AS A SURPRISE FOR THOSE WHO'D DO YOU ILL. SO WANDER WHERE YOU WILL, MIGHTY WIZARD.*

Elminster shuddered. Broken he might be no longer, but pain still racked him from a hundred lesser hurts. He was powerless to use his magic or contact Mystra or anyone else. Everything he did would be revealed to the devil riding his mind. He was doomed, just as soon as Nergal finished reaming his memory . . . and Toril would be doomed with him. He was free to drag his husk of a body around Avernus, if that could be called freedom. He'd felt enough of Nergal's questing thoughts already to tell himself the devil who'd violated him delighted in ruining minds.

So he stumbled away, uncaring, up a bare rock ridge. As he went, the ground trembled under him. A gout of flame spat up into the sky, sending an abishai squalling into frantically flapping flight.

Wincing at sharp stones underfoot, El reached the top of the ridge and looked out across a wasteland of rock. There, spinagons and abishai slunk and snarled at each other. Beyond loomed a high cliff where devils gathered.

A PATROL. THROW YOURSELF DOWN.

Elminster stood unmoving, peering this way and that. Now was a good time to test Nergal's control over him.

Without warning, his body surged sickeningly, as if an eel or snake were moving inside him. He crashed down hard onto unyielding stone, bouncing once with the force of his fall.

OBEY, GREAT WIZARD. BE AWARE THAT THERE ARE MORE PAINFUL WAYS OF TAMING YOU.

El shuddered. In his fall, he'd driven his hand into a tangle of thorns. As he struggled to pluck them out, weeping at the pain, he wondered how anything survived in this bleak realm of rock. What did devils eat? Each other, perhaps, but how did they ever birth enough to feed these hosts of . . .

THE WHORLSPELLS SUSTAIN US.

The what?

HELL'S LITTLE SECRETS. WANDERING, CAST BY NO ONE. THEY HAVE ALWAYS BEEN—LITTLE WHIRLPOOLS OF SNATCHING MAGIC THAT STEAL WATER, CREATURES, AND THINGS FROM OTHER PLANES, SPILLING THEM DOWN RIFTS IN THE ROCK. FOOD COMES TO US FROM THE WHORLSPELLS, AND TREASURE.

Elminster sighed, shook his head, and tried to get to his feet. He made it as far as his hands and knees before he felt the crawling sensation again. He pitched forward onto his face, scrabbling at the rocks with bleeding fingers.

STAY DOWN AND GO THIS WAY.

So much for wandering. El sighed—it came out as a hoarse gurgle—and started to crawl. A ball of fire roared across the sky, and the ground shook again.

He was standing on the wind-scoured battlements of a castle that no longer existed, watching something in the snow-covered garden below stir and suddenly rise, throwing off a thick cloak of ice, and reaching out a scaly claw—

Into a dark, dim hall where skeletons sat slumped in tall, arch-backed chairs, wan glows flickering about their bone fingers as the enchantments in the rings they wore finally died, letting loose spells that had been cast before Alaundo had been born . . .

The probing force in his mind faltered, and he was back in Avernus again. An angry mental roar echoed through him: *BY THE SEARING FIRES! YOUR MIND IS . . . UTTER CHAOS.*

El found himself grinning fiercely, and tried to send a firm, clear thought back at the wandering sentience within him.

Of course. I am a wizard.

A wordless slap came back at him out of the darkness of his own mind. It sent Elminster tumbling in a wet flow of what might have been tears or blood. He found himself screaming, or trying to, and shaking a head he did not have. . . .

Desperately, in the innermost cloak of comfort he'd fled into, he turned over a rock close to his heart and warmed his hand, just for a moment, on the silver fire lurking beneath.

Then, calm once more, he rose within the velvet darkness of his mind and went on, parting veils until he saw the blood-red sky of Avernus once more. Near the distant horizon streaked another ball of flame.

WHAT DID YOU—? THE FIRE—YOU USED MYSTRA'S FIRE! GIVE IT TO ME!

Crawling, Elminster kept silent, trying to get over the ridge before the awful compulsion to turn and look back at Nergal's glaring face overwhelmed him.

The outcast devil stood with arms folded and eyes like flames. His tentacles rose above him, trembling to strike. *YIELD TO ME, MAN!* The voice roared in his mind. *SHOW ME HOW YOU CALL ON THE SILVER FIRE!*

El crawled on, blind to Avernus once again as he struggled to think of all-cloaking darkness, of nights spent stumbling along dark forest trails, of moments lost wandering in wet, dripping tombs. . . .

There was brightness behind him, and shrieking cacophony. Nergal was coming, clawing through El's memories, tearing aside one after another until he unearthed what he sought in the dark, labyrinthine caverns of a wizard cursed to forget all too little.

Banners aflame, in a battle under bright sunlight long ago . . .

Elminster snatching aside rocks, turning them over to reveal fire beneath—the fire of smoking dragon's blood, spilled moments before in a spell duel that—

NO! NOT THAT REMEMBRANCE! THE SILVER FIRE, YOU PULING WORM!

Silver fire. Spilling through his fingers, amid tears, on another battlefield with a dying elf woman in his arms. Her head fallen back and her magnificent throat working, as silver fire spilled forth from her like glowing smoke, drifting down, running from her fingertips to blaze and gutter in the grass around them both . . .

YES! MORE! SHOW ME SILVER FIRE IN USE!

Silver fire, raging, roaring up hungrily . . .

YES! SHOW ME MORE! SHOW ME!

Silver flames whirling past a hundred disbelieving faces, screaming skulls as eyes melted and sizzled away and flames consumed all . . . hands reaching vainly for aid amid the roaring fire . . . slender, long-nailed, graceful fingers closing on nothing . . .

A SLAYING? USING MYSTRA'S FIRE? SHOW ME!
Though I hate to lose anything of my beloved, I can live without her remembrance of Orlugrym, aye....
SHOW ME, WIZARD! SHOW ME!

Whirling, snarling helices of silver flame around a thousand turrets and tumbling dragons and one grim and regal female face . . .
[mental chaos clearing]
She passed in a swirl of skirts.

The Red Wizard smiled. Like an eager shadow, he stepped out from behind the pillar. The Simbul might be half a world away, but this apprentice of hers would do. Oh, yes. . . .

Again he felt that soft sighing in his mind. A fluttering, almost a caress—not like any probe or mind-smiting spell he'd ever felt. No, this was altogether something else. Something that felt . . . satisfied. It was withdrawing, now, fading away.

A probe, sent by this lone, hurrying lass in the dark gown? Surely not.

She'd never paused or shown sign of wariness . . . or any aware-ness of what was around her. She strode away from him along the narrow passage, brow furrowed in thought, hugging herself as she hastened. Doubtless on some self-important mission.

Not one to match his. Steal something from the private quarters of the Witch-Queen of Aglarond. Well, why not the gown right off an apprentice's body?

Orlugrym smiled a velvety smile. She was pretty, this one. He could have some fun first.

He held up one hand and murmured a different spell than the one he'd been planning to use. Ahead of him, the apprentice stiff-ened and froze, the skirts of her gown whispering to a halt.

"Turn," he told her softly as he stepped forward, "and offer your-self to me."

Emerald-green eyes held amazement and fear as they met his. He tensed for a scream or a snapped spell, but she regarded him mutely for a moment, her eyes very large, before swallowing visibly and gliding forward. She lifted her face to him as she came, and her trembling fingers went to the laces of her bodice.

"Y-yes," she whispered, as they came together. "Yesss."

Orlugrym's smile tightened as she swayed back at her hips and pulled away the dark cloth, thrusting her bared breasts at him. His eyes fell to her soft skin—only to find it ablaze with shimmering silver. Silver that was suddenly blinding.

He staggered back, and found himself looking into a face that was melting and flowing, into . . . wild hair writhing like a basket of snakes . . . blazing eyes he knew—all Red Wizards knew.

"Why, Orlugrym, so inconstant?" the Simbul asked gently, not a trace of mockery in her voice. "You were so sure of your intent a moment ago, your mind empty of all schemes beyond this bold foray. Be bold, then: Embrace me. Something few of your ilk can boast of doing. Come."

Orlugrym trembled as he stared full into the face of his doom. Slender arms spread to encircle his own. Deadly lips parted as they moved to meet his, murmuring, "All you need do in life, Orlugrym, if you'd cling to it, is hold onto yourself—if, that is, you know who you are."

Their breasts brushed together—and his world became roaring, rushing flames of searing silver, flowing up and over all. Orlugrym's last memory was of her lips, floating disembodied amid the silver fire, and advancing to meet his, parted and eager. . . .

El sighed. It had been Alassra's memory, shared with him, and never his own—but to lose it and know it was gone still hurt. It fled from his mind, now, leaving him no longer knowing just what it had been. He'd felt such dazed emptiness before, long ago, and where was *that* recollection?

Ah, here. Archdevil, enjoy the show.

Silver flames and drifting darkness, like cloaks tumbled by lazy waves from which the sun had fled . . .

WHAT?

Elminster could feel the amazement in Nergal's voice . . . no, bafflement.

Bafflement. Aye, give him bafflement, over matters of magic and silver fire and Mystra herself . . . Mystra, now: three snippets of divine memory that had leaked into his own mind in a moment of shared passion. Memories of Khelben and of silver fire.

Roaring, ravening silver . . .

YES. SILVER FIRE! THE MYSTERIES OF THE SILVER FIRE! YIELD TO ME, ELMINSTER AUMAR! REVEAL ALL!

Darkness drifted away like the great black billowing robes of the Lord Mage of Waterdeep, windblown in his wake. He soared like an ungainly carrion crow over the spires, turrets, and rooftops of that proud city. His salt-and-pepper beard curled in the wind of his journeying. His dark eyes were as hard as dagger points as he searched for another flash of the magic misused below. . . .

Shrugging, he plummeted like a vengeful arrow at a familiar turret below: Blackstaff Tower. There Laeral waited, her eyes holding that sparkle that was for him alone. . . .

Come another night, years later . . .

Khelben and Laeral lay abed in Waterdeep, talking quietly in each other's arms of the day's deeds and plans to come. They looked up at summer stars overhead. The Lord Mage of Waterdeep had few conceits; one was the domed ceiling of their bedchamber. It twinkled with a thousand stars, mirroring the clear night sky overhead even when fog, snow, or cloud hid the real sky from view.

They both were restless tonight. Itches and tinglings sprang up in their bodies and shifted about, roiling inside them. Khelben frowned after a particularly violent surge of discomfort. They snarled in irritation, scratching furiously.

"Much power is moving this night," he said, staring about in the darkness. "Mystra's power—or Art that affects her, at least. What d'ye make of it?"

"Something is happening to our Lady, I am sure," Laeral said. "Look at us." She caught his hand and held it up between them. In the darkness, both bare arms glowed with a ghostly blue radiance. As they watched, it seemed to pulse, grow brighter, fade again, and then grow. The stirrings within them matched its changes.

"Should we try to speak to the Lady?"

Khelben was rarely indecisive, but he was puzzled and unsure now. His lady shook her head, long hair stirring and curling about her shoulders of its own accord, moved by the awakening Art within her.

"No," she said, "we might disturb her will at a dangerous time. She'll touch us, should she need us."

She pursed her lips and set her head on one side, thoughtful eyes on his. "But what if we reached to my sisters or to Elminster?"

Khelben shrugged. "Perhaps a good thing. Yet no doubt they feel what we do and know little more. Perhaps dangerous, if we are linked when the Lady calls on our power, or shifts power into us. I know not what to do . . . I have never felt this much—tumult—of Art before."

"Nor I," Laeral agreed softly, and drew him to her in a tight embrace. They held each other under the stars like two lost children, snuggling against the cold, and waited.

Sometimes waiting is all even archmages can do.

Silver fire dancing, in a little ring in the darkness above a tranquil pool, in a wood wherein no man has ever set foot . . .

STOP PLAYING GAMES WITH ME, HUMAN! The rage in Nergal's mind-voice overwhelmed the bewilderment. *HOW IS IT THAT YOU SHOW ME MEMORIES THAT CAN'T POSSIBLY BE YOUR OWN?*

Diabolic thoughts raced, dark and furious.

HOW CAN YOU EVEN KNOW SUCH THINGS?

Fear rang like cold steel from Nergal's coiling thoughts. A moment later the archdevil was plowing through Elminster's mind like a dragon intent on pouncing and slaying, heedless of the chaos he left. Archways cracked, and ceilings tumbled. . . .

TELL ME, WIZARD! YOUR TONGUE COULD LIE, WHEREFORE IT'S GONE, BUT HERE YOU CAN'T HIDE FROM ME OR DECEIVE! TELL ME!

All was bright lightning and red blood as Nergal came. El dimly knew he vomited blood out onto the stones he crawled over. The pain made his vision of the onrushing dragon pulse and fade, pulse and fade.

The pain. He hurled himself into it, sinking thankfully as if into cooling waters, plunging deep.

The dragon was coming for him, reaching out its talons, jaws gaping. . . .

El tumbled deeper through his memories, screaming out nonsense words as if deranged, wrapping himself in armor made of his own screams. . . .

DON'T GO MAD ON ME, MAGE! DON'T YOU DARE GO MAD ON ME!

Elminster grinned to himself in the heart of his wild screams. *I mustn't dare go mad, eh? Or what?*

A blustering quip from another world came to him, like a bright glimmering. The Old Mage hugged it to himself as he tumbled deeper, the dragon thundering in pursuit:

Only one of us is going to leave this room alive, and it ain't going to be me!

Three

THE DAY THE MAGIC DIED

A flame danced and guttered above the kitchen table in Elminster's Tower in Shadowdale, between two mages who were frowning and trembling in concentration.

The flame fed on empty air. Vivid blue tinged with purple and sometimes green, it seemed about to flicker out despite all that the Simbul and Jhessail—both leaning forward over the table, sweat running down their cheeks and dripping from their chins—could do. The air almost crackled with risen magic between the queen of Aglarond and the far less mighty in Art lady Knight of Myth Drannor. Nearby, the Bard of Shadowdale sat calmly, staring into the scrying flame. Elminster's scribe, Lhaeo, watched from one corner of the room, a cooling pot of tea forgotten in his hands. He was unable to stifle a long sigh of relief when the lady bard brightened. Not taking her eyes from the dancing flame, Storm Silverhand announced, "She—yes, it's Sharantyr, and she's laughing and chasing someone."

Jhessail frowned. "Laughing and—? Who would she be chasing about and laughing at?"

"Elminster," Lhaeo and the Simbul said flatly, together. Their faces wore identical, knowing expressions. At their tone, Jhessail sputtered in amusement. That sent everyone in the room laughing— including a faint, ghostly giggle from the empty air between Storm and the Simbul: their spectral sister Syluné.

Storm lost contact amid the mirth. She spread her hands helplessly as the flame exploded into a drifting cloud of winking purple and blue sparks . . . which faded away to nothing. She shook her head, sighed, and sat back, rubbing her temples with weary fingers. "Well done, you two," she said, "considering how unreliable all Art has become . . ."

"We *three*," the Simbul corrected. "Syluné provided the focus."

Storm smiled as she felt cool lips brush her cheek. "My thanks, Sister," she said to the empty air.

"Where are they?" Jhessail asked, leaning forward to push a decanter toward her.

The lady bard shrugged. "Somewhere south and west of us, more south, I think; probably Cormyr. Somewhere near mountains, in a castle or other fortified place."

The Simbul frowned. "The High Dale? Thunder Gap?"

Storm looked at her and frowned. "No, Sister. You must not risk yourself looking for them. Art could fail you at any time, and you could well attract unwanted attention to them. We must sit and do nothing—for once."

Shaerl grimaced. "When you're a lady at court, even in Shadowdale, you do a lot of sitting and doing nothing."

Illistyl shot her a look. "I'll bear that in mind when next the laundry must be done. I could use another pair of hands, betimes."

Storm snorted. "Enough, you two. We've the safety of the dale to consider. News is all over the North of great storms and earthquakes, of gods walking about and wild magic loosed. Many who harp are gathering to me. Whate'er befalls, you can be sure the Zhentarim and others—Mulmaster perhaps, or even Maalthiir of Hillsfar—will take full advantage of the general chaos to ride to war. We must be ready."

They all stared at her, except for Illistyl, who turned to Jhessail and said sarcastically, "And you wanted a little excitement this summer, didn't you? You had to wish it aloud, didn't you? You—"

Jhessail sighed, selected an apple of the appropriate size from the bowl of fruit on the table, and in one smooth, unexpected motion shoved it into Illistyl's mouth.

Her apprentice managed an indignant, muffled squeal in the instant before laughter reigned around the table again.

Don't toy with me, wizard! So you thrust at me a memory of yourself gone missing—amusing indeed! Yet another remembrance that can't be your own! Another shared with your fellow servants of Mystra! How came you by them?

Dark eyes, as large as all the starry night sky, looking down full of mystery . . . the Lady of Mystery, all his own. . . .

Elminster smiled at that memory, slowing his plunge to hang in the star-shot darkness.

Above him, like a great dark claw, Nergal slowed too. He smiled a brittle smile as he mastered his rage. Well, then, let the little human wizard play his games.

For a few moments more.

So these memories came from Mystra. So too did the silver fire. Well, then, let Elminster remember more of her. The secrets this future Lord of all Hell sought would inevitably be laid bare, around some waiting corner.

This one, for instance . . .

Stars falling in the night sky over Shadowdale, and the same stars seen from afar in Waterdeep, where folk on their balconies murmured and pointed, voices more worried than excited . . . to a high room in a tower in that city, where through clever magics the ceiling above the bed was lost in the sky of stars. . . .

* * * * *

Striding across her kitchen with a fresh-cut bunch of fragrant herbs in hand, Storm stiffened and stifled a soft curse. She was in a whirling hurry. A dying Harper's plea had made her late, spells could

not shorten the time that a good stew takes, and the good wives of the dale were bringing their children for an evening of tale-telling. They expected to see the Bard of Shadowdale in a nice gown, not bloodstained war-leathers crossed with recent sword cuts.

Why had that memory of seeking El come into her mind now? Alassra and Jhessail had strained so—she'd not soon forget, but why now?

She frowned, alone in the darkness, though in this place, she was never truly alone. "Sister?" she asked the empty air.

Syluné's touch was like the gentlest of breezes on her cheek and shoulder. *Aye,* the ghostly mind-voice came, *I just recalled that night, too. I wonder why.*

* * * * *

"Oh, love," Laeral whispered tremulously, arms tight about Khelben in the starry darkness of their bedchamber, "I could *feel* his pain. What a horrible thing to happen, to be stripped of all Art!"

"Aye." Laeral felt the Lord Mage of Waterdeep tense in her arms. With iron control, he stifled a shudder. He moved to quell her fear first, with the kind strength she loved him for. "I'd not wish that fate on anyone, even one who wore the robes of Thay or of Manshoon's serpents—and yet, love, our Lady chose him. He is the strongest of us all. Great Art has raged against him before, and done much damage—and he is still here, this day, to tell of it."

"If any mage in the Realms can hold Mystra's might and live to see the burden passed on—and resist the hunger to master it and, in the doing, be mastered by it—'tis Elminster of Shadowdale."

Khelben did shiver, then, and turned a white face to look into Laeral's. His eyes were large and dark with fear. "Mine will be the task to take up what of his work I can—and gather all the strength I can, here. If the Art does master him, and he becomes as wild and cruel a rogue as Manshoon, mine will be the duty to destroy him."

They held each other tightly in the large bed as tears fell. Neither could find words to comfort each other that were not empty.

Nergal stirred. *ARE YOU TRYING TO ALERT YOUR FRIENDS, ELMINSTER? DO YOU TRULY THINK SUCH MEMORIES CAN REACH THEM, TO WARN THEM OF YOUR CAPTIVITY HERE? GIVE IT UP, FOOL—NOTHING LEAVES YOUR MIND BUT THROUGH ME. I AM THE GATE OF FANGS, THE PORTAL THAT OPENS NOT. DESPAIR IN MY DARKNESS AND YIELD. YIELD UP TO ME YOUR SECRETS, LITTLE MAGE, ERE I GROW RESTIVE AND TEAR APART ALL IN SEEKING WHAT I DESIRE.*

Silver flames, flowing . . .

YES! MORE OF THAT! SHOW ME, CRINGING HUMAN! NERGAL COMMANDS! MORE, OR I'LL SNATCH AWAY YOUR SANITY WITH CLAWS OF FEAR!

Cold fear in spellcasting, fear of going mad . . .

YES! WHEREFORE YIELD! YIELD TO NERGAL!

Fear like a quavering flame in a dark room, where magic sputtered and failed in slender fingers . . .

Illistyl drew a deep breath and tried the spell again. Nothing happened—again. Her hands shook.

Magic had never failed her before. Oh, she'd failed *it*, a time or two, but always the error had been hers, something that more care or training could conquer. Not this wildness, this unreliability of her every spell.

Deep fear tasted like cold metal in her mouth. There was no Simbul here now, and Storm was half the dale away—there was only Illistyl Elventree, alone in a cold, dim stone room in the Twisted Tower.

"What's *happening?*" she demanded of the Realms around her, bosom rising and falling as fear took hold. "What have we done, that magic fails us?"

The door of the room resounded to a thunderous knocking, shook in its frame, and burst in upon her. She screamed.

"Oh, *gods look down!*" Jhessail scolded her, sweeping into the room like a vengeful wind, robes swirling around her. "Must you work such pranks of Art? Half the guards below have just lost every buckle and plate of metal on them—and they're now scrambling around in their boots and under-rags, looking very embarrassed indeed!"

Illistyl looked at her and burst into laughter . . . that soon dissolved into tears, and then twisted into laughter again. Jhessail held slim shoulders in her arms, cradling them, pulling her pupil close.

"There, there, kitten," she soothed. "Shadowdale still stands around us—take heart. It could be worse."

Illistyl drew a shuddering breath. "*How?*" she demanded tremulously. "I can't work even the *simplest* spell!"

Jhessail sighed. "Well," she said wryly, "all magic could fail us, and the gods could walk the Realms, and—"

Illistyl's arms tightened around her waist fiercely. "Don't *say* that," she hissed into her mentor's ear. "Don't even think about it! Jhess, I'm scared. *Scared.*"

Jhessail Silvertree held the younger mage tenderly in her arms and said, "We all are, kitten. Even the gods, now. Elminster used to tell me, when I cried: Walk with fear a little while. Get to know it, and know thyself the more."

Illistyl only sobbed in reply, and clung to her more tightly. "He's gone, too! Jhess—where is he?"

Jhessail felt wetness welling up in her own eyes. "I don't know," she whispered back. They clung to each other in the darkness. In a voice that was not quite steady, she said, "We're all scared. We should be, now, if we know what's befallen—and are sane."

Illistyl drew back and stared at her, eyes streaming. "You think mages are *sane?* You're crazy!"

Jhessail laughed until she had to cling to Illistyl for support, and they laughed together awhile longer.

There came the hurrying tread of booted feet, and Mourngrym rushed in, torches and guards at his back.

"What *now,* women?" he demanded, sword naked in his hand.

"The—sanity of mages," Jhessail gasped. "A . . . laughing matter, it seems."

"I've often thought so," the lord of Shadowdale replied, sheathing his sword. "Though with Elminster about, I've never quite dared say it."

Illistyl nodded. "And now that he's gone, who knows where . . . ?" Her voice was only a whisper.

Mourngrym looked at her. "I'm so afraid, lass, that if I stand still too long my bladder fills my boots right up to the tops. If you had any sense, you'd know that much fear, too."

He wondered, then, why the laughter of both lady mages was so wild.

MY PATIENCE IS NOT ENDLESS, MAN. DO YOU THINK SHOWING ME SUCH THINGS DELAYS YOUR FATE? THE UNLOCKING AND WIELDING OF MYSTRA'S POWERS ARE WHAT I SEEK, NOT THESE SCENES FROM THE EVE OF THE MADNESS OF MAGIC FAILING, NO MATTER HOW MUCH IT MATTERED TO YOU.

I try to reveal all, Nergal. I try. Much is tangled here, when the old Mystra passed and her powers were thrust into me to carry. Here alone is the time when I understood what I wielded. Believe me.

YOU MAKE SUCH BELIEF LESS THAN EASY, MAGE. DELAY ME LESS.

* * * * *

"Lord?" Darthusk pulled back on his swing a moment before his sword tip would have found Mourngrym Amcathra's throat.

The lord of Shadowdale stepped back, frowning. He shook his head as if trying to clear something out of it, staring at nothing.

Darthusk waved his hand in an urgent signal. All of the guards around the room stopped their sword practice and fell silent, looking at their lord in concern. Was this some sort of Zhent trick, or—?

Mourngrym shook himself again and caught up his belt rag to wipe the sweat from his face. "Strange," he said tersely as he raised his blade again, "but—'twas so vivid. A passing memory of our two lady wizards laughing until they were falling down. I went in to see why the noise, and . . ."

He shook his head again, wonderingly and said, "Cry pardon, Darthusk. I—magic. Strange, always."

"Aye, Lord," the guard said, as they crossed their blades to begin again. "Magic always is. I see it as a sword that burns at both ends—harming its wielder as well as the foe. It's a wonder to me that more mages don't end up aflame in earnest, screaming down in the Nine Hells!"

Mourngrym stiffened again, frowning at Darthusk. "What did y—never mind." He tapped his sword against the guard's. They swung at each other with real force, and the spark-striking clang of steel rose again around them. Mourngrym shook his head and growled, "Aflame in the Nine Hells, aye. Use magic I must, but trust it? Never!"

Their eyes met over their skirling blades, lord and guard, and they grinned and shouted in unison, "*Never!*"

*   *   *   *   *

[frustration like flame . . . aye, a flame burning in Hell with a too-clever mage in the heart of it]

WHAT'S THAT, LITTLE MAN? WHAT'S THAT THOUGHT OF FLAME YOU'RE TRYING TO HIDE FROM ME? YOU THINK FIRE CAN HARM ME?

Ah, no. "Never"

AYE, SO STALL NO MORE! SHOW US MORE OF THAT! THERE WERE GUARDS, YES, WITH DRAWN SWORDS, AND LIGHT—WELL?

[hasty swirl of images]

Brightness, long-barred doors opening, guards stepping warily back with naked swords bright in their hands, parting to let us stride forward . . .

Ahead, into the light . . .

ABOUT TIME.

The blue-white light of the Art, of Mystra's power unleashed . . .

SHOW ME!

Blue-white, and wavering . . . in a stone tower where an old man sat alone, spellweaving . . .

The spell had never gone wrong before. It was such a simple thing, the conjuring of light. Oh, wondrous to a farm boy, to be sure, the making of radiance where there had been none before—and a thing for a raw apprentice to be proud of. In the actual casting, mind, there was nothing very complex or difficult.

Taern "Thunderspell" Hornblade, Harper and mage of the Palace Spellguard of Silverymoon, stood up suddenly, then sat down again, frowning in bewilderment. In his mind he went over what he had done again, seeing clearly the clean, careful, precise steps. No, he had made no error. The spell should have worked.

He cast a detection spell, felt it range out from him. No fields or barriers, save those that were always in this place, met his probing. The scrying magic worked flawlessly, proof that no magic had been placed to drink or deny all Art. Everything seemed normal, the torches flickering in their braziers as they always did. Yet the spell had failed.

Either someone who could not be seen or otherwise detected had acted to steal or dispel his Art—hardly likely—or something had happened to Mystra or to his standing in the eyes of Mystra . . . or he was going mad. Happy choices, all.

With hands that shook only a little, Taern knelt in the stone-walled spell chamber and prayed to Mystra, his gray-bearded lips moving in entreaty. He felt as if a black gulf had suddenly opened beneath him, and he was helpless to avoid plunging into it, into oblivion. What had he done? What had happened to him?

He was still on his knees when one of the room's secret doors opened—the door that led to the chambers of Alustriel, High Lady of Silverymoon.

So upset was Taern Thunderspell that he did not look up or cease his prayers, even when a gentle hand came down to rest on his shoulder. He did stop, amazed, at the grief-choked, kindly words that followed.

"Make thy prayer a farewell and thanks to the Lady, Taern," Alustriel told him. "For she is gone forever."

Taern looked up, dumbfounded, and saw that tears rolled unchecked down the cheeks of Silverymoon's queen. A blue-white aura of power curled about her long hair and spilled from her brimming eyes.

"Lady?" Taern asked, reaching his hands up to her. "What do you mean?"

Alustriel took his hands in her own, and Taern felt a tingling of power. Great Art, she had, more than he had ever sensed before.

"Thy spell failed not by thy doing. It was lost, with all Art worked in Faerûn in that breath, in the passing of Mystra."

"Mystra is—dead? Destroyed?"

"Destroyed, aye." Alustriel knelt on the stones beside him, her long gown rustling. "While ye are down here, Thunderspell, ye could join me in prayer to Azuth, to guide the living."

"Living mages? Such as ye and I?" Taern was white-faced; the black gulf was all around him, and only the hands that clasped his kept him from sinking. Hands that glowed blue-white.

Alustriel smiled through her tears, and said softly, "For one mage, aye. The one who holds Mystra's power now. It burns him inside, and we must all hope he bows not to the temptation to wield it. And for the one who comes after, the one who must rise and grow to take Mystra's place and power. They will need our prayers, and whatever help we can give, in the days ahead."

Taern wished desperately that he did not feel so old and tired, the days of his greatest power behind him. None of his apprentices were ready yet. None would serve in any battle to come.

Alustriel put her arms around him and kissed his forehead. "Peace, Taern. The Lady's power has touched me; until it fades, I can see thy mind. Ye have done well, and it is thy wisdom, more than power of Art, that will be needed in the days ahead."

From where she had kissed him, Taern felt power flooding through him, awakening and soothing at the same time. He stared at his queen in awe and wonder and wished again he were not so old.

Alustriel's eyes held his in a steady, loving gaze.

He colored suddenly and brought hands up to his burning cheeks. If she could read his thoughts. . . . Taern loved her very much then, for she caught one of his hands and brought it to her lips and did not laugh at him.

MORE LOVEMAKING. DO YOU HUMANS DO ANYTHING ELSE?

Aye. We scheme and fight and work treason almost as energetically as archdevils.

MOCK ME NOT, ELMINSTER AUMAR. YOU ARE IN MY POWER. I HAVE BUT TO CLOSE MY HAND OVER YOU FOR YOU TO BE NO MORE. GONE FOREVER.

Promises, promises.

DO NOT PRESUME TO BANDY WORDS WITH ME AS AN EQUAL, HUMAN. MY PATIENCE GROWS SHORT INDEED. SHOW ME MORE OF GODLY MAGIC—NOW!

Pain! Pain in Avernus, of a tentacle become a talon and thrust through the breast of a crawling man, leaving him to stiffen and gasp in agony as fresh blood flowed . . . then to sink back, gasping in ecstasy, as the withdrawing talon healed its own wound, leaving the naked old man to fall on his face, shaking with weakness and pain. . . .

Weakness, and gods, and magic . . .

YIELD UNTO ME, LITTLE MAN!

Ah. Weakness in magic among the gods. Aye, let it be remembered. . . .

"I am ashamed to say it," Nouméa whispered, so faintly that mortal ears would have missed what she said, "but I am glad the Lady did not choose me. I would have failed her—and us all."

She stood in a dark cavern, lit only by a tall, slim conical column of silvery gray light. It replied in an echoing mind-voice.

Wherefore ye were not chosen. The Lady is—was—wise. Yet be not ashamed, Daughter. Differing natures decree different fates for us all.

"What now, Lord?"

The silvery cone flickered once. *We go on as before. None must know what has befallen. This seems wisest.*

"Seems wisest?"

I am not all wise or all knowing, Lady Magister. I can be sure only after I touch the mind of Elminster. It may become necessary, if the power he has taken twists him, that ye destroy him. Come with me now, as we speak mind to mind with the Old Mage. Merge with me.

The Magister looked at the cone in puzzlement. "Merge, Lord Azuth?"

Step into the space I now occupy, and stay entirely within this conical form. It is all that is left to me since the Fall. I must be ready to shield thee if Elminster has been . . . changed.

Nouméa shivered. She had not known that anything could bring fear into the voice of a god—especially her all wise, imperturbable teacher, the Lord of Wizardry himself.

Hurriedly she stepped forward and plunged—with a momentary, shocking chill—into the silvery cone, all that remained of the High One. Already his mind reached out like an uncoiling snake, lashing across great distances toward the slightly leaning stone tower in Shadowdale.

FULL OF TRICKS, AREN'T YOU? A FLAGON BRIMMING OVER WITH DECEIT. NEARLY AS DEVILISH AS ONE OF US. YOU KNOW FULL WELL I SEEK WHAT YOU RECALL OF MYSTRA. DON'T YOU? DON'T YOU? [searing fire]

[pain] *Aye.* [shuddering pain]

SHOW ME, THEN, SOMETHING SHE LEFT IN YOUR MIND—OR I'LL TEAR AND REND YOUR WITS IN EARNEST, WISE OLD ELMINSTER!

As ye command, Lord Nergal.

DO YOU DARE TO MOCK ME? [furious lashing fires]

[pain] *Not I, Lord. Gods, not I!*

Tears running down the sky from the dark, watchful eyes of the Lady of Mysteries, on a night before her powers failed, and she could only behold what befell as magic failed, all across Faerûn. . . .

The day was warm and bright—but all was decidedly not well in the Realms.

In Chessenta, the Sceptanar screamed in rage as three of his high wizards battled to control the wild transformations their Art had brought to certain ladies of the court. It was the Sceptanar's wont to have noble consorts altered by magic, to tint their skins with exotic hues, enhance their height and features, and give them something different—scales, or serpentine tails, claws, or even gossamer wings. This morn, the spells had gone horribly wrong. They brought on changes, yes—changes that continued, faster and faster, altering the ladies into monstrous things that screamed, bellowed, or burbled at the pain and stress of their shifting. The Sceptanar's most powerful high wizards scurried and cast spells and puzzled, hurling all they could find. No magic could stop these fell transformations.

Moreover, rumors of the gods walking the Realms grew ever more detailed with the passing days. The Sceptanar was beginning to grow very afraid indeed.

*   *   *   *   *

"Lady?" Taern's voice was rough with concern, and he half-rose from his stool under the lamp.

In the pool where Alustriel bathed, amid the spell glows and scented oils applied by deft servants, she had stiffened and gasped. She sat bolt upright, ripples racing away across the waters. She clutched at her head as if something had caught fire within.

"Lady!" Taern almost shouted. "Are you well?"

Alustriel raised a hand to stay his cry, and then asked, "Taern, did any memories come into your mind just now? Of the two of us, perhaps, on the night when the Art seemed to fail?"

Taern shook his head, his eyes large and dark. "The night I felt Mystra's power within you?" he whispered, heedless of the listening servants and the little murmur of wordless excitement that spread from them. "I'll never forget that night, Lady. Yet I tell you truth: It comes to me now, as you speak of it, but nothing until then. I was thinking of nothing but the ledgers and coins we'd been discussing."

"Nothing of Azuth, or the Magister, or far Chessenta?"

Taern shook his head. "No, Lady," he said in a low, wondering voice. "Why would I?"

"Aye," the lady wizard echoed, sinking back into the pool until the rippling waters lapped at her magnificent throat. "Why would I?"

* * * * *

[images spinning on, in the blood-red gloom of Hell]

In Aglarond, the Simbul forbade the use of magic against Thayan raiders, telling her men to trust instead in their swords. When the Red Wizards leading the strike against Aglarond tried to hurl lightning against the Simbul's men, their spells instead brought forth falls of flowers, crystal spheres, and mud. In the end, a Red Wizard sought escape by giving the raiders' stolen boat the power of flight, but his Art instead turned it to old and crumbling cheese, and it fell apart beneath them. They sank into the cold waters of the Sea of Dhurg. Only a handful emerged to the embrace of the Simbul's spell chains.

In Silverymoon, a simple spell to light the recesses of a dark cellar brought down the tower above it. The astonished caster was High Lady Alustriel, herself.

In Waterdeep, an apprentice's prank involving a dog charmed to fetch and carry pretty passing girls in to meet the lonely caster went wrong. Everyone the dog touched was transformed into another creature—serpent or rooster or centipede. When one became a hissing wyvern, the dog fled in terror. Nearby mages, alerted to the danger, cast spells to slay the monster. The enchantments instead brought down a rain of fire from the sky, turned gray stone buildings pink and translucent (mightily pleasing the owner of one, for it was a high-class brothel), and caused the street to be riddled with holes. The wyvern escaped, flying to the top of Mount Waterdeep. There, Khelben Blackstaff's spells restored it to its former shape: that of a terrified noble lady. Even his Art, though, twisted awry. Instead of clothes, the hysterical lady was covered with feathers of a vivid blue.

In Calimport, two female slaves with barbed whips dueled to the death for the amusement of their cruel sultan owners—and to settle a bet. Both weakened, panting and staggering, sweat beading their oiled bodies like clusters of gems. A watching wizard decided to aid his master's slave with a secretive spell. His furtive Art, designed to make her a shade faster, instead transformed her into a raging red dragon. In a trice, she devoured or smashed flat the sultans, the unfortunate wizard, and many of their servants. She then beckoned the other slave onto her back, and they flew away, northeast, toward the Marching Mountains.

All across the Realms, magic was going wild. Even in the High Dale, amid the chaos of weakening magic, fateful changes came. Perhaps the gods willed it, perhaps it was the deliberate work of Mystra . . . or perhaps it was mere chance. Heladar Longspear never had time to find out.

HELADAR LONGSPEAR? WHAT CARE I FOR HUMAN WARRIORS IN THE PIGSTY KINGDOMS OF TORIL? FOR THAT MATTER, WHAT CARED MYSTRA FOR HIM?

She was—is—a goddess. She cared. If ye cannot see the need to care for and nurture what ye rule, ye can never hope to be more than an outcast or a conqueror, Nergal. Never a ruler. Never for more time than it takes whatever world or plane that's beneath ye to find some way to be rid of ye.

LECTURE ME NOT, PULING HUMAN! [brutal mental bolt] *I THINK NOT!*

[pain; gasping, helpless, twisting servant to the pain]

HOW CROW YOU NOW, ELMINSTER? IS CLEVER SNEERING STILL YOUR TONE?

SHOW ME THE NEXT MEMORY MYSTRA GAVE TO YOU. NO TRICKS, NO DELAY. GIVE IT. NOW. [dark glare]

A dark head, glaring . . .

A dark, floating sphere amid racing shadows. . . .

Shadows falling away before torchlight, and old stone vaulting, and a room that had need of neither . . .

Khelben sighed and sat back from the crystal ball. It was three times the size of his head, glossy-smooth, and as dark and lifeless as death. There came an answering, feminine sigh.

Around them, the dome of the spell chamber winked and sparkled with stars—as it always did, no matter what the time of day or weather outside Blackstaff Tower.

He shook his head slowly, staring again at the empty crystal ball. "Nothing."

Laeral laid a comforting hand on his shoulder. "Easy, my lord. The fault is not yours. Magic seems to have gone rogue everywhere in the Realms."

Khelben Arunsun rose to pace the chamber. "It's not that, love. My Art held, I believe. I reached Lhaeo, the Old Mage's scribe, but Lhaeo knows not where Elminster may be."

Khelben shrugged. "He suspects—hopes—that a lady ranger of the Knights of Myth Drannor accompanies the Old Mage: one Sharantyr. Her I cannot reach, and in truth I barely remember her. We've met only a time or two, and always with many others in her company, whom I know much better."

Laeral glided up behind him and stroked his shoulders. "I expected no better result than this, and I'll be very surprised if you tell me in truth that you did. We can only keep trying and hope."

She gravely studied the man who was her lord, love, and master. "You are troubled more deeply, Lord—there is something more. I would know it, if you will."

Khelben turned and took her in his arms, unsmiling. Behind him, a star fell across the dark, unending void of the chamber. "I have tried to reach Azuth and the Lady, both. I have felt them. They are here, in the Realms, with us. Azuth's power burns but dimly, a mere glow where once there was a fire, and I cannot reach him. His Art has waned as he uses it; he is helping lesser beings as he always has—and will do so, I fear, until he is but a whisper and a memory."

Laeral turned her dark, beautiful eyes up to his. "Yet that is not what really troubles you. Is it the Lady?"

Khelben met her gaze and nodded grimly. "She is a captive. Magic imprisons her and drinks of her power—magic such as I have never felt before and do not yet understand."

Laeral stared at him in horror. "Who in all Faerûn has the power to hold Great Mystra captive?"

Khelben smiled bitterly. "Why, another god, of course."

So, you give me more of your friends worried about your absence. How touching. Well, then, clever wizard: Give me another of Mystra's memories, wherein we see some of these friends of yours trying to work magic to find you. Then, perhaps, we'll get somewhere in this sword play of crossed and clashing remembrances that amuses you so. . . .

As ye wish.

Mock me not, wizard! [mental slap]

I never mock, devil. [mental slap returned]

[pain; astonishment] *You dare?*

No, Lord Nergal. But Mystra does.

[confusion . . . fear] *She's aware, with you . . . within you?*

Not now. But she can be, if ye disturb the right—excuse me, the wrong—memory. Then she will come, and all thy work will be undone.

[fear, anger] *No. She can have no power over me here. Devils rule in Hell.*

Of course. Nice throne, by the way.

[red fires of anger] *So you never mock, little man?*

Never. Try to remember that.

[dark glare] *Unfold the memory, Elminster Aumar.*

"The gods alone know where they are, by now," Storm said quietly. "I think Elminster wandered westward—but he could have passed through any of a dozen secret gates. With a single step he could have reached the other side of Faerûn . . . or even another plane."

"A cheery thought," Shaerl observed sardonically. "Shall I tell Mourngrym to revise dale defenses to include a dozen unknown, invisible, but all-too-exposed gates that invading armies can rush through?"

"Easy, wench," Jhessail told her, patting her hand. "Have some more firequench." She pushed the decanter of ruby-red liqueur across the table. Illistyl made a silent grab for it as it moved away from her and was rewarded with a raised eyebrow from Jhessail. She returned it, with interest.

"Ladies, ladies," Storm sighed, shifting her feet down from atop the table. "Must we spit and snarl like rival kittens?"

Illistyl shrugged. "It's what we've always done before," she observed with impish serenity.

Shaerl giggled. A breath later, others joined her. The Lady of Shadowdale had brought the two sorceresses to Storm's farmhouse late, after most of the men in the Twisted Tower—including her man, Lord Mourngrym—were abed. Afternoon was a more usual time for these tongue-wag sessions, but they'd all been too restless to sleep and had met by chance, padding barefoot around the tower in their nightcloaks.

Storm Silverhand had also been awake when they'd come calling. As they approached, the three had heard her talking softly to someone, but when they'd gone through her open door, she'd been alone, a lute idle across her lap.

They'd sung a song or two, tossed around gossip of the dale's doings, and come at last to Elminster's sudden absence.

Illistyl had been surprised to see unshed tears standing in Storm's eyes. The lady bard had said little and continued to do so—but her sadness lay like a shadow in the room, enfolding them all. Illistyl felt it as keenly as any other but could think of no kind way to shake it away. Her gaze flicked down the table to find Storm's knowing eyes upon her.

Illistyl burst out, "Storm, what's *wrong?* I'd like to help, but I don't even know just—"

She broke off, startled, as a bat as large and black as a cloak flapped heavily in through the open doorway, circled low over the table, and writhed in the air in front of the fireplace. An instant later, it had become a tall, gaunt woman in a black, tattered gown. Her hair and eyes both danced wildly, and a fierce pride leaped in her face as she glided toward them.

"Sister!" Storm greeted her with a welcoming smile. "Will you take some firequench with us?"

The Simbul shivered like a cat after a fright. "Later," she said, taking a seat at the table. "After I try to learn what we both want to know."

"All of us, here," Storm replied quietly. "I've sent two good men out after them, too. Two who harp." Across the room, the strings of her harp seemed to sing faintly.

The Simbul looked around at them all, not smiling, nodded to each, and without pause bent her head and began whispering words of Art.

A heavy tension grew in the room. The candle flames shrank to steady, watching pinpoints. The Simbul sat at the center of the gathered power, black and unmoving. Her shoulders shook. She gasped, and the candle flames leaped and flickered again. The room was somehow brighter—and yet, Illistyl thought, looking at the Simbul's forlorn and ravaged face—it seemed no safer or warmer.

The Witch-Queen of Aglarond looked around at them all and said simply, "I'll need your help, all of you. Join hands with me, and I'll try again."

Without hesitation the women leaned forward around the table, the liqueur decanter standing like a red flame before them. The Simbul closed her eyes, shuddered again, and began to gather her will. As before, the room grew dim.

"Think," she muttered, "think of Sharantyr. Picture her face, her voice, what she looks like when she moves. We must key upon her, for Elminster is cloaked to seeking magic."

Obediently, they thought of Shar. Jhessail's eyes closed, her face calm. Illistyl and Shaerl both frowned, eyes scrunched in concentration. Linked to the Simbul, they could feel her draw in her power, feeding on their thoughts, emotions, and yearnings.

Power swirled around the room. Then the Simbul hurled her questing, searching thought outward, a long way. Like a fisher's hook into dark waters, she fell into a void of seeking where those linked to her could not follow.

After a long, tense silence, the Simbul shook herself like a dog coming up out of water. "We need more. All is twisted, all gone wild. Syluné . . . please?"

Three pairs of wondering eyes saw Storm and the Simbul's fingers part. Out of the smoky air between them, two slim, faintly glowing hands seemed to grow, gaining substance in ghostly silence. Each clasped a living hand.

A gentle whisper said, "I am here. Try now, Sister."

Shaerl, Jhessail, and Illistyl looked at each other for a frightened moment, stared at the half-seen, ghostly figure between Storm and the Simbul, closed their eyes, and threw themselves into seeking Sharantyr.

An eternity passed. The candles burned lower. They breathed as one, low and deep. Toril, with awesome slowness, rolled steadily beneath them.

They heard someone whimper, and the circle was broken.

Storm held only empty air, and the Simbul fell heavily facedown on the table, upsetting the decanter.

"Storm?" Shaerl asked anxiously, half rising. "Is she—?"

"Exhausted," the Bard of Shadowdale said faintly, leaning back in her chair. "As I am. It's a magic few know—thankfully, or there'd be mindless mages across half Faerûn, in short order."

Jhessail rescued the decanter and silently held it out to Storm. Storm stared at it dully for a breath or two, then deliberately took it, unstopped it, and took a long pull. When she replaced the stopper again and handed it back, it was almost empty.

"Storm," Illistyl asked quietly, her voice almost steady, "was that—?"

"Our sister, Syluné," Storm answered, as quietly. "Yes. It was, and what we tried did more harm to her than to either of us."

She turned dark eyes up to theirs, and added, "So now you know. Take up the weight of another secret, for the good of the dale."

Three pairs of serious eyes met hers, and three intent faces nodded silently.

The Simbul stirred. She spoke into the table her cheek was pressed against, "Is there any of that firequench swill left?"

After the laughter died away, Illistyl dared to lay tender, helping hands on perhaps the most powerful sorceress alive in Faerûn, raising her and wiping her sweat-soaked brow. The Simbul smiled silent thanks, looked at them all, and said, "Well—you know we failed. There's worse news."

Jhessail and Shaerl both looked at her sharply. "Tell," the Lady of Shadowdale said simply.

"All Art in the Realms is going rogue," the Simbul answered plainly. "Everywhere, and for all who wield it—we can unleash it, but our control slips and snatches and most of the time is lacking entirely. Magic has gone wild, and we cannot stop it."

Dread came and went on her white face. She reached thoughtfully for the decanter. "Across Faerûn," she added, "not a single mage, archmage, or hedge-wizard can rely on spells anymore."

Illistyl, Shaerl, and Jhessail exchanged looks. Illistyl and Shaerl spoke together, framing the same question as one. "In the name of all the gods, why?"

Storm answered softly, eyes on the flame of the nearest candle, "That's just why—all the gods. They've been cast down into the Realms, to contend among us, struggling and striving as we do; Mystra among them. It's why Elminster's gone away."

"Cast down?" Illistyl almost whispered. "By *whom?* Who has such power?"

Storm spread her hands. "In the oldest writings, he was called the Overgod. Nowadays, to those who know of him at all, he is 'The One Who is Hidden.' " She smiled. "If you meet him, you might ask his true name and aims—there are a lot of souls, mortal and divine alike, who'd like to know."

Illistyl drew a deep, ragged breath, and then smiled. "I'll get straight to work on it." Her hands trembled as they reached for the decanter. It held far less when she put it back down.

Shaerl shook her head. "Easy, lass, or we'll have to carry you back to the tower again."

Illistyl crooked an eyebrow. "Who, wench, will be carrying whom?"

Jhessail rose. "Come, ladies," she said. "We've done enough harm this night. Storm needs her sleep, even if we do not."

Storm thanked the mage with her eyes. Jhessail read the look and swept her companions swiftly out into the night.

As the candles died, one by one, the two sisters sat at the table unmoving, eyes faraway.

At last Storm moved unwilling lips. "Did you see or feel anything when you reached for Shar? Anything at all?"

"No," the Simbul said, staring down at her empty hands.

"Nothing. I was like the worst apprentice I have ever had—alone, wavering, helpless in the dark."

"I saw three things, Sister," came the eerie voice they had not expected to hear again. "Fire, and tears, and stars—overhead, it seemed, though they were all mixed together. Our stars."

Storm raised her head, and there were tears in her eyes. "Syluné," she said softly, "my thanks. They are not dead, then."

"Yet," came the voice of Syluné's ghost dryly, "yet."

* * * * *

Storm stiffened above her cauldron, almost dropping her knife. "There it is again," she whispered. "Sister, what's happening?"

Syluné was a silver shadow passing the firelight, just for a moment, ere gliding into gloom again. "I know not, but I've mind-spoken Jhess and Illistyl, and both are restless—but know not why. Could it be a sign from the Lady?"

The Bard of Shadowdale frowned. "She's never been so cryptic before!"

The ghostly figure of her sister smiled and faded away, leaving Storm staring at a bright copper pot. "And that habit will stop her being so now? We'll think more on this later. For now, best get your gown on, Lady of the Harp—your first guests are on their way up your path right now!"

Storm Silverhand wiped her hands dry, cursed cheerfully when she realized she'd used her gown, and then snatched it up and over her head, dampness and all, and thrust a herb-flower into the bodice as impish ornament. Later, for the love of Mystra! It seemed everything had to wait for later, these days. . . .

* * * * *

ANGER, LITTLE MAGE? NOW? RAGE IS IN YOU LIKE FLAME, STRONGER THAN WHEN FIRST I SMOTE YOU AND BOUND YOU! WHY?

Later, devil. I'll tell thee later.

NO, CAPTIVE, YOU'LL TELL ME NOW!

[pain]

[scream, trailing away to sobbing, images awhirl]

DON'T YOU COLLAPSE ON ME, PUNY HUMAN! I KNOW YOU'RE STRONGER THAN THAT! FEIGNING AND CRINGING ARE FOR DEVILS I TRAMPLE—FROM YOU, LET THERE BE INSTANT OBEDIENCE! INSTANT AND ABSOLUTE! DO YOU HEAR?

* * * * *

Khelben lifted his head sharply. "Did you hear something? A roaring, as of distant command?"

"Command, my Arunsun?" Laeral purred in his ear, almost playfully. "No, but I tell you true: Jerk your head like that again while my shears are so close, and it's not hair I'll be cutting, but your ear!"

With a frown of irritation Khelben flicked two fingers, and the glittering shears sprang upright. Laeral frowned at them, quivering in her hand, and then at her lord consort.

"Shall I finish this later?" she asked dryly. "The Lord Mage of Waterdeep is content to go out into the city shorn one side and not the other?"

"The Lord Mage of Waterdeep," Khelben said slowly, staring at nothing, "is troubled and knows not why. Put those away, love, and quell all castings, and feel. Just—*feel*. Something is amiss."

The shears clinked upon a table, and the glowing globes of light drifting all around them winked out, fading to nothingness as they sank toward the floor. In the sudden darkness Khelben could see Laeral standing like a statue, her eyes glistening, as they both reached out with their minds, seeking whatever it was that had brushed Khelben's thoughts so fleetingly . . . faintly. . . .

And then the door burst open, and an excited apprentice stood staring at them, framed against the light flooding in from the passage behind her.

"Lord and Lady Mage," she burst out, "I cry pardon! Ah, were you—?"

"Cutting hair?" Laeral asked calmly, as globes of light burst into being all over the room once more. "Yes." Her smile was only slightly wry as she asked, "So, Kareece: What news shakes all the Realms and requires our immediate action *now?*"

* * * * *

I hear, devil. By Mystra, how I hear.

CALL NOT TO HER, ELMINSTER! I KNOW YOUR GAME, NOW. YOU MUST HAVE SPELLS READY AND SEEK TO AWAKEN THEM BY RECALLING THEIR TRIGGERS. TRY ALL YOU LIKE—YOU'LL FAIL, BELIEVE ME—BUT REMEMBER THIS: MY PATIENCE IS NOT ENDLESS.

[mental lash; pain]

YES, RECALL AWAY, LITTLE MAN!

Longer, my memories must be longer—but each I call on is spent forever....

AYE, YIELDED TO ME AND LOST TO YOU FOREVER! NOT SO MIGHTY ARE WE NOW, HEY?

[echoing storms of diabolic laughter]

Aye, I've known better days—and nights. Much better nights.

Four

TO LOVE A GODDESS

The stench was unbelievable. Bones and blood—blood welling up from the ground and flowing in rivulets over the sharp rocks, as foul gases drifted over everything. A figure moved amid the tattered vapors: a lone, naked human crawling painfully down a hillside, like a shattered crab, headed he knew not where.

Elminster's fingers were bleeding stumps, torn by dozens of razor-sharp rocks, but the mental lashings kept him crawling, aimless and trembling. Stingfly after stingfly landed on his trembling flesh and drank deeply of his blood before leaving its eggs under the wizard's skin. With but one arm to lean on, the Old Mage had no way to dislodge them. Not that he could do more than groan and fling himself over on his back. He crushed one buzzing, squalling stingfly that way, but the others all sprang clear—to pounce on El's belly instead, ere he could right himself.

Ahead, the land fell away in a field of tortured rock to a gorge out of which rose darkly boiling plumes of smoke. Maggots as long as three men and as sinuous as snakes fell from some of those drifting clouds, to flop and slither across the rocks. Most seemed able to smell where the blood was strongest and glided thence, to a place where pale, amorphous bulks moved. Lemures, glistening palely, fed from a small pit of maggots—oblivious to the fact that other maggots burrowed into their own rear extremities.

An inspiring sight—not that Elminster cared much where he went in this land of death and cruelty. Perils loomed or lurked everywhere. Firebursts bloomed over distant mountains. From time to time spinagons and worse rose on flapping wings to cross the air above the gorge and glare hungrily at the struggles below.

Lower to the ground undulated something that looked like a lacework of odd jaws and claws and eyes, joined by ropes of mauve flesh. A hooked spear reached up to tug it brutally down to a waiting devil below. The fray that followed was brief ere the weird flying thing rose into the air again, larger and heavier than before.

It rose, drifted Elminster's way, and veered at him, descending in a swift dive with its many-toothed mouths swiveling to the fore. Lower it rushed, jaws agape, knowing its prey had nowhere to run.

The Old Mage watched it grimly. Would Nergal manifest power through him to defend the body he'd so shattered . . . or just let him be torn apart and devoured—salvaging only his head?

The many-jawed creature swept down, very close, trailing streams of green saliva. Dozens of black and gold eyes met his, gleaming with hungry anticipation. Well, his answer would not be long in coming. . . .

BACK AND FORTH I GO, ELMINSTER, OVER THE MEMORIES YOU HOLD UP BEFORE ME LIKE SHIELDS AND YET FIND NOTHING OF WHAT I SEE.

WHERE ARE THE SECRETS OF SILVER FIRE? WHERE ARE THE SPELLS AND SPELLBOOKS AND HIDDEN RINGS AND SCEPTERS AND ALL, GLOWING WITH POWER I CAN USE? WELL?

The archdevil rummaged again, clawing aside memory after memory. He shouldered impatiently through the dark, vaulted caverns of Elminster's memories.

An elf queen stands atop a cliff. The tatters of her sword-hewn, blood-drenched gown flap in the evening breeze. As she looks grimly out over a land the sun sets on, her arms cling to the broad, armored shoulders of a grim dwarf. He clutches her and weeps into her stomach. His bloody axe dangles by its war strap from one hairy, weary arm. . . .

GAHH! YOU'VE CENTURIES OF SUCH DROSS! WHAT CARE I FOR MORTALS NOW DUST AND REALMS LONG FALLEN?

A shining-eyed young sorceress delights in her first great casting. Her face glows as brightly as any lamp. She sweeps the brown-withered, skeletal body of her lich master into an enthusiastic embrace, showering his crumbling lips with kisses. . . .

ALWAYS AN EYE FOR BEAUTY, EH? NOW TO ME, WEAKNESS IS BEAUTIFUL—A CHINK TO BE THRUST THROUGH, A GOOD GRIP ON A FOE TO BE USED. YESSS . . .

Grim-faced warriors lean on their axes and broadswords. Flat menace fills their eyes as they watch wizards walk past, Elminster among them. One bladesman stirs too much. A cowled figure whirls to fling up an open hand. A green, glowing sigil bursts into being right in front of the snarling warrior, freezing him in midswing. The mages walk away, and the warriors glower silently. . . .

Here Nergal wandered, and there, rummaging through dusty darkness where small things scuttled and large things slept. The devil growled as he came on. El's lurking awareness stole away before him, ducking here and crouching there in mind shadows, memories like cloaking webs in his wake.

ANSWER ME, HUMAN! DO YOU THINK YOU CAN HIDE IN YOUR OWN MIND?

A world away, fangs bit and claws pounced, raking and clutching. El screamed, or tried to, sagging back as red pain flared in the dark vaults.

Nergal made a sound of irritated impatience, and lines of blue fire raced here and there through the darkness. There were singing sounds and echoes of what might have been snarls or shrieks. The claws and jaws were gone again.

Dimly, El felt himself collapsing onto sharp, uncaring stones.

ANSWER ME, ELMINSTER! HEED MY CALL, DAMN YOU!

Damned am I, indeed. Cringing here with my memories flowing away from me like water, slipping between my fingers to be gone, gone forever. . . .

INDEED. WEEP AND WAIL, WIZARD! WEEP AND WAIL.

[sudden vicelike mental probes, closing like claws]

BUT FIRST, SHOW ME MYSTRA SHARING THESE MEMORIES WITH YOU. HOW CAME THEY INTO YOUR MIND? HOW? LET ME SEE! SHOW ME NOW!

Dark eyes swim in dreams. Visions flood in, jolting a drowsing Old Mage awake. He sits bolt upright in wonder in his bedchamber, his eyes leaking blue-white fire. The flames reflect in the eyes of the one beside him—smiling Storm in early days, and later the fiery Witch-Queen of Aglarond. Her hair stirs around her slender shoulders like silver blades hungry for a foe, since . . .

YES, YES. WOMEN YOU'VE HAD AND TO SPARE! LET ME IN, WIZARD! NOT WATCHING YOUR FACE AFTER SHE MIND-TOUCHES YOU! SHOW ME!

[blinding, blue-white fire]

AARGGH! YOU DARE?

[mind lash red pain black agony dripping purple ruin]

STOP YOUR SCREAMING! THINK YOU'RE THE ONLY SELF-IMPORTANT MORTAL I'VE MIND-REAMED?

[reluctant healing]

THERE. STOP YOUR GAMES, OR TASTE WORSE.

No game. Ye wanted to see Mystra's mind-touch, and that's what I showed ye. The fire undying.

SHE COMES ONLY IN DREAMS, AND YOU SEE THE MEMORIES SHE LEAVES ONLY WHEN SHE'S GONE? BAH! DECEIVE ME NOT! SHE MUST IMPART DIRECTLY OR LEAVE YOU UNCONTROLLED.

Aye, so she does, most of the time. When we speak directly, I gain images of the moment, not memories worth sharing.

NOTHING MORE? EVER?

[glimpse]

AHA!

[confused images, swift racing]

HAH! WHAT WAS THAT?

[dwindling down, devil-ridden, to one brightness . . . of Mystra, long, long ago, in the land of Elminster's youth. . . .]

Eyes that swam with stars stared into his. Elminster fought for breath as lips that were both fire and ice kissed his throat, moved to his shoulder, and bit gently. Silver fire flowed from that wound. It roiled in the blue-white flame that was her hair, and in her hands, and in a regal cloak flowing endlessly from her.

In the air they drifted, a blue-white star high above Athalantar; El caught a glimpse of its flickering lantern fires far below, as they rolled together.

"Your defiant tenderness, El—aahh, I could drink of it forever. Give, Chosen of mine. Give unto Mystra."

"Gladly," Elminster growled, young and shining-eyed and supple.

As they surged amid the fire, memories that were not his own flooded into his mind. Images whirled, crashed, and raced in a welter of toppling towers and dragons locked in biting battle. Earth trembled. Rock shivered and rose into lofty peaks. Haughty mages brightened the sky with spells. . . .

SO, HER REMEMBRANCES LEAK INTO YOU WHEN YOUR MINDS ARE JOINED? SHE MUST MEAN TO SO SHARE, OR YOU SERVE A WEAK GODDESS INDEED. . . .

[weeping, falling from light into darkness, lost and alone]

OH, STOP THAT! YOU MAY HAVE LOVED A GODDESS AND LIVED, BUT IF YOU DEFY ME YOU'RE GOING TO DIE! SHOW ME MORE OF THE SILVER FIRE, FLOWING INTO YOU! YES! YESSS!

[mental probes lancing forth brutally, transfixing bright memory]

[weeping, shimmering tears, yielding]

Soft summer stars shone above Myth Drannor. El drifted thoughtfully beneath, looking down on magnificent, glowing spires. They were soon to fall, if Starym deceit and o'erreaching pride and dangerous meddling went unchecked. All this beauty to be lost . . .

As Netheril before it, said the thrilling voice in the depths of his mind. Blue-white fire kindled in the air around him. *It is the way of things, most precious Chosen.*

"Holy Mystra," Elminster whispered. The fire deepened and darkened to a blue-black scattering of countless tiny stars—her most private self. "I am most glad to see ye. I have been mournful and lonely."

I, too. Those eyes he could fall into, forever, opened in the air before him, dragging him in. *Let us comfort each other, bodies and minds.*

Silver fire coiled within the floating man, leaping up in quickening excitement to meet the greater flame that had birthed it. Stars shaped slender arms and lips, trailing away in dark glory as the flow of images began. Mind met mind. Silver fire rose and rushed back and forth, swifter and swifter. With a gladsome cry like a proud trumpet, Elminster Aumar shouted his own name aloud to cling to himself. . . . Aye, aye, it came. . . .

[fire, white and furious, overwhelming all, soaring up to bright, blinding glory]

Abruptly the fire was gone, and Elminster was wincing on rocks beneath a blood-red sky. A raw, wordless scream shredded the air of Hell behind him.

Lesser devils whirled up into the sky like bats flooding out of a cave at dusk. They winged toward the sound of shrieking agony, eager to see the mighty fallen.

Weak and sick, the one-armed old man rolled himself into a crevice. He pulled the ashen bones of some long-fallen devil over him. Its grotesque horned skull grinned at him with its eternal stare. If fair fortune or the grace of Mystra were with him, he'd now have no Nergal to protect him against the talons of passing baatezu.

Aye, it had come to that—rejoicing at the possibility of lying unprotected and alone in Avernus.

Closing his eyes, Elminster wrapped himself in that wry thought and descended again into the dark vaults of memory, seeking Nergal in his mind. The outcast devil had already shown himself to be a brute, with wits scarce swifter than a cunning sellsword of Faerûn. If a mere memory of Mystra's mind-touch caused him such pain, perhaps he was weak enough that a Chosen of Mystra—even a weak and exhausted one—might wrest free of him.

Cautiously El skulked through his mind, seeking the place that was a purple ruin—the part of his mind that was forever gone. The ruin was spreading. . . .

There, amid a blood-red glow, and riven shards of memories, he found Nergal. Hulking shoulders, barbed and mottled gray, tentacles stiff with still-fresh pain, great taloned hands fumbling blindly. . . .

[Pain—fury of the Nine, what pain! So that was what goddesses could do . . . and deceitful wizards. . . .]

Cautiously, El knelt. He called forth the tiniest amount of silver fire. With one fingertip, he traced a line on the worn and dusty stone. The line smoked as he seared his way across the floor of his memories, yielding yet more remembrances so as to keep well away from his shuddering captor. Around this pillar of things best forgotten, and this one, of regrets, then quickly down this dark way, soft and swift . . .

WHAT BEFALLS? MORTAL, WHAT ARE YOU DOING?

Now across this chamber, answering not, and down the steps beyond, hurrying, with walls trembling to the left, where the archdevil stirs. . . .

WHAT ARE YOU DOING?

Answer not, but race now, trailing silver fire in a bright and rending line, down more steps and left here, threading through the pillars and into the arch beyond—blast, but it grows light, red and bright ahead, and he's waiting—

Close hand on silver fire, will it down, sink into the stones, become dark and silent, a statue in this hall of statues. Brood, cold and silent. Be stone. Be not there. Be lost and forgotten.

Archdevils tread and slither both. Slow slither and footfall. Heavy, not hurrying. He comes. Footfall. Closer. Be stone. Slowly he comes. Slowly and carefully. Wary now, are we, Most Mighty of Avernus?

Footfall. Scrape of talon on stone.

ELMINSTER, RISE. I KNOW YOU.

Stone silence. Pain will come no matter what, so be stone, and let rage blind him.

[ice-cold probe, slow and sharp and deliberate, thrusting home]

[writhing, twisting agony]

YES. DECEIVE ME NOT, LITTLE SNEAKING CREATURE OF SILVER FIRE. NERGAL WAS PROUD IN HELL WHEN ATHALANTAR WAS YET UNBORN.

[pain pain pain]

[grim satisfaction, Nergal's claim echoing through a shattered mind, mortal mage writhing and drooling, rising up in Avernus like a grinning idiot, shedding bones]

An abishai loomed, claws outstretched, fanged mouth grinning, black wings and certain death. . . .

Red and purple fire blossomed in the fiend's gaping jaws, and its head exploded, spattering Elminster with wet foulness and shaking him to full awareness of Avernus around him. He stood in the crevice he'd sought to hide in. The headless body of the abishai flopped on the stones in front of him, muscles still trying to make it fly. Beyond, a huge dragon flew through the sky, black and terrible. It snapped at fleeing spinagons like a shark racing through a shoal of silverfin. Fire rose from the side of a black crag off to his left—

ONE LESS ABISHAI TO TEAR APART MY TOY. BE GRATEFUL, WIZARD. I'VE NOT SLAIN YOU YET.

I made no attack on ye. When ye seize on my memories, they are what they are; I cannot change them. Ye felt what I did, then.

IMPRESSIVE. NO WONDER YOU STAND AND DEFY ME.

Elminster was very careful to keep still and silent in the crevice and in his mind.

A JOINING OF MINDS, AND MEMORIES SHARED DELIBERATELY. IT BINDS YOUR LOYALTY ANEW AND IMPARTS ECSTASY, UNTIL YOU BECOME ADDICTED TO THE DIVINE TOUCH AND WILL DO ANYTHING TO FEEL IT AGAIN.

Elminster bowed his head. *That's one way of seeing it, aye.*

[grim grin] CAN'T YOU SIMPLY SAY I'M RIGHT, LITTLE MAN?

Mystra would see it differently, El said with as much mental dignity as he could muster. [image of arms crossed, body drawn up, chin lifted]

SHE CERTAINLY BRED DEFIANCE INTO YOU, OR CHOSE YOU BECAUSE OF IT. WHICH MAKES YOU BOTH FOOLS.

[sudden mental probe]

[wince]

[bright image, after image, after image]

SO, NO SUCH UNIONS WITH SHE WHO IS MYSTRA NOW.

Shared thought: *Which means no trace linkage remains that*

might let Mystra reach through her Chosen and do harm in Hell.

[relief] *So, LITTLE MAN, LET'S GET TO THAT SILVER FIRE.*

Sharp pain, and then numbness. Elminster reeled in the crevice. A maggot taller than he had reared up and sunk its fangs into his left shoulder. Its glistening body was undulating across his chest as it gnawed its way into him. . . .

Writhing in pain, he tried to claw at it, but Nergal's laughter was all around him now.

MAGGOT-RIDDEN! SUITS YOU, TREACHEROUS MORTAL! NOW, UP OUT OF THAT CREVICE AND CRAWL! YES, THAT'S IT!

Staggering, El found himself walking across broken rock again, the weight of the maggot that was now wrapped around him—and questing its way hungrily *inside* him—forcing him to lurch and falter.

MY MAGIC WILL KEEP YOU ALIVE, HONORED GUEST. HOWEVER, I REGRET TO ANNOUNCE THAT YOU WILL SUFFER. [gusts of laughter]

ADVENTURE, LITTLE MAN, IS WHERE YOU FIND IT. MY VENTURE WILL BE ON THROUGH YOUR MIND, MORE CAUTIOUSLY THAN BEFORE. YOURS WILL BE A LITTLE STROLL THROUGH HELL.

FEAR NOT, I'LL KEEP YOU ALIVE. I WANT THAT SILVER FIRE.

[pain, pain falling sharply, spreading pain, maggot tearing and thrashing]

UP, LITTLE MAN. THERE . . . MAGIC'S A WONDERFUL THING, ISN'T IT? NOW, LET US SEEK YOUR OWN EARLY DAYS, CREATURE OF MYSTRA, AND ADVENTURE THERE. SHOW ME AN EARLY TIME WHEN YOU WORKED WITH OTHERS, SO THAT I CAN SEE MYSTRA'S HAND AT WORK SHAPING YOU.

[friends' faces, castle battlements, a scudding moon, dark alley and drawn sword . . .]

THERE! SHOW ME, ELMINSTER!

[different battlements, different faces, one swimming to the fore: a bearded wizard, fat and frowning, lurching along full of importance . . .]

YES, THAT ONE WILL DO! SHOW ME!

Hear me, Vangerdahast. For the love of the Lady we both serve, hear me.

STOP MIND-MUTTERING, MAGE! SHOW ME!

[images, whirling up brightly, unfolding . . .]

"Th-through here, Lord Mage M-most High," the mouselike Keeper of the Vaults quavered.

"Yes, yes, yes," Vangerdahast replied irritably. Strangely enough, having laid his own share of protective enchantments on the Hall of Scrolls and Ledgers, albeit years ago, and being the only court official to often consult its contents, he did have a fair idea of where so vast and central a chamber *was*. As if he hadn't enough important worries right now, what with—

He stopped and stiffened, his mouth dropping open at what he saw. A moment later, he firmly closed it . . . far too late to escape the notice of the Keeper. The little man didn't quite dare to let a smirk show on his face but couldn't keep it out of his suddenly triumphant eyes.

"Leave us," the Royal Magician snapped, "and close the doors behind you."

He did not bother to look at the hastening courtier, and did not move a muscle until the huge and heavy bronzed double doors boomed closed behind him . . . and he was alone with the thing.

The thing that should not have been there.

His predecessors, generations of War Wizards under their command, and a rare few visiting mages deserving of such trust had cast spell after crawling and flickering spell on the walls, floors, and ceiling of the hall and the rooms surrounding it. Defensive magics, all, designed to foil each new method of scrying or translocation or other means of access. Growing thus over the centuries, they formed a complicated web that no man alive knew or could unravel without months of work and considerable personal peril.

Vangerdahast himself had overlaid the existing magics with several subtle misdirections designed to foil all but the most exacting users of wish spells. He had also cast far less subtle backlash enchantments that would twist intruding spells—unless preceded by a secret key—into paralysis, feeblemind, and smashing-blow effects against their casters. He would be loath to send even a magic missile at the thing protruding from the floor right now, lest each of its pulses come back at him.

The Royal Magician let out the breath he hadn't until then noticed he was holding. He took a few cautious steps to one side and peered at the mystery that had appeared in the hall.

A convulsed male human hand—long-fingered, bereft of the rings that had left pale bands of flesh, and with a few dark hairs adorning its back—protruded from the glossy-smooth marble of the vault floor. The forty-foot-square slab weighed many tons. It seemed that the owner of the hand was now entombed in that slab, for the hand did not look severed.

Vangerdahast had a sudden urge to give it a good kick to make sure, but royal magicians of Cormyr don't grow old and fat by undertaking stupid acts. Wherefore he did nothing more than peer around the hall until he was sure nothing else was out of place or missing He circled the hand, which hadn't moved in the slightest, and grew no wiser.

The Royal Magician let himself out. He sternly ordered the anxious Keeper and the ring of stone-faced Purple Dragon guards clustered outside to clear this entire wing of the palace, and then take themselves as far away as the Chamber of the Brazen Fool. He stood silently, waiting until the echoes of their obedient movements faded.

Vangerdahast spoke a quiet word. It awakened guardian magics that would reveal any hidden, lurking spy. He received with complete lack of surprise the lore that no such intruder existed within range. Making sure he was standing on a specific floor tile, he touched one of the rings on a hidden chain around his neck and spoke a word he'd hoped never to have to use again.

There was suddenly a taller, black-robed man standing on an adjacent tile, rubbing his beard and looking less than happy. "Yes?" he snapped.

Vangerdahast bowed slightly to his guest. "My apologies, Lord Khelben. Be welcome in the royal palace of Cormyr, in Suzail."

"Oddly enough, Vangy," Khelben growled, "I know where the royal palace is. I'll even accept that apology. The honor of your hospitality overwhelms me. It will do so even more if you unfold the reason for my summoning." The edge of his mouth curled. "A sufficiently interesting answer may even blunt Laeral's wrath at my abrupt disappearance. Note that 'may,' and speak accordingly."

Vangerdahast drew in a deep breath as their eyes met. "We stand outside the Hall of Scrolls and Ledgers. You had a hand in casting some still-active defensive spells here. Something has appeared therein; it's my hope that you can identify it and explain its appearance."

The Blackstaff raised one dark eyebrow, turned to face the massive double doors, and made a twisting gesture with one hand.

There was an instant of singing silence. Then the doors collapsed into shards and dust with a roar that swelled and shrank away to nothing again. The torrent of falling metal had vanished, swallowed up by thin air just above the floor tiles the two men stood on.

"How—?"

"One of the spells I cast, long ago. No door in this palace can stand against me."

It was Vangerdahast's turn to raise an eyebrow. "Oh? Why did you do that?"

Khelben shrugged. "We all have our own ways of doing things." He pointed across the mirror-bright floor of the Hall to the human hand jutting so improbably out of the smooth marble. "This, for example, is Elminster's work."

"*What?*" the Royal Magician snarled. "You're sure?"

Khelben strolled over to a certain spot on the floor and murmured a word. The air glowed for a moment, he raised his hand into the glow, and when the radiance faded, the Lord Mage of Waterdeep was holding a large, ornate decanter.

"Unmistakable. I've seen this spell before. Someone sprang one of his traps—probably cast on a spot where he meets with the Simbul."

"So, that's a Red Wizard," Vangerdahast mused. "Or . . . was."

Khelben nodded, sipping from the decanter without bothering with a flagon.

Vangerdahast looked at the decanter rather unhappily. How many more hidden surprises did the hall's web of spells hold? He asked rather hesitantly, "And to get rid of it?"

Khelben licked his lips and raised the decanter again. "I'm sure you know how to call on him," he replied. "Even if you don't want to."

Vangerdahast winced, as if something painful had struck him. Stepping reluctantly out through the entrance that the doors no longer guarded, he lifted one hand and murmured something.

Khelben watched, not quite smiling.

Abruptly a ring of light glowed on the floor tiles. A moment later, someone stood in its center.

She was tall and slender—some would almost have said bony, for her ribs showed clearly as she spun around. Unruly silver hair writhed about her like a nest of roused snakes. She faced her summoner. Vangerdahast swallowed.

The angry eyes of the Simbul, Witch-Queen of Aglarond, were barely three paces from his. She wore nothing and did not look amused.

"Vangerda—" she began, her voice dangerously low and soft. Blue motes of magical fire gathered above her left palm, and she turned to look into the hall.

Her face changed. She crowed in delight and raced across the floor on silent bare feet to where the hand reached up from the floor.

Bending over to peer at it—both men stared a moment, looked away, cleared their throats, and turned again to regard her—the sorceress clapped her hands and hissed happily, "Adrelgus, yes! Foolish enough to try to slay me!"

She spun around to regard the two wizards, planted her hands on her hips, and bubbled, "*This* is what El meant by my 'little present, reaching for me'!"

She clapped her hands, muttered something. The hand was abruptly gone, the marble floor as smooth and unbroken as if it had never been there.

The Simbul gave them a cheery wave, tossed her hair in a defiantly alluring pose, and snapped her fingers—whereupon she vanished too.

Inevitably, the two men stared in unison at where she'd stood, cleared their throats, and slowly turned to look at each other.

"If you're ever captured," Khelben said in a very dry voice, "try not to let it be by a woman . . . or at least, not that one."

Vangerdahast glanced involuntarily back to the floor where the hand had been. It bore no trace at all of ever having held a Red Wizard.

"How many palaces, vaults, and castles across Faerûn, which their owners think are secure," he asked, looking sick, "can be breached so readily?"

Khelben smiled with only a corner of his mouth. "Oh," he said quietly, "you'd be surprised."

No, no! [ripple of rage] *NOT MAGES YOU TAUGHT OR NOW TAKE TO BED! EARLY DAYS, I SAID!*

BAH! IF MYSTRA DIDN'T BREED YOU OR CREATE YOU, SHE CHOSE YOU. TAKE ME BACK, BEYOND YOUR BIRTH, INTO WHATEVER MEMORIES SHE GAVE YOU OF YOUR CHOOSING . . . AND LET'S SEE WHY.

STUPID WIZARD.

*   *   *   *   *

The Royal Magician of Cormyr looked up into Queen Filfaeril's eyes and found them just as sparkling with anger as he'd expected. *Thank* you, O watching gods.

"You were right to send for me, Highness," he said gravely.

The queen nodded, face frozen, and began pointing—at the door guards, her ladies-in-waiting, the two war wizards behind Vangerdahast, and finally, the door.

"R-royal Lady?" one of the guards dared to ask, earning himself a regal scowl and an imperious gesture toward the door. That was enough to start the hasty, wordless migration.

Vangerdahast stood motionless, facing the queen, until the stream of swift, quiet bodies was gone, and they were alone.

"Lady?" he asked, not bothering to hide his sigh.

"Vangy," the queen said with an exasperated sigh of her own, "call me Faeril or Fee or even 'stupid bitch,' but stop looking at me as if I've singlehandedly doomed the realm! What could you have been doing that can *possibly* be more important than uncovering another plot against the throne?"

"Lady," he said, stepping forward to clasp her hand, "I know not. I was on my way here, in answer to your call, when I—I remembered something."

The queen let her incredulous eyebrow speak for her.

Vangerdahast gave her a sour smile and added, "I'm not *quite* in my dotage yet, Faeril. It was a rather important memory—of the Blackstaff and the queen of Aglarond, here in these halls—and I can't think why it came back to me. So sudden and so vivid—all of it playing out in front of me as if I were living it."

The queen's eyes narrowed. "Khelben and the Simbul *here?* When was this, exactly?"

Vangerdahast sighed. "Lady," he said, "it's no part of present treacheries. I'll explain later, when you've unfolded whatever this latest plot is. Would it be Lady Kessemer's, by any chance?"

Filfaeril stared at him. "How did you know?"

The Royal Magician coughed. "Lady," he reminded her mildly, "I *am* a wizard."

That royal sparkle of anger was back, in full force. "You knew, and you didn't *tell me?*"

Vangerdahast took great care neither to sigh nor to roll his eyes. "Lady," he began carefully. . . .

*   *   *   *   *

"Ssso, Queen of Aglarond, at lassst you stray within my reach! One little missstake, but I fear 'tisss your lassst!"

The gloating devil's great bat wings struck her tumbling from the sky. She fell hard onto rocks. The cruel talons of dozens of laughing fiends held her captive and raked her mercilessly before she could rise, laying her bare—just in time for the great beast's whip to come down.

Mystra! What *fire!* Screaming and sobbing in the grasp of the fiend's minions, the Simbul could not even convulse under the lashing pain. Claws caught at her hair and her throat, dragging her head back, bending her over backward. Her blood-drenched front, laid open by the lash, turned toward a sky that matched its bleeding hue.

"Sssoo, what does a god-touched human taste like, I wonder," the great fiend purred, stretching down an impossibly long black arm.

Spread-eagled and helpless, the Simbul could only moan as that great taloned hand closed on her breast and tightened cruelly. Nails dug into her. The fiend's flesh was *hot.*

She could smell her skin sizzling as it burned, the stink choking her even more than the fresh pain. Somehow she managed to scream, "No! *No! Nooooo!*"

Her cry sent crystals and gems humming and singing all around her in the darkness. Gasping, Alassra Silverhand stared up at her own bedchamber ceiling.

No devils, no blood-red sky . . . she was alone, thrashing on her bed, drenched with sweat. Her hands were twisted in the samite beneath her, and there was nothing covering her but air—cool air. Yet she was afire, hot and burning, as if she had a fever—

No, the fire was raging in her breast! The Simbul gasped the word that made the ceiling glow. In its light, she looked down along her body. There was dark, dried blood all over her . . . but not enough to hide the horrible scar seared on her breast.

It was a deep burn—a brand she'd wear forever, unless magic banished it. It looked like it had been left by large, long, sharp-taloned fingers.

Panting with rage and fear and pain, she sat up and ran a hand over her twisted flesh. Aye, it was real.

Her jaw tightened in anger even before her hands flashed out to two of the gems set into the edge of her bed. Magic kindled within them. The flash of the first told her that no taint lurked within her, and she let the second do its healing work.

Breathing more easily now as the pain ebbed, the queen of Aglarond threw back her head, her hair writhing like soft snakes along her bare shoulders. "Tharammas of Thay, and his spell of nightmares! It *must* be!"

The healing gem winked out, and bare feet struck the floor. Imperious, furiously striding, the Simbul charged along darkened corridors, doors flying open—and almost cringing—before her.

Sleepy guards snapped to careful attention and dared not move another muscle as their monarch raged by. Rings and staves and robes and cloaks whirled to the queen of Aglarond as she went, clothing her for battle. A snarled word made spell-locked doors at the end of one last passage fly open, to let in the chill moonlight.

"Well," she told the cool night wind savagely as she stepped onto a moon-drenched balcony, "at least this time I *know* which Red Wizard isn't going to live to see the dawn!"

Spells sparkled around slender fingers. The robed queen melted away into a raging shadow. It quavered a moment under the moon, and then whirled away into the wind, east into the night, and was gone.

*   *   *   *   *

[Amid the raging of Hell, one Old Mage sinks back with a sigh and looks at his empty, broken hand.]

Aye. Stupid wizard, indeed.

Five

HERE BE WIZARDS

"If you please, Lord Mage," the lady servant murmured, turning with a swirl of cloth-of-gold and white silks to indicate an ascending side-stair, whose carpet was deeper and less worn than the dusty ways they'd been traveling, "to follow me . . ."

The doddering War Wizard straightened out of his customary stoop and inclined his head with a leer that he probably meant to be a pleasant smile. His hand unfolded in a grand gesture indicating she should precede him.

The lady servant kept her face serene as she gracefully gathered her gown and set off, soaring up the stair. The bony old mage watched. She was Vangy's latest apprentice, wasn't she? And a Crownsilver . . .

I SEE WIZARDS BUT NO ELMINSTER OR SILVER FIRE. YOU'RE HIDING SOMETHING FROM ME BEHIND THIS TOO.

I WARN YOU AGAIN, HUMAN, MY PATIENCE IS NOT INFINITE.

I appear in this soon enough, Lord Nergal—with secrets of magic, too.

[sneer] YOU SOUND LIKE A MERCHANT TRYING TO MAKE A SALE. THIS HAD BETTER PLEASE ME, WORM.

I strive to give satisfaction. Always.
AND I STRIVE TO REFRAIN FROM ENDING YOUR MISERABLE LIFE. ALWAYS.

A Crownsilver, wasn't she? Hmmph. As if that mattered a whit to him. Still, it had been long years since a maid as beautiful as this one had flown eagerly up palace stairs in front of *this* old War Wizard. That had been another lady, dust now, in a different tower.

Bolifar Geldert firmly set aside that memory and did not let either of the silently hurrying servants who brushed past him hear his sigh. Bolifar was studious, careful, and hard-working, more than most senior war wizards of Cormyr. That was its own reward and carried impressive weight in this place.

He'd dwelt long enough on past glories. Memories do not keep one warm nor fill one's hands with comfort, like the reassuring heft of a favorite dagger or the roiling power of a risen spell. It was his turn to mount the narrow stair.

At the top, standing ajar, was an arched gate of heavy iron. Its bars were as stout as his own forearms, and studded with blunt spikes. It looked like something made to hold dragons long ago.

In the cross-passage beyond waited the lady servant. She tried not to look nervous as she shrank from two restless panthers, who pulled taut the rattling chains that held them. They leaned forward, licking their lips and staring hard at her.

The other end of those chains was wrapped around the strong and hairy hands of a smiling man. Dark eyes, a goatee, and a cruel face between, the Master of the King's Beasts, looking every bit as dangerous as the two great cats he was walking.

Bolifar gave him a slow, deliberate nod and received the briefest of brow-inclinations in return. Not an unexpected insult, but something Vangerdahast should be apprised of nonetheless. It sat not well when beast-tamers thought themselves higher in rank than senior War Wizards.

Their stair crossed the hall where the panthers crouched and switched their tails. They stared a little less hungrily at a bony old wizard than they had at the curvaceous grace of his guide. The lady servant ascended the next flight, relief written plain down the splendid curve of her back. Bolifar Geldert followed, clutching his writing satchel a trifle more tightly than usual. He took care not to hasten—even when he heard the rattle that meant the master had loosened the chains. The first panther who dared to sink claws or fangs into *this* War Wizard would also be the last.

There were no beasts in the next passage their stair crossed, but silent hurrying servants and a pair of stiffly saluting guards. Gods above, hadn't he asked for a chamber with a door he could lock, somewhere off the "little-used, out-of-the-way upper passages"?

There was nothing at the top of this last stair but a closed door. Metal rattled as the lady servant turned her key. Her touch brought the glowstone adorning the doorplate to crimson life. In its ruby light, she turned and pressed a key, warm from its ride in her bodice, into Bolifar's hand. Without a word, she slipped past him down the steps and was gone.

Thoughtfully Bolifar watched her go. He unhurriedly turned and pushed the door open, stepping into the deep darkness beyond. Unfamiliar this turret-top room might be, but it was also heavily spell guarded and isolated—just the place he needed to write his report.

Vangerdahast had waited long enough—far longer than his patience was wont to stretch. What Master Mage Geldert had learned thus far of possible traitors to the crown in the minor noble family of Cordallar would have to be set down right smartly; Old Hammer-spells was undoubtedly pacing his chambers already and scowling like an Immersea storm.

Bolifar gave the warm and waiting darkness a rueful smile. Vangy's scowl was fated to grow darker soon. This old War Wizard was here, at the top of too many steps—rather than in his usual offices in the Royal Court—because he had his suspicions about the involvement of certain of his fellow War Wizards in the plotting of House Cordallar.

HUH. FEEBLE INTRIGUES COMPARED TO THOSE HERE IN HELL, BUT I CAN FEEL MAGIC NEAR—AND GETTING NEARER. NO LEADING ASTRAY, NOW!

None. The memories merely unfold....

Vangerdahast found himself yawning again. Quite deliberately he reached out to the nearest candle and snuffed the flame between his finger and thumb.

The pain brought him fully awake. Letting the smoke curl up undisturbed, he stepped back and shot a glance across the chamber. The tall, slender form was slumped and still: Sardyl, sitting patiently in her usual chair, had slipped into slumber.

It *was* late. Time had passed—too much time. The chambermaids would long since have begun clucking at the thought of the Royal Magician's personal messenger and scribe shut in with him this late, this long. As if the Lady Sardyl Crownsilver didn't trust Vangerdahast absolutely . . . almost as deeply as he trusted her.

"Wake, lass," he said, stroking her cheek with one finger, far more gently than the chambermaids would have believed Old Hammerspells was capable of.

Sardyl blinked awake and looked a silent question up at him.

Vangerdahast nodded impatiently, angry at the tardy Geldert. "Aye, fetch him," he growled and wheeled away to pace across the room once more, seeing not the desks littered with tomes and parchments, but his increasingly welcoming bed and much-needed sleep. "Give him no more time. I'll have whatever he's got ready *now*," he added, quelling yawn after yawn.

Without a word, his scribe rose, stretched like a cat, and set off to bring back Master Mage Geldert from the turret she'd conducted him to earlier. Vangy turned by his desk and watched her go. The Lady Sardyl Crownsilver might not have spells enough to best a good guardsman yet, but she was far more blessedly silent and tactful than a dozen of his most senior War Wizards—and more trustworthy, too.

Mmm. Trust. Always a rare commodity in Cormyr.

HO, HO! A LITTLE LUST IN THE OFFING, PERCHANCE?

[mental eyebrow raised] *Devil, ye make me look like a prude— and that, I fear, is an accomplishment.*

The door at the top of the stairs was still spell-locked. Sardyl lifted a shapely eyebrow and raised her hand again, feeling the faint prickling that told her she hadn't been mistaken. "Bolifar," she called softly, knowing how small the turret room beyond was.

There was no reply. Sardyl frowned, cast a quick look back down the stairs to be sure no guard was watching, and turned her hand in a swift circle as she murmured the words of a spell known to very few, even among the War Wizards.

The lock spell died with a tiny flash, and she turned the door ring and went in.

The lamp was lit, its soft light falling warm and steady across the turret room's rug, chair, table, and wall map. All of these things, and the lamp itself, occupied their usual places—but the chamber was entirely empty of Bolifar Geldert, his pens and ink, his parchment and blotter, and his writing satchel.

There were no corners to hide in. Sardyl looked up, found the ceiling every bit as bare as it should have been, and took two smooth steps into the room. She turned slowly, looking all around, reaching out to touch nothing. The windows were closed, their solid-slab shutters locked from within, and there was no sign of anything unusual in the turret room. Neither was there any sign of Bolifar Geldert.

The Lady Crownsilver's mouth tightened. She backed hastily to the doorway. From there she cast a magic-seeking spell into the turret room—and found only what had always been there: the old, many-layered magics on the map. Preservative enchantments laid down well before she'd been born, perhaps before her grandmother's birth.

Yet, standing here, she did not feel alone, somehow.

Eyes large and dark, Sardyl took several steps back and cast another spell, one that sought out invisible creatures. When it found none, her face grew white and grim. Securing the door, she spell-sealed its lock again. With the added flick of a finger, she made her seal different from another caster's, and went to find Vangerdahast.

Ah, a whiff of mystery! Show me more!
Of course.

"If what Lady Crownsilver says is true," the sage said, an edge of asperity in his voice as he knuckled the last sleepiness from his eyes, "I've been brought up several hundred stairs to see *nothing.*" He took two restless steps along the passage and then turned back to look up the last flight of stairs. At its top, the mightiest wizard in Cormyr stood glowering at a closed door.

The sage burst out, "Is there no trace of him? I mean—could the man not simply have taken himself away somewhere? There're over a thousand rooms in this wing alo—"

The Royal Magician turned and gave the Court Sage a level look. "Alaphondar," he said flatly, "we know our work. I'd not have summoned you to bear witness without trying to trace the man first. My spells would find him, if he were alive and anywhere in Faerûn, unless he's magically shielded." He turned his head to the third person present. "Is that your seal, lass?"

"It is, milord," Sardyl said quietly, her fingers poised over the door ring. "Shall I break it?"

Vangerdahast frowned. "No, let me." He made a little wave of his hand that everyone in the palace knew meant "stand back," and cast a spell that neither the sage nor the scribe had ever seen before. They heard a snarl of magic race away from the other side of the door, a faint whistling echo as if it had struck the walls and come shuddering back, and then—silence.

Sardyl and Alaphondar both looked at the Royal Magician. Vangerdahast stood with his head bent to one side, listening intently to the stretching silence. After a long time, he stepped forward and flung open the door.

The turret room was just as Sardyl had left it.

Alaphondar frowned. "Who lit the lamp?"

"Bolifar, apparently," Sardyl replied. The sage looked at Vangerdahast as if expecting a different answer but received no utterance at all. The Royal Magician was hastening to the shutters.

He held his hands over them for a moment before turning the thumb-keys on their locks and throwing them wide. Long-unused wood squealed and stuck momentarily. Dust curled up from the sill into the wizard's face. Vangerdahast sneezed like a bull bellowing in a thunderstorm. The sage and scribe joined the Master of the War Wizards at the sill. They looked down over a sheer drop of a hundred feet at the cobbled courtyard below and saw the faces of startled guards in the lantern light, gazing back up at them.

Vangerdahast let the sentinels get a good look at his face, watering eyes and all, but said nothing. These shutters hadn't been opened for some time. Anything entering or leaving by way of them would have been reported. He nodded sourly. He hadn't expected to see blood below or anything of interest hanging from the turret roof above, and his expectations were met.

The Royal Magician drew his stout body back into the room and turned, rocking slightly like a heavily laden cart dragged around a tight corner. "Is there anything," he snapped at Sardyl, "different about the room since your earlier look? Anything at all . . . the smallest detail or impression."

The shapely Crownsilver turned with more grace than the portly wizard. She wrinkled her nose as well as her brow when she frowned. "The rug . . . it seems different, somehow . . . more worn." She shrugged and added, "Yet how can that be?"

Neither man replied. Vangerdahast was already bending over the rug suspiciously, gathering its weave in his hand and plucking it up to glare at the solid stones of the floor beneath. Alaphondar knelt and almost angrily poked and prodded at hitherto-hidden flagstones, seeking a seam that would part or something that would shift.

After some fruitless time he sighed, straightened his back, and looked at Vangerdahast. "Well, O master of weaves?"

The Royal Magician did not bother to smile at the weak joke. "As an Obarskyr prince once said of a far grander gift than this," he said grimly, "it's just a rug. There must be forty or more like this around the palace. Woven in Wheloon eighty years back or so. Bought in bulk, in 1306, when the Lion Tower was built and all the furniture moved about. Proper chaos that was, too."

Feeling the stares of his two companions, Vangerdahast gave them both a glare and added, "*Yes*, I was here in 1306. The weather was fine that year, and the five before it, too, as I recall. I'll thank you to direct your disbelief elsewhere, and spare me any comments about wizards' dotage."

Sardyl sighed. "Secret passages?"

Her master gave her a weary look. "You've been reading too many fantasy books, my dear." Alaphondar, who'd been about to ask the same thing, shut his mouth with an audible snap.

The Royal Magician gave the sage a withering glance and waved his hand at the chamber around. "Look you: The stones are solid, with nothing to raise or lower them, floor or ceiling—and there's no room in the walls for secret doors or passages. The curve you see is because the walls here are the same walls that form the outside of the tower." One of his hands went to a belt-pouch, hesitated with visible reluctance, and then dipped within.

There was a small glass sphere in the wizard's fingers when he raised his hand again. He murmured a word over it. Sudden light winked and moved within its depths.

"Stored magic?" Alaphondar asked, leaning forward for a better look.

Vangerdahast nodded. "These hold but one spell—and it's a spell that works only once in a particular place. Once I've called this forth, another spell of the same sort will never manifest successfully in this room."

"And it's a . . . ?"

The Royal Magician left the sage's question hanging unanswered in the air as he went to the windows, closed and latched the shutters, and put his back to them. "In a moment," he announced, "we should see an image, a person. Identify it if you can—and fix its features in your mind if you can't." He felt Sardyl's question without bothering to meet her gaze, and added, "My magic will be seeking the likeness of the last person to use translocational magic into or out of this room."

As he spoke, the glass sphere flashed with a vivid golden flame and shattered, tiny shards tumbling musically through his fingers.

A moment later, the air in the middle of the room shimmered, seemed to *flow* for a moment, and suddenly grew misty. Gray wisps coiled, lengthened, and became—very suddenly—sharp and distinct. They were looking at a woman, or rather at the faint, flickering image of a woman's upper torso, the rest of her lost in the mists. She looked determined, even eager, as she raised slender bare arms and moved her fingers in the most graceful casting Sardyl had ever seen. Suddenly, she was gone, leaving two fading motes of starry light.

It was a long moment before she realized the woman hadn't been wearing anything but rings and a necklace. It was another before she heard Vangerdahast swallow in a way he rarely did.

Sardyl knew what that sound meant and turned in time to see grief in Vangerdahast's softened face. The Royal Magician looked like just what he was: an old man struggling not to cry. That was all she saw before his face hardened.

He looked up at her with what could only be called a defiant glare. Wordlessly she put a comforting hand on his arm—something Alaphondar would never have dared to do—and asked her question with her eyes.

"Amedahast," he replied gruffly. "High Magess of Cormyr, into the reign of Draxius. This was her 'by-herself' chamber, long ago. No one's used translocational magic here since her time—not really a surprise, that, given the wards."

The wizard strode a few paces to the wall, peered at the map, and touched a tiny monogram in one corner of it. "Aye, here's her mark. She drew this . . . more than seven hundred summers ago."

Alaphondar looked around the room once more, and shook his head. No, it really was too small to hide anything from them. "If your missing Bolifar *were* in this room," he said carefully, "and didn't just go back down the stairs after you left him, perhaps he left by way of the window, in wraithform."

Vangerdahast shook his head. "No holes in those shutters, and no gaps for air to slide through. Saw you the dust when I opened them? No. Something darker happened here. I can feel it."

His scribe was nodding. She could feel it, too, as strong as when she'd been here before. There was something about this room. A *watched* feeling . . .

Alaphondar shrugged irritably, and said, "I'm for my bed. I've seen your nothing and have far too much to do tomorrow to stand here yawning any longer. The gods give you good slumber—though for the life of me, you don't deserve it."

As the sage turned and left, the wizard and his scribe looked at each other. In unspoken accord, they frowned and turned to prowl the room again, searching for what must be there.

With a sudden growl of impatience at his own failing wits, Vangerdahast cast a magic-seeking, advanced on the map and the lamp, and sighed sourly. He leaned back against the wall. The map held its complex weave of old spells, and the lamp, flame and all, was bereft of enchantment. The rug also bore only the magics of long ago.

Bolifar Geldert, it seemed, had simply vanished from this room.

Simply and impossibly. "Impossible," in Vangerdahast's experience, always meant magic.

"The sage's desire for bed seems wiser than before," he said quietly. "Come, lass. Let's spell-lock this room and go. There'll be plenty of time to search fruitlessly on the morrow."

Sardyl nodded and said nothing, but then she usually did.

YOU DON'T SEEM TO FEATURE IN THIS YET, MAGE. YOU WILL BE TEACHING VANGERDAHAST ABOUT MAGIC BEFORE THIS IS DONE, WON'T YOU? OR IS A LITTLE OF THIS NECESSARY?

[mind slap, red pain flaring like flames in the vaulted darkness]

If ye refrain from that, Nergal, 'twill unfold faster!

[diabolic growl of warning]

[fresh images flaring]

Between great paintings and tapestries, sheets of polished copper striped the palace walls. Lamplight reflected from the metal, throwing a warm glow onto its face and flashing back onto carefully motionless, watching guards. Standing in pairs along the walls, the guards kept their faces expressionless as the Royal Magician escorted his scribe past them to the door of her chambers.

"Get some sleep," he told her grimly, his voice low enough to reach her ears alone. "There'll be plenty of time to worry about Bolifar's fate in the morning. Set your spell shield."

Sardyl nodded and bowed to him. She looked pale and on the verge of tears, her eyes large and dark.

After another wordless moment, Vangerdahast put a comforting hand on her shoulder.

Lady Crownsilver slid gently out from under it and went into her room.

The Royal Magician stood like a statue, listening as his scribe closed and bolted her door. It was barely a breath later before he heard the tiny singing sound that meant she'd set her spell shield within.

Vangerdahast nodded grimly at the closed door and cast a spell of his own. As he turned away for the long trudge to his own chambers, the guards were startled to see a fist-sized eye hovering behind the wizard's back, keeping a lookout for him.

The conjured eye saw nothing suspicious on the journey, nor was there anything amiss as the Royal Magician entered his familiar rooms, set his own wards, passed into an inner spell chamber, and turned to his workbench. Without even pausing to light a lamp, he worked a mighty magic to trace Bolifar Geldert.

The mighty magic collapsed into darkness, failing utterly.

Vangerdahast frowned down at the fading ashes and wisps of smoke that had been his spell. He sighed for perhaps the hundredth time that night and headed for a closet he rarely opened. A hooded thing waited there.

The spell on the closet door gave him enough dim red radiance to drag the hood off and toss it aside. The revealed speaking-stone atop its pedestal was a chipped, sloping mass of rock, not the polished crystal sphere favored by the fashionable mages of Sembia and Calimshan. Just now, Vangerdahast couldn't have cared less what it looked like. Six guards whose minds were free of magic had agreed that Bolifar had gone up those stairs—and not come down.

Wherefore the answer to his whereabouts lay somewhere in that little turret-top room, almost certainly hidden by a magic older and greater than his own. To find out what that might be, the Royal Magician of Cormyr needed to talk to someone who'd remember Amedahast alive—how she talked, how she'd thought, how she'd lived.

The wizard sighed again and ran his fingers through his beard. Like it or not, he could think of only one person yet alive who, if the gods smiled, might have known her well enough. . . .

A rug in the corner flickered, rippled, and reared up from the floor like some sort of menacing monster. Vangerdahast blinked wearily at it for a moment, whirled away from the speaking-stone, snatched up a wand from his workbench, and aimed it grimly at the rippling pillar of cloth.

The rug blinked back at him reproachfully, and then fell away to reveal a tall, gaunt, white-bearded man in worn robes. With one hand on his hip and an eyebrow raised, he regarded Vangerdahast. Even a slate-cutter in the westernmost reaches of Cormyr could have identified the visitor: the Old Mage of Shadowdale, Elminster.

"Thy wards need a little work," Vangerdahast's onetime tutor observed in a dry voice. "I could reach through them without difficulty, having so used this rug before."

Vangerdahast's eyes narrowed. "You did? Why?"

Elminster raised his other eyebrow. "To visit Amedahast, if ye must know," he said, with what was almost a grin. "Yon rug lay beside her bed."

The Master of the War Wizards rolled his eyes. "I might have known," he snapped, starting to pace. He brought himself to a halt, drew in a deep breath, wrestled down the anger that always gripped him when he faced Elminster's easy smile, and said abruptly, "We—I—need your aid. There's been a disappearance."

"Heir? Crown jewels? Azoun's second-best codpiece? Or is it serving maids again?"

Vangerdahast gave Elminster a dark look. "A War Wizard," he said quietly. "A good man. Come." Without a backward glance at the rug or the speaking-stone, he set off toward the doors, striding hard. Elminster shrugged and followed.

A LONG TIME TO THE MAGIC, LITTLE WIZARD. WHAT ARE YOU UP TO?

Trying to call up memories for ye, devil. There are many, buried deep. But there's magic enough in this one. Watch and see.

On his second circuit of the little room, El bent over, sniffing. He dropped to his hands and knees and prowled, like a boy playing at being a stalking wolf. His snuffling became constant, his beard trailed along the floor, and his eyes narrowed. "D'ye have much trouble with rats?" he asked the stones.

"Running about? No. Or do you mean dead rats in the walls?" Vangerdahast frowned down at the crawling wizard. "There's naught but air outside these walls . . . why? What can you smell?"

"Rotten meat. Decay. Very faint." El sprang to his feet, his prowling done, and asked sharply, "The lass said the rug was different?"

Vangerdahast nodded.

El nodded back at him, the barest grim beginnings of a smile playing about his lips. "No doubt, no doubt."

The Cormyrean wizard's eyes narrowed. "What do you know, or suspect?"

"A trapper on the floor, who ate the rug atop it along with your War Wizard and his papers. His bones, ink bottles, and such will pass through it soon. Lurker-beasts give off such stinks at will."

"A trapper? I'd have found it," the Royal Magician of Cormyr said sourly, waving at the floor, "and it's not there now. I took care to make sure that rug was just a rug. Spin another dream, Old Mage."

"The murderer put it in here before your Bolifar arrived, and took it out again after the lass ran out of here to come looking for ye."

"Someone who can carry lurker-beasts around like carpets or bid them follow like pets? You strain credul—"

Vangerdahast stopped speaking in midsnap, and left his mouth hanging open. The color drained slowly out of his face.

"Kaulgetharr Drell," he said, very slowly. "Master of the King's Beasts. He has a trapper; I've seen it devour butcher scraps and the like. When he casts the right spells, it follows him about like a hunting hound."

El smiled and spread his hands. "Well then," he said briskly, "I've work of my own waiting, back in Sh—"

Even as he raised one long-fingered hand, Vangerdahast barked, "Wait!"

The Old Mage raised an eyebrow again, and the Cormyrean wizard said hastily, "My scribe Sardyl spell-locked this door! Drell couldn't have just—"

The rest of the color left his face. Vangerdahast looked suddenly very old, as yellow and as brittle as crumbling parchment.

"Sardyl," he murmured. "Is she in it too?"

Elminster shrugged. "Mayhap . . . but she needn't be. That's not the way the trapper and its handler came in."

He waved at the map on the wall. "That's one of Amedahast's portals. All of her maps are. Have ye never known?"

Vangerdahast gaped at him.

"Ye can also see and hear through them," Elminster added with a tight smile. Turning to look at the map, he drew his fingers inward like a crone's grasping claw. He seemed to beckon or to pull something unseen toward him.

The map shimmered. Out of it stumbled a man in a rich, open-front shirt and tasseled leather boots and breeches. The newcomer's face was twisted in a snarl, and he lunged atop Elminster. One arm—the one that held a gleaming dagger—rose and fell in a blur. Blows thudded as hard as galloping hooves as he stabbed the Old Mage repeatedly.

Elminster raised his other eyebrow. "Are ye done?" he asked calmly, watching the blade pass into and out of his chest, as harmless as smoke.

The dagger-wielding man stiffened. His blade fell from trembling fingers, struck the toe of his boot, and clinked its way to a tumbling halt along one wall.

"Baerune Cordallar," Vangerdahast said in a voice of doom from just behind the man's ear, "surrender your person and the truth your tongue can speak to me, now, or face everlasting torment in beastshape!"

The motionless noble could move only his eyes.

Elminster stepped forward almost lazily, touched Cordallar's forehead with one long finger, and murmured, "Three others with features like these—one a woman. His kin. And a cruel man with fine features and a goatee. Two others—one of Arabel, one of Marsember—with ambitions but only slight involvement, to be used as dupes later. The woman's thoughts have shaped the plot, but this one was to be the chief instrument. He is to have wed the Princess Alusair . . . then brought about the death of her elder sister, Tanalasta."

Vangerdahast growled, a low rumbling that rose in growing fury. Baerune's eyes became desperate. He struggled to speak, face quivering, but managed only whimpers, like a muzzled dog.

"How many plots against the crown has it been, this tenday?" Elminster asked almost merrily. "Now I really *must* go."

Vangerdahast drew in a deep breath and said simply, "Thanks. This is one more I owe you." He raised an eyebrow of his own. "How did you know about the maps?"

Elminster smiled. "If I were a gentlesir," he told his onetime student mildly, "I'd not tell. Amedahast was . . . very beautiful. I'll take care of your beast-master, ere I depart; this map leads to the one in his chambers, in the back robing room."

"You can see that, through the map?" the Royal Magician of Cormyr asked curiously. He strode forward to peer at Amedahast's drawing of the kingdom.

In the wizard's wake, Baerune Cordallar was jerked along helplessly, stiffly upright and unable to do anything but move his eyes about, which he did wildly.

"No," El replied sweetly. He stepped forward and melted into the map. "I recall where the matching map hangs. That robing room used to be mine."

It seemed to Vangerdahast that the last he saw of the Old Mage of Shadowdale wasn't the airily waved hand but that old sardonic smile. As always.

I LOOK AND SEE NO MYSTRA, NOR SILVER FIRE. ONLY MORE CLEVERNESS OF ELMINSTER.

[red anger, ebbing]

YET YOU ARE A CHOSEN OF MYSTRA AND MUST HOLD SOME OF HER SECRETS IN YOUR MURK OF A MIND.

SO REVEAL WHAT I SEEK, OR DIE.

Well, we must all perish sometime. Slay me, then, if ye care so much for my present comfort.

I'LL GIVE YOU THE COMFORT OF DEATH, CHOSEN OF MYSTRA, WHEN THE SILVER FIRE IS MINE. IF YOU CEASE DISPLEASING ME, IT MAY EVEN BE A SWIFT ONE.

Have my thanks.

GET ON WITH IT, MORTAL! [mental slap]

[pain, reeling, the maggot gnawing, gnawing . . . aaghh]

[healing, purging fire, frying maggot]

THERE. NOTHING VITAL. PROCEED.

* * * * *

"Vangy," the princess in gleaming armor growled as she drew on her gauntlets, "this had *better* be good. I've a little treason to ride and attend to, and—"

The Royal Magician raised one bushy eyebrow. "You think this is news to me? Alusair, where *do* you keep your wits? In your codpiece, like all the blades riding with you do?"

The princess stared at him and chuckled. "Well said, wizard. Just don't start a series of jokes about 'What does the wayward princess carry in her codpiece,' hey? Mother's been through enough lately."

Vangerdahast gave her a severe look as he came close to her. "I know that well. Unlike some oh-so-important young lasses, *I've* been comforting her."

Alusair rolled her eyes. "Vanj," she said, employing a nickname she *knew* he hated, "the queen is stronger than any of us. She needs comfort like a dragon needs more scales. Now, what do you need me for—oh. What're you doing?"

The Royal Magician of Cormyr had unlaced her gorget and flipped it aside, and his thick fingers were now busy with the laces of the leather jack beneath it.

Alusair arched one eyebrow. "Really, mage! Have you not heard of courting? A glance, a few honeyed words, perhaps a glass of wine for a girl—"

"Alusair Nacacia," Vangerdahast growled, "behave. Blast—look you, lay bare your throat and fish out that pendant I gave you." He distastefully eyed the pointed double-prow of her breastplate and rubbed at his forearm where he'd bumped the sharp-sculpted Purple Dragon adorning it. "Your breastplate leaves me very little room to work."

The Steel Princess gave him a wry grin. "It's not supposed to. Some men who come close to me use swords and daggers, remember?"

"Huh," the wizard growled. "They're the wise ones."

Alusair let out a roar of laughter.

Vangerdahast had to shoot a severe look over her shoulder at the Purple Dragons who'd leaned in to see why their warrior princess held her armor aside and her throat out to the Royal Magician.

"Now this," Vangerdahast said, carefully clipping a new pendant onto the old one, "will protect you against some rather nasty spells that I'm afraid our latest crop of traitors will try to fell you with. It's . . . it's . . ."

"Wizard?" Alusair snapped, putting out a hand to steady him. She'd never seen Vangerdahast's face go so grim and ashen before. He looked afraid and old. Afraid and . . . ashamed.

"Vanj," she murmured, shaking him as she stared into his eyes, "what is it? What ails you?"

With a growl, the Royal Magician broke free of her and stepped back. "I—nothing that need concern you. It's a wizardly matter."

"Oh, I see. Like a knight staggering into his hall with two swords through him. That's a 'warrior's matter'?"

"Alusair," Vangerdahast said heavily, with signs of personal distress, "leave me. Please. You cannot help in this. No one can."

Alusair stared at him, clapped his arm wordlessly, turned, and strode out. In the next room he heard her murmur, "Jalance, lace this up for me, will you? And this time, *try* to keep your fingers on the thongs, hmm?"

Several men laughed, and the old wizard heard them moving away. He stood alone in the center of the room, feeling close to tears.

"Mystra save me," he whispered, "but I cannot. I'm old. I would not have lasted five breaths in Avernus at the height of my reckless youth. My place is here, in Cormyr, where I am needed for a little time more. Oh, Lady Mystra and Lord Azuth, forgive me. Elminster, forgive me."

He looked wildly around the deserted room and saw the brief glimpse that had been twisted into the fading edge of that second memory. The sharp rocks of Hell jutted like dark teeth against a blood-red sky. A broken thing crawled, the sharp ends of bones protruding from its tortured limbs. A shaggy face drooled and bled and wept, with deep-set eyes he knew. His old teacher, Elminster.

The Old Mage of Shadowdale was trapped in Hell, his magic gone or captive, reaching out with his mind to those he hoped could aid him. It must be all he had left.

Vangerdahast took two swift steps across the room, shaking his head. Those eyes . . . with an effort he banished that image from his head. It had been wrested from the gaze of some lesser creature of Hell, to be sure, who'd been watching Elminster. That meant El was probably dead by now, half-devoured. Yet he should make sure, should try to do *something* to aid the old meddler. He should . . . should what?

"Mystra, Mother to Wizards," he whispered, the words of a very old prayer, "what should I do?"

Silence was his only answer.

"*What should I do?*" His shout rang around the chamber ceiling and brought startled servants and Purple Dragons alike running.

When they reached the room, it still echoed with anguish, but the Royal Magician was gone.

Six

ANOTHER WARM DAY IN AVERNUS

It seemed he'd been crawling forever, in pain forever, wandering in Hell with an archdevil tramping through his mind.

MY, MY. NEITHER THE USEFULNESS NOR THE ENTERTAINMENT I'D EXPECTED— OR BEEN PROMISED. SHOW ME MORE! SHOW ME WHAT SHAPED YOU, LITTLE BEING OF SILVER FIRE! SWIFTLY, BEFORE I GIVE IN TO THE GROWING URGE TO MAKE THINGS MORE ENTERTAINING.

[mindworm thrusting, mental fire, bearing down, tightening]
[shriek, welter of images, howling failure to flee]

A grim man in black strides warily through a dripping wood, his hand on his sword hilt. His cloak, drawn up around him, is pinned with a brooch in the shape of a silver rose. From time to time, his alert and peering eyes seem to flame with silver.

YES! MORE SILVER! GET TO THE SILVER THAT FLOWS AND BURNS! SHOW ME!

A silver harp pin, bobbing on the breast of someone running, in shadowed darkness where hounds howl and men curse, close behind . . .

DON'T TWIST AWAY FROM ME, WIZARD! SHOW ME THE SILVER MAGIC AT WORK, NOT EVERY LAST CURSED SILVER THING THAT HOLDS MAGIC! YOUR MIND IS LIKE A LIBRARY WHERE EVERY TOME'S BEEN SHREDDED, AND NOW YOU HURL HANDFULS OF TORN PARCHMENT IN MY FACE!

SHOW ME SILVER AND MAGIC TOGETHER. NOW.

A silver-handled cane, black and slender, hangs in the hand of a fat, bearded mage. Heavy-lidded and sighing, he trudges down gleaming marble-floored halls, past high-arched windows whose uppermost glass is worked into stained reliefs: images of a purple dragon in flight. The Purple Dragon of Cormyr.

"Honored Vangerdahast," a voice murmurs from ahead, "the queen has need of you, and in some haste."

The mage glares at the unseen speaker but quickens his pace.

NOT THAT DODDERING FOOL! I WATCH OVER HIM MYSELF!

Another bearded man in robes, taller and grimmer, strides through a room of many beds where young lasses are hastily dressing. Robes, sashes, high boots, and garters form a flurry. He sees them not, though he snaps orders obviously meant for them. He paces on, his gaze intent on a small blue sphere that floats in the air before him, flying slowly and smoothly elsewhere.

KHELBEN OF WATERDEEP IS NOT UNKNOWN TO ME EITHER. IS THIS LEADING SOMEWHERE, ELMINSTER? OR ARE YOU BUT WASTING MY TIME ONCE MORE AND COURTING FRESH TORMENT?

The two bearded faces, together, wear expressions of irritation as they whirl down a rainbow-hued well. . . .

A slender feminine hand reaches with firm, unhurried confidence through blue moonlight to touch the black-robed shoulder of Khelben Blackstaff Arunsun. The wizard stiffens, wonder warring with apprehension on his face. The hand dissolves into a flurry of small stars that swim and dance and spin to become a circle of nine stars.

Khelben goes to his knees in reverence, his eyes never leaving them.

The nine stars race around in their circle to become seven, and the seven one. One that's not a star, after all, but a single blue-black eye, shot through with many racing motes. It winks coyly, once, then is gone. . . .

NO! NO MORE TEACHINGS OF MYSTRA! WHAT'S THIS, OVER HERE—WHAT YOU'RE DWELLING ON BEHIND THIS CAVALCADE OF SNATCHED GLIMPSES THAT AVAIL ME NOTHING! SHOW ME WHAT YOU'RE RUMMAGING THROUGH!

[whirl of images, swept aside]

THAT'S BETTER. I'LL JUDGE WHAT I SHOULD SEE, CAPTIVE.

[bright scene unfolding]

THIS LOOKS INTERESTING. I'LL SEE ALL OF IT.

The news spread through the city like wildfire. The Company of the Wolf was riding into town. The Wolf himself would be at their head, fresh from defeating the armies of Amn in battles at far Six-trumpets and the banks of the Winding Water. Behind that grim war captain would be horse after horse laden with plate, coins, and other booty of far-off wars: Calishite silks, spices, wines, and all manner of strange things. They would come to spend and carouse, and forget fallen friends and much hard riding and spilled blood. That was good for the girls who frequented the Slipper.

Mirt the Merciless, slayer of a thousand thousand, took his usual route from South Gate through the twisting streets of Dock Ward, at the head of a proud procession of battered men on battered horses. Men who had stared down death eye-to-eye two days before rode wearily into the shadow of Castle Waterdeep and turned at last into their usual stopping place: the old and rambling inn known as the Scarlet Slipper.

The Wolf sat patiently on his saddle while the wounded were carried to hire-nurses in South Ward. Three trusted captains rode to buy fresh horses, food, and drink. Others arranged rooms for the yeomen of the company. Only then did Mirt dismount, with a creak of protesting leather. He strode stiff-legged into the dimness of the Scarlet Slipper to call for his first jack of wine.

BAH! MORE LOVE AND TENDERNESS! WEAKNESS! IS THAT ALL THIS WIZARD IS FULL OF?

THIS IS AN UTTER WASTE OF MY T— BUT HOLD. THIS CANNOT BE FROM YOUR OWN REMEMBRANCE. IT MUST HAVE COME FROM MYSTRA. PERHAPS IF I FOLLOW IT, I CAN TRACE OTHER LEAVINGS OF HERS, UNTIL AT LAST—NESSUS, AT LAST—I REACH SOMETHING USEFUL.

The Scarlet Slipper was well known in Waterdeep, City of Splendors. Hither came many night maidens of the less expensive sort—young or old, fat or thin, from near-beauties to heavily painted exotics of all eccentric descriptions. Those female citizens whom merchants called "ladies of the evening" kept to the gentler wards of the city. The Scarlet Slipper had a less exclusive reputation.

As the day drew down and dusk crept catlike along the alleys, they began to appear—night maidens strolling alone, in pairs, or even threesomes. Like softly scented shadows, they stole down from their upstairs rooms everywhere in Dock Ward—and a surprising number from wards farther afield. Word of the company's arrival had brought out what sailors called "a full hunt," well endowed with perfume, furs, and gowns of silk, satin, and musterdelvys. Inside the inn, wine flowed apace, and the gathering night grew loud.

HUMANS SEEM TO SPEND A LOT OF TIME FEASTING ... BUT SO WOULD I IF AVERNUS WERE NOT A PLACE WHERE TO LINGER OVER A MEAL IS TO BECOME A MEAL. HMMM ...

Scarred and hardened warriors laughed and roared and tossed dice. Some, emboldened by wine or youth or great need, took to dancing with tavern-girls amid the crowded tables. Others disappeared up dark stairways or into side alleys before full dark was come.

In the center of the tumult, silent and watchful, the one called the Wolf sat nursing a jack of wine. He ignored calls and caresses and flirtatious displays. Several men who sat with him looked interested. With a curt nod, Mirt allowed each in turn permission to leave duty behind for a time and join the frolics.

The burly, hawklike leader of the company sat warily at his table, hand never straying far from his blade. He took no companion from the many who approached him. His eyes no more than flickered once or twice.

So the evening passed. The Slipper's regulars trickled in, emboldened, to join the merriment and broad minstrelsy of the house. Ale and wine flowed freely. Others came, too; watch officers and urchins, passersby and sailors. They stood quietly along the walls near the doors, watchful and curious. Mirt returned their stares, calmly and quietly, but nodded to few and spoke to none.

The less bold night maidens, too, drifted in by the door to stand staring, timid and yet hopeful. One or another was whirled away for a dance, or caught the eye of a favorite and left escorted. Most just stood, watching longingly.

Mirt looked at them all, expressionless, as the wine in his jack grew steadily less. Young or old, short or tall, buxom or slim—he'd seen them all, or their like, many times before. Sooner or later he'd choose one—who or why he did not know, for none had yet caught his interest—to spend the remainder of the night with. He was in no hurry. Wolves can seldom relax.

Then, with quickening interest, he noticed a new arrival among the night maidens. With the quiet grace of a lady, she slipped in behind louder, bolder wenches. She stood with the others in the shadows. He noticed her because she was far plainer than the rest.

Her gown was simple and gray. She wore no face paint, made no gesture, and took no preening or beckoning stance. Mirt looked at her again, meeting her eyes squarely. She seemed momentarily taken aback at his interest, then returned his gaze with steady calm.

Mirt looked at her more closely. She was much older than most of the girls. He watched her move aside serenely as a warrior pushed past. She had a beaklike nose that would have sat better on a man's face than on the serene visage whose gray-green eyes met his so steadily. Unexcited, yet not derisive or uninterested. Faintly curious, faintly—something else, but hiding all behind a steady mask.

Without hesitation Mirt rose. As he passed, he skirted bolder hands that stroked and plucked at him and ignored familiar entreaties husky and shrill alike. In a few strides, he was among those women who had hung back. Some were shy, or affected to be so. Some were young and unsure, or intimidated by more experienced rivals. The one he sought had as yet spoken to none. Most of the other girls thought her a wife or creditor come to seek one man of the company, not a night maiden at all.

Eyes widened in surprise and dawning hope at his approach. "Mirt," whispered a dozen excited throats. "Mirt the Wolf!"

There was shifting to straighten hair or best display a shapely leg, but the lady in gray moved not at all, nor spoke. Something flickered behind her eyes, but her expression did not change.

Girls moved aside, looking more surprised still, as the object of the Wolf's attention became clear. He came to a stop, hand on belt, and raised an eyebrow in silence.

This one was old indeed for the Scarlet Slipper. He had never seen her before.

In like silence, the lady nodded her head, once. Mirt stepped forward smoothly and took her arm as though they were old friends of high station at a dance in Piergeiron's Palace, not strangers in the course of an old trade at a rundown inn. The amulet around the Wolf's neck remained still and cool; there was no magic here.

"Whither?" was all Mirt asked as they stepped out into the moonlit street.

Amid the shadows, dark figures drifted a step or two closer, saw the scabbarded sword ready beneath the man's other hand, and moved away again.

"This way," was the cool reply. "It's not far." They walked slowly up the street toward the castle, looming high above. Mirt seemed in no hurry; he was intrigued.

"How much, milady?" he asked, in a gently neutral tone.

"I am no lady, sir," was the tart reply. "Two gold—one before my door . . . and one in the morning."

Mirt's eyebrows rose. "You've not done this long," he said flatly.

"Is the price too high?" came the cool challenge from beside his shoulder. But she walked on as before.

Mirt shrugged. " 'Tis not that," he answered. "You spoke of morning. Long indeed for but one gentleman-guest."

"I have not been doing this long, sir."

Mirt stopped and turned to look over his shoulder. His companion made as if to draw free, but he held her arm firmly.

"Have you changed your mind, sir?" she asked, slowly.

Mirt shook his head, raised his hand, and made a sign. Two men who followed them returned it and turned away, one raising his drawn sword in silent salute.

"Nay," Mirt replied. "My men," he added, and began walking again. "They'll follow us no more."

"Why—no, you need not answer that," his companion of the evening replied. "It is just here, sir. Your gold?"

Wordlessly Mirt opened the hand whose arm was linked through hers. In it gleamed a gold piece.

AND HUMANS CALL US EVIL! AT LEAST WE MAKE NO PRETENSES ABOUT THE EVIL WE DO!

What, is Nergal telling me there's no deceit in Hell? No lies? Hmm?

THE LITTLE HEALED ONE WAKES! WELL, WELL . . . ENJOY THE RIDE. I'M OFF THROUGH YOUR MEMORIES AGAIN, LITTLE MAN, THOUGH I'M BEGINNING TO FORGET WHY!

Ah, my spell's working!

[SNORT, MIND LASH, GROAN OF PAIN, DIABOLIC CHUCKLE] *IDIOT HUMAN, SHOW ON . . .*

"Still awake, milady?" Mirt asked gently later, into the darkness. She turned from the window where she had been watching the moon sail above the harbor, laid down something long and thin that gleamed in the moonlight, and came back to bed.

"Yes," she said very softly, getting in. Mirt put an arm around her and drew her to him, to warm her. After a moment or two she relaxed, and lay still against him. Mirt traced the fall of her hair past her shoulder.

"How are you called, milady?" he asked.

"Nalitheen," she replied, a curious tightness in her voice.

"I am Mirt," Mirt said. After a moment, she chuckled.

"So half the girls in the Slipper said, when you came over." She lay against him, warming, unmoving. "The Wolf, they call you. Slayer of Thousands. I had thought to find you more—savage."

Mirt shrugged. "Why so? If I am angered, my trade is battle. . . . I get my fill of lashing out." He coughed, and stared into the night in his turn. "Some of my men are cruel, aye, and will always be so. Some bluster and swagger because they are too young to know better."

"I have hosted some of those," Nalitheen agreed, in neutral tones.

"Those who have fought longer," Mirt added, patting her shoulder, "would never treat you ill. The greatest thing a woman can give a soldier is safe rest, so that he can sleep deeply and relax, not fearing a knife in the ribs."

"I know that," Nalitheen said quietly. "My husband was a soldier. He was killed two summers back, near Daggerford. Borold was his name. He rode for Waterdeep and was well thought of. He was slain by mercenaries sent to seize the city's bars of silver that he was guarding. Every man in his command was cut down, and the lords were very angry." Her voice was thin and bitter as she added, "Angry for the loss of their silver."

Mirt lay still, looking into darkness. A small chill of sadness added its weight to earlier sorrows, deep within. The Company of the Wolf had taken that silver, under hire to the merchants of Amn. If Borold had commanded the guards that day, Mirt the Merciless had slain him. A stout man, with bristling sideburns and eyebrows. He had been fast enough to get his saber into Mirt's arm before he died. He stirred, and almost spoke—but Nalitheen's voice had been so bitter.

"Men who swing swords have no idea how many women go hungry because of them or are left behind, forever alone. Many I know here will never know if they've been abandoned or how their lord died," she said softly.

"How is it that you heard of your—of Borold's fall?" Mirt asked.

"They told me; soldiers at the palace, when they summoned me there and gave me his pay." She shrugged. "I know not how they learned it, or even if it is the truth. They gave me forty pieces of silver for the life of my husband."

"Then why, milady," Mirt asked softly, "sell yourself? Is it—forgive my blunt asking—loneliness?"

Nalitheen shrugged again. "I have two daughters. They must eat. For myself, I don't care anymore, now that Borold is gone. I used to think I'd hear him call, and he'd come up the street again as he always did, singing. But I know he won't now. Ever again."

They were silent, for a time. Then Mirt asked again, roughly this time, "But why—sell yourself?"

Nalitheen turned in his arms to face him, in the darkness. "What else have I?" she asked simply. "I can cook, aye, but there are a hundred hundred folk this side of the castle who can cook better than I. I have no skill at handiwork, nor strength to load or unload goods in the streets for whatever coin is offered. All else in this city is guild work, and I lack the coins even to apprentice to a guild. And 'prentice wages won't feed two younglings, even if I near starve."

Mirt ran a hand along her ribs. "Naught else to spare, have you?"

Nalitheen chuckled. "Borold used to say that. I have always eaten little."

"I've no complaints," Mirt assured her, and they chuckled together. He fell silent then, and soon after began to snore. Nalitheen lay still in his arms, looking into the night—and surprised herself by falling asleep almost immediately.

You humans certainly rut a lot. If you wasted less time talking your way into each other's arms, you'd have more time for killing and plundering.

My thanks, Nergal, but some in Faerûn, as it happens, have noticed that already.

[snort] *Reveal more, wizard. My patience is a shorter thing than it was when I first captured you.*

And as it happens, I've noticed that.

[diabolic chuckle, images flying by]

When Mirt awoke and rolled over, it was gray dawn. Beside him, the bed was empty. He looked first for his sword and laid it by long habit close within reach. Then he dressed quickly and quietly, as was his wont, stretching once or twice as cats do.

Nalitheen came into the room before he was done, with two steaming tankards of what smelled like bull-tongue broth. She stopped suddenly at the sight of him fully dressed.

She was barefoot, and as a warming-robe wore a once-fine, patched gown, open down the front but loosely belted at the waist. She handed him one tankard with what might have been a smile and sat down on the edge of the bed, pulling what she wore more tightly around her.

"You'll be leaving, then?" she asked, raising her eyes to his. There was something strange in them.

Mirt nodded slowly. "I must. The company rides again, this afternoon, after we've bought food enough to ride on." He sipped, and nodded appreciatively. "My thanks—this is welcome, indeed."

Nalitheen looked at him. "So was your kindness last night," she said. Mirt met her gaze steadily, and then deliberately drained his tankard and rose. A gold piece fell from his hand to clatter inside it as he set it down.

"One more thing, if you will," he said slowly. Nalitheen raised her eyebrows over her tankard, as she sipped her still-steaming broth.

"Show me your daughters," Mirt said softly, almost pleading.

Nalitheen looked at him for a moment, the tankard suddenly forgotten in her hand, and then nodded and led him to a curtain in one corner of the room.

The door behind it was locked. Expressionlessly, Nalitheen put one end of the curtain into Mirt's hand. Then she bent and took a slim key from beneath a floorboard in a corner nearby, fitted it to the lock, and swung the door wide. A ladder led upward into soft gloom.

Nalitheen waved him forward. Mirt nodded and climbed the ladder slowly and carefully. The rungs creaked under his weight. The ladder ended in a little room under the eaves of the house, rosy now with the first true light of dawn. Great, wondering dark eyes waited for him there, as two sleepy, tousle-headed lasses stared at him from their shared bed.

"Naleetha and Boroldira," Nalitheen introduced them from behind him. Mirt turned at the harshness of her tone and saw her knuckles white around a dagger she clutched, its wickedly sharp point toward him. "Borold's," she added, flatly, nodding down at it.

Mirt met her burning eyes for a long, silent moment, then deliberately turned his back, to face the girls in the bed. "Ladies," he greeted them gravely, bowing as if they were high ladies of a court, "I am Mirt the Wolf. Pray accept my apologies for disturbing your slumber. Naleetha, Boroldira; I am pleased to have met you."

He smiled and turned back to Nalitheen, the smile still on his lips.

"Thank you," he said simply. He stepped past her blade as though it was not there and went back down the ladder, not hurrying. He strode on, with Nalitheen behind him, on and down the stairs below, to the front door of the house.

When he turned, Nalitheen was standing on the lowest step of the stair, trembling, the dagger in her hands. Tears glistened in her eyes.

"Put the blade away, milady," Mirt said softly. "There's no need for that."

Nalitheen shook her head, slowly and helplessly, and let the dagger fall to the floor. She stared down at it silently, her hair fallen around her shading her face.

"How long have you known?" Mirt asked her quietly.

"T-they told me who killed him," Nalitheen whispered, and then looked up at him angrily through her tears, head to one side. "They told me Mirt the Merciless killed my man. I've waited for you. Two long seasons, lying alone and crying every night. I wondered if you'd ever come close enough to me for this dagger to reach."

"And now?" Mirt asked, unmoving, holding her gaze.

"Last night was different," Nalitheen sobbed, and looked away, striding along the bottom step of the stairs. She wheeled at its end, and cried, "How long have *you* known? Who I was, and wh—that you'd killed my husband?"

"Last night. When you told me how he died," Mirt told her truthfully.

"And you stayed?"

"I'd paid," Mirt replied mildly, and then added, "No, that was cruel. I trusted you with my life, Nalitheen. Then and now."

He drew his blade, slowly. Nalitheen flinched but did not draw back. Meeting her eyes steadily, Mirt upended his scabbard and shook a cloth bag out of its depths. The coins inside it clinked heavily as he put it into her hands.

"This," he said gently, closing her fingers around it with his own, "is for you, and Naleetha, and Boroldira. I'm sorry. I'll come again, and there'll be more. You have my word on that."

Nalitheen looked at him, unmoving and expressionless, the gold in her hands. Mirt kissed her forehead gently, resheathed his blade, and fetched down his cloak from a peg.

"Gods bless you for your charity, Mirt," Nalitheen whispered, sounding more weary than bitter. She shivered, shook her head a little, and closed her eyes, leaning against the door frame.

" 'Tis not charity," the Wolf of Waterdeep told her almost fiercely as he turned to go out into the brightening street, "for I'll be back."

AH, SO TOUCHING! THE MISPLACED PITY THAT HUMANS CALL "HONOR," I BELIEVE. OR LOYALTY, OR SOME OTHER WEAKNESS LIKE THAT. AND YET—MINDS LIKE MAZES, THIS ONE ESPECIALLY.

REST NOT, CAPTIVE WIZARD—NERGAL CRAVES ENTERTAINMENT! SHOW ON!

*   *   *   *   *

"You offend me, pig of a merchant," the Calishite said, his accent as heavy as his perfume. Though Velzraedo Hlaklavarr of Calimport was hardly slimmer than the wheezing figure sprawled with his boots up on the chair, Velzraedo was far better dressed. His spade-beard wagging, the Calishite added a delicate stream of curses that called into question Mirt's ancestry, personal hygiene, dietary habits, the hobbies and judgment of his mother, and his familiarity with camels. "Kindly," he added with a sneer, "remove yourself from this seating you so indolently occupy. Its use is required by myself—Velzraedo Hlaklavarr of Calimport, First Finger of the Masked Vizier!"

Mirt's reply was a repetition of the mellifluous, echoing belch that had first offended the silk-clad envoy. "My," he told his fingernails, not moving from his sprawled position at the best table in the Brave Bustard, "but it certainly seems mustard and quince were not meant to be in a sauce together—at least not in *my* stomach. Why, stop me vitals: my very proximity seems to have a marked effect on the sanity of visiting Catamites—or is it 'Calishits'? I can never recall! Why—"

The envoy interrupted this airy observation with a roar of rage. He snatched one of the dozen or so wicked silver-bladed throwing knives from the gleaming row adorning his belt. His arm was a blur of purple silk—right until the moment it crashed down on the table in the violent and bouncing company of Velzraedo Hlaklavarr's nose.

The Calishite's generous behind and gilded boots rose into the air, driven up by the chair that Mirt the Moneylender's boot had thrust into his guts. In the suddenly silent tavern, everyone heard the loud sob of pain and robbed breath that Velzraedo Hlaklavarr announced to the world.

Almost lazily Mirt plucked the knife from the Calishite's numbed fingers, used its point to skew aside the envoy's turban, and delicately brought a decanter of firewine down onto Velzraedo Hlaklavarr's balding head.

In the wake of that wet, solid blow, the Calishite jerked once, arms flailing weakly, rolled to one side, and lay still. His tongue hung loosely over the edge of the table.

Mirt looked up at the six grandly uniformed warriors the envoy had brought with him. He smiled, Velzraedo's throwing knife waggling ever-so-gently between his fingers. "Pity overwhelm us all, but he's collapsed. It must be the air in here—very bad, very bad. I fear my own offerings do nothing to improve that state of affairs, so perhaps His Fingerness will revive most speedily and completely elsewhere, hmm?"

The envoy's guards glared at Mirt, hands clenched on the hilts of their blades—then surveyed the dozen or so armed, scruffy men sitting tensely at the tables all around, weapons ready and bottles hefted for hurling. Dark eagerness burned in their eyes. Even the serving wenches had turned to glare, clay wine-jacks poised in their hands.

The largest and most grandly mustachioed guard looked at Mirt and bowed his head. "Perhaps there is wisdom in what you say, merchant. We'll take our master elsewhere, in peace, and remember your *kind* concern—and your *face*—in our prayers, for later."

Mirt's smile was wintry as he replied, "As I will yours . . . and with two sets of gods heeding fervent entreaties, our next meeting should come soon, hey? I know I'll be ready."

The guard froze for a moment to match stares with him, then slowly and deliberately dragged the senseless envoy back off the table and into the arms of the other guards. They went out, the two rearmost men facing back into the dining hall, hard expressions on their faces. Various gestures offered them a swift and eventful journey—even before a sudden tumult and clang of arms in the passage outside heralded their fate.

Breathing heavily and wearing a smile as broad as the sun, Beldri-
garr Stoneshield of the watch burst into the room. "Did those Calishites cause any trouble in here?"

A dozen smoothly expressionless faces adorned as many shaken
heads, telling him no.

Stoneshield grinned. "Thought so. Well, two of them tried to cut
down a serving lad right under my nose, there by the door—and we
were already looking for that envoy for passing crooked coins in the
Sunset Sail!"

The tavern master of the Bustard cursed heartily and scooped his
hand into the bowl under the bar. He brought up a fistful of coins and
peered at them.

The watch officer shook his head, chuckling, and sat down across
from Mirt. "So, Old Wolf," he growled. "I might have known I'd fi—hey!
What's amiss?"

Mirt the Moneylender, most famous roisterer on the Docks, was
frowning and shaking his head, an odd expression on his face. The
Calishite throwing knife fell forgotten from his fingers to clatter on
the table.

Stoneshield drew back from it as if it were a coiling viper. "Is it—
poisoned?" he rumbled, his eyes darting from it to Mirt and then back
again.

"N-nay," the moneylender said slowly. "No, I—something just
touched my thoughts." He lifted one scarred hand to tap the side of
his head, and added slowly, "Just about—here."

"Magic!" the watch officer spat, boiling up out of his chair. "Why, I'll
have those Calishites in chains in two hot moments, see if I don—"

"No," Mirt snapped, putting out his hand, "it's not them. No. I hardly
think they'd know of Nalitheen or her daughters." His frown deepened, and he rumbled, "I'd best go check on them. Perhaps they're in
need, an' the gods've sent me a sign." He rose, tossed a handful of gold
coins toward the tavern master, and said, "Top up all flagons, will ye?"

A roar of approval followed him out of the Bustard, but it didn't
cheer him up much.

*　*　*　*　*

He set his hands on soft shoulders.

Silver hair whirled around and coldly imperious eyes looked into his. "Do you have any idea what a foolish thing that was to do, Elminster of Shadowdale?" the Queen of Aglarond asked, anger lifting her voice like a drawn sword. "I might have slain you in an instant."

"I've spent my life doing foolish things and stepping into the path of peril," the Old Mage replied gently. "I'm not going to stop now—no matter how beautiful the lady who admonishes me."

That brought a smile. "You flatter like a Thayan," The Simbul observed, making the words almost a dagger-thrust.

"They, Lady, learned flattery from me," Elminster said in dignified tones. "They failed, however, to learn any good judgment from me if they are so foolish as to offer violence to a queen so powerful and passionate and wise."

Silver hair stirred as soft words fell like stinging blows. "And what if I like violence, old man?"

"Then you may offer it to me," replied the wizard in the patched and stained robes, spreading his hands. "Mystra has made me into an old anvil, to take the blows of many. Lady, do your worst."

A sudden smile like silver moonlight split the room. "I think I'm going to enjoy this," the Simbul told the air around her. She plucked off her crown and sent it spinning into a corner. As she started toward him, she crooked one shapely eyebrow. "Which shall it be, now—my worst, or my best?"

"Lady," the old man replied in a purr that matched hers, "let me, I pray, be the judge of that."

WIZARD, DO YOU HAVE ANY IDEA HOW BORING THE FLIRTATIONS OF HUMANS ARE TO ME? NOW, IF YOU'D KNOCKED HER OVER WITH A SPELL-HURLED HORSE, OR ACCIDENTALLY BURIED HER UNDER DUNG OR ROTTEN FRUIT AND HAD TO ENDURE HER FURY AFTER, THAT I'D LIKE TO SEE. BUT HONEYED WORDS ... D'YOU THINK DEVILS KNOW NOTHING OF SUCH BANDINAGE?

MOREOVER, IT'S HARDLY A REVELATION TO ME THAT YOU CONCERN YOURSELF OVERMUCH WITH THE LADIES. WHAT RANDY OLD HE-WIZARD DOESN'T?

MY IMPATIENCE GROWS. I THINK A LITTLE LESSON IS IN ORDER.

AND IN HELL, WE TEACH WITH PAIN.

*   *   *   *   *

"All Faerûn bows before the beauty of the—the queen of
Aglarond," the Purseroyal of Tantras said tentatively, the sweat of
fear glistening at his temples. Did one daresay "Witch-Queen" to
the Simbul's face? Or call her "the Simbul"? Indeed, what at all did
one dare do in the presence of a lady who could be a purring
kitten one moment and a castle-shattering tempest the next?

The Simbul lounged barefoot on her throne, clad in a plain robe
that hung open from her shoulders to the sash at her waist, and
fell away from her magnificent legs high on her thighs. In both
cases, the Tantran ambassador could tell with distressing clarity
that the fiery ruler of Aglarond carried not an ounce of spare flesh
on her body. Why, he could see every muscle and tendon, rippling
as she shifted lazily, clear down to . . . *Holy Sune! Guard my
thoughts. . . .*

"An appropriate wish," the Simbul murmured, loud enough for just
the ambassador to hear. "Know that your musings do not offend me,
but know also that I am in some haste, and would hear with rather
less formality and more speed the wishes of Tantras toward our fair
realm. In plain speech, get on with it, man."

"Wah—I—ah, that is—" the purseroyal began auspiciously enough.
Irritation and then anger stole across the regal face before him. The
blood drained right out of his own face. His mouth trembled in
uncontrollable terror.

One slim, long-fingered royal hand rose in a clawing, sweeping
motion, as if to rake him away.

The Tantran was suddenly aware that he might have only moments
longer to live. The courtiers of Aglarond, ranged tightly around the
walls of the throne room, had fallen tense and silent—and were *leaning forward* in unison to see every detail of his fate.

He whimpered once, wondering where to run and knowing that
such flight was doomed, and—and—

Then it was all too late. The Simbul lifted her head almost in defiance, stiffened, her face going dark and her eyes starting to blaze.
Abruptly she rose and turned away from the quaking ambassador.

She strode a few catlike paces across the open stretch of floor around the throne, clawing at the air in frustration.

What *was* it? Thrice now, whilst this fool gabbled and shook before her, it had touched her, stirring something in the depths of her mind. Oh, so faint a touch, but troubling, setting her nerves to jangling and the silver fire to flowing impatiently. When this happened, it always betokened something bad. It always made her restless, too. Part of her wanted to hurl off her clothes and fly, shifting from shape to shape, dragon and falcon and wyvern and pegasus, on and on as the spirit moved her, as she tore across the skies of Faerûn, seeking . . . *something*. Something she knew not what.

Alassra Silverhand stood silent, motionless except for the shivers running up and down her body. She was clenching her hands so tightly that her fingernails pierced her palms, and blood began to drip through her fingers. She stared at the floor as if her gaze could burn through it. . . . From one courtier, a tiny, hastily stifled shriek ran around the throne room as smoke curled up from the floor tile that bore the brunt of the Simbul's regard.

The Purseroyal of Tantras shrank back, weeping as quietly as he could, visibly struggling to keep control of himself. Writhing in the icy claws of his own fear, he was on the brink of screaming his headlong way back to his ship, through closed castle gates, plate-armored guardsmen, and all. In a moment or two he might be blasted by the Witch-Queen of Aglarond in one of her fits of destructive fury—or as some folk called it, "insanity."

There was fear on many of the faces along the walls now. When the Tantran ambassador saw that, his nerve broke. With a raw wail that would have done justice to a banshee plummeting down a long, long well, the purseroyal whirled and fled for the door.

As his despairing cry rose to its height, the Simbul looked up—and froze, astonished. The throneroom was almost deserted, with only a few of her most faithful retainers trembling by the door. Their eyes were on her, their faces white and set.

"Whatever—? Oh," the Witch-Queen said, stopping in midsnarl as she caught sight of her image in one of the tall, narrow mirrors on the throne room walls. Silver fire licked forth from her eyes and her mouth. Blue lightning crackled from her fingertips.

"Mystra," she murmured aloud, "but this is serious. Either grave matters are stirring, somewhere—trying to reach me, I'd say—or I'm finally going as mad as folk say. Well, one way or another, El will tell me soon enough."

She moved her hips restlessly and laughed and waved reassuringly to the sorceresses by the doors. "I'm growing to need him," she announced, "and that's a weakness I cannot indulge further. Thorneira! Phaeldara! Fetch back that screaming Tantran fool, and soothe and clean him up if he's no longer presentable! Bring me envoys and treaties and wrangles to settle! It's not nearly time to take ease and dine yet!"

With uncertain smiles, her apprentices scurried to obey. After they'd gone, the Simbul stood alone amid deserted splendor and frowned down at her empty palms. The lightnings were gone now, but fire still surged and roiled just below the surface.

What—or who—could have brought on that troubling touch? It was so distant, so . . . strange, like a horn-call from Hell. . . .

Shaking her head, the Witch-Queen of all Aglarond went back to her throne, and to the decanter of mint-water that rested beside it on a bed of ice. Well, if it was like all the other troubles that had flailed her with thorns all her life, 'twas a stone cold certainty that if she ignored it now, 'twould come back to smite her all the harder soon. And "soon" would become "right now" whenever its arrival would be most inconvenient.

*   *   *   *   *

Elminster threw back his head and screamed again as the imps tore away all of his fingernails and began gnawing on the bleeding ends of his fingers.

MORTALS WHO PRESUME TO WASTE MY TIME SHOULD EXPECT TO PAY FOR THEIR EFFRONTERY.

Nergal's mind-voice seemed almost to hold a sigh or a yawn. His rage amid El's memories, this time, had been brief, leaving behind a fiery headache. Blood still ran from El's ears and nose and welled up in his throat . . . but at no time in this last torment had he lost awareness of who and where he was.

No, he'd been spared that blessing. The endless brawl and slaughter that was Avernus raged around him unabated. El and the swarm of imps were writhing together on a rocky height whose stains and scattered bones attested to its usual use as a feasting-perch. From this height he could see far across the land of tortured rock. At least three dragons were flying across the blood-red sky, surrounded by swarms of winged devils that sought to slay the wyrms even as they savaged and devoured devil-flesh.

THEY'LL HAVE YOUR TOES NEXT, THEN YOUR HAND AND FEET. I THINK THE DISOBEDIENCE OF EVEN THE GREAT ELMINSTER MAY BE TEMPERED BY A LITTLE TIME SPENT CRAWLING AND DRAGGING ALONG ON RAW STUMPS.

El did not bother to muster his will for a mental reply. He was too busy spinning a maelstrom of remembrances to deceive his captor into thinking his sanity was failing—to hide the slow seepage of healing silver fire he was releasing, oh so gently, within himself. El had to keep the pleasure of its healing relief out of mind, so Nergal wouldn't see it and pounce on what he so hungrily sought.

Something large and dark and terrible suddenly rose over the edge of the rock. The imps fled with frightened squeals. Naked and holding up bloody stumps in futile array, Elminster faced the pit fiend. Nothing but the vapors of Avernus separated them.

A slow, cruel smile quirked around man-rending fangs. Dark eyes flickered with mirth. *Curse of the Nine, it wants to play. Mayhap I'll be torn apart slowly.*

With an almost lazy flap of its wings, the hulking devil lifted itself over the lip of the rock, tail curling like that of a cruel cat, and landed before Elminster, as light as any feather.

Nergal, Elminster cried, putting all the fear he could find into that shout, *aid, and swiftly—or your toy will be gone, silver fire, memories, and all—and whoever sent this fiend will know of your scheming!*

Red rage flared in the back garden of his mind. *YOU DARE—?*

OH. GABBLE, MAN. QUAVER, SCREAM—AND THEN MOVE YOUR HAND AS IF WHELMING A SPELL. FLEE NOT!

Instants became long minutes of frenzied thought—flash and shimmer among the dark inner pillars—as Elminster did all of those things enthusiastically. Nergal shouldered forward through the wizard's ravaged mind, gathering his own strength for what was to come, and his captive saw much.

Deep rage calmed Elminster and fed him, rage at this ultimate violation. Nergal must be utterly destroyed. Not for the satisfaction of a certain mage of Shadowdale but for the memories the archdevil had already rummaged through and taken. Nergal now knew far too much about far too many people for civilized Faerûn to survive. A Nergal free to play could now manipulate important folk and, with them, entire realms.

Nergal must be destroyed, before anyone else can learn what he now has or read the stolen memories . . . but how?

That question rang through Elminster's mind again as the pit fiend pounced. Magic so great that it left the wizard sick and shaking swept through him, laced with Nergal's triumphant laughter. It rode Elminster's bloody spittle down the fiend's gullet, to explode within.

El arched over backward, tumbling through the air, cloaked in a shield of Hell-magic as blast after wet, spattering blast heralded Nergal's triumph over the hapless fiend. Spells upon spells resounded, enough to shatter even the rock upon which they'd been standing and leave ashes of the mighty devil. Elminster meanwhile tumbled unscathed out of the wrack.

Nergal must be destroyed. But *how?*

Seven

NIGHT COMES TO TAMAERIL

Panting, in pain, the half-healed worm that was Elminster, weary beyond the power of pain to keep awake, now, swaying . . .

Aye, fall down! What care I that your face be unbroken or not? But keep me waiting no longer, wizard. You live yet for the memories you yield to me—so show me more. Mind you're not wasting my time again, though. I find you're teaching me one thing all too well. Impatience.

[shimmering of many images, shifting and tumbling like black silk scarves blown aside in a bright breeze . . .]

It was the fourth of Flamerule, in the Year of the Harp. In the clear night sky over the great city of Waterdeep, a sky the color of royal-blue velvet, stars glittered like tiny, far-off torches. A warm breeze slid gently past the spires and stone lions of the city rooftops. On a certain high balcony, doors of copper and black bone had been left open to let it in.

There came a sudden stirring, a movement at the balcony rail. A shadow rose, blotting out starlight, to glide forward with silken speed into the dark room beyond.

A vigilant watch-eye floated silently in the soft gloom of the bed-canopy. It saw the shadow. Peering, the eye perceived more clearly in the near-darkness. The intruder was a man in smoky gray leathers, gloved and masked, who carried a long, slim sword naked in his hand. Moonlight gleamed down its steely length as the intruder turned this way and that in a cautious search about the empty bedchamber.

All was still. Whatever he sought was not here. The masked man listened at a door and silently drew it open. Darkness hung beyond, in a room lined with clothing hanging on pegs like bats in a cave. Not what he had come for.

The intruder closed the door with slow care and crossed the room to a larger, grander one. There was a tingling about this portal, a tension that grew as he laid a gloved fingertip on its dark surface and eased it ajar.

From where he stood, a broad stair descended into a high-domed, cavernous hall. Darkness reigned save for the faintest of steel-blue glows. It came from a full-armored guard who stood in front of the door. He faced away from the masked intruder and grasped a great blade.

Stood? Nay, floated. No feet joined the dark greaves of that armor to the stone step below. No flesh joined its gauntlet to its fluted elbow and shoulder guards. Moonlight shone faintly between the helm and the high collar of the back plates beneath it.

Behind the intruder, moonlight grew. The guard's floating helm turned slightly, the blade rising.

With a small, silent shiver, the masked intruder drew his finger-tips slowly back, letting the door close. His own blade rose, ready, as he backed two cautious paces, and waited.

Silence. Moonlight grew slowly brighter in the bedchamber. The intruder cast a last look around the room, stooping to peer beneath the canopied bed from afar. No one hid there, and nothing moved. His straining ears heard no sound but faint music from the night outside.

Away, then. In three swift strides, the masked man regained the balcony, to rejoin the night shadows outside. There would be blood enough to spill elsewhere.

THIS HAD BETTER SHOW ME SOME USEFUL MAGIC AT LAST, WORM OF A WIZARD—OR I'LL BURN YOUR MIND LIKE A TORCH AND BE DONE WITH THIS TIME WASTING!

Ye'll see magic, Nergal—and blood and cruelty, too, enough to suit even ye.

DO YOU SEEK TO GOAD ME OR APPEASE ME?

[silence]

COY HUMAN! SHOW ME MEMORIES, OR DIE FORTHWITH!

[images, whirling in profusion]

Laughter floated softly up to her from below. Distinct words, and the magic that some words release, could not penetrate her spell wards, but Tamaeril could hear the murmur of speech. The servants seemed happy tonight.

Tamaeril half-rose to open the door and listen—then sat back in her high-backed chair and smiled wearily. Hadn't she heard enough talk in her years? Whispers in alleyways, clack and clamor in the bazaars, and cold debate in the mercantile offices of the noble house of her birth. She'd heard more high words these past nine winters through the masked helm of a lord of Waterdeep as she sat in judgment, her name and face secret.

Perhaps some of the younger sons of the Bladesemmer blood had returned early from the pleasure barges and the lantern-lit dancing parties in the streets of North Ward.

If they had come back to Bladesemmer House this early, little doubt they'd be chasing the maidservants. Later returnees often entered the forecourt hall on litters carried by menservants of the house. Snoring or moaning out the sickness in their stomachs, such sons had had too much fiery wine and too little sense.

In earlier days, when sterner Bladesemmer men had ruled the House, no such unruly merriment would have been permitted. Time changes all things, and its unending march had carried away those stern brothers, uncles, and cousins, Tamaeril's husband among them. The younger folk laughed more and grudged less. They cared less about piling up gold coins and grimly holding to old traditions and old feuds. So the world turned again, and who was Tamaeril to stop it?

A lady of a noble line, yes, and a lord of great Waterdeep to boot, though her lordship was a secret to all but a few. Still, age had relegated her to these spell-guarded chambers and a role of dispensing advice, approval, and disapproval that went gently unheeded alike.

Tamaeril sat back in her chair and remembered parties and suitors long ago. She reached for the tall, slender drinking jack on the table beside her. Its sinuous silver-sheathed length caught the candlelight. She raised it in age-dappled hands and looked thoughtfully at her gray-haired reflection.

Not four nights ago, Mirt had spoken to her of mounting one last adventure. "One last toss of us old dice." He'd been restless in his lord's chair a long time and had said such things before, but never had she felt such quickening, eager excitement at Mirt's talk. Perhaps . . .

There was a sudden flickering of cold, white light beyond the drinking jack—light where there should be none. Tamaeril lowered her wine to look.

An expanding oval of white, shifting light stood in midair, flickering as if it were a ring of flames that gave off no heat. A gate! A portal to span distance, perhaps even to link this plane with another, stranger one. Danger enough, and an effect that should not be able to form here, within her wards!

Tamaeril set down her jack and shifted to rise. Her hand went to the ornamented knife at her belt—but she was old and slow.

Too slow for the slim, gleaming blade that leaped at her out of the flowing flames of the gate, driven by an eager gloved hand. It slid into her soundlessly, with shocking ease. Its kiss was so cold that all the breath went out of Tamaeril's old lungs. Half-disbelieving, she felt the shock of the blade's tip biting into the chair behind her.

She stared at the masked face of her slayer—a young one, a man by his scent and build, gloved and clad in gray shadow-leathers. He smiled down at her fiercely, a smile cold with hatred.

Letting go of the sword that pinned her to the chair, the man reached with his sword hand to the cuff of his other glove, where several small pieces of silver gleamed.

"Don't you know me, Lady Tamaeril?" he asked in a soft, almost purring voice. Tamaeril knew she'd never heard it before. "I'm surprised. Ladies, by and large, seem to know nothing—but you are both lady and lord. And lords of Waterdeep—or so I'm told," he added mockingly, "know *everything*."

The gloved hand was approaching her breast now, reaching over the blade that transfixed her even as the numbness of death crept swiftly outward from it. Helplessly Tamaeril watched it bring a small silver pin toward her, a pin in the shape of a harp.

A harp? He was pinning it to her gown now, gently and delicately, taking care not to prick her with the pin. Tamaeril smiled at the irony of that, even as she felt strength ebbing away. Blood slid into her lap and down her thighs, ruining her favorite gown. . . .

"Why are you smiling, Lady Tamaeril?" came that soft voice again, this time with an edge of rising anger in it. "Do you find me *amusing?*"

There was a brief silence as Tamaeril swallowed and found she could not speak.

The masked man seemed to master himself. When he spoke again, his voice was once more soft and controlled. He stepped back a long pace to study her, wearing the pin, and seemed satisfied with what he saw.

"Know, Lady, that you must die to atone for the shame done to my family. You had no hand in it, true, but you are a lord, and you could have undone it. You did not, and so you die. More sudden than I would have preferred, perhaps, but I'm still learning this 'revenge.' As the bards say, it's rather sweet."

The gloved hand went out again as he approached. "They tell me that you were once beautiful," he said almost approvingly, as he picked up her drinking jack and swirled the wine left in it. He stepped back again, toward the cold fire of the portal, and added, "You look pretty now, with your color back. My apologies for the gown . . . but you wouldn't want anyone else wearing it after you're gone, would you? No common born or outlaw"—his voice went momentarily steel-hard— "should be seen in the streets in Lady Tamaeril's fine gown!"

Tamaeril's murderer sipped her wine thoughtfully. "I'll stay until you're quite dead, of course. Is there anything you'd like to talk about?"

Tamaeril sat helpless in her high-backed chair, strength failing. A venturesome ribbon of blood was sliding coldly down her ankle now. Talk . . . hadn't she grown weary enough of talking? And yet— *you are a lord*, and *could have undone it*. She was no more powerful than any other lord, and—*I'm still learning this revenge*. This one would slay as many lords as he could!

Most lords had Art or strength or skill at blades far more than her own to command, yes, but most were old or very busy or both. They were apt to sleep soundly when they retired to chambers warded against magic and guarded with loyal swords. How many would he kill before he was stopped?

A tiny, chilling voice asked within her, *Would he be stopped?* One last adventure, Mirt had urged. Well, she had not chosen it, but it, the Lady of Luck willing, had chosen her . . . both the "last" and the adventure.

Tamaeril smiled wryly, even as the drowsiness of her last great slumber stole up behind her eyes. Spells she had still, though none to harm this one or anyone. She must use them, for the sake of Mirt and Durnan and the others, even young and stern Piergeiron. . . .

Tamaeril worked her lips to speak, even as she exerted her will in a silent command. A door she could not see, behind her chair— a door she would never see again—swung open by itself, in answer to her will.

"Wh-who . . . ?" she managed to say, as the blood poured down her ribs more slowly.

The masked man lifted the drinking jack again.

Her night hound smelled the blood and the unfamiliar man and Tamaeril's fear all at once and came through the door in a silent bound. The shrieking howl of warning and battle rage was still rising in its throat as its jaws opened wide to tear out the intruder's throat. Borgul's front paws raked down the arm that the man threw up to ward off those jaws.

They fell together in front of Tamaeril. She tried to raise her hand to the blade that held her there. Her hand trembled and fell back. Numbly she bent her will again, to the crystal stopper of the wine decanter on the table beside her. It shifted, just a breath. Yes!

Borgul's jaws closed on the drinking jack, thrust between them for the crucial instant as he and the masked one rolled together on the floor. The intruder hissed one word. Many small lights pulsed, and Borgul stiffened without another sound. The man he'd sought to kill rolled free and found his feet.

The great hound lay spread and still as the masked man, breathing heavily, faced Tamaeril. "Have you any more *pets*, Lady? Anything else I can slay before your eyes? Well—can you no longer speak?"

Tamaeril turned weary eyes to him. "Young man," she said, raggedly, breast rising and falling with the effort of breathing as blood filled her lungs, "I would know who you . . . are . . . and . . . why—why—" She coughed, a racking agony that forced her head down and made her eyes flood with red tears.

Through it all she heard her killer say softly, "Tell you who I am? When I can let you die never knowing? Why, Tamaeril, gracious lady, I find I cannot afford you this satisfaction. Pray accept my deepest apologies." He laughed, a mirthless rasp that made her shudder.

Tamaeril forced her head up again and watched him through dulling eyes. Her will carried the crystal stopper silently on, on across the room. She would have only an instant once he discovered it. She dare not look until the very last moment.

Tamaeril forced herself to shudder again—it was not difficult, but the pain it brought was sickening—and turned her head, as if in agony. There. There it drifted, straight on, inches away from the servants' gong. *Goddess, aid me!*

Tamaeril turned her head back to look at him. The gong rang. He smiled. "Oh, by all means, Lady, summon aid. I want eyes to see you and loyal retainers to strike down with my Art! I want to enjoy this to the full! My thanks!" There was a sudden rustling behind him.

He spun with that thin-lipped smile still on his face. A spray of magic missiles darted from his hand to blast away the life of her just-awakened songbird, in its cage. Her tormentor hummed merrily as they heard the thud of a maid's slippers on the stair below.

Tamaeril raised a hand and spoke a cantrip of her own devising; the first magic she'd created for herself, under the tutelage of the one called Elminster, long ago. The elegant carpet beneath her slayer's feet jerked suddenly, sending him stumbling off-balance, back toward his flickering gate. Her other hand, slow and trembling, found its way to the cold steel in her breast.

When he regained his feet, the masked man was snarling with rage. "Enough, old cow!" he snapped. He strode forward and wrenched his blade free, twisting it savagely in her breast as he did so.

Tamaeril gave a little scream and doubled over, spitting blood. The hand that had been climbing past the blade found its destination by accident. Her convulsing fingers grasped the amulet about her neck. Dimly Tamaeril was aware of her murderer backing up to his gate. The door of her chamber swung open. The wards shone suddenly bright across it. Her maid's thin scream rose shrilly. Shouts and pounding feet came in answer.

The amulet glowed, faint and blue-green and soothing. Pain ebbed as Tamaeril stared into the light and lost herself in it. She scarcely felt the magic missiles that tore into her old and broken body, lifting her back up into a sitting position in the high-backed chair. Tamaeril made a gift of the last of her strength. With the few fading instants of her life, she whispered a warning to her colleague and friend Mirt.
Mirt, Beware! Masked one . . . comes slaying lords . . . has Art . . . took me, Tamaeril . . . .

And so, with the pride of accomplishment, Tamaeril, oldest Lord of Waterdeep, slid into the embrace of death. The crystal stopper shattered as it struck the floor. The chamber was silent for a moment before the small, grieving wail of Tamaeril's favorite cat began.

[Somewhere in Hell, the fallen human—sprawled on rocks drenched with his own blood—sinks hungry and yet sick, parched and yet awash, into waiting oblivion. . . .]

DON'T YOU FAINT ON ME, TREACHEROUS HUMAN! WE'LL JUST TASTE THE MIND-WORM TOGETHER AGAIN, SHALL WE? YOU WERE FINALLY GOING TO SHOW ME SOME MAGIC, AFTER A TOUR THOUGH ALL THE DYING LORDS OF WASTERDEEP, AS I RECALL. . . .

[mind lash, mental pincers clamping down furiously, images streaming]

Mirt the Moneylender, who had once been called Mirt the Merciless, stared around the darkened wizard's parlor and swallowed.

"Gods take us all," he rumbled, broad blade already gleaming in one hairy fist. "What are we coming to, that lords of Waterdeep can be struck down in blood, in their own cozy-rooms? And a wizard, too!"

He glared about the room like an angry hawk, bristling. A battered hand-axe seemed to find its own way from his belt into his other hand.

"Keep close now, lass," he added. "I can't protect you if I can't reach you, as some smart-tongued prince or other said to his concubine, just before I spilled his brains out. . . . I forget me just where that was, now. Gods, but I *must* be getting old!"

"Now, my lord," Asper reproved him softly, her own slim blade in her hand as she put her back to his, eyes darting warily about the room, "remember that ballad of Randal Morn's: 'You're only as old as the one who feels you'!"

Mirt grunted, and then chuckled reluctantly. "Aye. Aye, I recall. But hush, now, as we prowl a bit. If any buck's going to try and gut me, I want to hear him coming!"

They stood together in the dim, cluttered parlor of Resengar called the Whitebeard (and, by some of his apprentices, Old Baldpate), a lord of Waterdeep and one of Mirt's friends. Or rather, he had been.

Not the width of a hand from Mirt's battered, flapping old boots lay Resengar, eyes gleaming sightlessly up at the star-decorated ceiling above. The old wizard's hands were drawn up as if to ward off a foe. His mouth was open in disbelief. Just beneath it, someone had opened another mouth in his throat, a red sword slash that still leaked blood onto the dark furs underfoot.

Looking down at him, Asper almost expected Resengar to cough his dry little cough, look all about with beard bobbing, as he always did, and apologize for having nodded off. But as silent moments followed, one after the other, he did not move. Those staring, sightless eyes grew dull. Resengar would never cough again.

Mirt had liked the shy, fussy old wizard perhaps best of all his fellow lords, after Durnan. He'd been looking forward to swapping ancient tales over even older wine tonight with the aging fusspot, watching Resengar stare longingly at Asper as he treated her with elaborate courtesy—until the wine took him and he began to snore, whereupon they'd quietly leave. As usual.

Now someone had cut Resengar the Whitebeard down in the middle of his cozy-room, his most private chamber, amid all his wards and defenses of Art. Someone who had left a silver Harper's pin behind on the breast of the wizard's robes. Resengar—who had never worn his own rune, let alone any other insignia—did not even own such a thing.

Someone was going to pay. Pay in blood, if Mirt the Merciless had anything to say about it. He hadn't realize he'd snarled that aloud until he heard Asper's soft but firm, "Yes, Lord. I am with you and will stand with you in this."

Mirt turned to smile at her, and Asper saw tears glistening in his angry old eyes. He met her understanding gaze, saw her expression, and tossed his head, turning away quickly. "Well, then," he said gruffly, "let's be looking about, then! We won't be finding anyone while we stand here, growing old!"

Asper only smiled and nodded as her lord turned and stomped away into the dim corners of the chamber, weapons raised. He had been a lion of a man once. Iron shoulders swung axe and long sword from the saddle on many a battlefield in those days, with force enough to cleave armor and bone. Or so the old warriors' tales told, in the taverns.

Men had called him Mirt the Merciless, and when he rode, fear rode before him. The Wolf, he was, and his men the Company of the Wolf. They looted and slew with grim efficiency. Butchery was never their mark, except against those who did not pay the Wolf his promised fee, or dealt him treachery. Those he hunted down and slew—mercilessly.

No man can stop the seasons, it is said, or escape their slow but certain claws. Winters pass, uncaring, and with them strength seeps away. The Wolf became the Old Wolf; Mirt grew old and gray—and rich. Men no longer feared his name. He rode no longer to war. The coin he had won by the hire of his sword he lent out, at fair rates, in the city of Waterdeep. Those who tried to cheat him learned that his sword had not grown so slow as all that, and that over the years he had learned a trick or two and picked up a useful magical bauble or three.

When honest debtors could not repay loans, he lent them more in return for a share of this and a share of that. In such a way he saw many old war companions to comfortable graves, who would otherwise have starved or frozen, homeless, in winter gales. Mirt said prayers over their failing foreheads or unhearing remains, paid for the burials, and turned over what they had left to their descendants. What he owned a share of—hovels, shops, or ships—he bought outright and took as his own.

In this patient way Mirt the Moneylender grew richer without making over-many enemies, and became as well loved as a moneylender can. Well loved? Aye, and in the end a lord of Waterdeep, for many small kindnesses revealed in his grayer years, and one greater one.

The homeless girls of the city were always welcome at Greygriffon House, once the quarters of Mirt's mercenary company. Mirt spent much gold hiring good women to see to the girls' upbringing and tutelage, and himself sponsored them to apprenticeships as they desired or gave them dowry when they were taken to wife.

"Mirt's Maids" were always to be seen wearing gowns as fine as any goodwife when out in the streets. When of seventeen summers, they were free to take their weight in silver and gold and make their own way in the world. Some stayed happily at Greygriffon House. Others asked Mirt to sponsor them as apprentice smiths, or warriors, or ship captains. The Old Wolf proved to have a heart as soft as his pockets were deep, and did so.

If he grumbled and bristled and blustered through his days, those who knew him saw past that and valued his friendship for what it was. Mirt grew fat and wheezing from hours at the flask and belly-up to well-laden tables, but he never laid aside his weapons or let down his guard of wary eye and sharp wits.

Asper looked at her lord now and saw wrinkles and stubble, his paunch and wild-flowing, mostly gray hair. She saw too the anger smoldering in his eyes as he looked around the room with drawn sword raised, and loved him all the more.

She had always loved him, since that day many years ago when he had come loping through the streets of a burning city, while his troops looted and slew all around him, and scooped her up from under the wild hooves of a riderless horse.

Hardened fighting men had looked on amazed as their general, the cold and deadly Wolf himself, caught up the crying toddler. He had held her close against his stubbly cheek as he snatched the reins of the terrified horse, hauled it near enough to grab a brutal fistful of mane, swung into the saddle, and spurred out of that ruined place.

Women he had taken, that night and many nights later, but always he bathed and cuddled his stolen child before he slept, telling tales and hoarsely whispering coarse songs to her in the night.

"Asper" was all she remembered of her name. Asper she was to him. She rode to battle strapped to his back, wrapped to the chin in thick, sweat-stained leathers. A great steel shield covered him from shoulder to shoulder and kept her safe, if half deafened and much bruised, within.

He fed her on mare's milk and such wine, fruit, and cheese as she could suck from his fingers. Later she ate bread and half-raw meat, and choked on the fiery wines he plundered from a hand's-worth of cities. Scarred and loud-voiced warriors tickled her and showed her tricks of knife-throwing and string-knotting and drawing in the dirt around a hundred campfires. She laughed a lot and grew to love the man who made her laugh so.

Winters passed, and Mirt's riding and fighting came less often. Asper finally lost count of the battles she'd been big enough to actually see and grew steadily sadder at what her eyes beheld. One after another, many warriors she knew and liked groaned or gasped their last moments away or lay twisted and still in the dust. Mirt grew older, too, and slower, and at last he came to vast, noisy Waterdeep to stay, not just for a roaring ride of drinking and wenching and hiring on new swordsmen.

Asper grew taller. Mirt took to buying her gowns and fine slippers and one day awkwardly presented her with a canopied bed and a room of her own. He had held her, too, when she came howling from night-terrors or sheer loneliness to interrupt his snoring, and told her gruff and bracing truths and marched her firmly back to her own bed. He even took to calling her his daughter.

So she had been the first of Mirt's Maids, Asper reflected, even if he saw her more as his daughter and less as a consort. She would never leave his side, if she could manage that. She would die for him, gladly, if the gods willed it so. She would do anything—anything—to take the tears she saw now away, forever. But Resengar lay dead, and she could not bring the dead to life.

Mirt's angry prowl around the parlor ended on his knees beside his old friend. He carefully examined blood and wound and the body that bore them. He took a silver pin carefully into his hand. Asper could see nothing more in the sudden, silent flood of her own tears.

A strong, familiar arm went around her shoulders. "Now, lass," Mirt rumbled in her ear, "smile! Remember Resengar leering at you and showing you that little cantrip he was so proud of, that made the circle of stars. . . . When Mystra thinks of her follower Resengar, she'll remember such things as those . . . and she'll be smiling, mark you!"

Asper did, despite herself. Ah, Mirt! she thought, the gods smile upon me, indeed, to give me you as father and lord and perhaps husband someday, all at once!

"No!" he whispered, slowly. "Gods, no! Tamaeril!" Asper spun to look up at him, blinking away tears in sudden foreboding. *"Tamaeril!"* Mirt cried suddenly, his voice sad and soft. Defeated. Axe and blade hung forgotten in his hands.

"Lord?" Asper whispered, hesitantly. Mirt looked off into the shadows a moment more. Then he turned his head slowly toward her voice, as if dragging himself back from a far-off place. His eyes were haunted.

"Tamaeril is dead," he said roughly. Anger burned in his eyes again. His chin came up. "Someone is slaying the lords of Waterdeep," he said, jaw set coldly, eyes dangerous. "Someone able to pass wards"—he waved his blade impatiently around the room—"whose magic should be impassable. Someone who may be a Harper or wants all to think him one. Or her. It may just as easily be a maid or an illithid or worse. It goes masked, is all I know." He shook himself, as if awakening, and strode toward the doorway with sudden energy. "Come, lass!"

"Where?" Asper asked, following him out of that room of death.

"To find Piergeiron. The lords must be warned." The Old Wolf strode down the worn stone steps toward Resengar's oval front door and the many-shadowed back alley beyond.

"Tamaeril? The Lady Tamaeril Bladesemmer?" Asper murmured her question, her back to Mirt's shoulder as he crouched by the door's way-slit, peering into the night beyond.

"Aye. She managed a sending to me as she died." Mirt kicked the door open grimly and thrust a cloak on his axe out into the alley. Silence. No shadows moved. He shrugged and tossed the cloak aside, crouching to hurl himself out into the night. "Fast, now," he whispered softly. "And stay low."

"My lord," Asper whispered back urgently, "shouldn't we go home for armor and friends, better weapons, magic? You are not the least of the lords! You stand in great danger!"

Mirt grinned wolfishly. "The gods must know I grow bored, these days. I would share that danger, lass! If this one who slays lords knows I am a lord, then let him find me! I want to be found . . . for if he finds me, then it follows that I will have found *him!*"

The blade he held lifted a little, a snake eager to strike. "I feel in some need of finding this lord-slayer, right now," he added softly, and Asper shivered a little in spite of herself. Then he was gone, out into the night. She set her trembling lips together in silence, raised her blade, and followed. As always.

Eight

FRESH TORMENTS

Elminster stumbled forth over sharp stones into full wakefulness once more—and into the claws of a red haze of pain.

It seemed he'd been lurching and scrabbling and crawling along forever, his guts sick with agony, his thoughts a chaos of grim scheming and involuntary remembrances, goaded by the archdevil riding his mind like some exhausted, tatter-winged bat steed. . . .

YOUR MIND IS LARGER THAN I'VE SEEN IN A HUMAN BEFORE, Nergal mused, his mental-voice as silken-smooth as ever. Cruelty thinly cloaked in grace . . .

This reaming could take forever, and I weary of it.

Elminster drew himself up so he could lean against a stone thickly smeared with old, black blood. The cracked skulls of devils crunched and rolled under his feet. *And so?*

AND SO, DEFIANT MAGE, 'TIS TIME TO BURROW THROUGH YOUR TWISTED TANGLE OF A MIND IN EARNEST. Nergal said in a mind-voice that was a sharp biting sword. I SPURN THE VISIONS YOU LAY BEFORE ME TO WASTE MY TIME. I CARE NOTHING FOR LONG-AGO ADVENTURES OR ROMANCES. I DESIRE MYSTRA'S POWER—I KNOW YOU MUST HAVE WIELDED IT, AND FROM YOUR MEMORIES OF SUCH USAGES, I CAN LEARN! SO GIVE ME, MAN—YIELD AND CRAWL!

Shouldn't that be yield or crawl? All ye need do is—aaarggh!

[dark lances stabbing, bright pain flashing, tumbling, memories surging, falling, wild pain, screaming screaming amid devil's laughter, rising to outbellow all]

LITTLE WORM, *I* COULD HAVE DONE THIS TO YOU FROM THE FIRST!

[mind lash, raw screaming]

HAH! *I* SHOULD HAVE DONE THIS TO YOU FROM THE FIRST!

[bright whirling chaos of torn memories, shards and scraps a-tumble]

. . . Across the fields she saw him go, a bent and tattered gray form. He dwindled, striding steadily on, became a tiny figure, and was gone. **And she shivered, sighed, and turned away.**

[images dwindling, falling, fading, lost and forgotten forever, now, in the wake of an archdevil's wrath]

The warrior looked down at the gathering vultures and the heaped bodies of the fallen and leaned on his spear.

Far they stretched from the height where he stood, far across rolling hills and the plain beyond; a hundred hundred souls and more this day. Davalaer thought on the wailing and grim sorrow that news of this battle would bring to the dales, even though victory had been theirs. Too many men would never return home. Too many were gone forever.

Aye, there would be lamenting in the houses of the dalefolk. Davalaer sighed, looking out at the still forms below. "But they will forget," he said heavily. "And then—somewhere, sometime—this will happen again."

BAH! YOUR MIND IS A CESSPOOL OF THESE MISTY-EYED MOMENTS! WHAT CARE *I* FOR THE TEARS OF WEAK AND FOOLISH HUMANS?

[shards of remembrances hurled, broken, away . . .]

HOW CAN YOU HIDE WHAT *I* SEEK, WHEN MAGIC IS YOUR POWER AND YOUR LIFE'S WORK? HOW? HOW?

[red eyes glaring through the darkness of shattered chambers, memories strewn broken on the floor like shards of glass and torn cobwebs]

MYSTRA. THAT'S IT. YOUR GODDESS AIDS YOU.

[diabolic eyes raging up into pyres]

SHOW YOURSELF, GODDESS!

[darkness, silence, eddying dust]

COME FORTH, COWARDLY WENCH!

[darkness, memory shards sighing down to rest]

ELMINSTER AUMAR, SHOW ME MYSTRA! REVEAL TO ME MEMORIES OF MYSTRA! SHOW ME!

[cringing, faltering, pain-ridden]

Aye . . .

"The Starym are apt to be overproud fools," the Lady Laurlaethee Shaurlanglar said calmly, "but they are right in one thing: to allowing these stinking bears of humans into our midst is to sully and doom us. That's why I invited you here, plaything of the Srinshee. That moonwine you drained oh so elegantly was laced with enough srindym to kill a dozen overambitious human magelings."

The man they called Elminster cast three swift, hawklike glances behind and before him, gliding a pace to one side to peer behind a hanging as gracefully as any young warrior of the People.

The elf lady laughed lightly. "We are quite alone, doomed one. I've no need or desire for witnesses—no guards to keep at bay the paws of a dying brute. I am the last of a proud warrior line, and I can protect myself."

Elminster gazed silently down at the slender wisp of gowned elven beauty in the chair. The Lady Laurlaethee was frail even as elves measure such things. Standing tall, she'd be little more than half his height. Sapphire-bright eyes looked coolly back up into his with no trace of fear. He gave her the slightest of smiles and asked, "And ye did this thing—why?"

"Hatred," the matron said, rising with supple grace. "For you and the likes of you. Beasts who seek to steal what they haven't the wits to learn. If the Srinshee wasn't so besotted with lust, you'd still be scrabbling and straining to call forth a little glow from your fingertips—in the brief moments before you found your corpse decorating the end of a Cormanthan spear."

"Well, that's certainly blunt enough," Elminster observed. "Being a thirsty beast—and one of course quite devoid of proper manners, I wonder if I might have some more of this excellent wine. I believe the srindym improves it somewhat."

Sapphire eyes flashed. "She protected you!"

Elminster bowed his head. "Lady, she did."

"That traitoress!" the Lady Laurlaethee spat, striding to a corner where large and small spheres of crystal turned slowly, chiming faintly as they spun. "Once word of thi—"

"Lady, I must guard ye against thy own foolishness," Elminster said swiftly, raising his voice a trifle. "Ye seem to think I speak of the Srinshee. I do not. She neither knows of our meeting nor provides me with any defenses. My spell cloak is my own."

The exquisite beauty of an elven face is shattered when perfect lips twist into a sneer. "You presume me foolish indeed, ape-thing. You wield no magics of any accomplishment that you did not seize, steal, or cozen from this elf or that. Who is this 'she' who protects you, if not one of the People?"

"Divine Mystra, the goddess I serve," Elminster said quietly. He watched for her response as calmly as if he feared nothing.

"Pah!" The Lady Laurlaethee spat, coming to a halt behind her crystals and glaring at the guest she hoped to slay over them. Their radiance lit her face strangely from below. "All sorcery streams from those *we* reverence—the True Gods! If this 'Mystra' of yours has any power at all, she must be but a face and a name extended to you unwashed humans by divinity that cleaves to elves, the Chosen Folk!"

"And if this is so," Elminster said with a smile lurking in his eyes that did not—quite—touch his lips, "and my magic triumphed over thy magic, it would mean that a goddess we both revere, by whatever name, has chosen me over ye—would it not?"

"Be still, ape!" his hostess snarled. "Lie down and die! How dare you profane the air of my home, to say nothing of my own ears, with such a suggestion!"

She made a clawlike gesture with one hand, and the air seemed to sparkle and freeze in place, just for a moment, around Elminster. He gave her a lazy smile and strode forward.

The Lady Laurlaethee stiffened and went white, her eyes blazing. There was a sighing in the air around the advancing human. Her eyes widened, and she drew back a pace.

Elminster Aumar stepped gently around the spheres of crystal and continued to advance on her. Furiously she wove magic with nimble fingers and hissed incantations. The air became alive with tiny silver lances and curling, half-seen dragons . . . but still he came on.

"Back, beast!" the elf matron said, her voice rising in real fear. "Stay back, or—or—"

A ring on her finger winked and vanished. Suddenly great hands reached up from the floor beneath her guest's boots, and down from the ceiling . . . hands that faded into trailing dust before they could close on the human.

Laurlaethee's lips tightened. Other rings flashed. She shouted a sudden incantation and dashed one hand across her other palm, gashing it with the thorn-barb on a ring. A swift word made the drops of blood she flung into the air catch fire and hang motionless between them.

Elminster smiled gently and stepped through them, wincing not at all as they exploded.

The Lady Laurlaethee was almost in a corner now, her mouth trembling with fear. The next words made the room rock and roar. They left her visibly wrinkled and withered . . . but seemed to touch the advancing human not at all.

Slender shoulder blades brushed a flower-girt wall, and the last of the Shaurlanglars shuddered, drew in a deep breath, and closed her eyes. She did not need or want to see what she did next.

Her hand swept down like a striking adder, plucking the tiny dagger from its sheath at her loins and bringing it back up to her breast in one flashing movement. As it went home, she would spit her death blood in his face and bring down a curse on him that no mage shield could turn aside. Laurlaethee Shaurlanglar did not want to live in a world where beasts rose to rule. To think that it had come to this, that—

She knew just where to strike, but she'd not thought it would feel so icy.

Cold, so cold, the blood spurting and—and—sudden glory!

Warmth, a rising song, ecstasy such as she'd not felt for years, since the arms of her gone and gathered beloved Touor had last clasped her close . . .

She blinked her eyes open—and stared into those of the hated human, inches away. His hand was on her breast, the magic that had healed and restored her curling up from his fingers. Those fingers trailed down to her wrist with infinite gentleness and captured her fingers.

He knelt and kissed her fingertips. "Lady," he said from his knees, looking gravely at her, "I came here hoping to win a friend, not to shatter a foe. Does it matter who we worship if we do good to each other? I hope to call on ye again . . . and that ye never have proper cause to use this on me."

He rose as swiftly as her hand had sought her own death, and dropped something into her palm: her blade of honor, still dark with her blood. As she watched, that gore vanished like smoke, leaving the silver-steel as bright as before.

She closed her hand around it and raised it, ashamed at her trembling. He stood regarding her, well within her reach, and did nothing but look into her eyes.

Laurlaethee Shaurlanglar flung her blade away blindly and was sobbing as hard as she'd ever wept in her life, almost blinded by the flood of her tears. Through them, she dimly saw the human walk away across the room, through the tatters of her mightiest spells, to the balcony whence he'd first come.

The human Elminster stood there, looking back at her, and raised his hand in a salute used by elves of older times to show respect to their elders.

As he did so, every spell he'd broken whirled once more to life, restored and singing bright and mighty around her. The room rocked once more with the force of their contesting powers. He held them in check, one doom upon another, and then, with a wave of his hand, spun them all back to nothingness. Her ring reappeared on her finger, undrained. Her spells and her spilled blood returned to her, thrilling her once more with their waiting power.

Laurlaethee gaped at him in astonishment. No one could do thus. No one.

"Mystra is nothing if not merciful," he whispered, the sound carrying loudly to her ear. "Be at peace and of good cheer, Lady Shaurlanglar. Neither of us is angry with thee."

Then he was gone. The ancient elf raised her fingers to her cheeks to brush away tears. For the first time in centuries—long, long centuries of lonely pride—she felt wonder.

She turned her head to look at herself in the lone mirror in that room, and stood a long time lost in thought. Even the withering was gone. She looked—younger! She turned to show one flank to the glass, and then the other. Younger, firmer, taller . . . she threw back her head and laughed, caring not if it sounded a little wild. Then, impatiently, she did off her gown and let it fall behind her, striding bare to the balcony where she sniffed at the decanter of moonwine, and found it, of course, purged of all srindym.

Laurlaethee shook her head, smiling a little, and leaned out to watch birds flit and whir and sing. A cool breeze had risen from the shadows to ghost past the rail, but she stood proud against it, not chilled in the slightest.

Wonder makes a very warm cloak.

LITTLE MUMBLING GODS, MORE PRETTINESS? MY HEART TREMBLES, BUT MY GORGE RISES! FIRE OF THE PIT, HUMAN, BUT YOU TRY ME SORELY! I SUPPOSE THAT WAS MYSTRA WORKING THROUGH YOU, AND THUS—BY THE THINNEST, MOST TWISTING THINKING—A FULFILLMENT OF MY COMMAND.

Indeed.

SILENCE! WHEN I HAVE NEED OF YOUR CLEVERNESS, WIZARD, I'LL NOT FAIL TO INFORM YOU. YOU CAN AVOID TORMENT RIGHT NOW BY SHOWING ME YOURSELF WIELDING—OPENLY AND AS A WEAPON IN A MANNER USEFUL TO ME AND CLEARLY REVEALED—POWER GRANTED YOU BY MYSTRA. IMPRESSIVE POWER, MIND, NOT IDENTIFYING THE FRAGRANCE OF FLOWERS OR SOME SUCH FRIPPERY!

Thy command becomes my wish.

AND THY MOUTH REMAINS FAR TOO SMART FOR THY COMFORT, IDIOT WIZARD! DO AS I COMMAND—NOW!

[flow of bright images, like stars poured down a well, quickening and growing broader, deeper . . . slowing, slowing . . . one radiance wells up to outshine all]

The line of blue fire blazed down the doors, sealing them. Ancient magics girded the hall, for all its ruined state, against wider Faerûn outside. Here the most mighty had contended in formal duels for centuries upon centuries, fusing the stone into glassy flows, embedding desperate radiances . . . and leaving behind the smell of fear and the prickling tension of watching, bound and helpless spirits.

A smile crossed the face of the tall, impossibly thin combatant. It held no trace of mirth or friendliness.

"Did you think," the lich hissed in triumph, "that I'd come alone?"

A stalactite behind and above one bony shoulder blurred and descended—and became a floating sphere of many eyes. It drifted forward with dangling tentacles and many jaws snapping on stalks. From nearby shadows flew a bat-winged gargoyle waving a sword of black flame. A vast snake slithered out and lifted its gigantic, cruelly beautiful, human-seeming head. Near it stood a graceful she-elf with obsidian skin and spell-spun daggers whirling about her slender wrists.

These creatures strode or glided or floated down the hall to menace the lone challenger—a human not so tall or thin as the lich. He had little of a warrior's build and nothing about him sharper than his hawklike nose.

The human's eyebrows rose. "Strange bedfellows, indeed," he observed calmly. "Thy falling into league together—*that's* a tale I'd like to hear." He sat down on a piece of the tumbled stone beside him, propped his dusty boots on another stone, and got out his pipe. "Well?"

The lich stared. "Are you insane?"

The mage shook tobacco out of a little pouch and commenced to tamp it down into the bowl of his pipe with his thumb. "Probably," he replied cheerfully. Death advanced on him, spreading out with stealthy grace to outflank and surround him. "Are ye surprised?"

The lich did not bother to reply but instead snapped hurriedly, "Before Mystra and the Mages Arcane, I claim right of subsumption in this duel, that all my opponent's powers be granted to me—*attack!*"

Though the presence of allies and the failure to allow one party to claim before commencement were blatant breaches of the rules of

Spelldown Hall, and though the creatures arrayed against him made death a swift certainty, the human puffed on his pipe and made no move.

As the first spell touched him—a bright bolt from the death tyrant—the hall was suddenly full of blue-white fire and a wordless singing that was both feminine and exultant. Drow limbs roared into flame and were gone. The gargoyle melted away into a brief whirling chaos of black flame and melting shards of sword. The gigantic snake burst like a boiled sausage and crumbled to dust. Silently, the beholder winked out.

As the last of its allies vanished, the disbelieving lich gasped, "How—?"

"Mystra gives ye greetings," the reclining human said pleasantly. He blew a smoke ring in the direction of his opponent before following it with the innocent question, "Does this mean ye don't want to tell me the tale of this little alliance?"

The lich's scream of fury was as wordless as Mystra's swelling song. Black flames and red roared out of its bony hands and snarled across the hall at the man with the pipe.

Elminster watched the flames come. As they struck home, he jerked his body this way and that in spasms that made his pipe shoot up to the ceiling. Smoke curled from his lips as he announced calmly, "Mystra makes reply."

He closed his mouth. When he reopened it all the blue-white fire in Faerûn poured forth, sweeping away one end of Spelldown Hall, frantic lich and all, in a single roaring instant . . .

Blue-white and so bright . . .

AARGH! RRRAAAAAGHH! OUGHHH!
[writhing flailing red-eyed pain, shuddering horns and tentacles, rocking and keening in helpless slithering agony, dying slowly to gasps]

[cautious peering, stealing forward from shadows to look at the smoking ruin of too many memories, with the smarting sentience of an archdevil smoldering at their heart]

OHHH. URRHH. [slow roll over, curling of stiffened talons, flexing of torn tentacles, unfolding in the sudden absence of pain] *SWEET FIRES OF NESSUS!*

Nergal?

IF I THOUGHT YOU'D DONE THAT DELIBERATELY, WIZARD, I'D TEAR YOU LIMB FROM LIMB AND SAVAGE YOUR REMAINS!

I but yielded what ye forcefully sought.

SO YOU DID. THOUGH IT SHOWED ME NOTHING USEFUL. SUCH FURY RARELY COMES FORTH WHEN I OPEN MY MOUTH.

Oh, I might disagree with ye there....

HAVE YOUR SMILE, LITTLE MAN. TORMENT WILL COME TO YOU AGAIN SOON ENOUGH.

[rising from the ruin to stand and then stagger, tentacles questing forth, the light growing more as the search begins once more]

SO THAT'S WHAT THE FIRE OF A GODDESS TASTES LIKE. SPARE ME NO WARNINGS IN FUTURE, WHEN I TAKE HOLD OF ANY SIMILAR SURPRISES!

I know not, devil, what can surprise thee.

REALLY? NEITHER DO I. [grim mental smile] WELL, WE'LL JUST HAVE TO LEARN TOGETH—

Spinagons swooped and tumbled out of the blood-red sky. They fell upon a hulk and stabbed with forks and raked with feet. The thing reared up, scattering them with two thrusts of its tentacles, and bellowed, "Who *dares*—?"

Shrieking, the devils flapped out of the hollow, fleeing in babbling panic.

Nergal glared after them, able to snatch only one of his attackers. Snaking tentacles slowly tore one limb after another from that hapless, shrieking spinagon. One end of a tentacle thrust into its mouth, breaking the jaw to keep from being bitten, and remaining. That muffled the shrieks. Nergal shook his head.

Whether agents sent by a rival or merely brainless hunters, these flapping annoyances were an overdue warning. Lost in the enjoyment of rummaging human memories, he'd been leaving himself vulnerable. Not all the denizens of Avernus were wise enough to avoid an archdevil. Others might well decide to try their luck with a wounded, reeling Nergal—to say nothing of the naked, puny crawling thing that was Elminster. Alone amid smoke and scuttling things a few gorges off, he was well on the way to blundering into the arms of Tasnya, or Oomrith, or Skeldagon, or half a dozen others.

Caution was in order. Nergal moved across smoking fissures to a more defensible place. A pack of nupperibos had gathered there. Nergal gave them a many-fanged smile full of fell promise. The nupperibos fled from him in grunting haste. Nergal flung his awareness back to the dark caverns of Elminster's mind.

Back to the human's youth in Hastarl, and from there no doubt a long, tortuous chain of memories wherein the wizard knew ever more of Mystra's power, and magic mastered and then hidden. Magic that would soon belong to Nergal.

Diabolic laughter echoed in a cavern around the tentacled lord. The sound filled also the riven chambers behind the eyes of the Old Mage. Spines bristled, granted by Nergal to make Elminster a less obvious morsel.

Languid limbs stretched, cherry-red and glistening with the blood of the gutted, half-crushed lemures that filled the bowl-shaped bed.

"So," purred their owner, as little flames licked from between her lips and rose from the tips of magnificent breasts, "Nergal has a new toy—one alluring enough to distract him from his usual hunts and cruelties. Such a toy Tasnya must have."

She rolled over on the lemuran corpses, arching away from the razor-maws of the land lampreys whose gnawing brought her such pain and pleasure. She-devils knelt eagerly at the foot of the bed. She fixed one with a look that had fire in it. Its human-seeming tongue licked both its lush lips and the dainty fangs behind them, in anticipation of a pleasurable mission.

Tasnya did not disappoint her slave, though her voice dripped with irony. "Do you go forth, *loyal* Sressa," she told the erinyes, "and take an interest in Nergal's doings. Harm him if you can, and snatch away unharmed his human captive if possible, bringing it here to me. Tasnya has uses for mortal wizards—and blundering archdevils who come raging hence to recover them, too."

Nine

WHO'S KILLING THE GREAT LORDS OF WATERDEEP?

Many-spined, tormented, crawling . . .

[images of a fat, wheezing man and a slender lass, hurrying through a city at night]

YOU'RE TAKING ME ON THROUGH ALL OF THIS? THERE'S BEST BE SOME VIVID AND USEFUL MEMORIES OF MAGIC BY THE END OF IT, ELMINSTER, OR I'LL GIVE YOU MEMORIES OF AGONY THAT WON'T SOON FADE.

AND DON'T TELL ME YOU'VE HEARD SUCH THREATS BEFORE.

[silence]

WELL?

I but follow thy wish, devil, and so remain silent.

HUMMPH. INSIDE, YOU BURN AS DARK AS ANY DEVIL, DON'T YOU?

[smiling silence]

GET ON WITH IT, WIZARD!

"We'll use the tunnel," Mirt rumbled. "I've no time for pleasantries with courtiers."

"Do you ever?" Asper replied, amused. Mirt merely grunted. He'd been hurrying through the darker streets and alleys, his old boots flapping, for some time now, and retained little breath left for talk. For once.

Asper could hear him wheezing along ahead of her, his breath a constant whistle in the night. The Old Wolf waved his sword carelessly in one hand and moved with surprising speed. Asper tried to keep her eyes on all the night's darker shadows, tensely alert for an attack she hoped would never come.

Mirt made no attempts at stealth or caution. He charged through the night like an angry bull, heading around the rocky arm of Mount Waterdeep on which the Castle stood. He scrambled through alleys, rubbish heaps, and backyards hung with washing. Mirt began to growl deep in his throat, a rising and falling rumble that boded ill for whoever—or whatever—got in his way. As usual.

They crossed Gem Street at a lumbering run, nearly bowling over a watch patrol. Mirt plunged down a side street. Asper ducked under a grasping watchman's arm and scrambled after him, ignoring angry shouts to stop.

Mirt was fumbling with something at his belt. "Here," he snarled at her, thrusting his sword into her hand. "Hold this!"

"I hear those words at least thrice a day," Asper panted. She turned . . . to face watch officers charging down the alley. Trust her lord to relieve himself at a time like this. But, no—

Mirt turned with a louder growl than usual and dived at the ankles of the foremost officer. That unfortunate shrieked in protest as Mirt heaved him up into the air and flung him like a child's doll back into his colleagues. They crashed together with a meaty smack that made Asper wince.

Mirt spun back toward her. In one hairy hand he held a length of silken cord that ran up to his belt; its other end was tied to a key, which he had hidden in his codpiece. He fetched up against one wall of the alley.

"Hah!" he said an instant later. A stray beam of moonlight winked on the key as he let it fall and dangle, turning back toward her. "Come on, lass!" he roared. "In with you!"

Without waiting for a reply, he spun about to boot aside the reaching staff of an officer of the watch. "We haven't time for these fools!" he snarled, wrestling the man aside and slamming him into the nearest wall.

Asper dived past him into deeper darkness. Mirt's fingertips trailed along her shoulder. He followed, kicking aside the grasping hand of the man he had felled so that it wouldn't get caught in the door.

"Perhaps later," he said with a ferocious smile. He leaned close to the watchman's startled face, displayed his discolored teeth, and slammed the door shut.

"Where are we, Lord?" Asper whispered softly and urgently in the darkness. Mirt chuckled.

"In Shyrrhr's house," he replied. "Stand still, lass, while I find a lamp." He deftly plucked his sword out of her hands, as though he could see perfectly.

"There's no need," a cool voice said out of the darkness. "I've one ready." A door opened with the faintest of grating noises. A hood rose from a lantern perhaps four paces away. "Welcome . . . Mirt?"

"Aye, Lady." Asper could hear her lord smiling. "Your alarm still works, I see."

Before them stood a tall, beautiful lady in slippers and a sleeping gown of emerald green worked with gold. She held the lantern in one hand and what looked like a wand in the other. Her eyes matched her gown. She smiled.

"Up to your tricks again, Old Wolf?"

Mirt unconcernedly stuffed the key back into his codpiece. "Lady, meet my lady, Asper. Asper, this is the Lady Shyrrhr. I know you've seen each other from afar many times at court, so perhaps we can dispense with all the tongue work. We're in a hurry, Sheer, to reach the palace."

Shyrrhr's eyebrows rose. "Come," she said simply, and led them through several doors and down a steep spiral stair. "If you were not who you are, Mirt," she added softly, as they descended into cool dampness, "I would not let you pass this way. All is not well at the palace."

Mirt stared hard at her bronzen hair, as if the weight of his gaze could lay bare the thoughts in her head. "Nor outside it," he grunted shortly. "Watch officers followed us here."

Shyrrhr chuckled musically. "I know I can always count on you for an entertaining evening, Old Wolf. No offense, Lady Asper."

"None taken, Lady," Asper replied.

The stair ended in a stone-lined tunnel. Shyrrhr handed Asper a lamp from a shelf where a row of them stood ready. "*He* always drops them," she said, looking with her eyes to Mirt as she lit it. "Go in speed. Gods watch."

"And over you, Lady," Asper replied.

Shyrrhr waved and smoothly slipped back up the stairs. "I'll talk away the watch for you," she called back softly.

Mirt grunted. "Tamaeril Bladesemmer and the wizard Resengar are dead this night, Lady. Guard yourself."

Shyrrhr turned. Her eyes were very green. "I always do," she said softly. "I thank you for the news, Mirt. Tell me more when you can." She turned again and was gone.

Mirt nodded in answer. "A good lass, Sheer. No doubt she has some envoy or other upstairs, spilling news they never intended to as they empty her wine decanters."

Asper crooked an eyebrow. "I take it you've emptied her decanters a time or two, without spilling whatever she wished to learn."

Mirt grinned. "She's Piergeiron's best agent," he said dryly, "but not a lord, if you take my meaning. If Piergeiron were to marry again, though, I'd not be surprised to find Shyrrhr at his side kneeling before the priests."

He grinned again, and strode forward down the tunnel. "Watch sharp, now. The stones're none too level." He wheezed and moved faster in a lumbering trot. "Hold that lantern high, lass, and pray to Tymora that we're in time!"

I'VE WAITED MORE THAN LONG ENOUGH FOR EVEN A PALTRY THING OF MAGIC. THERE HAD BEST BE MORE—AND BETTER, TOO! WIZARD, YOU ENTERTAIN ME, BUT YOU WASTE MY TIME.

Ye have other pressing engagements, Lord Nergal?
[growl, mental slap]
[pain gasping pain]
[teeth bared; satisfaction]

Torgent was old for a man trusted to guard the lord's person. His mustaches were snow-white, no longer gray, and his shoulders lacked the bulk and weight of years gone by. He still stood as proud as ever in his livery, and none had ever seen him as much as yawn on a night watch.

The three men under him could not match his years with all of theirs put together, but it was his old ears that heard it first: the soft scrape of a leather sole on one of the stones down the tunnel.

"Ready, lads!" Torgent snapped. "Someone comes!"

Ready-loaded crossbows were snatched up. Torgent drew his sword and raised his shield before him. He stood behind the great spiked and iron-barred gate to challenge whomever was coming. Waterdeep the Mighty depended upon him, and he was ready.

"Stand and declare yourselves, in truth and without omission," he issued the traditional challenge. His deep voice boomed in the tunnel. Through its echoes two came forward in haste, one rotund and puffing, the other slim and lithe. Both bore drawn blades.

"Torgent! 'Tis I, Mirt of Waterdeep, with my lady, Asper," Mirt roared as he came up to the gate. "We must see Piergeiron, speedily, so tell your lads to put down those bows and open the gate as fast as they know how!"

"Mirt! Well met, Old Wolf!" Torgent chuckled, tossing sword and shield aside. The gate clanged and clattered as all present heaved at it from both sides to raise it.

"Not so much of the 'old,' youngling," Mirt growled as he rolled up from under the gate's iron spikes to clasp Torgent's gauntleted hand. "Where's Piergeiron, this hour?"

Torgent looked troubled, even as he smiled and handed Asper to her feet. "Lady," he said automatically, bowing. His face fell grim again. "The lord is no doubt in the Inner Audience Chamber, under heavy guard. I'm glad you've come. He's not himself, these last few days." The other guards murmured agreement. They wrestled the gate down again. "Keeps his armor on day and night, with the visor down. He's always been one to use words sparingly, but he says even less lately. Just 'yes' and 'no' and 'next' and 'enough.' I'd take it kindly if you'd let us know what's amiss."

Mirt's frown was black.

With a little shiver, Asper saw him in memory—once again in the saddle in his mercenary days, hearing of the treachery of a Tethyrian noble and vowing to repay it.

The blade in Mirt's hand leaped a little. Seeing it move, one of the younger guards reached for his own sword out of habit.

"I'll tell you what I can, when I can," Mirt said, striding on. "My thanks, Tor. I know the way." And he was gone, boots flapping. Asper danced at his elbow on lighter feet.

Torgent turned back to the gate, a fierce smile on his face. "Now, by my sword, we'll see something! I'd see the back of all this mystery, lads—and that man'll do it where others would strike stone and fall back. There'll be some wild times ahead, or I miss my guess!" He sat down again whistling a jaunty old marching song.

The younger guards exchanged glances, shrugged, and grinned. More than one of them stole a look the way Mirt and Asper had gone, Not one remarked on Asper's beauty. Torgent looked just a mite stirred up for that.

MAGIC, ELMINSTER. WHEN DO WE GET TO THE MAGIC?

Soon, devil, soon.

THAT REFRAIN HAS COME SO MANY TIMES, IT'S ALMOST A CHANT.

That it is, Nergal. Would ye like the entire ballad?

[disgust] *GET ON WITH SHOWING ME REMEMBRANCES, WIZARD. I'LL NOT SIT STILL FOR YOUR SINGING.*

[amusement, bright images flashing]

They took a secret passage, and another, and avoided most guards and almost all servants. Mirt was known, and his ready passwords and display of a signet ring of Waterdeep carried them swiftly to the doors of the Inner Audience Chamber.

The guards held ready blades and moved them aside not a finger's width while their captain went in to announce them. He was a long time coming out again. When he did, his voice was cold.

"The Lord Piergeiron will see you both. Reluctantly. Lay down your blades and follow."

Mirt shrugged and dropped his blade. He had others, to spare, about him. Asper handed hers hilt-first to the nearest guard.

"Cheery greeting, indeed," Mirt said, matching the guard captain's cold stare with the steel of his own anger. Were he not a lord of Waterdeep, he'd have little way of even reaching the First Lord. These guards did not know his true standing.

Were they not lords, his friends would not now be dead—nor would warning Piergeiron be necessary.

Mirt's face was as dark as his mood as he stalked into the gloom of the Inner Audience Chamber. Ahead, Piergeiron sat in full armor under a single lamp.

"Dismissed," Mirt snapped at the guard captain.

The guard ignored him. Who did this fat moneylender think himself to be, anyway? Lord of all lords in Waterdeep?

Piergeiron's silent gesture reinforced Mirt's order.

Mirt waved to Asper with one finger to keep her eyes on Piergeiron. No sooner had the guard closed the door than the Old Wolf spun about, a dagger appearing from somewhere about his person to flash through the air and transfix the bell-rope not four inches from the First Lord's hand.

Asper gasped.

Mirt stomped forward, leaped on Piergeiron, jammed iron fingers into the visor-swivel, and jerked it upward as they crashed together to the floor.

"I thought not," he snarled, staring into shocked brown eyes within. "Who are you, and what have you done with Piergeiron?" Without waiting for a reply or shifting his gaze, he snapped, "Take that wrist, lass, and hold it up over his head! 'Ware daggers!"

The struggles beneath him were feeble. In another instant he had the helm unbuckled. He tore it off with more haste than gentleness—to reveal the frightened face of a lass younger than Asper!

"Now just who might—*Aleena?*" Mirt growled, hand bringing yet another dagger up to the bare throat of the girl in armor.

"Y-yes." Aleena swallowed, face marble-white, jaw trembling. She lifted her chin and looked angrily at him. "Is—did *you* try to slay my father?" When she spoke, her voice had the full, deep boom of a large man of middle years: Piergeiron, defender of Waterdeep. It sounded odd indeed, coming from such delicate lips.

Mirt frowned and rolled off her, waving Asper back. "Nay, of course not," he growled. "What befell? Come girl, quickly! Tell! Lords of Waterdeep have died this night! What happened to your father, and why are *you* wearing his armor? Piergeiron would never agree to using you as bait to trap a blade that missed him once!"

Aleena nodded, sadly. "Father's in no condition to agree to, or forbid, anything. He lies in Blackstaff Tower, deep asleep. Someone almost slew him, three nights ago."

Mirt bristled. "And we were not *told?* How *is* he?"

Aleena shrugged. Her eyes were moist. "He lives. Laeral poured a good seven healing potions down him. He'd—been run through, more than once. He—oh, gods weep, Mirt!" She clung to him and burst into tears. Mirt patted her awkwardly, turning to Asper with an appeal in his eyes.

Asper fetched the nearest decanter and poured out a glass of whatever it was.

Mirt thanked her with a glance and held it to Aleena's lips. She shook her head violently through her tears. "Too much already," she said. Mirt shrugged and drained the glass himself.

"I've been so *scared!*" Aleena sobbed. "Sitting here, waiting for the killers to come again . . . I can't even *touch* this sword! It's father's holy blade, even if I knew how to fence as the warriors do!"

Asper gently shouldered Mirt aside and knelt to put her arms around Aleena. The grand plate armor was cold and hard as she embraced it.

Aleena blinked at her with a watery smile. "M-my pardon, Lady," she said desolately, "I—it is not right to weep before strangers. I am Aleena, daughter to Piergeiron. Might I know your name?"

Asper smiled. "I am Asper. Mirt is my man. We came here to warn your father, I fear: two lords of Waterdeep, at least, have been slain tonight. The Lady Tamaeril Bladesemmer is dead; she managed a sending to my lord, and we know that one man, masked and able to get somehow within her wards, slew her. Earlier, the wizard Resengar was killed in his own parlor. Do you know of others?"

Aleena shook her head. "I do not even know the full count of who is a lord and who is not. Laeral did tell me that Mirt was, ere she sent me here."

Mirt stared, the decanter already half-empty in his hand. "Laeral sent you? What foolishness is this?"

Aleena lifted her chin again. "Lord," she said softly, " 'tis my duty to Waterdeep, as your service is yours. The palace throne could not be seen to be empty, else this man or men, and their backers, would know they'd succeeded—and what might befall the City of Splendors then? An army, attacking? Fleets? All slaughter that we might prevent!"

"Men, you say," Mirt said, frowning, ignoring her other words. "How many attacked your sire?"

Aleena shrugged. "None here know. He used a teleport ring Khelben gave him long ago, to come to us in Blackstaff Tower. The Blackstaff is gone walking the planes these nineteen days now, on some work or other he spoke nothing of, to me. Laeral and I nursed him. When we had done what we could, she told me I must wear father's armor and sit the throne here, being of height to do so. I agreed. We washed it up, and she laid a spell upon me, so that"— a smile touched her lips, and slid away again—"I sound like father when I speak. A comical effect, I'm told."

Mirt grinned. "I'd think twice about embracing you, with your visor down, aye. So what now?"

Aleena spread her gauntleted hands. "I-I don't know. I can't sleep for worrying over father. I'm sick at heart over deciding who should hang or who owes who what damages or—all of it! I know not how father or anyone does it, day upon day! I-I can't go like this much longer." She wrinkled her nose. "As well, I stink to the very heavens in this armor, and soon enough those who know father will know that the smell is not right for *him*."

Mirt and Asper chuckled. "Yes, it grows strong, with your helm off," Asper said. "Let's go to Blackstaff Tower and talk with Laeral, then, or we've reached a trail's end."

Mirt nodded. "Aye, indeed. Put on that helm again, and we'll get you a bath if nothing else."

Aleena smiled. "How did you know, so quickly?"

Mirt shrugged. "The way you sat. The way you waved to the guard. The way you didn't look offended beforehand at the dirty joke you would've known I'd be making as I greeted you—all that on top of what Torgent said."

"Torgent?"

"One of the palace guards. He's on Shyrrhr's tunnel gate, tonight. If you need a friend or protector in the palace, Lady, you could find no better than he. Look for an old man with a white mustache. He said you'd said little and kept to your armor these past days; he knew something was amiss and as good as told me that it wasn't Piergeiron inside the armor. Folk can tell, lass. Folk can always tell." He shrugged. "Besides, if I'd been wrong, your sire owes me a turn or two. 'Tis not my habit to leap upon every lady I meet, you know."

"Lately?" Asper asked him, eyebrow raised. "Is there not a tunnel from here to Blackstaff Tower that we might use?"

"Aye," said Mirt and Aleena together and chuckled. "Come," said the fat moneylender, striding toward a pillar. "This way."

Aleena frowned. "Here? But it's down—"

Mirt grinned at her. "Trust me, Lady." He said. "There're ways and ways, in this place. You'd want to miss a chance at giving that surly grim-chin outside the door a fright, no? When he finds you gone, it'll give him a short breath or two!"

Shaking her head, Aleena joined them. "Father *warned* me about you, once. But I had no idea—"

"They never do," Mirt purred, as stones parted to open a narrow, secret way. "Mind your heads, ladies. . . ."

A hungry mouse in a corner of the room had time to draw only three breaths after the secret door closed and before a midair flickering filled the chamber.

Cold flames raced outward and around. Out of them leaped a masked figure, blade ready in hand. The room was dark and empty. After a quick and silent look around, it shrugged and stepped within the flames once more. The fire and light dwindled to nothing, and darkness returned.

The mouse scurried out in case the strange visitor had left something edible, but there was nothing. Not like the old days. Things were never like the old days, the mouse reflected, slowly and dimly. Perhaps that was the way of the world.

LORD OF THE PIT, WIZARD, WHERE IS THE DEVIL-DAMNED MAGIC?

[silence, mindworm burrowing grimly on through vaulted darkness]

"Through here," Mirt wheezed, trotting bent over low. "The way opens out—"

"So it does! All the more danger for someone who's a lord of Waterdeep, but Faerûn is a dangerous place!"

The voice was cheerful and unexpected, very close to Mirt's ear. The Old Wolf was faster than he looked. He had his sword raised and ready, in just the right spot, and he ducked back with a snarl.

His would-be slayer hissed out a curse. Slender steel sang out in a vicious thrust that skewered only air.

Mirt's stouter blade lashed in over it, biting hard into leather and flesh beneath. The man sobbed at the sudden pain. Mirt brought his sword back trailing a dark ribbon of blood and batted his attacker's sword down.

They strained, steel against steel. Mirt used his free hand, candle and all, to deliver a punch to where the wound must be. His foe groaned and shuddered, reeling back. For the first time, Mirt dared to scuttle out of the passage into the room.

Asper snapped his name, tense and low, from behind Aleena.

Mirt growled, "Still alive—and dancing with a masked *man*, for a change."

"My turn," Asper replied. "You killed the last ruthless slayer who attacked us, remember?"

"Huh," Mirt grunted in reply. He swung steel with all his strength to parry another deadly thrust. The blow struck the slender sword. It clanged from stone to stone and must have numbed his foe.

The gloved and masked man waved his sword as if he was fanning flames, staggered backward along the side passage he'd attacked from, spun around, and raced away.

Mirt scrambled after him, thankful that this new passage was full-height.

"Who is it?" Asper called, pelting after him.

Aleena clanked and stumbled along in their wake, clumsy in her armor.

"I know not," Mirt snarled, bounding down a short flight of steps with his wounded attacker stumbling along just out of reach. "Someone who knows what I am and how to find me, obviously—ho! Your name, Sword-for-Brains! A lady demands it!"

Gasping, the slender masked figure scrambled across a chamber and plunged into the stinking darkness of a sewer-arch. Mirt bounded after him with grunting enthusiasm.

Ahead, a flickering light flared. Mirt glimpsed his leather-clad foe lunging through a wheel of cold white flames. The flames blazed in a slowly turning ring, perhaps a handspan from a stone wall. A gate, gods be thanked again.

He came to a lurching halt, ignoring a rat that scurried out to see if his boots might be supper, and peered around the chamber. Reeking pipes let into it. Channels carried sewage along one side of the room. The vaulted ceiling was webbed with old, tiny cracks. There was no way onward that didn't involve cold flames.

Mirt eyed the rat that fearlessly nibbled his boot, and peered at the gate again—ere his blade stabbed down.

Its curving length rose an instant later when Asper burst into the room. She spun away from his steel even as he snatched it back, and skidded to a halt within easy reach of the flames.

"You didn't have to wait," she grinned, nodding at it. "We could hardly have gotten lost with no other way on, hey?"

The Old Wolf's blade barred her way. He held up a warning finger, dipped his sword to transfix the rat, and tossed it lightly into the ring of fire.

There was a flash, a loud sizzle, and a smell that made the armored warrior entering the chamber gag and sag back. Aleena raised a disgusted hand. She winced in the sudden blazing light of the whirling wheel of flames. It flared bright, shrank, flared again . . . and was gone, leaving nothing but a little smoke behind, and the stink of cooked sewer rat.

"That might have been you," Aleena gasped hollowly, between gulps of nausea.

Asper tossed her head. If she was frightened, she gave no sign of it. Only anger was on her face as she glared around the room. "He could be in the lowest of the Hells by now," she said bitterly, "or in the next sewer over—and we'll never know."

AMUSING, ELMINSTER. I LAUGH. NOW SHOW ME MAGIC.

Somewhere in Waterdeep, a vial clattered onto a tabletop. There came a sigh of satisfaction. A moment later, a gloved hand reached down to the table and took up a silver harp pin. Chuckling, the figure waved, bringing cold flames to pinwheel out of nothingness. The leather-clad form leaned through this fresh flickering and was gone.

MAGIC, YES, AND ANOTHER MEMORY GIVEN YOU BY MYSTRA, BUT AGAIN I FIND NOT WHAT I SEEK! THIS IS RIDICULOUS! WIZARD, GET ON WITH IT!
The tale unfolds, Lord Devil.
[bright images flying]

The time before dawn grew more difficult as he got older. Durnan stood in the cold, getting dressed for another long, long day. The Yawning Portal was his home and his life, and he loved it dearly, but sometimes—these dark fore-dawns, usually—he wanted to be somewhere else. Somewhere that did not allow innkeepers to rise before highsun, when their old aching feet and shanks were thoroughly warmed by the sun, and someone *else* had the cooking fires lit long ago, and a hot meal ready, and—

The high, ragged scream made Durnan jump half out of his hose. Tamsil, from the taproom downstairs! He hopped awkwardly, kicked his garments away with a curse, snatched up his sword belt by the hilts, and launched himself bruisingly through the door frame into the dimness.

In the brief whirl of his naked charge down the stairs, he shook the hilts in his hands for all he was worth until the belt fell away, roaring wildly all the while to distract whoever might be attacking his daughter. Tam was more than old and curvaceous enough to catch the eye of a thief who might think that innkeepers are actually allowed to sleep, and—

Skidding through a doorway with sword and dagger glittering in his hands, Durnan found himself with no foe to fight.

Tamsil and her mother Mhaere both looked up at him with eyes large and dark with fear. His wife was holding a double crossbow in her hands, its strings still thrumming enough to tell him that both quarrels had been fired. No foe lay dead or groaning on the floor before them—but it did offer the discerning naked innkeeper's eye a lavish display of broken crockery and fresh blood.

"Are you all right?" Durnan snapped. "And where is—" He gestured at the wreckage on the floor. "—he?"

Mhaere smiled thinly. "Yes, and gone. A masked man, armed with a blade. He—"

She drew in a deep, shuddering breath that told him she wasn't half as calm as she appeared to be, threw back her head to gasp for air, then resumed speaking as gently as if she'd been discussing the weather. "In leathers, alone, not familiar to me. An oval—an upright oval, like a lady's gazing-glass—of flames that were cold white, not hot, was suddenly right *there*, and he stepped out of it and charged at Tamsil. Thank Tymora, she was carrying water—yon ewer you see in pieces on the floor—and flung it in his face."

Durnan turned slowly to peer around the field of battle, nodding. "Whereupon you," he replied, "took up the ready-bow from behind the bar and gave him both bolts."

"Chest and shoulder," Mhaere added, and he could hear the satisfaction in her voice. "He fled back through the hole in the flames, and they were gone, just like that, and him with them."

Durnan stalked across the room like a hairy panther and pounced on something small on the floor. "Dropping something as he left you," he growled in bafflement, as he picked it up. He was holding a silver harp pin.

"Papa," Tamsil said in her high, clear voice, "I don't ever want to see that man again. How can we stop him ever coming back?"

"The only way you can ever really stop any foe," Durnan muttered, staring at the pin in his hand. "I must find him—and he must die."

MY, MY, MYSTRA'S MEMORIES CERTAINLY MAKE YOUR TORIL SEEM AN INTERESTING PLACE. I'M NOT SEEING THE MAGIC I SEEK YET, THOUGH, AM I?

Ten

HARPERS HUNT BY MOONLIGHT

The Lady Mage of Waterdeep bent over the silver harp pin on the table, lying amid the eerie, softly raging glows of her spells, and murmured, "There. In a moment, we'll see—"

Obligingly, the pin exploded, bolts of lightning snarling hungrily across the room as the world went white and Laeral's body was hurled helplessly away.

A certain Old Wolf scrambled up out of his chair as the lightning that should have slain Aleena melted and toppled a brazier instead. It was still falling across Mirt's seat when Laeral smashed into him and drove him back into the tangle. They crashed to the floor together, bouncing with tooth-jarring force. Flames flickered briefly here and there around the room and then went out.

Pinned under a brazier, splintered furniture, and a wizard sobbing in pain, Mirt glared briefly up at a blinding-bright sphere that floated near the ceiling: Laeral's safeguard. Having absorbed most of the unleashed magic, it was slowly fading back into invisibility. The ceiling above was decorated with a collection of scorch marks that told him little disasters like this one had occurred a time or two before. He wasn't sure if that was reassuring—after all, Blackstaff Tower still stood.

"Lass?" he asked roughly, struggling to get out from under. "Are you well?"

He was answered by three sets of moans and curses, one of them from atop his breast. He took gentle but firm hold of the Lady Mage and thrust her up into the air so he could slide to freedom. "What befell?"

"There was a trap on that pin," Laeral said, panting. She rolled off his hand and found her own wincing way to her knees, "left behind deliberately to harm anyone using spells on it. No Harper would do such a thing. Someone is trying to mislead us all into thinking a Harper killed Resengar."

Mirt nodded. "This fails to surprise me," he said, turning his head to see how Asper and Aleena fared. Beside him, Laeral toppled silently over onto her face.

Flames flared up from her body as it struck the floor, writhing, and Mirt roared out a heartfelt curse and a cry for aid. As he rolled the Lady Mage over, Asper ran for the door—and the alarm-gong on the wall just outside it.

Only his smallest belt flask held water, and Mirt dashed it into Laeral's face and pawed at her nose and cheeks to try to keep the flames at bay—greenish-yellow tongues of hot fire that seemingly rose from nothing. Magical fire, of course, damned wagonloads of praise be to Mystra, and all that. It ignored all of his ineffectual attempts to douse it; though it somehow didn't spread to him, the Old Wolf was heartily glad when the room suddenly filled with stern-faced Tower apprentices.

He was thrust aside in an instant, and the room erupted in tense castings and snapped orders and suspicious peering. Their health assured, Asper, Mirt, and Aleena were thrust into chairs in the most distant corner of the room and sternly bidden to wait and not stir.

Just now, none of them felt like doing anything but sitting dazedly and letting the numb tingling die away. Young apprentices were still scurrying in with more chairs. Hard questioning lay in the future of Laeral's three unexpected late-night guests.

Amid the nervous tumult, a tall figure limped into the room. Aleena rose in a flurry of clanking armor to run to him.

"Gently, 'Leen," Piergeiron cautioned as she rushed to throw her arms around him. Scowling apprentices reached out to claw her back. Piergeiron made straight for the nearest chair, wobbling a little as he came. His face was tight and white with pain.

"Well, young lion?" Mirt said, looking into his eyes.

Those eyes were oddly green, a strangeness that seemed to grow as the Open Lord of Waterdeep collapsed into the chair and gasped, "Perhaps I'll live." As his daughter reached him at last and rained kisses on his face, he caught hold of both chair arms and shook himself, wincing.

"Weak as a gutter kitten," he hissed, waving Aleena back to her chair. "Now, will all the watching gods—or any of the rest of you— kindly tell me just what is going *on?*"

Mirt held up a hand to forestall anyone else saying anything and turned to the apprentice standing watchfully beside his chair. All four of them had acquired such sentinels, he noted, and they did not look entirely friendly.

"How fares the Lady Laeral?"

"That's not for me to say, merch—" the young wizard began, his voice as cold as the edge of a drawn blade. He fell silent in astonishment as a long, slender hand took hold of his arm from behind, and its owner followed, giving him a quelling look.

"I, too, perhaps will live a bit longer," Laeral told them, a wry smile on her lips. "A clever trap *beneath* the Harper enchantments— or at least, what I thought were Harper spells." She gave Piergeiron a friendly nod and turned her head to regard Mirt. "You were about to say something important, I believe?"

Mirt nodded and looked in turn to Piergeiron. "Tell us what you last remember—of what befell before you ended up here."

The paladin drew in a deep, quavering breath, lifted his head to stare thoughtfully at the spell-scorched ceiling, and said, "I was . . . charmed by a spell, cast by one who came on me unawares, in private. A man, by the mind-touch, young and full of rage and excitement. He forced from my mind the names, faces, and abodes of all the lords of Waterdeep."

Around the circle of chairs and apprentices, there was a silent bristling, a sudden tension that was almost a gasp.

"He thanked me . . . mockingly," Piergeiron said slowly, remembering, "and then came around from behind me to bow—all sweeping arms and snooty flourishes, a parody of a courtier—and swept a sword from behind his back and ran me through. He wore a mask, and I don't think, if he'd removed it, I would have known him. His blade went through me—"

Aleena hissed in disgust and fear, and her father threw her a smile as he continued, "—and struck the back of my chair. That broke the charm, and I roared at him and rose. He tried to slash open my throat, but I managed to draw my own blade—"

Aleena was already holding it out to him, hilt first, in its scabbard. Piergeiron gave her another smile, took it, and laid it across his knees.

"—and he seemed disinclined to cross swords. He threw a spell into my face—force bolts that burned, like daggers stabbing. It threw me to my knees. He fled into the next room. I got there crawling— just in time to see his back foot vanishing through a gate."

"An oval of flickering fire?" Asper asked. "Cold flames? Shrank away after that?"

Piergeiron gave her a thin smile. "Indeed. Is he a friend of yours?"

Asper gave him a withering look, and his smile broadened. "Forgive me, Lady," he said, "that was unworthy of me—and an insult to you. I fear my jests are apt to be awkward."

"Yet, look you here, Paladinson," Mirt growled, beckoning one of the Tower apprentices over. The wizard blinked back at him until Laeral gestured that he should heed the summons; Mirt gave him a false, sweet smile and plucked the silver harp pin from the man's hand, holding it out to Piergeiron with a flourish. "This matter does question friendships, as it happens."

The First Lord of Waterdeep peered at it. "Yes, the Harpers have always been friends," he said slowly, frowning. "Or perhaps had been until now."

"This has gone on long enough," Mirt growled, and lifted his gaze to Laeral. "Get Elminster to the palace, away from all your wards— and take all of us there, too, to meet him. Now."

As quickly as if she'd been his youngest maidservant, the Lady Mage of Waterdeep nodded and trotted from the chamber, leaving her apprentices staring from her dwindling figure to Mirt, then back again.

"Elminster," someone muttered, in tones of awe.

WELL, QUITE THE MIGHTY SAVIOR WIZARD YOU WERE. A PITY I'M NOT SEEING MUCH OF THE MAGIC YOU PROMISED.
[mind lash]
[pain]
[mind lash]
[writhing pain]
[mind lash]
STUPID HUMAN! THINK I'LL SIT PATIENTLY TO BE DUPED FOREVER?
[mind lash]

Half a world away, in a tomb deep under Myth Drannor, a glowing ring of wraithlike figures flickered like so many man-high candles, cold and white in the gloom.

Two darker figures stood unafraid in their midst, a man and a woman. "Enough talk for now, I fear," Elminster was saying reluctantly, raising his staff. "You've quite filled my brains with old spells and lost lore—and I'm sure you must be more than weary of my gossip."

"*Nay*, man," the closest baelnorn said in swift reply. "You two are the only visitors who bring us news of the passing world—the only ones to remember us. Even we grow lonely." He turned to face Storm Silverhand and added fiercely, "Lady—oh, 'twas good to hear songs again! Your voice is lovely."

"Aye," several other ghostly figures sighed in eerie unison.

The Bard of Shadowdale turned to give them all a smile, and replied, "My thanks. I cannot hope to match even a fair singer of Cormanth—"

"Ah, Lady," another of the tomb guardian spirits said, waving a dismissive hand, "our spells can bring back at any time the sounds of past songs sung to us. What we lack is new songs, and the singer alive and here, performing for *us*. Your kindness will give us much joy ahead, much to talk over—"

A sudden radiance of sparks kindled about Elminster's forehead. The wizard stiffened and swayed, pain flashing across his face.

"What befalls?" a baelnorn snapped, raising hands that glowed suddenly bright and dangerous. "Can we aid?"

Elminster's gaze rolled down, and he shivered. "N-nay, friends. A new peril has come to light. We shall return in time to come, if we can. For now, we must go. Farewell."

Blue sparks swam before Storm Silverhand. She barely had time to be startled before they washed over her. The world became a place of endless falling through a blue glow.

Her boots were suddenly on uneven ground. Blue sparks were fading, and the smells around her were now dung and the sea, rotting fruit and cooking smoke.

"An alley near Piergeiron's Palace, in Waterdeep," Elminster explained as her hand went to the blades at her belt. "Laeral farspoke me."

"And?" she asked simply, putting hands on her hips and pivoting to look around.

"Time to use thy tracing spell, lass—take thyself to any Harper pin in this city that's been tampered with or had other spells laid atop it. There'll probably be a man there who's good with blades. Keep thyself alive until I teleport to thee." He kissed Storm while she was still blinking and frowning at him, then whirled away, striding along the uneven cobbles toward the palace.

Its grand and lofty entrances seemed strangely—deserted. The doors to the private wing, however, were closed and guarded by two huge men who stood like expressionless titans in their closed helms and mirror-bright armor.

The Old Mage strode up to them without hesitation and reached between them to lift the ring-bar from the doors—and almost lost a hand to the halberds sweeping down.

The point topping one followed him as he scuttled back. Its wielder's voice was less than kind as he said, "None may enter without leave."

Elminster sighed. "Leave I have, goodsirs. Pray stand aside for Elminster of Shadowdale. I am in great haste, and for good reason."

"Elminster?" The guard's voice dripped with the skeptical sneer hidden behind his helm. "Aye, and I'm the Grand Pasha and Vizier Most Mighty of all Calimshan!"

"Who are you, really," the other guard snapped, his own halberd leveled menacingly, "and who gave you leave to pass? Of those not

known to us by sight, our pass-list is very short, and I very much
doubt you're anyone on it!" He backed to where he could easily and
swiftly slap an alarm-gong with one swing of his gauntlet. "Well?"

"I am Elminster in truth," the straggle-bearded man replied quietly, "and I have leave to pass anywhere in the city—leave given to
me by Lord Ahghairon of Waterdeep, long ago."

"Pah!" the first guard responded, throwing back his head. "You
expect us to believe *that?*"

"I care not what you do or do not believe," the old man told them
mildly, "but if you delay me longer, know this: I'll send you forthwith to where you'll end up anyway, if you retain the stupidity to
deny an archmage anything."

The first guard drew himself up in triumph. "You would *dare* to
threaten a Guard Confirméd of Waterdeep, in the very palace?
Why—"

He thrust ruthlessly with his halberd at the old man—and the
world suddenly changed.

Elsewhere, in dusty near-darkness, the two guards found themselves blinking at each other over their halberds, and then, slowly,
trembling in fear.

They both knew very well where they were: the trophy hall that
gave entrance to the Hall of Heroes, the warriors' tomb in Waterdeep's City of the Dead.

Elminster strode straight through lofty halls, anger and magic crack-
ling around him. He scattered guards and courtiers like so much dust.
As chamber gave way to chamber, the guards he faced were older.
Not a few of them recognized him and stood aside with salutes.
"Piergeiron," he snapped at the first pair of them not to do so. They
swiftly opened the doors they were flanking and waved him in.

"No, Lord, I cannot," Laeral was saying firmly. "There are too
many enchantments hereabouts, layer upon layer, hundreds of
them, and many old and forgotten. If I could but touch him, I could
put a tracer on him that few mages could break, but—"

Heads turned as Elminster joined the small, tense group of folk.
They gathered by a lone lamp, within a watchful ring of silent Tower

apprentices. Laeral, Mirt, Piergeiron, and Durnan nodded to him. Asper bowed her head and murmured, "Lord Elminster, be welcome."

At her words, Aleena and Durnan's wife and daughter stared at Elminster as if he'd suddenly grown several heads, each of them spitting flame.

"I may have a solution to that," the Old Mage told them, "but we must move swiftly; Storm is our bait, and stands in peril. All who would see battle and this affair done, gather around me now, touch me, and hold that contact steady. Apprentices, back to the Tower."

The ring of novice wizards wavered.

Laeral turned her head and said crisply, "Do as the Lord Elminster directs, please. *Now.*"

The Old Mage did not wait for pleasantries or to watch the apprentices hasten out. Brief magefire flashed. The room was suddenly much emptier than before, leaving only Mhaere and Tamsil staring at their father, who stood alone by the lamp.

Mhaere frowned a little at her husband. "You . . . didn't go," she said, a question in her voice.

Durnan strode over and put an arm around her and Tamsil. "You left your crossbow behind," he replied softly. "What might have befallen if the slayer had come here, after we'd all gone?"

With his free hand, he drew his sword. It gleamed in the lamplight. "Whatever else befalls in this world, I'll *not* lose you, if I can prevent it."

BAH! WEEPY SENTIMENT EVERYWHERE! THIS HUMAN'S WITS ARE ADDLED— ADDLED! WHAT SORT OF FOOL LIVES HIS LIFE WRAPPED IN LOVE OF OTHERS?

The human sort of fool, Nergal. It's what we are, just as ye are the creature of Hell ye are.

GRRRR! FALL SILENT, CAPTIVE WIZARD!

They were suddenly elsewhere—a dark and cold elsewhere, with dust rising around them and the smell of stone strong in their nostrils. Underground.

Piergeiron slapped his armor, startling his daughter rigid, and willed it to come alight. It awakened in a pale blue glow.

By its radiance and Laeral's glowfire they could see they were standing in a high-ceilinged hall that looked empty but for the drifting dust.

Many dark archways marked led to passages that ran off into gloom.

The radiance coming from Laeral's hands flared to almost blinding brightness. The Lady Mage of Waterdeep reached up to touch Piergeiron's head.

He gasped, shuddered, and stumbled away from her.

Laeral reeled and sank down to her knees. Aleena bent to catch hold of her, but Asper was swifter.

"Lady?" she asked quietly.

"I'll be fine," Laeral said calmly. "Piergeiron needs to be hale and whole right now, and I've made him so. I'll just be a little weak for awhile."

"Aleena," Asper said, "stay with her. Guard her—and if anyone wearing a mask comes anywhere near, scream your head off."

Piergeiron's daughter looked at Mirt, Elminster, and her father, collected their nods of assent, and knelt down by Laeral with an audible sigh of relief.

Mirt slapped Piergeiron's chest gently. He rumbled, "You know where we are, don't you?"

Piergeiron was staring at a coat of arms carved over a nearby archway. "I think so," he replied quietly, "and I begin to suspect why."

He drew breath to say more—but Storm's long, raw scream came echoing down to them from somewhere far beyond the arch.

Asper, as always, moved first, racing like a dark wind through the archway. Piergeiron soon caught her up, his consecrated blade glimmering as he willed it to shine. Elminster sprinted along close at hand, leaving behind the puffing and astonished Mirt.

Along a passage they ran, then through two chambers of cobwebs and dust, and a third where a lone, scuttling spider fled their furious approach. In the fourth, light shone amid vaulted pillars, casting forth the shadows of two dark, struggling figures in leather. One was masked. His sword, glistening with blood, stood out of Storm's back. Impaled, she was struggling forward in agony, trying to reach him.

The masked man saw the new arrivals and raised his other hand. The many-hued flames of a ready spell were racing around it.

"Sssambranath," he said clearly and carefully, the first word of an incantation that would define what part of the chamber erupted in a racing storm of lightning bolts. "Naerth—"

His incantation broke off as Storm spat blood into his face, making him choke. The hilt of his blade was almost against her breast, now, and she clawed weakly at his masked face. He shook his head violently, ducking away from her as much as he could without letting go of his sword—but his spell was ruined.

No such misfortune befell Elminster. Swinging around a pillar to a panting stop, the Old Mage caught his breath and cast a careful spell. The room suddenly fell shimmering and silent.

Striding past where Asper was frozen in midleap, the Old Mage reached the two bodies joined by steel. He cast another spell with the same fussy care, touched Storm Silverhand to visit its effects on her, and gently took hold of her shoulders and tugged.

Wetly, she slid back along the masked man's sword, her eyes unseeing and her face twisted in pain. Elminster kept on pulling, wincing at the feel of the steel sliding out of her.

The longer he kept this ancient Illuskan spell going, the more pain he would feel. Yet it could be nothing compared with what Storm must be suffering. He'd sent her into this—the most rebellious of the three lasses he'd raised as his daughters, albeit centuries ago.

Gods above, but he'd forgotten just how much this could *hurt*.

The Old Mage set his teeth and dragged the Bard of Shadowdale a few unsteady, trudging steps farther, past the statue that his spell had made of Mirt. The Old Wolf was frozen in midstride, arms swung wide for balance and drawn steel in both hands.

Elminster knelt beyond him, wrestling with a snarl against the rising surges of agony that made his hands tremble. Mystra, *how* many times had he done this for this lass? And she for him? On her riven breast, he carefully laid out what he'd need for the healing spell. When he was done, teeth chattering with pain, he banished the spell.

At once the world was all loud, racing movement again. The pain was abruptly gone. For him.

El let Storm half-crush his hand in her own as she stared up at him, agony like fire in her eyes. Then he drew a deep breath and drowned out her scream with an iron command of his own. As Asper, Piergeiron, and Mirt charged at the masked man, the Old Mage's voice rang out over them like a battle trumpet: "*Don't* kill him. Yet."

FIRES OF NESSUS. A ROOM FULL OF CLEVER-TONGUED HUMANS! DO I GET TO
SEE THEM DIE?

No, but ye get to hear their talk of powerful magic—and I do
mean powerful.

AH! ABOUT AVERNUS-FREEZING-OVER TIME!

Helpless the man hung in the air above them, masked no longer.
Spread-eagled and furious, frozen in the grip of Elminster's spells,
he was running out of obscenities to spit down at them.

That seemed almost fair, because fewer and fewer questions were
occurring to those below. His answers thus far—most given proudly—revealed him to be Amril Zoar, of the noble family exiled from
Waterdeep long, long ago. He'd armed himself to destroy all the
lords of the city with the spells and an enchanted sword he'd gained
from a man who bore a silver harp badge, and he wondered how
to reach them ere they gathered together to hunt him down.

For years he'd schemed and brooded until by chance his spies
found a book. It turned out to be a lost tome of Ahghairon, the
"Founder of Waterdeep," that detailed how to create "ring of fire"
gates. These short-lived gates were but echoes of certain ancient,
long-hidden portals moved into the cellars of early Waterdeep by
Halaster Blackcloak. Echo gates could be created only within a
short distance of the ancient portals, but—Mirt's eyes gleamed at
this news—they could bypass many modern barriers and defensive enchantments. Once a master of echo gates, Amril had taken
his tutor's harp badge as his own and begun slaying lords of
Waterdeep.

Mirt peered up at the floating man and said grimly, "Right. Enough.
Kill him. We can spell-talk to his corpse about his kin and kill them, too."

"No!" a voice rapped out from behind him. Storm's face was pale,
but she strode forward as swiftly and smoothly as if she'd never felt
the bite of cold steel. "I must know more of the man with the silver
harp, who taught this Amril magic!"

Elminster looked up. "What happened to your tutor, and who
was he?"

Amril Zoar glared down at him and said bitterly, "I never knew
his name. He was killed by a knight of Waterdeep, who came

seeking my father's death—and mine. He found my father's, but my tutor bought my life with his own."

Elminster let his hand fall to his side, and the spread-eagled noble sank, still spellbound and motionless, to hang a few feet off the dusty stone floor.

Mirt stepped forward in grim silence, axe in hand, and looked to Piergeiron.

The First Lord nodded. "For Waterdeep, then. For Tamaeril, and Resengar," he intoned.

The axe swept up, glittering.

A leather-clad form sprang in front of Mirt, bare hands raised. "No!" Storm protested. There were tears in her eyes. "Do not kill this man. His cause was just in his eyes—and his task nigh impossible, for one alone. I would have him for the Harpers."

Mirt frowned at her. His gaze strayed to Amril's sword, still lying in a dark pool of Storm's blood, and then back to the Bard of Shadowdale. "Why?" he asked bluntly.

"He saw his cause as just and did what he thought he had to," Storm replied. "Who are we to think ourselves better than he?"

Mirt's frown grew. Something that might have been a growl stirred deep in his throat—then, slowly, he stepped back, lowering his axe, and bowed to Storm.

"Methinks yon youngling enjoys slaying overmuch, Lady," he said darkly, "but enough. I grow sick of killings. Mind you get that book of Ahghairon's from him, though . . . I don't want his cousin or squire or trained dog coming through a gate beside my bed in the midst of my snoring time, one or two nights from now!"

Storm nodded. "If he cannot or will not change his ways," she said softly, "he *will* find death. At my hands."

"So be it," Piergeiron said, almost wearily. "Just take him far from Waterdeep." He looked down at what he was turning over and over in his fingers, as if seeing it for the first time. "A silver harp," he said thoughtfully. "I thought the badge of the Harpers was a silver moon and a silver harp."

"The silver moon was my mother's badge . . . her kin came from the city of Silverymoon," Storm said softly. "But Harpers have a better answer. Mirt?"

Mirt smiled. He put his arm around Asper and growled, "The harp is the Harper. The moon need not be part of the badge—for as the motto says: Harpers hunt by moonlight."

SO WE SEE SOME WHISPERS OF MAGIC, BUT HARDLY THE SILVER FIRE I SEEK OR ANYTHING I CAN SEIZE AND MAKE USE OF. I WEARY OF LASHING YOU, IDIOT WIZARD—SO I'LL DO NOTHING TO YOU, NOW. TRY NOT TO FOOL YOURSELF INTO THINKING I'LL FORGET THIS AND THAT YOU'RE GETTING AWAY WITH SOMETHING. YOU'LL LEARN DIFFERENTLY SOON ENOUGH.

Mirt found himself blinking at the ceiling, all silver in moonlight. "No!" he gasped hoarsely. "Gods, no!"

He was still dressed. The hilt of his sword was ready under his clenched hand. Amril Zoar's blade dripped with Storm's gore . . . He'd half forgotten the details, but they came flooding back, with a face behind them: Elminster. Or rather, what was left of Elminster.

A desperate, wavering mind, less than it had been, pleading, and in a ruined body . . . in a stinking stony waste under a blood-red sky. Avernus. It had to be.

"When I'm ready to look for a place to die," Mirt told his sword as he drew it and watched the moonlight gleam along its bright length, "Hell will not be where I start. Just so long as that's clear."

With a grunt he rolled off the bed, stamped his feet to settle them in his boots, and set off down the passage. This might be one walk he didn't come back from, and he was damned if he was going to leave before he saw—

Asper, a pale flame in the gloom, burst bare out of her bedchamber. Her hair was wild. She held a sword in one hand and boots in the other. "Thieves?" she gasped, almost falling in her haste to bar his way. "Lord work?"

"Worse than that, lass. Elminster needs me."

"Elminster? Why?"

"Because he's trapped and in torment in Hell," the Old Wolf growled. "Where I dare not go."

"*No*, Mirt," Asper cried. Her face went bone-white. "Not to Hell! You'll never even get near him before the devils get their talons on you, and you'll be—you'll be—"

She flung away her boots and clutched his arm. "No friend is worth dying for—when your death isn't going to help him!"

Mirt scowled at her, eyes gleaming like two old torches. He tried, and failed, to shake off her grip. Her fingers were like claws. "Aye, true enough—and with Khelben and Laeral gone off the gods alone know where, that leaves me just one weapon swift to my hand that's sharp enough to hew down devils."

Asper's face was wet with tears. "What?"

Mirt set his jaw, freed himself from her hand, and strode toward the stairs, hefting his sword. "Halaster Blackcloak. I have to find him, down in Undermountain, and—ha—convince him to fight his way into Hell and bring Elminster back here to me. Without delay, so he might just still be alive when Halaster gets there." He chuckled, a dry, terrible sound.

"Mirt, *no!*" Asper almost screamed. She gnawed at her knuckles and sobbed. "You *can't!* He's mad! You—"

"—Have to," he finished her sentence for her, softly. "For—live or die this night—if I fail my best and oldest friends, what am I? And what have I lived for?"

Eleven

OLD DEVILS, NEW TRICKS

Bare, thorny branches of stunted trees stabbed like despairing fingers into the blood-red sky. Elminster Aumar sighed at them. Well, at least he could move, seeing new sights on the probably short remainder of his journey toward death. Such mobility afforded him a deep and abiding consolation, of course.

El crawled forward on raw, bleeding knees, his body bristling with greasy, green-black spines that he hoped looked half as unappetizing to devils as they looked to him. He tried not to think of the trail of gore he must be leaving. Twice now, he'd had to turn and roll over to transfix and slay maggots nipping at his feet, and he'd lost count of the times he'd retched and spewed in helpless nausea at the sights and sounds all around.

Devils were clawing and disfiguring each other overhead right now, slitting eyes and tugging out entrails with eager savagery, spattering the rocks below with thankful lack of attention. Elminster crawled on, smiling inwardly at his looks. Well, he'd been a raven-haired, silken-hipped lass when that wasn't his true shape, either, so he hadn't much cause for complaint. Not that rocks listened to the complaints of broken archmages any more than they heeded the curses of other beings.

The ground trembled in the throes of a violent underground explosion. El tried not to think of what death traps caverns must become at such times. Another snarling fireball crossed the sky.

Sooner or later in this tortured landscape of rock and flame and bitter fumes, where devils roamed in search of too-scarce food or traveled in ruthless patrols—in the distance, a flying phalanx of abishai swooped in unison to spear squalling nupperibos—his luck would run out.

Sooner. Even as he slipped for the thousandth time and lost his wind in a belly-landing against saw-edged rocks, a spade-barbed tail rose in front of him. It was glossy-black and as large as his head. The body it was attached to must have been large indeed. El ground his face into the stones a moment before the razor-sharp tail cut across his head. The resounding slap set his skull ringing and drove him into a wavering upright posture. It had sliced open his scalp far enough back for his own blood not to blind him with its first drenching flood.

What a stroke of luck, indeed. With that sarcastic thought held in the forefront of his mind to keep Nergal from noticing what he was doing, El leaked a tiny amount of silver fire slowly out to stanch the bleeding. He lifted his head to see what was attacking him.

"Well," purred what could only be another outcast archdevil. It reared up from the rocks in front of him. "What have we here?"

Three long, sinuous serpent tails rose from where they coiled around and amid rocks, to meet in an obsidian-hued body that had the shape of a lush human female torso. From the shoulders spread bat wings, dark beneath and ruby-red on their sleek outer surfaces. A forked-tongued and horned head swayed on the end of a neck that was too long, but otherwise looked both human and attractive. Unfortunately, the fingers extending in his direction ended in hooked, hawklike talons. Each was as long as Elminster's arms.

Three barbed tails flipped up to slap the rocks in unison and propel the devil in an undulating charge. The swaying head came within a foot of Elminster's own. Ale-brown eyes with flames flickering in their depths stared hard into blue-gray, weary human ones . . . and beautiful red lips snaked into a smile.

"A spell-twisted human, if I'm not mistaken . . . transformed why? I'd best see just who you are before I cook you for dinner or remake you into a more pleasant shape for my own amuse—"

The serpent-devil stiffened and hissed, rustling her wings with a single, convulsive shudder. She sent a mindlance into Elminster . . . and found Nergal.

[ruby sun, blossoming and widening, serpentine awareness questing forth]

[tentacled giant turning to face the intrusion, gathering ominous strength]

"Ho-ho, a wizard of great power . . . memories aplenty here, both entertainment and something I could use, if I can but find the right remembrance . . . but hold: Here's a taint that's somehow famili—"

MALACHLABRA!

"Nergal!"

DIE, SERPENT-BITCH!

"Your turn to feed worms, Lord Most High of *Nothing!*"

[mind bolt, turned aside, raw agony, Elminster screaming as walls smash down, ceilings fall, chambers collapse . . . mental arrows, leaping one two three, struck aside and hurled back in bright array . . . El still screaming]

"Human, I am Malachlabra, Duchess of Hell and daughter of Dispater! Cleave to me, and I'll rid your mind of this tentacled brute!"

[mind bolt strikes mind bolt, great flash, long despairing shriek of agony, El writhing as fires are hurled back and forth in his burning mind]

"Human, I . . . ah, your name is—*Elminster!* Elminster Aumar, cleave to *me!*"

Abishai veered away, spitting and shouting, as the serpent-devil reared up and spat ribbons of fire far across Avernus. She drove one long, cruel talon into the ungainly creature at her feet. His raw screams died into frothy barking, and even maggots shrank away from the thing of churning flesh, erupting limbs, and wetly jetting gases.

Far away, the ground shook. Malachlabra shouted in triumph. She was still laughing, raised upright into a sky she was raking with her talons, when Nergal's reply came down upon her.

The red air shimmered, bled purple, and rolled back for an instant. It vomited huge purple spheres of roaring, trembling flame on all sides of the serpent-devil.

Then, of course, they exploded.

Convulsing talons whipped and cartwheeled past the ropy thing that was Elminster. Stones lashed at him, and he was drenched with she-devil gore. Torn and gutted lengths of serpent danced in macabre trembling long after they'd fallen among far stones. Where Malachlabra had been there was nothing but smoking, fresh-tumbled rocks—and black and crimson slime spattered on the stones.

All at once, as Nergal's laughter thundered through Elminster's mind, the thing of teeth and odd-shaped limbs and lumpy bodies shuddered. It ceased its shapeshifting chaos. Arching and snuffling, the transformed wizard writhed on blood-spattered rocks. Maggots reared up hungrily, yellow-white and glistening with slime. El, adrift in blood-shadows of suffering, never felt their gnawing.

SO YOU CAN CHANGE SHAPE AT WILL, LITTLE MAN? WELL, WELL. ANOTHER SECRET IT'S TIME YOU YIELDED TO ME. I'LL HAVE ALL OF THEM IN THE END, YOU KNOW—BUT BY THE FREEZING STYX, YOU MAKE IT HARD WORK, TEARING EVERY LAST ONE OUT OF YOU!

[Through rivers of blood, the tentacled creature shoulders fearlessly forward. Through many dark and shattered rooms, he seeks bright memories of shapeshifting.]

Silver fire threaded out, oh-so-subtly—mere droplets where rushing floods were needed. Face twisted in pain, Elminster Aumar writhed on the ground, slapping at maggots. As Nergal's thought bored on, probing ever deeper into El, the long and fissured torso dwindled. Its limbs became human arms again.

El groaned and let a little wash of silver fire sear the maggots gnawing him. They fell away, slain instantly. He collapsed again with a groan. *Let Nergal think the shapeshifting was my doing and not Malachlabra's. Anything to keep him from noticing the fire . . .*

[A great horned head looks sharply this way and that as it presses on through a mind where red rivers recede. Tentacles trail through the gore as it paces and peers.]

"Die, evil mage!" Cruel spears thrust like tongues of flame into his back. El snarls a curse that turns into a helpless spewing of blood. Spear points transfix him. They shove him forward, between the merlons, to plunge out into emptiness and down, down toward the stinking moat.

There are ragged cheers as he plummets, but they become shouts of alarm ere he reaches the ground. That landing will come somewhere else.

The ring on his finger has done its work. His very bones are rubbery. His skin itches, his body feels wet and empty and sick . . . and it's flowing, changing as he struggles for breath. He watches the ground and the scum-cloaked water hurl itself up to meet him. . . .

Less than the height of a man away from smashing into that water, the black-robed body becomes a black star. The burst of dark radiance freezes for a moment. The watching crowds murmur. It drifts sideways in the breeze ere it winks out and is gone. . . .

* * * * *

Black, stinking pools bubble with sulfurous stinks. Cruel wasps alight on the heads of submerged, spellbound captives and thrust home their long stingers, trading venom for blood. The thrashing, foaming victims drown.

A sudden whirlpool pierces those waters. It turns up gigantic ribcages black with slime, and odd-shaped, unidentified things that are flung far and wide from the muck. At the heart of that whirlpool rises a cloud of red and black. It spins swiftly at first and then more slowly, to stand at last, revealed as—

"Malachlabra, Duchess of Hell and daughter of Dispater," murmured the watching Tasnya. She banished her scrying image with a lazy wave of her hand before the distant serpent-devil would have a chance to feel her scrutiny. "You are *such* a headstrong fool. Almost as bad as Nergal."

She gave her own cleverness a crooked smile and rolled over again to bite out the throat of an erinyes. As the others whimpered and shrank away from the gore-filled bed, the imps hovering above Tasnya never paused in their work, flogging her just the way she'd commanded, with the little barbed whips she'd fashioned. By the Nine, but she loved pain.

*   *   *   *   *

AGAIN YOU TRY TO DUPE ME, HUMAN! JUST HOW STUPID DO YOU THINK I AM?
[silence]

*YES, YOU'D BETTER KEEP SILENT, ABOUT NOW. FIRE AND BLOOD, HOW HAVE
YOU EVER FOUND ANYTHING IN THIS WALLOW-PIT YOU CALL A MIND? EVERY LINK
HAS A SIDE TRAIL, EVERY MEMORY TWO OR THREE OVERLAPPING IT, AND YOU
DANCE IN FRONT OF ME LIKE A LITTLE YAPPING IMP, THRUSTING ONE THING INTO
MY FACE WHEN I SEEK ANOTHER! WHEN I'VE GOT YOUR SECRETS AT LAST, I'M
GOING TO TAKE GREAT PLEASURE IN YOUR SLOW, PAINFUL DEATH. I'M GOING TO
TEAR TENDER ORGANS OFF YOU AND OUT OF YOU THAT YOU NEVER KNEW YOU
HAD!*

[silence tinged with weary amusement]

*YES, I KNOW YOU SNEER AT DEVILS FOR THEIR UNSUBTLE CRUELTIES, LITTLE
HUMAN WORM, BUT CREATURES CAN'T SNEER WHEN THEY'RE TOO BUSY SCREAM-
ING. . . . YOU'LL DISCOVER THAT TOO! NOW, I WANT TO SEE MORE MEMORIES—SO
GET ON WITH IT!*

Steaming bowls of soup sat on the weathered kitchen table
before them. Hot tankards of cider stood to one side. The two
silver-haired women ignored both in favor of chuckling over the
latest "Heartsteel" novel out of Sembia.

" 'Eyes flashing,' " a voice on the tremulous edge of helpless
laughter announced unsteadily to the world, " 'she flung dweomers
that flashed brightly at the otherworldly apparition. . . .' "

The other woman groaned in derisive disgust and fell into helpless gales of laughter a breath behind her sister.

Storm, who held both the book and the current title of
Reader Aloud to the Assembled, mastered her mirth first. Tossing long hair back out of her eyes, she eyed her sister's shaking shoulders and said gruffly, "None of that laughing,
now—we've an epic to finish!"

" 'A bodice-throbbing saga of broken hearts and blazing spells!' "
Syluné quoted with a fresh whoop of laughter. "Wherein boldly
thrusting blades strike at the heart of evil, smiting aside chastity belts
in the way!"

Storm looked up at her. "It *doesn't* say that," she protested mildly, her own lips trembling on the edge of laughter. "It says 'along the way,' I'm sure." She did not bother to flip the book over to check.

Syluné descended into a fresh fit of giggles, buried her face in her hands, and waved at Storm to read on.

Storm gave her a dubious look, adjusted the ornate and rimless spectacles lower along her nose (they went with the post of Reader Aloud, for reasons both of them had forgotten some centuries ago), and cleared her throat loudly.

Syluné obediently sat up, eyes streaming, and stared at the ceiling to avoid meeting Storm's eyes.

Storm gave her an amused look, and then raised the book once more and resumed the tale. " 'The gallant, rippling-muscled blue-black steed neighed as loudly as a temple bell as the knight in shining armor hurtled bravely down out of the balcony, tumbling through the crossbeams with sounds like unto an entire armory crashing into the same midden-pit, and slammed into his place in the high-cantled saddle—but facing backward. The clangor of tortured metal and the scream of the tortured knight that quite outsang it, startled the faithful war charger even more than the sudden heavy weight on its back, and it reared—almost spilling Sir Taen from his seat once more—and then galloped wildly down the length of the bedchamber. The startled princess sat up in bed just in time to see—' "

"Oh, *stop!*" Syluné sobbed, howling. Her rocking-chair creaked as its pace quickened into a near-canter; Storm watched with amusement as it commenced to walk across the floor, bringing the ribs of Syluné's new body hard against the edge of the table.

Her laughter never faltered—even when the chair tipped forward and Syluné's chin came down on the spoon with a clatter. It soared toward the rafters, and Storm waited for it to come down again, fielded it with a deft hand, and asked, "Could you kindly refrain from hurling the cutlery? We're not dining at a royal table, you know!"

Syluné's laughter redoubled. She threw herself backward, chair and all. Not surprisingly, the rocker took this as a signal to rock. Violently.

Storm rolled her eyes, sighed, and told her farmhouse ceiling, "It's not much to ask, but it might just be too much to ask . . . if you take my meaning."

The ceiling evidently did. Something small and light fluttered down from somewhere amid its loftier, dustier beams, dislodged in all the hubbub. Storm caught it and raised her palm to stare at it: a folded paper jumping frog that one of her Harper trainees had made three summers ago. He'd obviously flicked it aloft before leaving.

As Storm regarded the clever little thing, her mirth gave way to sadness. She'd buried that Harper's gnawed bones in the Teshen backlands last winter; this little frog was all that was left of him now.

"Sister," Syluné murmured, bereft of all humor, "I must go—Alustriel can tell you why!"

Storm lifted her head from the frog to stare at her older sister. Sylune's head lolled, drooling and empty-eyed—before she pitched face-forward into the soup.

Storm stretched out a long arm to grab a good handful of hair, muttering too late, "Not in *my* soup, you don't!"

She hauled the body back into a sitting position and set down the frog as if it was the most precious thing in the world. Then she sighed and took up her discarded apron to wipe the soup from Syluné's vacant face. Lifting her sister's discarded body up in her arms as if it weighed nothing, she gently carried it upstairs to a bed.

The Bard of Shadowdale looked down, sighed, and arranged the lifeless hands to clasp the Heartsteel novel to the still breast, in case she wasn't around when Syluné returned.

Then she went downstairs and outside, to look across the dale she loved. She plucked up her tankard of cider along the way and wondering how long it would be, this time, before she too was called to war. . . .

NO! NO! MORE TIME WASTING! BEAUTIFUL HUMANS, BUT WHAT INTEREST HAVE I IN SUCH? MAGIC I WANT, CURSE YOU, HUMAN! HOW CAN YOU STILL DEFY ME? HOW?

[growling, firmly quelled]

NO, I'LL NOT TEAR AND SNARL. I'LL DIVE INTO YOUR MIND ONCE MORE AND THIS TIME SEEK BEINGS YOU RESPECT BUT DO NOT CONSORT WITH SO CLOSELY. WHAT ELSE WOULD EARN YOUR RESPECT BUT REAL POWER? MAGIC TO TAME KINGDOMS WITH! MAGIC I CAN USE!

[red eyes burning, striding into dark rooms and tearing down what images are found there, clawing aside and seeking more . . .]

*   *   *   *   *

"L-lady Queen?" The young lass quavered, her face dissolving into terror. She trembled violently, too frightened to move. She desperately wanted to be anywhere but here, anywhere but kneeling and proffering flowers to the queen of Aglarond in the royal gardens.

Her mother looked on with a face as white as chalk.

The Simbul, the witch whose spells tore Red Wizards to blood and bones and smashed down towers and made mountains shatter, had suddenly scowled. She scowled even now, her hair rising and twisting along her shoulders as if with a life of its own—no, many lives, all of them eager to blast and destroy and lay waste to little girls who dared to offer flowers.

A small sob dragged the Witch-Queen of Aglarond back to awareness. Her gaze met the wild, trapped eyes of the little girl who'd made the sound.

A chill went through the Simbul. Nothing should ever happen to make little girls look like that. She mustered the warmest smile she could, knelt to say, "My thanks," and bestowed a royal kiss on the trembling forehead. "Be welcome always in our gardens," she added, raising the still-fearful girl to her feet and turning her head to give the anxious mother a smile.

The courtiers standing around visibly relaxed. The girl darted away like a rabbit from under the royal hand, heading for the safety of her mother's skirts.

At the Simbul's elbow, the oldest of her guards dared to murmur, "You scowled, Majesty?"

The Simbul nodded. "I did. At a memory."

"Ah," the guard said, stepping back. No doubt a woman who'd slain hundreds of Red Wizards in frantic spell battle over years upon years had more than a few grim memories that might come to mind unbidden.

So she did, but what made the queen of Aglarond frown again as she turned away to walk a garden path was the fact that the memory was not her own. She could still hear her sisters' helpless laughter over a romantic book, a fancy-novel . . . a moment new to her, but tattered and elusive in someone's store of remembrances. But whose?

Whose mind could have touched hers so feebly? Whose?

Twelve

THE HARPER WITHOUT

The easy thing to do would have been to hurl herself over the cold stone sill, into the night and the rain. Out and down, down to the courtyard below. Alustriel gripped the stony edge with fingers that trembled, pale white. Why then did she not do it?

Pride. Just that—a small thing to stand between her and a quick doom. It would be swift, yes, but dishonorable, a shame as sure as that Irlar sought to bring on her, with his mocking smile and honeyed words. She looked down again. The night hid the stones she'd stared at for hours. It would be an easy thing now, in the dark, alone. In the morning they'd find her lying on those stones. "Aye, she jumped," her uncle would say. He'd spit out of the side of his mouth, shake his head, and turn away, waving at the servants to bundle her body to be burned.

I will not have him think that of me, Alustriel thought.

She turned away from the night to face her waiting chambers. Irlar would come to her soon. Irlar the laughing lordling, a sneer bright in his eyes. Irlar, who'd take her to wife not for love—though no doubt he'd force the attentions of love on her, this very night— but for the lands and wealth held in her name. Hers to surrender but not hers to enjoy; her uncle saw to that.

Uncle Thamator. The Wolf, men called him, and dared not meet his eyes when he was in a fury. All knew him for a fearless warrior, matchless in the field, and a bitter man—and all knew him to be a Harper. Alustriel shrank even from the memory of their last meeting. Together in his chambers after a feast, sharing wine—her first taste of such things, amber fire that warmed her throat like spiced sauce—she'd asked him eagerly, innocently, when she would be made a Harper.

Thamator fixed her with eyes like colorless glass. "I gave my lady for the Harpers, girl. My lady, and my son not yet born, who died with her. Too many comrades to count have followed them. I've given the Harpers this strong right arm, these thirty winters since. I have given them friends with my sword, too, when it was necessary. *What* have *ye* to give them?"

He spoke the last words with biting anger, almost spitting his contempt. She stood silent, shocked, face white—and then red. He saw her mounting color, stared at her deliberately, and went on. "Ye are not a warrior. Ye are pretty, but beauty is not something so rare that it will aid the Harpers. Ye do not believe that one god is the right and true one above others, and cannot then serve as a priest; a good one, at least. Ye have the silence to steal but no strength or speed—and ye lack the craft to lie glibly."

The lord of Bluetower strode angrily across the room, and turned to confront her again. "So I paid good coin to see ye made something of a mage. The wizard Thurduil said ye had a way with the power. Eight years! Eight years of coins out of this purse, one handful after another, too many of them gold—and to show for it? Ye can make a servant *sneeze*. A prank I can match with a pinch of pepper! No doubt Gaerd has managed to get ye to do some other tricks of the like by now. He's a master; the fault's not with him."

Thamator's eyes were like the points of two swordblades. "And ye want to know when ye'll be made a Harper," he minced with boiling sarcasm. She couldn't turn from his eyes as he lowered himself into his chair and added with terrible softness, "Get out of my sight for a time. Ye look too much like your mother did to be saying such idiocy to me." His face twisted briefly in a spasm of pain or regret. A passing shadow left his features as smooth and blank and unyielding as stone.

Alustriel turned and stumbled out, wiping vainly at the tears that streamed down her cheeks. . . .

Two days ago, Irlar had come riding at the head of a company of laughing young men in finery, swords bouncing at their hips. When he offered for her hand in marriage, her uncle had not even bothered to see her. He'd sent a servant to give her the simple message: "Heed." No more—and that before all the house. Her cheeks still burned at the memory.

Irlar! The same lordling who'd once spat on her at a Shieldmeet feast and hissed, "Get away from me, unclean one! Witch blood! *Harper!*" Alustriel had never forgotten. It was clear from his barbed sidelong questions these last two evenfeasts, neither had he.

If she could have worn the silver moon and harp badge of the Harpers, the badge her uncle said she did not deserve, Alustriel was sure Lord Irlar would have shied away like one who has seen a ghost. Or if she could have worked magic strong enough simply to push him away when he approached, his fear would poison his greed. But she was a weak, defenseless prize, and he knew it.

Not so easily mastered as all that! Irlar had taunted her tonight, saying over wine and minstrel music that he would come for her when the house was asleep, to taste what he would own when they were wed. He added that if she was at all reluctant, her magic would protect her. She could have screamed out her rage and frustration at him then. As surely as an animal in a forester's cage, she was trapped—trapped! Only tiny victories were within her grasp. She had said nothing to his taunts, only smiled as serenely as she could manage, hoping to discomfit him. After a moment he had laughed—a short, ruthless bark—and turned away contemptuously.

All her magic, aye. Alustriel looked down at her slender, empty fingers, bone-white in the dimness. Only faint torchlight came in the window from rooms adjacent to her own. She could make people sneeze. Irlar had made a little joke of that; she had refused to demonstrate. She could also make sounds out of empty air, but only in a very limited way: she could mimic a single harp string, plucked note by note, choosing the tune and whether it played softly or loudly by how she imagined it in her head. She could also make the source of the noise shift from very near to something from afar, perhaps a hundred paces. Gaerd had told her she wasn't a Harper yet and suggested she keep this ability a secret from all until she'd mastered something more to go with it. She had done so.

Barely ten days ago, under the master wizard's kind tutelage, Alustriel had managed to make a great blue spark snap from one of her fingers to a metal coin set on a table several paces distant. She'd felt only a tingling, no pain . . . but she could make a spark appear only when she was excited or frightened or upset. Its creation always left her shaking and drenched with sweat. Great magic, aye.

Yet it was all she had. Alustriel turned in the darkness and strode into the little room where she kept her spell components— harmless ingredients for this or that. A sudden instinct made her hand close on a certain vial of iron filings and slip it into the hidden pockets in her skirts. Perhaps she could blind Irlar with it. She could not make herself pick up the tiny, bejeweled dagger that she knew lay on the table near the vials. He would only slash her face with it—or toss it laughingly aside.

There was a sudden scraping sound at the door of the other chamber. Irlar had come for her.

Irlar was a servant of Bane. He had a tiny brand under a ring that he turned around and around on his finger. Irlar meant to take her to a temple tonight, to forswear Mystra for Bane and quench any magic she might have forever. No doubt, he would also force his love on her at the dark altar, to claim any child she might bear for the dark god. . . .

A sudden shiver shook her so much that her teeth chattered. Alustriel bit her lip, stilled her quaking limbs, and forced herself to move calmly and silently into the main chamber . . . to meet her doom. Her uncle might never be proud of her, but she would not see him dismiss her as a light-headed wench, a nothing. She heard a gentle sighing sound, and knew it for an unseen blade cutting the bell rope so she couldn't summon aid or rouse the house.

She made her face as dignified as she could and looked to the door. She deliberately unhooded the tiny oil lamp before her on the stone window-table. The sudden light caught him sliding home the flimsy door bolt of brass filigree. His look of alert surprise rose into a smile as he saw that she was alone.

"Well met," he said with gentle sarcasm, "my Alustriel." He stared at her eagerly, hungry for a reaction. Waiting to feel her fear.

Panic and nausea rose together within her. Alustriel looked back

at him, keeping her face calm. She dared not speak; she trusted neither tongue nor voice to be steady and loyal. Irlar grinned at her
indecision and advanced.

"Come, now," he asked, "is my offer of marriage such a hated
thing? Or a matter so trifling that it wakes no spirit in you at all?" At
that, Alustriel smiled, though inside she felt more like weeping. It
was meant to be an unsettling, catlike smile, but it wavered. He
grinned, not wary at all. Why should he be?

She was helpless, and they both knew it. Slowly she hooded the
lamp, plunging the room into darkness as she gathered control of
herself. Again.

"Welcome, my lord," Alustriel managed, finding her voice at last
in the polite phrases of her childhood training.

"I hoped I would be," he answered triumphantly. With a sudden
stride he reached her, putting his arms around her. He kissed her
fiercely. His lips were those of a proud conqueror.

Alustriel fell back a step. He advanced, keeping their bodies tightly pressed together. Her rising anger made Alustriel's heart and
breath quicken. Irlar took this for excitement, and his hands began
to move. Boldly, to her hip and breast, pushing her back.

She retreated toward her high-canopied bed. Furious resolve
made her breath shudder and misled him into renewed boldness.
Onto the sleeping furs he bore her. Eyes closed, lips glued to his,
Alustriel concentrated with infinite care on her harp spell. It had to
sound just right.

There. He stiffened atop her as he heard it. Far away it sounded,
and muffled, as if in another room. Slowly it grew louder. Alustriel
held Irlar to her with feigned caresses and bent her will with aching-
ly careful precision. The unseen harpist was coming nearer. Irlar
pulled his lips from hers and gripped her arms with bruising force.
"What—*who's that?*" he hissed, shaking her.

"My uncle," she whispered with false urgency. "In the secret passage! On his way here; he only plays so when he comes to speak
with me!"

With an oath Irlar rolled off her, drawing his dagger. Alustriel
seized her chance, heart pounding. In her skirts, her fingers found
the vial and uncorked it.

Irlar turned his head and hissed, "Where?" at her commandingly, to learn where the nonexistent passage was.

She flung the contents of the vial into his face. She stabbed a finger at his eyes, gathering her will with that peculiar surge she always felt—and there was a snap. A blue spark leaped into Irlar's eyes, crackling for an instant among the filings there.

Irlar roared, clutching at his eyes.

She felt his dagger swing around, missing her in the darkness as she flung herself back and away, rolling along the edge of her bed. As always, casting the cantrip left her weak and trembling. She found her feet and fled unsteadily across her dark bedchamber, hampered by her skirts, trying to keep ahead of his reaching blade.

Cursing, Irlar came after her. He slashed wildly with the dagger, still blind but heading straight for the passage door. She'd have no time to throw the bolt and escape from her rooms. She whirled around her unseen guest table, bending her will again to the harping, bringing it louder and nearer.

Irlar followed. His cursing sounded scared now, more than angry. Alustriel breathed a prayer to Tyche as she bumped her shins into her little side table, stumbled, and caught herself on it with both hands. She swept it up desperately, spilling a mint-water decanter and two drinking horns to the floor. She held it like a shield.

Irlar charged toward the noise, slashing wildly. He slipped on one of the horns and flung his arms up to hold his balance. Alustriel stepped forward to bring all her weight to bear, as she'd seen her uncle's axe men do, and brought the little table down as hard as she could on the hand that held the dagger.

Irlar screamed on the heels of the sickening crack. The dagger rang off the glass decanter somewhere underfoot.

He lunged upon her, grabbing at the table with his good hand. She held to it, but he jerked impatiently, tore it from her grasp, and flung it away. It crashed against the far wall.

Alustriel dodged away again, desperate now.

"Bitch!" Irlar hissed at her savagely. "I'll kill you for that!"

She knew his words for simple truth. His thoughts of abduction on horseback to a temple of Bane were gone. Nothing less than her blood would satisfy him now. He crashed into another table, toppling statuettes and jars, but did not upset it and stopped, holding to it to steady himself. Alustriel heard a jar roll across it with almost lazy slowness—before it toppled over the edge to the floor.

Then she was pulling at the bolt of her chamber door with all her strength. It squealed, and he roared at the sound. Some instinct made Alustriel duck away. An instant later a perfume bottle crashed into shards against the wall just above her head, showering her with glass and a stinging mist. Then came another and another. In her hampering skirts, she scuttled sideways seeking a weapon . . . or a refuge against his murderous fury . . . and knowing she would find neither.

A rushing, whistling sound in the darkness told with cold certainty that Irlar had found her riding whip.

She *had* to get out of these long skirts! With shaking fingers, she unlaced and tore at the garment, crouching low and biting her lip. Irlar panted and thrashed the darkness furiously with the whip, seeking her.

Nearer he came, and nearer. Alustriel rolled out of her skirts at last. He heard her and charged with an exultant roar. She twisted on the floor and brought the cloth up before her in both hands, as a shield. The whip cut into them with a sharp crack, and one of her arms burned with sudden, stinging fire.

The whip came down again—and again and again, in a rain of blows too wild and rage-driven to be precise. Alustriel rolled and crawled and writhed on her luxuriant rugs, but could not elude him. When she got the edge of a table between her and the whip, Irlar kicked her savagely in the face and breast until she was out from under the table's shelter—and pressed on with his whipping, grunting with the effort of his stroke.

Alustriel sobbed as she made for the table. This time the whip missed her. She crouched motionless in the dark, gathered her tattered will, and bent it to her task.

In the darkness above, Irlar sneezed. Alustriel gave a little crow of triumphant laughter. Again she felt the surge—and again he sneezed, the whip swinging wildly. She rose swiftly under the table, catching it on her shoulders and driving it into him. Irlar stumbled back into furnishings and went down, losing the whip. Alustriel danced away from his flailing limbs. She headed for the door, her only chance.

She pulled on the bolt with sudden, rising hope—but the brass jammed in her haste and wouldn't budge. Looking back, she saw Irlar silhouetted against the dim torchlight of the window, leaning on the stone table and reaching for the bell-hood of her tiny oil lamp. She could not let him lift it, or she was lost! With light enough, he could stalk her at leisure. . . .

His eyes must have recovered. As his hand settled on the hood, Alustriel ran at him with frantic haste, heart pounding. She crashed into him just as he saw her in the blossoming lamplight. He struck her on the brow with the hood. Alustriel reeled . . . but her hands were on the hot metal, and she swept the lamp up and out the window, heedless of the spilling oil—and the room was safely in darkness again.

She was too close to the window. Irlar could see her outlines in the faint torchlight. He shoved her away so he could land a blow with his good hand: a solid punch that sent her reeling, eyes stinging and wits dazed. Her jaw felt as if it was broken . . . gods, the pain! He was after her triumphantly, reaching out to throttle her.

Alustriel fled from him—had she been dodging him in the darkness *forever*? In sudden determination she turned and fled no more but ducked in under his arm, ramming her head into his belly as hard as she could, charging forward.

Irlar was in pain, and unsteady. She carried him before her rush, back, back to the window. He kicked out wildly as his back hit the low sill. He lost his balance. Alustriel punched his groin, grabbed his foot, twisted, shoved—and suddenly she was alone in the room.

There was a sickening crack from the courtyard below. Lord Irlar struck the stones and bounced, once. A moment later, Alustriel heard the sudden shout of a guard. Torches began to flicker and move.

She leaned on the sill for a moment to catch her breath, watching them, and then turned deliberately for the door. The harp's song began as a few happy notes and swelled around her. She walked, uncaring of her appearance, down the long dark passage, through the heavy doors, and around the turn to her uncle's door. As she approached, it was thrown open.

Thamator came out into the night gloom, his sword drawn.

"Who be ye?" he challenged roughly, blinking into the darkness. The music of the harp swirled around him.

"I still want to be a Harper," Alustriel told him, surprised at how calm her voice sounded.

"*Ye*, girl? Must ye wake me with such tricks at this time of night? Hast aught else to do?" her uncle demanded thickly. She knew from his tone that her music reminded him of someone else, from long ago. The sword in his hands began to glow palely. In the growing radiance she saw his jaw drop.

His gaze was on her bloody state of undress, and roved to take in the red whip weals crisscrossing her body. He took a step forward, peering at her in disbelief. "What, in the name of all the gods, bef—"

Then there was a clatter of hurrying boots, and a waving torch came around the corner, its light gleaming on helms and spear points . . . and anxious faces. "My lord!" snapped one of the guards, his voice high with tension. "The Lord Irlar! He's dead! In the court-yard, belike he's fallen from a window!"

"Aye," Alustriel said into the astonished silence, "he did." Ignoring the startled looks from the men crowding around her, she added, "After he was pushed."

Meeting her uncle's eyes steadily, she added, "I was disinclined to become a bride of Bane—and before my wedding night, too."

She turned her back on them all with newfound dignity and left then. Her uncle's astonished curses faded behind her as she sought her room again. His voice sounded, she thought, amazed and . . . and a little pleased.

Now to ask Gaerd how to become a Harper. Alustriel looked down at herself, shrugged at her state of dress, and turned her aching, whip-scarred legs down a different passage. Why not now? Why should her uncle be the only one roused this night?

When she knocked on the wizard's door, it opened, and Gaerd was smiling at her—sleepily, but smiling nonetheless.

There was a crystal sphere in his hand, and in it she saw, with a little shock, the open window of her room as seen from within . . . captured as a tiny scene within the globe. The mage waved her to a chair, beaming at her proudly. On the table beyond the seat, a harp of silver hue was playing softly, by itself . . . and with a smile, she recognized her tune.

Thirteen

NERGAL SURPRISED

Adrift in a dream of pain, Elminster gradually came awake to the real-ization that it was real. He was floating, or falling, through a cloud of red and black smoky foulness shot through with crackling fires. Bolts of bright fury lanced out of it from time to time to transfix him. He was falling through Nergal's mind.

AWAKE, LITTLE WORM? WASTED MY TIME AGAIN, THANK YOU KINDLY.

[mind bolt jabs repeatedly until the human writhes and curls in shuddering pain, and then jabs still more]

WHAT DID I THINK OF IT? CHARMING. [SNEER] *DEFEAT A MAN BY LUCK, AND TAKE YOUR REWARD FROM THE GODDESS.*

[gasp]

WELL, MIND-SLAVE, I'VE LOST PATIENCE. AGAIN. PREPARE TO BE TAKEN APART. I'M THROUGH DANCING TO YOUR LITTLE GAMES. I'M GOING TO FIND AND TAKE THE USEFUL MEMORIES FROM YOU AND BE DONE. DIE, MIGHTY WIZARD!

[bright arc of mind bolts, raining down like fire and splashing back up to overwhelm all, searing the tumbling, howling, fading form of the human host]

GIVE ME, FOOL! GIVE ME WHAT I SEEK!

[bright ring of fire, tightening into a noose around the falling, dwindling, limbless essence of Elminster]

Give me that silver fire!

* * * * *

In the void where stars fall endlessly, a head lifted, blue-black hair swirling behind it in a great wave. Stars shaped themselves into a frown. "Something is amiss."

The Weave quivered once more. Mystra's eyes blazed in sudden silver.

"Elminster! Old Rogue, what befalls?"

She reached out for the familiar sly warmth, the impudent whimsy that always met her touch with a wink and a caress . . . and found nothing.

"*Elminster!*"

Alarmed, the goddess of magic gathered her strength around her in bright array and quested forth in earnest.

Pain . . . the silver fire spilling . . . in the Hells!

Her teacher, the root of much of her power, her surest link to the Mystra who'd been before her—in peril!

"*No!*" Brightness blazed up amid the stars, and the void shook.

* * * * *

Across Faerûn, altars to the Lady of All Mysteries erupted in blue fire that consumed nothing and seared no hand caught in it but jolted all sworn faithful into full, restless wakefulness. Locks on spellbooks failed, and tomes boomed open. Runes blazed up to trace spinning mirror glows of themselves above their pages, and dragons rumbled and growled and looked this way and that for foes or visitations.

In a clearing in Neverwinter Wood, the young mage Dethaera Matchlass drifted wonderingly in the grip of her first Magefire ritual. She soared in sudden bright array high above the astonished heads of her fellow worshipers. She sobbed in pain and wonder as spell after unfamiliar, mighty spell unfolded in bright glory in her mind.

In the green depths of Myth Drannor, a lone and leaning tower collapsed with a roar.

In Waterdeep, a young girl staring up at Ahghairon's Tower walked through the hitherto-impenetrable barriers around it. Its door swung open at her approach. Eagerly she stepped inside and came not forth again.

In Luskan, one of the overwizards of the Arcane Brotherhood, in the midst of ordering a cruel fate for a clumsy apprentice, suddenly acquired the head of a lion in place of his own. In baffled horror, he commenced to roar helplessly, his means of working magic and of conversing both snatched from him in an instant.

In Suzail, while stepping curtly past a barely concealed Harper spy in a little-known passage in the palace of the Purple Dragon, Vangerdahast stiffened. The lady almost stepped out of hiding to steady him as he reeled, but the gruff old wizard strode on, slamming a door hastily behind him. In the chamber beyond was a chair, a writing-desk, a cloak stand, and a mirror. He leaned on the desk, wondering why his blood was afire, and happened to look into the mirror. The face that looked back was not his own, but female, with eyes both wise and beautifully young. Breathing heavily, Vangerdahast blinked— and the mirror shattered. He turned away grimly, knowing that at last it was time.

In Avernus, a ball of fire raced down to burst amid scorched pinnacles. It suddenly veered aside. Out of the air before it stepped a tall, slender female form, as bright as a beacon.

In a hundred gorges and on a thousand mountainsides below, devils lifted their heads, stiffening. They took wing in great hosts and saw a human woman standing alone in midair, as tall as a dozen devils and cloaked in her own blue-black hair.

"*Where is he?*" her voice rolled out across all Avernus.

Pit fiend generals winced and growled. Lesser devils cringed. Those flying against her faltered. Black whips lashed them on. The intruder watched them come and did nothing.

Forks and lances and fire-daggers plunged into her as if into nothing, tearing her bright raiment. Where bared flesh should have leaked blood, there was only darkness in the air, shot through with rushing stars. The eyes of the floating lady flared silver.

"*Where is he?*" she said, more urgently. "*What have you done with him?*"

Dragons came, flying hard and fast, jaws agape in hunger. They were goaded by archdevils whose hosts mounted the skies in their thousands and tens of thousands, blotting out the bloody vault with their bodies.

Mystra glared at those who thrust their weapons into her. They blazed away in wisps of silver smoke. Magic snarled and spat at her. She twisted it and struck back through it. More devils died.

Died forever, seared away as though they'd never been, gone in their hundreds. Beneath the converging hosts, Avernus trembled as archdevils deeper in the Hells looked up in real alarm and gave orders. From the very rocks of Avernus, pit fiends erupted, leading armies of winged devils.

Hell was aroused. The sky split with lightning and the smoking mountains roared fire. In the heart of a million devils and more, Mystra glared and slew, glared and slew, until those flying three ranks back of the vanished were singed. They fell from the skies onto Avernus in a dark, wet rain of broken bodies, cloaking the peaks and choking the blood rivers.

Terrible trumpets sounded. Dark chariots ascended the skies. From their fanged maws poured hordes of winged monsters, horrible hydras seldom seen in Avernus.

Mystra slew and slew, a bright silver flame against a tightening sphere of black bloody death. The air itself began to shatter and fall away around her like smashed glass. Rifts opened around the embattled goddess. When she saw Faerûn bright and fair through them, below and behind her, Mystra knew that she must go or lose Toril in her trying. The harrowing of Hell—and the snatching of Elminster—must wait for another day and another way.

Like her faithful Chosen before her, she bent her attention to closing rifts between Toril and Avernus. Unlike Elminster, she passed through the last, closing rent with a parting gift in her wake.

The blood-red sky of Avernus flashed silver and then blue-white. All over that tortured land, every flying devil fell, torn apart in an instant.

Black, smoking blood drenched and drowned the land. Mystra never knew that she almost drowned the man she'd come to save. An erinyes had swooped out of the slaughter moments earlier to embrace and shield a blindly crawling Elminster ... and when she fell away from him, torn apart and dying, he was unscathed. He staggered to his feet to see the last silver glow fade.

"Mystra," he whispered. "Great Lady . . . all this, for me?"

Weeping, he fell back among the dead. The air for as far as the eye could see was filled with dark explosions. Countless pit fiends arrived from Nessus, full of the fury of Asmodeus to slay the lone intruder who no longer stood in the sky. Hell shook with dark rage from below. The flames rose high. The sky became blood-red for another eternity.

* * * * *

Azuth.

In the drifting darkness of a space that was not a plane, formed by the magics of all the enchantments of Candlekeep, the Lord of Spells glided like a bright serpent from one rune to another. They stood like sculptures in a void. He restored the fire of this one, and subtly reshaped that one, shifting its powers and meaning slightly to safeguard the fabric of Toril and to guide mages in slightly new directions, thus . . .

The voice in his blood, as he drifted as a thing of fire and risen magic, was so soft that it might have been an imagined thing.

High One, I have need of you. This time the mind-voice was clear and strong. Mystra, near at hand, sought him.

"Great Lady, I hear. How may I serve?"

The void suddenly blazed with silver fire. A blue-white glow rolled to the horizon like a wave seeking a far shore. Two eyes, as dark and star-shot as a warm summer night, regarded him from a spot within easy reach of his hand.

Azuth restrained his sudden desire to embrace the goddess and taste of her love; it was a feeling that washed over him at their every meeting, the call of her power to his.

"Great guide," she said softly, "our most mighty Chosen is fallen into Avernus, and Hell is risen against me. We must take him back. How?"

Startled, Azuth shaped himself into a tall, young mage with robes of shimmering white and eyes both large and dark. "You're sure—but of course." There was a flash as Mystra shared with him what had befallen her, her mind-touch with Elminster . . . and how feeble the mightiest of her Chosen had been. The Lord of Spells frowned.

"Well?"

Azuth winced. "Great Lady," he murmured, "with Hell roused, force is not the way. Stealth, too, is doomed for a time. If he survives, a small, swift rescue might succeed—but know, and forget not, that whomever we send, we shall be throwing away. Even those who escape Hell physically are often driven mad."

*   *   *   *   *

So your Mystra has missed you and wants her little lapdog returned. Yet even goddesses find Hell too warm in its welcome and flee empty-handed. She'll never have you now.

You're mine, little chained wizard.

Mine, while your sniveling ruin of a mind still totters along, vainly trying to hide things from me.

There's not much of you left to resist me, is there?

Let's see if we can uncover your memories of control over magic by seeing you teach novices, hmmm?

Glass burst into the room in a thousand sparkling shards. Sighing, Elminster put one hand over his teacup.

"*Die*, cursed mageling!" The mage in the window thrust her hands forward in claws, and lightning burst from her long fingers.

They snarled across the room amid the customary blinding flashes and spitting sparks, and struck something unseen a foot or so shy of the Old Mage's nose. He calmly watched them rebound and waved cheerily to the Red Wizardess as her own spell smashed into her and drove her—shrieking—back out of the room.

"Lhaeo," Elminster announced calmly, "the window. Again. An ambitious Thayan, as usual."

"I know," a sour voice floated in from the gardens outside. "My roses—why must they *always* land in my roses? Half an acre of lilies and wort to lie and smolder in, but oh, no, into my roses it is, enthusiastic plunge and all the thrashing . . ."

"It's thy turn for the casting," El reminded him sweetly. He stuck a thumb into his teacup to do some serious stirring.

"I don't have to do this, you know," Lhaeo muttered. "I could be earning a whole copper piece a month digging graves in Voonlar."

"Ye *could* be ruling a *kingdom* somewhere not so far away, lad," Elminster told the ceiling.

"Don't tempt me," Lhaeo grunted. "Glass everywhere, roses shredded and smoking, and several dozen young Sembian ladies coming to tea! Couldn't you just slay me now and get it over with?"

"And *what* would I be doing for fun *tomorrow*, eh? Ye princelings—always thinking only of thyselves, sparing not a thought for the welfare of feeble old wizards, worn out from saving the world for a few thousand years. . . ."

"Oh, belt *up!* The only thing worse than a gushing gossip is a puffed-up wizard! You've already eaten half the sandwiches, and they're not even *here* yet!"

" 'Twas the *least* I could do, lad," Elminster replied in hurt tones, "after ye went to all that trouble, trimming off the crusts."

Lhaeo's head rose into view through the glass-toothed window frame. "And that's another thing! Off you go to another of these 'other worlds,' and pick up *another* utterly crazed idea! Cutting my perfectly good egg-glazed crust off bread sliced so thin I can *spit* through it! What idiotic sort of folk do *that?* I—"

"*Could* spit through it, as a mere supposition, I hope," Elminster said reprovingly, one eyebrow lifting.

"Could and *did*," Lhaeo told him. "I had to try it, once I thought of it."

Elminster emitted a sort of incredulous "eep," and looked down at the neat piles of crustless sandwiches on the plates before him.

Lhaeo gave him a disgusted look. "You don't mess about much in kitchens, do you?"

At that moment a fat-bellied copper frog statuette on a nearby shelf opened one eye and its mouth, cleared its throat, and said in flat tones: "Bong."

Lhaeo groaned. "They're here." He waved a hand wildly, murmured something—and all the glass in the room rose back into place in a smooth, glittering swirl.

Elminster raised a sardonic brow. "Getting a little showy now, for the ladies?"

The window made a very rude sound in reply.

Elminster ignored it. Lifting two fingers in a swift little gesture, he said to the empty air. "Pray enter and be welcome, ladies fair. Let my humble home be a refuge to thee, however unworthy its accoutrements. As ye walk about my home, I bid ye remember only this: If ye don't touch it, it can't hurt ye. Tea is served in the room whose door is now glowing blue."

Blue mists roiled for a moment at the far end of the chamber. The door there swung wide.

Something large and lace-trimmed and seemingly triple-bosomed sailed in through the mists before Elminster could finish putting a kindly smile on his face. "Oh, so YOU are the GREAT Elmin-STAH! SUCH an honor, SUCH a rare joy to meet you! My friends back in Selgaunt will be SO jealous! A REAL live archWIZARD, sitting in his own parlor with all his books and funny hats and skulls and JARS of frogs and . . . oh, well, yes, it's SO exciting! ISN'T it, girls?"

There was an obedient chorus of "Yes, great lady" from the doorway, but Great Lady Calabrista wasn't waiting to hear it.

"I want you to know, sirrah, that we have come SUCH a long way just to see YOU, and that I've chosen only the FINEST of my young ladies! I'd not DREAM of wasting your time on anything but the BEST! Oh, yes, I think you'll be HIGHLY satisfied at the sort of young lady my little school produces—if I DO say so, myself! Girls? GIRLS! Dally not at the doorway, but come in, come in, so the GREAT Elminster can see you!"

The teacup in front of Elminster muttered, "Sounds like a slaver I once heard in Tharsult." The voice sounded suspiciously like a tiny, tinny replica of Lhaeo's.

Elminster smiled and said, "GREAT Lady Calabrista, ye must be SO hungry after such a LONG, ARDUOUS journey!"

The teacup sputtered, but Elminster ignored it. "PRAY enter in and sit in my BEST chair, and partake of these SUCCULENT sandwiches and a little light berry cordial. . . . Thy young ladies, too, I'm sure, would not take such fare amiss. . . ."

Before he finished speaking, the owner of the high-prowed

gown and helm-high hairdo had whisked herself into the pink silk cushions of a gilded high-back lounge. It had been a rotting mushroom in the forest out by Harper's Hill only that morning. She swept sandwiches onto a silver self-platter faster than raindrops fly to earth. A dainty decanter of cordial floated gently off a shelf to fill a fluted glass at the Great Lady Calabrista's elbow, causing her to emit a surprised little titter.

Four young and silken-gowned beauties drifted into the room, making hand-courtesies as they came. They ranged themselves before the four empty chairs farthest from their tutor. Their beauty was as gilded as fine court furniture, but at least two of their smiles held a touch too much superior sneer. All of them affected slight boredom and languid ease. All of them would soon catch cold in the gowns they had chosen to impress. Watching pearls glisten, slippers glide, and pendulous gem-cluster earrings sway and dangle, Elminster was beginning to be reminded of Tharsult too.

"Come along, come closer, girls! DON'T be shy; great men have no time for shy little girls! Sirrah Elminster, these sandwiches are QUITE the most EXQUISITE morsels that have passed these my lips in weeks! Why, whatever are they made of?"

"Snail, Great Lady," Elminster said with the sweetest of smiles. "Laced with a green paste made from only the largest tree-slugs of the forest around us, garnished with pepper and lemon-squeezings, of course."

"Of course," the Great Lady Calabrista echoed, faintly and haltingly. Elminster put a firm hand over his teacup to muffle its snort of mirth. Four gracefully extended hands stopped, quivered, and withdrew, leaving platters untouched.

The Old Mage raised his brows. "Oh, but they're GOOD! Nobles in Waterdeep prize nothing else more highly! And if the gods smile upon thee, and grant their *brightest* luck—" He leaned forward eagerly, peering at the sandwiches upon the platter before him, until his hand stabbed suddenly down, to peel back bread and reveal a hurrying slug undulating out of the heart of a sandwich— for just a moment, before he slapped the bread back into place, snatched the sandwich to his mouth, and bit down, hard—"ye find a *live* one! Ah, there's nothing *like it!*"

As he spoke, the green head of the slug poked out of the corner of his mouth, twisted this way and that questioningly, and then vanished within again. Elminster chewed heartily, beaming at his guests. The little illusions get 'em, every time.

"I-I think it would be best," the Great Lady Calabrista quavered, "if we proceeded with the burden of our visit. Men of great influence in Sembia—not to put too fine a point on it, men of great WEALTH—have enrolled their daughters at my school for some years now, seeking to find those who are GIFTED BY THE GODS with an aptitude for magic . . . an aptitude that I flatter myself I can draw out without recourse to dark altars and midnight fires and sacrifices of, er, snails. . . . THAT IS TO SAY, I am confident that these, my BEST students, will not disappoint any competent practitioner of the ART! I was REQUESTED to bring them before you by VERY highly placed individuals, for your examination and—ah, approval."

"Ye have done well and wisely," Elminster said with a smile. "I approve of all of them."

"You DO? Without eve—that is to say, their fitness at magic shines forth so BRIGHTLY?"

"Indeed, Great Lady," Elminster said with a gracious smile, gently slapping his teacup (which had begun to emit small sounds that resembled hiccups), "it doth. Indubitably. Had ye not had so GREAT a hand in the shaping of their glories, their power would blind EVEN YE! Let me tender my apologies, ladies four, for discussing thee as one does cattle, or fine gowns, or the luster of china. . . . What concerns me most is not thy grasp of spells but thy thinking, and characters, and the daily flight of thy hearts. Perhaps we can assay a beginning in learning that, here today. I—"

Glass burst into the room in a thousand sparkling shards. Sighing, Elminster put one hand over his teacup again.

"*Die*, cursed mageling!" The mage in the window thrust her hands forward in claws, and lightning burst from her long fingers.

They snarled across the room amid the customary blinding flashes and spitting sparks, and struck something unseen a foot or so shy of the Old Mage's nose. He calmly watched them rebound, amid the screams, crashing headlong flights, sprays of loose pearls, and the Great Lady Calabrista clawing her way up the back of her grand chair, which promptly overbalanced to reveal far, far too many silk and gem-beaded gauze petticoats to the world. Lightnings clawed at the Red Wizardess who'd cast them. They scattered before her shield as she snarled in angry triumph and lashed out at random around the room, causing a certain teacup to dance, chairs to slump back into mushrooms again, and the frog to open both its eyes very wide and inquire, "Bong?"

In three breaths the room was empty of four Sembian ladies. Elminster reclined at ease in his chair, sandwich in hand. He watched with interest as the last of his young visitors, trembling and white to the very lips, held forth a wand she'd snatched out of a hitherto-hidden hip sheath, gritted her teeth, and hissed out a word that brought the stick of wood in her hands into furious life.

A white beam smashed across the room, caused red fires to rage about the Thayan mage for a crazed instant, and then smashed the Red Wizardess, window, spell shield, and all, out into the garden, leaving a large and smoking hole in its wake.

The young Sembian stared at what she'd done, unshed tears bright in her eyes.

A weak voice groaned from somewhere outside, "My *roses!*"

"Are ye all right, Lhaeo? I wasn't expecting this spitfire here to have a wand of ever-searing flames. . . ."

"That wasn't me," his scribe told him wearily. "I was still being a teacup. That *was* a Red Wizard—or Wizardess, whatever."

Old and magely brows rose together. "Two, in one afternoon? I'll have to start charging a toll." Elminster's head turned slowly, and he asked the astonished young lady, "Nouméa Fairbright? That is thy name, is it not?" At her nod, he continued, "Nouméa, wherever did ye get a wand of ever-searing flames? They're not *safe*, ye know."

The young lady gaped at him for a few moments longer, and then found her voice. "*Safe?* SAFE? After you set your apprentice on us hurling lightning? To trick us and scorch us and scare us like I've never been scared before? Why, you—"

Elminster grinned, and Lhaeo's face, as it appeared at the window, wore an identical expression.

"Ye'll do," they said in chorus. "Yes, ye'll do just fine. Sit down, feet up, and have a snail sandwich; they're really mustard, cheese, and pickles. We've much to talk about."

Nouméa glared at them both for a moment longer. Then she sat down firmly on a mushroom and brought two spike-heeled golden slippers down on Elminster's table with a crash. "Well?" she asked, raising a severe but amused eyebrow. "Wasn't there some cordial?"

Fourteen

ONE HELL OF A BARGAIN

Tentacles tightened—and a devil's head flew. The spinagon's neck fountained black, smoking blood as its body whirled around in grotesque spasms. Its staring head bouncing wetly on the rocks some distance away.

Disgusted, Nergal turned away. Even slaying things gave him no satisfaction now. Avernus was in an uproar, with pit fiend generals riding dragons here and there, legions of cornugons flying in their wake, and barb-tailed osyluths stalking everywhere, spying and prying. Thrice he'd escaped attack only by the swiftest of shapeshifts and masterful acting. Sooner or later he'd end up trying to impersonate a particular general to troops who reported to the *real* general.

Almost as bad as that prospect was the likelihood of his encountering a spy of the Lord of Lies—a margrave or overduke or demichancellor who'd been sent to scour out the truth of things in Avernus.

All this because of one old, weak, smart-tongued mortal wizard who was *still* successfully resisting all attempts to plunder his mind of anything useful. A wizard who even now was wandering Avernus, blundering along into trouble. Trouble for Nergal, too. As long as Nergal was riding his mind, there was a link between them that even an amnizu could follow.

He'd best pounce on the worm and leash him in chains, and then take the shape of one of the pit fiends he'd slain himself—Gorkor, or Jarleil, or Tharthammon. Yes, Tharthammon would do: a slow, grim, close-mouthed giant among pit fiends. Few, even among the dukes, dared to question when he gave them dark looks.

So farewell tentacles, and fair greeting to great arching wings and a bulk as large as four Nergals. It was high time to call his wandering mind-slave back home.

Mind-twisted Faerûnian bastard.

HO, LITTLE WORM! HOW ARE THE FAIR SIGHTS OF HELL?

[guilty swirling of silver—silver fire? *HAD THAT BEEN SILVER FIRE?* But softly . . .]

Unprepossessing.

AH, THEN YOU CAN SEE ME AGAIN?

I'm not bleeding into my eyes just now.

[growl] *YOU TREAD DANGEROUSLY ON MY PATIENCE, WIZARD. . . .*

An erinyes swooped down and healed me—see the memory if ye believe me not.

WHAT?

[mental scrabbling, frantic haste, images flashing past in a roar, hard slow staring, then bitter cursing in the tongue of Hell]

ELMINSTER, HEED! CEASE MOVING ABOUT. FIND SOME CAVE OR CREVICE TO COWER IN, AND STAY THERE. I'M RECLAIMING YOU.

I'd hate to miss the pleasure of shared company.

YOUR TONGUE, MORTAL, WILL BE THE BLADE THAT STABS YOU YET. JUST YOU BIDE IN ONE PLACE UNTIL I REACH YOU. I'M LESS THAN PLEASED WITH YOUR STALLING. YOU KNOW VERY WELL WHAT I SEEK AND PERSIST IN GIVING ME MEMORIES OF THIS WENCH AND THAT—IS LUST ALL THAT CONSUMES YOU?

No, but 'tis one of my favorites.

[growl] *THAT CLEVER TONGUE . . .*

IT OCCURS TO ME THAT I'VE BEEN SEEKING YOUR MEMORIES OF WIELDING POWER IN THE WRONG WAY. HUMANS SEEM SO DIRECT, BUT PERHAPS YOU WIZARDS DO MORE AS WE OF HELL DO: MEDDLE, ACTING AT A DISTANCE THROUGH AGENTS, UNWITTING AND OTHERWISE . . .

I've quite a collection of memories of my meddling in things— busy centuries' worth, in fact.

[mumbled curse] *I FIND MYSELF UNSURPRISED. LET US BEGIN. . . .*

[mind lash, fiery eyes moving forcefully forward, cries ignored, images flashing past . . .]

* * * * *

Torchlight flickered off glistening mauve slime as a tentacled head turned. "Well, what have we here?"

"Mhulker," Baergrim snapped from behind him. "It's still you, isn't it? That—that *thing* isn't taking you over, is it?"

"My guest has . . . needs," the mage with the mindflayer's head replied in hurt tones. "Were you in a particular hurry to descend yon stairs and die deeper in Undermountain? Or is hereabouts exclusive enough for you?"

"I'm in no particular hurry to die anywhere, thank you," the warrior replied sourly. "I just wanted to remind you that this *is* the lair of Halaster the Mad, and things are seldom what they seem. I mean, if yon lady's been chained for long, how is it that something else hasn't come along already to devour her?"

The wizard, breathing heavily, pushed through the bead curtain in the archway. He entered a room where a chained woman was spread-eagled over a pedestal. Her large eyes were terrified, pleading over the tight leather gag that covered the lower half of her face.

"My guest only wants her brain," the wizard snapped. "You may have the rest of her when I'm done."

Baergrim came to a halt well back of the pedestal where the woman's torso rested, and exchanged warning looks with the other two Blades: a small darker-skinned warrior named Eltragar and a slim woman in worn and patched leathers. Mheriyam was a nervous thief. She had daggers in either hand, and her face was white with fear.

Together, the three Blades watched the wizard approach the pedestal. It was surrounded by a glowing circle of green dust on the floor. Runes of a similar hue had been painted on the woman's arms.

The wizard gave the ring a quick, sneering glance and strode right across it. As he leaned over the woman with a tight smile growing on his face, she jerked her head from side to side, sudden and frantic flailing making her chains rattle. Yet, arching and twisting, she could not escape the tentacles now reaching out. . . .

"*Mhulker!*" Baergrim snapped suddenly. "Mhulker, get *back!* That gag's covering her mouth *and her nose!* She can't be breathing—so *she can't be human!*"

There was a sudden confusion of writhing tentacles, jouncing chains and roiling lights around the pedestal—and then a brief roar of flame.

When its flash died and the Blades could see again, they found themselves blinking in horror at something lurching toward them. Mheriyam screamed.

Mhulker's legs and pelvis were staggering back from the pedestal with nothing left above them but a little cloud of drifting ash.

Three blades came up in unison, but no one made a move toward the pedestal. As Mhulker's remains stumbled and sagged to the floor, the cloud of winking lights and rushing smoke above the pedestal coalesced suddenly into—a man.

A bald, elderly man with long white hair and wrinkled brown robes stood beyond the pedestal. His fierce eyes softened not a whit as he folded his arms across his chest and gave them an eager, welcoming smile.

"Halaster!" Mheriyam howled in terror, whirling around and breaking into a frantic run. "Halaster Blackcloak!"

Baergrim and Eltragar did not need to hear her warning; they were already running hard, bouncing bruisingly off stone walls as they gasped and stumbled. Cold, cruel laughter pursued them a long way down the passages they fled through.

When the echoes of frantic boots had faded, the mad wizard shaped one of his arms once more into slender femininity and with a glance spun a chain out of nothing to link it with the wall once more. Someone else was coming, and the old ruses were the good ones.

In a few moments, the woman lay spread-eagled in her chains on the pedestal once more, eyes pleading above the gag that once more covered both mouth and nose. One had to give the alert ones some small chance at survival, after all. . . .

The chained woman turned her head and stared in swift fury at the figure who came through the beaded curtain next. It wore his own true likeness, a bald, elderly man with long white hair, fierce eyes, and wrinkled brown robes—and it leaned against the archway, folded arms across its chest and smiled at him. "Halaster Blackcloak, I presume?"

Halaster did not bother to drop his womanly disguise as he snapped, "Aye, so who are *you?*"

The spell that cracked out of him stripped away the intruder's disguise and sent him flying helplessly across the room. A fat and unlovely man struck the far wall with a groan and slid slowly down it, face tight with pain.

Halaster rolled off the pedestal, becoming himself as he strode forward to deal death. No, best learn how and why this fool had taken his semblance first. And then—ah, yes, and then . . .

Blue bolts of lightning were already whirling and spitting around one of his hands as he came to a halt above the wincing and struggling man. That face . . .

"Mirt? Mirt of Waterdeep? What by all of Mystra's whims are you doing *here?*" Halaster held the lightning where the old merchant could see it and said softly, "I asked you a question. Answer swiftly or die—I shan't stand here waiting for you to ready an attack."

The Old Wolf spat blood and said, "Found y-you. Knew I would." Then his eyes became two blue-white flames, and he began to rise from the floor, floating upward even as he—no, *she*, for shapely limbs and hips were beginning to spin into being out of what had seemed his own tattered brown robes—glided forward.

Halaster raised his hand full of lightning and snarled, "Who—or *what*—are you?"

"Call me Mystra," his visitor said gently. The rolling echo of that voice shook Halaster to the depths of his soul.

He found himself on his knees, trembling, tears threatening. . . .

The hand that touched his was firm, solid, and smooth. It sent a wash of power through him that drove back the dark curtains in his mind for a time and left him blinking in grateful awe.

"Don't thank me," the goddess of all magic said to the mad wizard. "We need to talk."

"Because?"

"I have need of a task swiftly done," Mystra said. "A hard task, and one suited for a madman."

Halaster's lips lifted in what was almost a smile, and he asked, "If I live, will you give me sanity?"

"If I can."

"Will you give me magic enough to have a chance of succeeding?"

Mystra nodded. "I will. Thrice as much power as you've ever tasted or wielded before, and more."

"That's what made me mad, I think," he whispered. "I'll do it."

It was Mystra's turn to not quite smile. "Would you like to know what the task is, first?"

Halaster shrugged. "No, but tell me."

"I need a wizard brought back from the Nine Hells. As alive and as intact as you can make him. He's a living man and an intruder there, not a denizen."

"I'll do it. Who is he?"

A face and a name and a more secret name whirled into Halaster's mind, and he staggered and caught at his head. "Elminster," he said in surprise. "Lady, is he not one of your own?"

Mystra nodded. "He is—as you shall be."

"L-lady, I have been touched by Shar," Halaster dared to whisper.

Mystra tossed her head impatiently. Small winking stars scattered from her long, flowing tresses to stream about the chamber. "I know. Touch me."

Halaster Blackcloak swallowed. He rose and extended one hand timidly toward her. The power that jolted through him made him shriek and go blind. It seemed to him, just for a moment, that his body struck a wall with bone-shattering force. . . . By then, all was blue-white fire, roaring on and on, and Halaster was laughing in exultation at the power racing through him. He rode it far and away, across planes and great voids and past shadowed, reaching things . . . or perhaps it rode him.

* * * * *

WELL, NOW, WHAT'S THIS? MANY FOLK, SOME SORT OF FEAST, SPELLS GOING OFF . . . YES.

Though the hour bells had rung but nine, the revel was in full swing. Laughter, snatches of off-key singing, and fond shouts of friendship echoed off the high ceiling in an unending din. The minstrels had long since given up trying to be heard and joined the crowds around the drink trays. The ring of empty goblets rolling around tiled floors was the loudest music now.

Sir Sabrast Windriver watched servants carry a hopelessly drunken noblewoman past on a gigantic fluted silver platter and smiled. Someday, the younger Lady Hawklin might learn to gracefully spew ruby wine all over herself, but she hadn't learned it this night—though she *had* been practicing.

Beside him, his good friend Andemel sighed and said, "Such a waste of good wine. She could be so beautiful, too . . . in green."

Sir Sabrast winced. "And waste that much elven menthe? At six lions to the bottle, ruby wine's bad enough, but . . ."

"Ah, but if we were truly noble," Master Andemel Graeven said slyly, "we'd not care a whit about costs and prices."

"If we were truly noble," Sir Sabrast retorted, "we'd be out of business in a month and a tenday . . . at about the time the Crown loans ran out. 'Tis a pity, to be sure, that honest merchants can't get wagonloads of free lions from the Crown to indulge *their* mercantile whims!"

Andemel led the way back through the curtains into the cozy dimness of their favorite alcove. By the gods, *both* of the pillars that held up its arched ceiling had been moved. There was a new and stonily regal bust of Azoun standing in one corner, too. Did they ever stop rebuilding things at the palace—with tax coins taken from those in Cormyr who actually had to work for their living? Probably not. Andemel shrugged and asked his friend, "Just who in Suzail, now, would you be calling an 'honest merchant'?"

"My apologies," Sabrast replied with a smile. "Let us say 'common-born,' then."

Andemel nodded. "Better. Ah, but I'll forgive many haughty nobles a lot of things so long as their vanity keeps them hosting revels like these. Did you see that lass with the glowing gown? When the mock flames died away right down her front, I'd thought I'd choke! How does she keep those emeralds glued on?" He shook his head in remembered admiration. "She's still around, isn't she? Mayhap I'll ask her if she'd like to see the new Graeven garden topiary, hey?"

"Well, friend," Sabrast told him, "old lion you may be . . . but she's even older."

"What? Magic? She looks not a day over twenty winters—if that!"

"Magic, indeed. Kept you from seeing her beard quite effectively, didn't it?"

"*Beard?* Sabrast, what're you drinking?"

"Excellent firewine, thank you," Sir Windriver replied. He stepped out through the curtain to deftly procure an entire platter of oysters drenched in garlic butter. The servant carrying it looked very surprised but departed in swift silence. "Andemel, you've met that young lass in the gown of flames before . . . and, as I recall, you didn't stop shuddering and cursing for a tenday. Yon lass is the wizard Elminster."

"*What?* Sabrast, you're . . . serious. Oh, gods!"

"How did you think he learned all the Cormyrean gossip? Can you see him spending days sitting in front of a crystal ball when he can have the fun of spying into our minds in person?"

"But . . ." a shaken Master Andemel Graeven replied, bravely struggling with the shock of how close he'd come to trying to win the charms of one of the oldest and most feared mages in all Faerûn. "But . . ."

Another brace of servants struggled past, gasping under the weight of a fat and snoring noble burden. Under the strain, the metal of the silver-plated platter was groaning more loudly than they were. The hairy arm dangling over its edge might have belonged to Lord Blester . . . or Lord Staglar. No one else at court was quite grossly fat enough.

Sir Windriver drew the alcove curtains firmly shut. "Glah! I'm not so eager to see more brazen young ladies that I have to watch all of Cormyr's most corpulent being carried off to bed. Sometimes I wonder how this kingdom staggers along from one day to the next, with the likes of Blester leading the converse at court. Bah—enough of it. You lured me here, Andemel, with talk of something that would interest me greatly. I trust 'twas more than the pleasure of seeing Elminster in a fine enspelled gown!"

Master Graeven settled himself back among the cushions of the most comfortable seat and crossed his silver-toed boots atop the gleaming polish of a handy side table. "I don't recall having to lure you all that hard, Sir Windriver . . . but aye, there is something of import I wanted to share with you. Something I've just acquired, called a 'Godsfrown Shield.' "

"A 'Godsfrown Shield'? Explain!"

Andemel reached for an oyster. "If you should have a valuable cargo stolen, wagon and all, or have a warehouse burn with all that is in it, the gods frown on you, no? So Baerusin takes a stiff fifty golden lions and undertakes to intercede with the gods for a month, or a tenday, or whatever you agree upon. If the wagon goes missing or the building burns, he gives you several thousands of gold pieces to replace your loss. *He* is your shield, your 'Godsfrown Shield.' If all is well—and he has agents who watch *very* carefully over your wagon or warehouse, to keep all well— he keeps the fifty lions."

Sir Sabrast frowned. "Hmmm . . . a theft on his part, it seems at first—but no; guards come all too expensive—especially when one must pay them more than a rival slips them, to avoid betrayals. Shields are always expensive—and if it fails, this one comes expensive to Baerusin."

Andemel nodded. "Exactly. Wherefore, I've purchased a shield on my shop that lasts un—"

The alcove curtains were thrust open, and a face that bore the latest stylish wisps of mustache and beard, adorned with tiny golden rings, peered in. "Ah!" it exclaimed in delighted recognition, a scant second before a servant stammered unnecessarily, "Master Raurild Sarpath!"

Raurild turned and made an unmistakable gesture of dismissal to the servant, one that involved the transfer of a golden lion, then strode into the alcove, pulling the curtains firmly shut behind him. "Andemel! You're alive, by the gods! A thousand thanks to Tymora for that! I've just heard about the fire in your shop yestereve, and I—"

Master Andemel Graeven peered nervously into the shadowy corners of the alcove, seeking spy holes with eyeballs gleaming in them . . . and thankfully finding none. "Hush!" he said urgently. "By Oghma, let the record be straight: the fire was *not* yestereve, but this night. About an hour from now."

Sir Sabrast Windriver filled the momentary silence with a chuckle and poured himself more wine. Ruby, of course.

"Raurild, this is late out for you . . . your good wife grant permission for once?"

Master Raurild Sarpath grimaced. "Yes, as it happens. 'Possibly good for business, so long as I drank but little,' she said—so here I am."

"Your *wife* decides whether or not you can go out to a revel?" Andemel asked incredulously.

"Aye, quite so," Raurild told him. "In marriage, I leave all of the small decisions to my wife—in fact, she insists on it. The larger matters are mine to deal with."

Sir Sabrast Windriver crooked one eyebrow. " 'Larger matters'? Such as?"

Raurild smiled thinly. "I don't know. We've been wed only sixteen summers; no larger matters have come up yet."

Sabrast and Andemel exploded in mirth. When he was recovered enough, the knight poured another glass of wine and held it out to Raurild, just as the alcove curtains parted again—and a sudden stillness descended upon the cozy scene. A quiet that bespoke tension. The four grim and fully armored Purple Dragons who held the curtains open might have had something to do with the sudden change of atmosphere. Two officers raised glowing maces, flanking the slender, oily-haired figure of Suzail's most senior tax collector. Those court weapons could paralyze or turn aside other spells, and they were borne only by the most able and high-ranking soldiers of the realm. Precept Immult Murauvyn wore the thinnest of crooked smiles.

"Ah, Sir Sabrast Windriver," Murauvyn said softly, "what a pleasure finally to look upon your face. A hard man to catch up with in all sprawling Suzail. They warned me, and I certainly found it to be so. Yet we meet at last. I bear a fond greeting from the Crown—and the request that you surrender unto me the thirty-six thousand lions in last year's unpaid taxes that you, Sir Sabrast, owe to the Royal Treasury of Cormyr!"

Feeling the sudden weight of interested gazes upon him—those of Andemel and Raurild foremost—Sir Sabrast Windriver grew a whit pale. "I seem to have failed to carry such funds about with me," he observed smoothly. "It's these new form-fitting tunics . . . they leave precious little space for thousands of coins, y'see . . ."

Precept Murauvyn interrupted witheringly. "Sir Sabrast Windriver, my agents have failed to find you with coins enough in your tunic at your villa on Turnhelm Street, your stables on Sarangar Lane, your city manor in Ambel Row, your business offices on Waervar Street, your little romantic hideaway on Westchapel Way, the cottage that so sumptuously houses your mistress on Brightstar Street—"

"Ahem," remarked Sir Sabrast Windriver, hastily.

"—the cottage of your *second* mistress on Undelmring Street—"

"Ahem, hem, hem," Sir Sabrast Windriver added, more vigorously. "Now, just a—"

"—your country estate at Gray Oaks, your yacht moored at Moonever, your hunting lodge at Mouth o' Gargoyles—and oh, yes, the cottage of your *third* mistress, in Waymoot. The port rolls in Suzail record sixteen sailings of vessels owned by you so far this season, and *twenty* returns; at least two of the ships that were unloaded at the docks to your enrichment shared a name and charter but were quite dissimilar in size and age. Fellow agents of the Crown report that the ledger of landings in Marsember that records the particulars of your fleet is mysteriously missing. They have thus far failed personally to examine any of the offloaded cargoes, which would, of course, add taxation to the amount I've just mentioned—to say nothing of any personal transactions you may have accomplished that may also be of interest to us. I speak now merely of the face value of annual land taxes on the properties I've just named, though one of my colleagues reports that you own at least two score houses in this city and some hundred or so upland farms. How is it—with so much land that you could readily sell enough to meet almost any royal demand for monies—that you seem to habitually forget to render unto Azoun what is, undeniably, Azoun's?"

Andemel and Raurild, whose eyebrows had risen at this astonishing catalogue of wealth, looked with interest at their colleague, wondering what Sir Sabrast would say or do now. Without thinking, in an instinctive move to distance themselves from financial embarrassment and Crown suspicion, they'd stepped a pace or two away from him, so that the master of Windriver House now stood alone in a little cleared spot of gaudy Thayan carpet.

Taking one slow stride to where he could lean against one of the recently relocated pillars, Sir Sabrast Windriver managed a smile.

"Actually, Murauvyn," he replied calmly, "you appear unaware of my fourth, fifth, and sixth mistresses, my Olde Lace and Glitterswash chain of souvenir shops throughout Sembia, and the current needs and dispositions of my large family. My eldest son, Falorian, is hard at work founding his own shipping line out of Selgaunt, my middle son Arastor is fast becoming the largest builder in stone in Westgate, and my youngest, Bralzaer, has founded a mercenary company in Impiltur, Bralzaer's Bold Basilisks. I have six daughters, all of whom are in Sembia going through three or four new gowns each a day, trying to snare wealthy Sembian husbands. My sickly wife—of whom I'm sure you've heard—is busily trying every medicine that can be suggested by man or halfling, searching for a cure for . . . living, it seems. Do you have any idea how many golden lions they can all spend in a day?"

He smiled archly and added, "If I don't give any of them so much as one worn copper coin, why should I give anything to you?"

Into the tense silence that followed, Raurild couldn't help but snort as he tried to smother his mirth. The tax collector gave him a cold look before bending an even more icy gaze upon the unrepentant knight.

"Sir Sabrast," Precept Immult Murauvyn said in cold, precise tones, "your treatment of your family is not the concern of the Crown. Your failure to render tax monies, however, is. In fact, it has become a concern so grave that the Royal Magician of Cormyr has gone so far as to grant me permission to seize whatever of your properties I choose, to meet the outstanding debt—*after* you have rendered menial labor on the royal roads of the kingdom for a month, as any penniless debtor must. You act the part of the destitute man all too well and drive us to treat you as one."

Sir Sabrast stepped away from the pillar, casually moving one hand to cover the rings he wore on the other, and asked softly, "And if I refuse to submit to your demands upon my properties and person?"

The other pillar in the alcove suddenly twisted and blurred. Glowing maces swept up, and Purple Dragons reached for their weapons on all sides. They paused as the pillar resolved itself into the unmistakable figure of Vangerdahast, the Royal Magician of Cormyr.

"Sabrast Windriver," the old and pudgy mage said calmly, "be aware that daring to cast any spell or commit any acts of violence at this time will earn you a year or so of additional service as a toad . . . in the palace dung-Middens."

Even as Vangerdahast spoke, the pillar Sabrast had been leaning against became a whirling chaos. An instant later it snapped into the shape of a beautiful maid who was *almost* wearing a gown of leaping flames.

Purple Dragons gasped and swallowed as those flames died away, shrinking to nothing, to reveal a body that was covered with a shapely tattoo of the Royal Arms of Cormyr. The painted maid blew Andemel a kiss, flickered, and was suddenly a bearded, hawk-nosed old man in plain gray robes.

"Elminster!" several armsmen gasped in startled recognition.

"Just another pillar of the palace," the Mage of Shadowdale told them dryly. "Well met, Vangy, loyal armsmen, and good merchants of Cormyr. Is this a private party?"

Vangerdahast glared at him with a look as sharp as a drawn sword. "Elminster," he asked in a dangerously soft voice, "what are you doing here?"

"Paying Sabrast's tax debt—with handsome interest, ye'll note—and advising ye, in a *friendly* manner, to reconsider thy rightful demand for his performance of hard labor."

Precept Murauvyn opened his mouth to say something, licked his lips, and looked at Vangerdahast.

The Court Wizard asked softly, "And just why would you do this?"

The bust of Azoun in the corner was suddenly surrounded by a vivid amber radiance that drew every eye. It winked, twisted into the shape of a harp for a fleeting instant, and then slumped into a gleaming, slithering heap of gold coins and glass-topped coffers full of gems.

"Rogue he may be, but I—as well as many unwitting folk of Cormyr—are indebted to this knight of thine for certain supportive actions he hath rendered."

A clearly furious Vangerdahast snapped, "And if I refuse to accept your payment? What *then?*"

"Well, then," Elminster replied mildly, "I'll be forced to end my protection over certain treasures here in the palace . . . and, I'm afraid, they'll revert to their true forms."

"Elminster," Vangerdahast snarled, "are you threatening me?"

The Mage of Shadowdale looked shocked. "By the gentle mercies of Holy Mystra, no," he purred. "Just volunteering some more friendly advice—about consequences, this time. Some of those treasures, ye see, will no doubt be angry when they awaken."

"Angry? Awaken? Elminster, you've placed monsters in the midst of our palace?"

"Nay—am I to blame, if various kings of Cormyr have an eye for valuables others fail to nail firmly down, and bring them home?"

"Elminster Aumar," Vangerdahast said tightly, "enough bandinage. Just what sort of monsters are in our halls under your control?"

The Mage of Shadowdale resumed the shape of the curvaceous maiden in the gown of leaping flames and gave the nearest Purple Dragon a welcoming, pouting wink. "Ah . . . dragons," he told the ceiling innocently.

"*Dragons?*"

"Only three—or was it four? And only a small sort of dragon," El replied.

In the shocked silence that followed, the lady in the flaming gown took Sabrast's arm and added sweetly, "I'll just go and tell the chancellor ye accept Sir Sabrast's belated but generous payment, shall I?"

Vangerdahast swallowed, closed his eyes, and croaked, "Wine . . . I need wine. Lots of it."

As she glided through the curtain, the lady in flames snapped slender fingers. Full wineskins appeared out of nothingness and rained down on the Royal Magician.

It was hardly the fault of the Mage of Shadowdale that the third wineskin burst when Master Raurild tried to catch it—and that the fourth hit the momentarily blinded merchant on the head and also broke, drenching Vangerdahast and Precept Murauvyn, and spraying everyone else in the alcove with wine.

Ruby, of course.

BY ALL THE FIRES OF HELL, IS THERE NO END TO THESE TRIVIALITIES? MAGE, HOW DOES ONE LIVE YEAR UPON YEAR AND DO SUCH . . . SUCH WASTE?

[furious volley of mind bolts]

[wizard screaming down into torn, broken darkness, and dripping, motionless silence]

[diabolic satisfaction]

Fifteen

HALASTER COMES CALLING

Black talons closed cruelly on shuddering, cringing white flesh.

THERE YOU ARE! AGAIN YOU TOY WITH ME!

Bulging arms plucked and tore at the thing that might have been human, shaking it furiously—so violently that some bleeding appendages fell off.

[whimper]

HAH! SOME VAUNTED ARCHMAGE YOU ARE!

[spell flash, rattle of spell-spun chain]

[sizzle of burning flesh, howl of pain]

HAH! THAT JOLTED YOU, DIDN'T IT? YES, I CAN HURL SPELLS BETTER THAN MOST MORTALS. BEHOLD, YOUR VERY OWN COLLAR AND CHAIN. GOOD DOG.

[laughter]

What . . . have ye done to me?

PUT YOU ON A LEASH, TO KEEP OTHER DEVILS FROM EATING YOU—OR WORSE.

There's worse? [wry amusement]

OH, YES. WHY, IF Y— BUT NO. WE'LL NOT SPEAK OF SUCH THINGS. TRYING TO WORM THE SECRETS OF HELL OUT OF ME? MORTAL, WHAT THE HELL ARE YOU PLAYING AT?

[mental chuckle] *Well said.*

There was a moment of menacing silence, there on a smoking ridge in Avernus, before Nergal laughed too.

HUMAN, I BEGIN TO THINK I'M GOING TO MISS YOU.

You're leaving? So soon?

[mental snort] *IDIOT. A JESTER AMONG WIZARDS, YOU ARE. DOWN, DOG, AND COME BACK THIS WAY WITH ME, AND I'LL HEAL YOU A LITTLE. I DON'T WANT A TRAIL OF BLOOD TO BRING US UNWANTED ATTENTION.*

Where are we going?

SOMEWHERE ELSE. [bellow of laughter] *STEW ON THAT, CLEVER WIZARD. THINK HUMANS ARE THE ONLY ONES MIGHTY IN MAGIC? WHY, I KNOW A SPELL THAT CAN BIND A DEMON FOR A HUNDRED YEARS IN THE SHAPE OF A SWORD. WE CALL THEM "DOOMBLADES." THERE ARE A DOZEN OR MORE WANDERING AROUND YOUR PRECIOUS TORIL RIGHT NOW, IN VARIOUS UNWITTING HANDS. YOU STEAL ANY SWORDS LATELY, WIZARD?*

Ah, how recently?

[gusts of laughter] *AH, ELMINSTER, YOU'LL SLAY ME YET!*

Ahem. A figure of speech, of course.

EH? INDEED, INDEED. LITTLE HUMAN BASTARD.

Silently, a pointed rock behind the archdevil moved, curling out like a dark finger. . . .

Nergal let healing fire wash briefly over the shuddering human in his hands. He bent his will and watched his magic turn the scrawny man slowly into a creature of Hell: a nupperibo, bloated and dirty and yellow-white. With a tight smile he dropped Elminster to hang, choking and strangling, at the end of the spike-studded chain. Fresh blood flowed as his captive's new bulk was dashed helplessly against the barbs.

Nergal shook the chain, rattling his struggling captive against a rock. El clutched frantically at the chain to avoid having his neck broken. He danced for his life as the archdevil threw back his head and laughed.

With a sudden, dark surge, the point of rock stabbed forward—and thrust through the laughing pit fiend like a gigantic spear tip.

Nergal screamed.

Impaled and aflame, the pit fiend flailed vainly at the skies, beat his great wings in agony, and staggered frantically forward. He dragged himself gorily off the rock. The spear of stone flashed blue-white, searing the shrieking devil each time.

When the outcast devil staggered free, it was visibly smaller, and trembled violently with each step. A sudden flurry of small explosions—erupting magic left in it by the stone—rocked its guts. Gore and entrails spewed in all directions. Shuddering and bent over, Nergal sagged to the stones of Avernus. He groaned and dwindled into a shuddering thing of tentacles.

The stone that had pierced the archdevil moved again. It arched over to touch the ground, its matter visibly flowing. The tip grew thicker, and straighter, standing tall and then . . . breaking away and taking a bold step out onto the sharp rocks of Hell.

A white-haired, bald wizard stood above the chained heap that was Elminster. His eyes blazed with blue-white flame as he spun a web of the same glowing hue around the captive mage.

The net touched the chain, crackled angrily along it, and collapsed. Halaster muttered a curse and raised his hands to weave another spell.

He was three murmured words into it when a cloud of stones streamed up from a ridge behind him. It hurtled down and smashed into the wizard, sending him flying with a startled cry. The stones crashed onto the rocks of Avernus and stopped bouncing. Halaster was somewhere beneath them, unseen . . . and unmoving.

"In Hell, human, you get only one strike," Nergal spat, rising into view from behind the ridge, his eyes flaming red. Four more boulders were clutched in his tentacles. "It's best to make it a good one."

The heap of stones he'd hurled heaved once, twice—and then flew apart, a blue-white flame roaring up out of their heart.

Nergal sneered and fed it flames of black and ruby-red, hungrily clawing at the stones. They shattered into deadly spraying shards.

The pain-wracked worm that Elminster had become undulated frantically away. Hot shards sliced into him and sizzled where they sank in.

The blue-white flame stood like a knife-blade in the heart of Nergal's spell flames. It erupted into a flurry of bolts that beheaded the tentacled devil.

"Hah!" roared a face that promptly grew on the end of a tentacle. "Thought you'd slain me, wizard? *This* is how you hurl a brightbolt spell!"

A flurry of bolts twice as large and numerous as Halaster's streaked back at the mage. The very stones on which he stood vanished in blast after blast that hurled the agent of Mystra into the air. Leaking blue-white flame, he fell back into the inferno of creaking, red-hot rocks and landed in a frantic whirl of magic. He staggered upright.

"I'm here for your blood, devil," Halaster snarled, raising hands that crackled with lightning.

"And I," Nergal snarled, growing scorpion-sting tails to match his many tentacles, "am here for yours!"

Halaster's spell—a bright net of silver lances linked by lightning and girded about with spirals of holy water—crashed down on the outcast devil. Nergal roared out his pain.

The ground under Halaster thrust up in huge fangs of dark, smoking devil bone, much as the mad wizard had first attacked Nergal. Like that attack, those fangs transfixed their target.

Screaming hoarsely, Halaster wriggled, impaled on what proved to be one of Nergal's tentacles—a tentacle that ended in a long, slender spike of bone. Shuddering off the effects of the archmage's spell, the outcast devil managed a short, ugly laugh and thrust his foe up into the air.

The thorn of bone was twice as tall as the man it pierced. Striking between the wizard's legs, it had thrust its way up through guts and lungs to burst out of Halaster's throat, shoving his head aside. Blue-white flames leaked from the mad wizard in a dozen places as his failing, darkening eyes sought Elminster.

"I'm . . . sorry," he gasped hoarsely. "I—tried."

Blue-white flame blazed up and spun Halaster away from the bone-fang, leaving it bare. Fire whirled in a small, spinning sphere in the air. Nergal raised a taloned hand to rake it—but the sphere suddenly grew very small and very bright. Halaster tumbled inside it like a broken doll . . . winked out, and was gone.

Elminster and Nergal both blinked up at the empty blood-red sky. In unison, they dropped their gazes to peer around at the scorched and smoking rocks, seeking little dancing blue-white stars or some other evidence of Halaster's survival.

There was nothing like that to be seen.

Nergal laughed, a sound that began out of relief, and became gloating.

SO FLEES YOUR LAST HOPE, ELMINSTER. ANY MORE RESCUE PACTS? MAGES WHO OWE YOU ENOUGH TO RISK THEIR LIVES COMING HERE?

[weary silence]

I THOUGHT NOT. WELL, THEN, LET ME DIVE INTO YOUR SHATTERED LITTLE MIND AGAIN AND SEE MORE MEMORIES OF YOU MEDDLING—ONLY THIS TIME LET IT BE WITH RULERS AND MAGES AND ADVENTURERS, NOT ANY COMELY LASS WHO HAPPENS BY . . . IT'S MAGIC I'M AFTER, REMEMBER? REMEMBER?

[mind lash, red pain, hasty flourish of bright images, fading and falling, then whirling up into a single display once more . . .]

"My lord," said the Simbul, and tears shone in her eyes, "I cannot stay longer. Those fools of Thay would try to wrest my land from me again. I am needed."

Elminster smiled.

The bard Storm Silverhand sat near, thoughtfully putting a better edge on her old and battered long sword. Only she and the Simbul knew him well enough to see the sadness hidden behind his eyes.

"Of course," he said simply. "These things—as always—must be." He stepped forward with surprising speed and embraced her.

The morning sun shone bright and clear through the trees of Shadowdale. Leaf-shadows dappled the rocks on the rising flanks of Harper's Hill. Storm's blade flashed back the sun as she turned it, keeping silence.

In his old and deep voice, Elminster muttered things into the Simbul's hair, and she whispered words back. No other was meant to hear them. Storm took care that she did not. That was the way she was.

The two great archmages half-turned toward her as they parted. Storm saw the brief gleam of a large blue gem that Elminster put it into the Simbul's hand. " 'Tis a rogue stone," she heard him say. "It will bring ye to wherever I am, should ye need to see me in haste. Go, now. These partings grow no easier to me as the years pass."

The Simbul nodded, slipped the gem into a pocket of her girdle, and turned back to kiss him impulsively. She whirled away in silence and leaped into the air, her black robes dwindling and flapping. A black falcon rose on swift wings into the sun, banked sharply eastward, and was gone.

The Old Mage stood silent and unmoving for long minutes, watching where she had gone. When the birds in the trees started their calls again, Storm slid her shining blade into its sheath and went to him.

In silence the two old friends linked hands and turned to go down the trail together.

After about a dozen paces, Elminster asked, "D'ye mind, lass, if I cry?"

Storm kissed his cheek softly and said, "Of course not. I think you should do so far more often."

"Romantic," he growled back, in mock disapproval.

"Fellow romantic," she replied, and put her arm comfortingly around him. He growled but did not pull free. She did not have to glance his way to know how wet his face had become.

How sweet. More lust and sugared words. Weep, little wizard, weep. I suppose such remembrances comfort you now, but I can't think why. I'd be raging. How much time you've wasted over females—just rut and move on, and save me all this "love." There is no such thing as love.

For devils, no. I'm not a devil, Nergal.

But well on your way to being one, Elminster. Believe me.

Oh? Is this something I should make a habit of?

[diabolic chuckle] *On with it, wizard! You're wasting time again! Give it up, idiot—no one's going to rescue you now! Show me what I seek, or at least what happened after you stopped embracing and crying and kissing.*

As ye wish.

[bright images, flittering down, down]

She was young, slim, and very beautiful. Tarth swallowed and tried not to stare.

Silvery-gray hair flowed from her head in long waves, curling smoothly about arms and tiny waist and long, long legs. She reclined in a low bough of an old indulwood tree, smoking a clay pipe and regarding him in thoughtful silence. Her eyes were blue-green, flecked with gold, and very large.

"Ah . . . well met!" said Tarth awkwardly, leaning on his staff. He'd plundered old magic in forgotten tombs across the Dragonreach, and peered into forbidden tomes in places both dusty and dangerous, but he'd never been so close to a beautiful female moon elf before.

Tentatively he bowed and smiled. She returned his smile, enchantingly. Tarth stared deep into those exquisite eyes and cleared his throat.

"I—I've traveled a long way, good lady, to reach this place. Could you tell me, please, where the tower of the sage Elminster stands?"

The elf-maiden nodded. "Up yonder path, past the pool," she replied, her voice husky, yet dancing. She giggled.

Tarth stared in helpless wonder.

A long, slim arm reached out to him. "This is his pipe, which I . . . borrowed. Will you return it for me?"

Tarth nodded. In a silent whirl of flashing limbs she vanished into the leafy shade overhead, leaving him holding the still-smoking pipe. He stared down at it for a moment, then peered vainly up again into the tree, shrugged, and went on.

HO, HO! I THINK I'M GOING TO SEE SECRETS OF MAGIC AT LAST! OR IS THIS JUST ONE MORE OF YOUR TRICKS, MAGE? HEY?

[silence]

STILL IN THE THROES OF AGONY DOWN THERE? TOO BAD.

The little path turned off the main road through Shadowdale just in front of Tarth's well-worn boots. No sign or runestone marked it for what it was, but the directions given him had been clear enough. The young wizard stood alone for a long time, staring along the line of worn flagstones in the grass, before he stepped onto them.

The way led him between two tumbledown cottages and across a grassy field toward the great, rising rock of the Old Skull. A still, peaceful pond glimmered off to the left. Birds sang, and chipmunks called. Tarth Hornwood, known by some as "Thunderstaff," walked slowly and fearfully up the garden path. He could see what lay at its end now: a squat stone tower that leaned slightly to one side.

Tarth held his staff menacingly in one hand, hoping he would not have to use it. Its power seemed to have been growing weaker of late. On his other hand gleamed the Lost Ring of Murbrand. Tarth hoped there would be no need to call upon its powers, either.

Despite days of research and experimentation, he did not know how to command the ring to do anything.

At the spot where a trail of moss and beaten grass branched off and ran down to the pond, a large flat rock lay beside the path. Its top was worn smooth, as if many folk had sat upon it over the years. Just now it held a curved, smooth-carved pipe, twin to the one he carried. It was lit, smoking quietly in the morning air all by itself.

Tarth stared at it. Was it some sort of trap? The Old Mage himself, perhaps, shapechanged to avoid prying intruders? The young wizard looked at the pipe for a long time and then with a shrug reached down. He'd faced danger enough and lived to tell the tale—and this was only a pipe. He hoped. His fingers touched it, warm and hard and smooth, and he almost jerked his hand away.

His fingertips tingled against it as he waited. A bird flew past; silent minutes lengthened. Carefully Tarth picked the pipe up and quickly looked all around. Nothing menaced. Nothing was altered. It was exactly the same as the one the elf had given him.

Two pipes that smoked by themselves. Tarth held them carefully out before him to avoid breathing in their smoke, and walked on toward the waiting tower.

Its small, plain door faced him blankly. Tarth leaned his staff into the crook of one elbow and reached out with his freed hand toward the pull ring of the door, to knock.

His fingers were still inches away when the door swung open silently.

Tarth stepped back in alarm. After a few breaths of silence, he stepped forward again, and then hesitated, peering into the darkness.

"Well, stand not on the threshold, welcoming flies in! Enter, and unburden thyself of whatever matter ye have sought me out for, mageling!" came an imperious voice from within.

Tarth swallowed, and took a step forward. "How—how did you know I work magic?" he found himself asking, before he could stop the words from spilling out.

" 'Tis written in foot-high letters on thy forehead, of course," came the dry answer. "Have ye not noticed it before?" A sort of grunt followed, and the voice continued. "Hmm . . . ye must be an adventurer . . . such pay the least heed to the world around them

. . . Well? Come in, then! 'Tis not so difficult—advance thy other foot, as ye did the last, use thy staff for balance, then boldly reach ahead thy first foot, again, and the deed is done!"

Tarth did so, and found himself in a dark, dust-choked chamber piled to the ceiling with parchments and thick leather tomes. Upon a stack of particularly massive books perched an old, straggle-bearded man in flowing robes. One gimlet eye fixed on Tarth.

In one hand the old man held a tiny bird, cupped carefully. The bird, too, regarded Tarth. It cheeped once disdainfully.

The old man's other hand reached out. "My pipes," he demand-ed simply. "Ye must have met Aelrue."

Wordlessly Tarth handed over the pipes. The mage's fingers brushed his, and Tarth felt a brief tingle of raw power. He stood awed in the dimness of the cluttered chamber, as the old man spoke softly to the little bird in words Tarth did not understand. It cheeped again, briefly, and flew into the darkness at the back of the room.

When it was gone, the old man looked up. "Tea?" he asked, almost roughly. "Ye look dry." Without waiting for a reply, he called, "Tea, Lhaeo! For two."

He waved at an old barrel, atop which were stacked several wrin-kled maps of Thay and the Utter East, the hues of their magical inks glowing faintly in the dimness.

"Toss those aside and sit ye," the old man commanded. "We may as well get started. Time not spent is not saved. Thy name?"

Tarth gave his first name, looking around for a place to set the maps and finding none. The old man sighed and waved a hand, and the maps wafted out of Tarth's grasp and glided out of sight behind towering stacks of parchment. At the same time, the two pipes, which had hung patiently in midair at the old man's shoulder, winked out and rose into the darkness, where they were lost to view.

Tarth sat hastily, leaning his staff against his shoulder.

Elminster nodded. "Elminster of Shadowdale," he replied. "Your business with me, lad?"

Tarth swallowed, and tried to look fearless and uncaring. "I seek training to further my mastery of the Art," he said softly. "If you are willing, and find my payment sufficient, I'd like to learn from you what I can, by the passing of the next moon."

The famous sage raised both his eyes this time to fix Tarth with a long, cool considering gaze. His eyes were very blue. Tarth soon felt uncomfortable, but dared not turn his own eyes away. Finally the Old Mage nodded slowly.

An instant later, Tarth found a steaming jack of tea floating silently down out of the darkness, past his nose. He closed a hand around it rather shakily.

"Ye mentioned payment," that dry, imperious voice rolled out. "Would it trouble ye overmuch, lad, to be more specific?"

"Ah—this!" Tarth said, thrusting forward his hand. "The Lost Ring of Murbrand!"

Silence fell. The expected astonishment was not forthcoming. Elminster's blue, clear eyes regarded him steadily. Out of the darkness overhead, another jack of tea floated down into the archmage's waiting hand. The old eyes never looked at it, but remained fixed on him. Expectantly.

Tarth rushed to fill the silence with excited words. "One of the greatest treasures of the lost magecraft of Myth Drannor! A thing famous in bards' songs and in old tales across the Realms! A—"

"A thing whose wielding is far beyond thy present powers," Elminster replied dryly. Tarth looked back at him, crestfallen.

"Well, yes," he admitted. "Yet its gaining was not easy . . . and I have Art enough to tell that it *is* a thing of great power, the greatest I have ever seen."

Elminster nodded. "So it is." He regarded Tarth steadily over the top of his jack as he drank. Silence grew and lengthened.

Tarth let his hand fall back to rest on his thigh. "Well?" he asked, suddenly afraid. The old man's gaze seemed dark and menacing and somehow angry. With cold certainty Tarth knew that the great archmage could probably seize the ring and destroy Tarth Hornwood utterly, in a very short and simple time. Those eyes held his, now seeming somehow amused. Death must look like this, so close . . .

"Is it sufficient?" Tarth heard himself asking, calmly and firmly.

"Aye—and nay," was the reply. " 'Tis a thing of worth enough, aye. But I don't want it. Ye keep it." A hint of a smile twisted the mustache. "Ye may grow to have power enough to use it. Ye may even need it."

Tarth stared briefly down at the ring upon his finger, remembering for an instant the crumbling, bony hand that had worn it. The rest of the ring's former owner had lain shattered and hidden beneath a huge fallen block of stone, in a deep and cobweb-shrouded crypt of Myth Drannor.

Tarth had not expected to keep the ring for long. He swallowed, suddenly afraid again and suspicious. "What do you want, then?"

"In return for thy training? Why, thy staff, of course," came the calm, dry voice.

Tarth's breath froze in his lungs for a long, trembling moment. The staff he bore, a plain spar of smooth-polished, shadowtop wood, was the most precious thing he owned.

Tarth's first tutor, in far-off Amphail, had given it to him long ago. Old Nerndel's Art had been feeble and forgetful with great age, but he had warned Tarth to keep the staff safe all his days. "It is a thing of great power," Nerndel had said. "Guard it well. Perhaps it will make you happier than it did me."

"My staff?" Tarth asked, heart sinking. "No. No, I cannot part with it. I will not! I refuse."

"The door, as I recall, lies just yonder," Elminster said dryly. "Ye found a way in . . . those bold feet of thine may serve to find a way out again."

"No!" Tarth said. "No, no—name some other price, some other payment . . . if you will. I've come so far. . . ." He leaned forward. "Please? A service, perhaps? To ask that a wizard give up his staff is a very great asking—and what good is such a staff to you, a great archmage?"

"More importantly," Elminster asked quietly, "what good is such a staff, Tarth, to you?"

"What do you mean?"

"Thy staff," the Old Mage demanded, "grows weaker and weaker as ye use it, does it not?"

After a few breaths of startled silence, Tarth nodded reluctantly.

"Ye, too," Elminster went on, "grow weaker and weaker in Art, Tarth Hornwood, as ye come to rely upon it more and more."

Tarth frowned. "You know my last name?"

Elminster grinned. "Aye. A while back, a friend of mine, young Nerndel—eh, old Nerndel he'd be, to ye—told me he had chosen his heir-of-Art, a bright one. He asked me to look out for ye, if ye came this way."

"Then—then you'll train me?" Tarth asked, hope rising suddenly into his throat.

"Aye. In return for a service."

"I can keep my staff?"

"I did not say that. The service ye can do me, mageling, is to destroy thy staff. Ye have come to depend on it overmuch, methinks, to have survived the perils of Myth Drannor and won that ring ye wave about so boldly. 'Tis time to learn to trust thine own power, without frozen fire to aid thee. Thy service will be to undertake a simple but precise ritual, to bring about the destruction of thy staff."

"And if I refuse?"

"Then ye must go," said the old man mildly. "On down whate'er roads thy overconfident feet lead ye . . . until ye fall, as ye are sure to, to some brigand quick with a rock or two, or a lone goblin creeping while ye sleep. No man who bears such power openly can have friends, nor trust companions overlong. If ye try, 'tis a cold and open grave ye'll find soon, lad, as someone else seizes thy baubles."

"I've not done poorly so far," Tarth said, nettled. "I can protect myself."

"Can ye?" came the soft response. "What defenses did ye prepare, then, before venturing into easy reach of my power?"

Tarth sat in silence, cold fear slithering within him again. The Old Mage's eyes gleamed steadily in the dimness, watching him.

Finally Tarth shook his head in defeat, and spread his hands. "Only the spells I carry."

"And thy staff, of course," Elminster added pointedly. "Come, lad—thy tea is growing cold. Have we agreement, or will ye walk?"

"If I destroy this staff," Tarth said, trying not to look at it, "do you promise to make me a more powerful wizard—and let me walk free?"

Elminster nodded. "Aye. I do so swear. Mark ye: Only by the unmaking of thy staff will ye give and find freedom and learn true power and happiness."

Tarth nodded, slowly and reluctantly, as his thoughts raced. "Then we have agreement," he said. A moment later, he added, "I must rejoin my companions-of-adventure for a few days, then I shall return."

Elminster nodded. "Aye, neglect not thy share of the loot," he said with a smile. Tarth smiled back, thinly, and drained his jack.

"My thanks for the tea," he said, getting up. Dust, disturbed, rose around him in a clinging cloud.

"The tea was the least of the things ye should be thanking me for," the Old Mage told him mildly, waving a finger. In slow silence the pair of empty jacks rose out of sight overhead. Uneasily Tarth nodded, and strode for the door a shade more hastily than he'd intended to. It opened for him by itself. He sighed and did not see Elminster smiling at his back.

[sigh] *YOU DON'T HURRY THROUGH THIS, DO YOU?*
If one does, it doesn't work. Like certain dealings in Hell.
CLEVER AS EVER, MIND-SLAVE. MIND THE BACK EDGE OF YOUR OWN TONGUE DOESN'T SLICE YOU.
[silence, images flourished almost mockingly]

There came a knock upon Sarlin's door. Sarlin the Supreme heard it and rose in haste. Times had been hard of late, and coins all too few.

Tarth Hornwood stood outside, his face tanned and a ring gleaming on his finger. His eyes looked somehow older than they had when he'd visited Sarlin before. He'd been adventuring, surely.

"What do you want, Tarth?" Sarlin asked plainly.

Tarth regarded the old, evil sorcerer calmly and said as simply, "Business. And no tricks, this time."

Sarlin did not smile, but nodded. "Well, then: what?"

Tarth thrust forward the splendid staff he held, dark and smooth and straight. "I'd like you to make another of these."

Sarlin raised his eyebrows. "That could well take years," he began. "Do—"

"Not its powers," Tarth said quickly, "though it must bear a dweomer and be able to, say, bring forth radiance, and quell it again. I need a staff that looks like this one, so close that not even the greatest mage of the Realms could tell them apart."

Sarlin raised his eyebrows again. "Expensive," he said, after a moment.

Tarth nodded. "I'm willing to pay you with this," he said, extending the fist upon which the ring gleamed. "It is the Lost Ring of Murbrand."

Sarlin leaned forward to peer at it. "Truce?" he asked.

"Truce," Tarth agreed. Sarlin extended his hand, and Tarth put the ring into it. The old sorcerer examined it carefully, turning it in his fingers to read the runes Murbrand had put there long ago. It was unmistakable, or all the books of lore were wrong. He held in his hands a ring of power. Sarlin almost trembled with excitement.

But that was not his way. He merely raised his eyebrows again, and—slowly, reluctantly—handed the ring back. "This staff must be valuable to you," he said.

Tarth nodded. "Almost as valuable as the ring I'm offering," he replied pointedly, "to one who knows how to use it."

Sarlin grinned. "As you know, of course, how to wield the ring," he returned. "Give me the staff now and the ring when I've done, in exchange for the two staves. Come back four mornings from now."

Tarth raised his own eyebrows. "That soon?"

Sarlin shrugged. "I am a master of what I do. You know that."

Tarth nodded. "You are. Agreement, then?"

Sarlin nodded back, almost eagerly. "Agreement."

AND NOW THE REVEALING . . . OR YOU'LL PAY IN PAIN, MAGE . . .

"Ready, lad?" Elminster asked gently. Tarth nodded, face expressionless. The Old Mage waved his hand. "Begin, then."

Tarth stood in the circle Elminster had prepared, deep in the forest near Shadowdale. On a tall, flat stone at its center lay the staff Tarth had brought here. Beside the staff lay a sharp knife.

Tarth stepped forward to stand over the stone. Sweat was suddenly cold upon his neck and forehead. He could feel the sage's watchful gaze like a weight upon his back. The young wizard breathed deeply, then shrugged and began the ritual Elminster had taught him.

It began with a spoken charm, soft and precise. Tarth pronounced it and carefully took up the knife.

As he did, his eyes fell upon the staff. Dark and smooth and gleaming, it was the familiar and comforting thing that had earned him the name "Thunderstaff" in Arabel. Half in derision that name had begun—but he had made it a term of respect. Now, if Elminster's will reigned, he would be leaving it all behind.

Tarth sighed again, forced down his irritation, and raised the knife, beginning the chant. Soft and light, to begin with. The knife caught the light and gleamed briefly. He raised his other hand to it and drew blood with a firm, deliberate stroke.

There was a cold tingling in his palm as the blood began to flow. Tarth stepped back and carefully drove the knife hilt-deep in the ground, whispering another charm in time with the chant. When he approached the stone again, blood had begun to drip from his fingers.

Carefully, still chanting, he moved his hand so that the drops fell upon the staff. "Ye have come for the wisdom of sages," Elminster had said to him. "Yet it alone is not enough. The blood of heroes also is called for, to win freedom. So ye must shed a little blood, mageling."

Tarth could feel the Old Mage watching him as he bled on the staff. Each drop that landed on stone or turf remained, but those that fell on the staff vanished utterly as they touched it.

Elminster had warned him, whatever happened, to keep on with the chant. Tarth did so, even when the staff began to glow on the stone before him. A faint red-gold radiance stole slowly into being down its length, grew brighter, and took on a white hue.

Tarth stepped back, as Elminster had instructed, and made his chanting louder and faster. He knew, without looking, that he bled no more. The magic was healing his hand.

The staff lifted an inch or so from the stone and began to hum as it floated in the air, glowing ever brighter.

The ritual required his tears now. Tarth stared at the staff, blinking and remembering all the adventures he'd survived these past few winters, staff in hand. Its magic was a shield against danger. He'd miss it.

The memories came fast now, and his chant wavered. He'd miss it indeed. Tears came to the young wizard's eyes. His throat grew thick as he recalled the comfortable weight of the staff in his hand, after many a battle. Sometimes he had almost thought it a living thing, a person.

Tears fell freely now. He moved forward as Elminster had told him to, so that his tears fell upon the glowing staff.

In answer, the staff pulsed brightly. The hum rose in a thrilling surge, into a singing sound. Slowly and majestically, the staff rose, turning in the air until it hung upright. The very air around it began to glow until it was surrounded by a bright aura. Tarth chanted on, fascinated and hopeful.

The staff rose above the stone, pulsing. Bright and then dim, bright and then dim again, its light almost faded entirely.

Behind the young wizard, at the edge of the circle, Elminster frowned. He crossed his arms as he stood watching.

The staff pulsed more quickly now, brighter and then completely dark before it became bright again. Its singing faded. Suddenly, it crumbled into nothing, and was gone, falling in ashes upon the stone.

Tarth's chant ended uncertainly. In the sudden silence, he turned to look at the Old Mage, almost angrily. "Is that all? It seems a waste!"

Elminster smiled sadly. "The waste, young master of Art," the sage said softly, "was thine, in spending the ring for so little." He gestured, and there was a sudden flash in the air above the stone.

A staff hung there, dark and gleaming—and very familiar. It was Tarth's staff, the real one—that Tarth had left safely hidden in a study-cell in the nearest temple of Mystra, guarded by the most potent wards Tarth knew. Tarth gaped at it.

"The true staff, young hero," Elminster said gently. "Honesty is best, even in magic. But that is a lesson one must teach oneself. Start on it whene'er ye feel old and wise enough." As he spoke, the staff turned in the air and glided down to rest upon the stone in utter silence, the knife leaping from the turf to join it. Elminster spread his hands questioningly, his eyes on Tarth's, then in an instant vanished, leaving only empty air behind.

Tarth stared at the fern-clad bank where the Old Mage had stood. Then he looked slowly all around, trembling. He was alone in the forest circle.

The path he had come here by ran invitingly away into green stillness amid old trees. Tarth looked down it and swallowed, his mouth suddenly dry. He took one hurried step toward the path, then looked back. His staff lay gleaming upon the stone. Tarth stood wavering an instant, then ran back and snatched it up.

Its familiar weight was reassuring in his hand. Tarth knew it all too well: It was his own staff, indeed, brought here by Elminster's magic. The young wizard held it raised for a moment as though to blast an unseen foe, then turned and dashed down the path.

As he ran, Elminster's parting words ran through Tarth's head. A lesson one must teach oneself . . . start on it whenever old and wise enough . . . Tarth came to a halt, panting. The staff was heavy in his hands. Sweat ran slowly down into his eyes.

Tarth blinked until he could see again. He stared wildly around at the trees. No one stood watching. There was no sound but his own breathing. He thought briefly of the spell in his memory that could take him in an instant far from this place, and it stirred in his mind. Tarth thrust it from his thoughts, stared down at the staff in his hands, and turned around. He started to walk slowly and deliberately back to the circle.

The knife lay on the stone. The clearing around remained empty and still. Tarth walked into the circle again and stopped. His breathing was loud and ragged in his ears. Raising the staff, the young wizard looked at it long and lovingly, feeling its heft and power in his hands. Then he sighed and stepped to the stone. It took a very long time to let go of the staff after he'd laid it down.

White-lipped, Tarth Hornwood stood alone in the circle for an even longer time. Then he stepped forward and softly spoke the charm that began the ritual all over again. Reaching for the knife, he never saw Elminster reappear on the bank behind him.

The Old Mage smiled and nodded approvingly.

The staff rose again. This time Tarth's tears flowed so freely that he could scarcely see the staff through them. He was filled with an aching sense of loss and a wrenching, weak feeling that grew worse in waves, in time with the pulsing of the staff.

It climbed above the stone. The singing was loud in Tarth's ears. Suddenly it flared into blinding brilliance. Tarth cried out, breaking off the chant. He fell helplessly to his knees amid the singing, and slid sideways to the turf, and beyond. . . .

[growl] *HOW MUCH LONGER, WIZARD? HOW MUCH FIRE-LASHED LONGER?*

Cool air whispered past his brow. There were gentle hands on him . . . two, three—had the old sage grown more hands?

Tarth blinked and found himself looking at a clear blue sky and dancing leaves overhead. He was lying on his back on uneven ground. The aroma of warm tea came from somewhere very near at hand.

"With us again, lad?" Elminster's familiar voice rolled out. Tarth turned to look at the Old Mage, opening his mouth to reply. It stayed open for some time in utter astonishment.

The Old Mage was sitting on a stone, tea in hand. He wore a worn and patched cotton under robe above his battered old boots. Sitting with him was a slim, gray-eyed lady regarding Tarth with interest. She held two jacks of steaming tea in her hands and was clad only in Elminster's flowing outer robe.

"Well met," she said, in a low, gentle voice.

Elminster grinned. "Tarth Thunderstaff," he said with gallant grandeur, indicating the lady, "meet thy staff. The Lady Nimra. Known in her day as Nimra Ninehands, after a spell she favors."

His grin broadened. "Ye've been draining her strength to work thy Art these long years, so I had ye give much of thine back to her, ere ye destroyed her entirely. Now, I've wasted time enough. Evenfeast awaits ye both at my tower, when ye find the way thither. I imagine ye'll have much to say to one another."

He chuckled at Tarth's stunned expression. "Now, lad," he reproved, " 'tis not every day a wizard has a chance to speak so freely to his staff. Use that glib tongue of thine." With that, Elminster waved a hand, and was gone.

Wordlessly the lady held a jack out to Tarth.

He took it gingerly, managing not to spill any on himself, and cleared his throat. "Ah . . . well met!" he began uncertainly. A wavering smile spread itself hesitantly across his face . . .

GAH! LOVING AGAIN? YOU HUMANS!

Much later that night, Tarth sat again with the Old Mage amid the dusty stacks of parchment. "How long have you known about her?" the young wizard asked curiously, gesturing upwards. The Lady Nimra slept in Elminster's bedchamber above them.

"Nimra was imprisoned in the form of a staff over seven hundred winters ago, by a rival in Myth Drannor," Elminster said slowly. "We never freed her, for her imprisonment let loose a number of fell creatures that had been in her power. They searched everywhere for her and would have found and destroyed her in the end, if she'd walked the Realms in her own form. Her imprisonment was the best disguise she could have found."

"What happened to these creatures that search for her?"

"Destroyed in their turns, down the years," the Old Mage replied. "Nerndel slew more than one of them."

"Master Nerndel? How did he come to have the staff?" Tarth asked in astonishment.

Elminster grinned. "He was Nimra's rival. It was his trap that imprisoned her. He hoped one day to free her and woo her—but I laid spells on the staff, so that I could find it where'er it might be hid and so that its making could not be undone while Nimra's enemies yet lived. I also took from Nerndel the spells he used to entrap her—so ye are stuck with her, young Master Mage."

"Stuck with her?" Tarth echoed, not understanding.

"Aye. She owed Nerndel six services, and the first he set her to do was to train him. The second was to undertake a certain ritual. It trapped her in the form of a staff, while her first task lay incomplete. She is not free of the web of spells he laid until she completes the training—of ye, since ye are Nerndel's heir."

"Me?" Tarth asked, dumbfounded. "But what then?"

Elminster shrugged. "That is between the two of ye. She has served ye these past few years, willingly, even if ye knew it not, and I think likes ye. Thy ways may well run together a long time yet."

"Together," Tarth said wonderingly, looking up at the ceiling. "But how should I treat her? What do I say to her? Should I try to make her do me the services that remain? If I try, what will she think of me? Need I fear her—ah, attacking me?"

Elminster smiled slowly and spread his hands. "In this, ye must be your own guide. Ye have already shown that ye can take the proper course, alone."

Tarth stared at him. Then his eyes narrowed suddenly. "You did agree to teach me until the passing of the next moon. Tell me, then, what I want to know!"

Elminster nodded. "I agreed, aye. Yet I fear I can help thee little, Tarth. I know not the answers to any of thy questions."

"You are said to be the wisest of living sages, in most fields!" Tarth protested. "One who knows all the answers!"

They heard a light step upon the stair. Tarth turned and stared at the Lady Nimra, who smiled at him. Tarth looked deep into her clear blue eyes and was lost.

"Only fools know all the answers," Elminster told him quietly. He silently vanished, the dust swirling up around him.

"And so, Master Tarth," Nimra said softly, as she sat where the Old Mage had been, "your questions are your own to answer, and your choices your own to make, and you must live out the results. That is what being a mage is, after all."

Tarth nodded, and cleared his throat. "Ah, uh—well met!" he began brightly.

She started to laugh. . . .

THAT'S YOUR "POWERFUL MAGIC"? YOU CLAW TOO HARD AT MY PATIENCE, LITTLE WIZARD!

HOW DOES IT FEEL WHEN I DO THE SAME TO YOUR CHAIN? AND MAKE IT TAKE FIRE AT THE SAME TIME! HEY? EH?

[screaming, raw and wild and in vain, dying away]

OH, NO! NOT THAT EASILY! A LITTLE HEALING AND A JOLT AWAKE, AND YOU'RE READY TO TASTE TORMENT AGAIN!

[roaring diabolic laughter, screams rising]

Sixteen

FOR THE LOVE OF AN OLD MAGE

Tentacles reached angrily toward the dirty, naked chained heap that was a man ... then, reluctantly, drew back again.

I REMAIN SOMEWHAT BEWILDERED AS TO WHY SOME OF THE MEMORIES YOU'VE SHOWN ME ARE OF LASTING INTEREST TO MYSTRA—OR TO YOU. WHY IS THIS IN YOUR MIND, ELMINSTER? DOES MYSTRA PLACE THERE ONLY WHAT SHE WANTS YOU TO SEE, OR ALSO SOME THINGS YOU DESIRE TO SEE?

Out of love and grace, the Lady I serve gives to me memories of things I could not witness but desire to. The doings of Mirt, for example—I felt the need to understand the character of this man, as a fellow Harper.

AH. JUST AS I WATCHED YOU FROM AFAR, YOU WATCH OTHERS. [growl] I'LL NOT TRY TO HIDE FROM YOU, MANLING, THAT RAGE RISES IN ME AS I SCOUR YOUR MIND AND SEARCH OUT MEMORY AFTER MEMORY, AS IF I'M SEEKING ONE STONE IN ALL THE ROCK THAT IS AVERNUS, AND FIND NOTHING OF THE MEMORIES OF MAGIC I SEEK. MEMORIES I NEED.

YET YOU MUST HAVE THEM, OR YOU COULD NOT BE WHAT YOU ARE. PERHAPS MYSTRA IS THE KEY. I DO NOT THINK SHE REACHED OUT TO CHANGE YOU, IN HER BRIEF VISITATION HERE ... I WOULD HAVE FELT THAT. SO YOUR MEMORIES MUST SURVIVE—AND FINDING THE ONES SHE GAVE TO YOU MUST BE WHERE THE TREASURE LIES.

SHOW ME A MEMORY FROM MYSTRA. IT DOESN'T MATTER WHICH ONE; I CAN TASTE THE DIFFERENCE NOW AND FOLLOW THE TRAIL YOU LEAVE ME. MAKE IT TOO LONG, AND I'LL GIVE YOU MUCH PAIN. LEAD ME TO WHAT I SEE, AND YOU'LL LIVE LONGER. A SIMPLE BARGAIN, EH?

Clear enough.

I HEARD YOUR TONE. REMEMBER THIS: I HOLD YOU IN MY HAND. I DECIDE THE TERMS . . . AND THE PUNISHMENTS. FORGET THAT NOT.

Oh, I'm unlikely to. Believe me.

HUMAN, DO YOU DARE TO THREATEN ME?

I never threaten, devil. I promise.

[growl] *I HAVE A PROMISE FOR YOU. WHEN I HAVE WHAT I DESIRE, YOUR SUFFERING WILL BE LONG.*

DO YOU DARE TO HAVE ANY PROMISES FOR ME?

Not yet.

[smoldering diabolic glare, whirl about, plunge into vaulted darkness once more, scattering images like forlorn stars . . .]

* * * * *

The sky was gray over Aglarond—slate-gray and cloudless, like a vast sheet of armor plate. The Simbul scowled up at it from her favorite balcony. She set down a goblet of something she'd cast spell after spell on in a vain attempt to make it taste like a certain ancient vintage El had spell-stored from fallen Myth Drannor. The bracer that was all she wore had begun to glow, telling her the seneschal had lost patience in stalling envoys and courtiers and wanted the afternoon throne session to begin.

The Simbul strode back through her chambers. Snatching a robe from the nearest hook as she passed—a rich purple and cloth-of-gold affair of many entwined dragons that would have been better given to someone who'd admire beautiful garments a trifle more—the Witch-Queen of Aglarond shrugged herself into it. She strode along a back passage, vaulted over a railing in front of a carefully impassive guard, landed on a harlounge, bare inches from a sleeping cat, marched away heedless of its spitting wakefulness, and found herself crossing the last few paces of carpet to the side doors of the throne chamber. Without a sash, her grand robe billowed open around her.

The guard by the doors had served her for a very long time. He looked at the Simbul's face and down at her bared body for just an instant. He set aside his glaive and unbuckled his sword belt with frantic haste, stepping forward to hold it out to her in one gauntleted hand in time to receive a dazzling smile from his queen. Her whirling embrace spun him around in the passage.

She murmured, "Buckle me." During another turn in her arms he did. She saluted as they parted, thrust the door wide, and was gone.

Only then did he stoop to retrieve his breeches from the floor, recall that he'd worn his second-best sword belt, and cringe at the thought that the Witch-Queen of all Aglarond was even now striding to the throne with not only a sword and a dagger bouncing at her hips, but a bag of dice, a bit of string knotted around some cheese with which to entice a pet mouse out of its hole to visit him, and an undone pouch with his best deck of air solitaire cards in it—the ones with the unclad beauties of Thay on the backs, guaranteed to float in the air for at least three breaths after being released.

With a grin, Thaergar of the Doors decided that if his queen noticed, she'd probably be greatly amused. Thank the gods.

Or at least, so he hoped.

* * * * *

So I have called, and my friends come not—or cannot reach me, through the legions of Hell. I am lost. It is cruelty on my part, sheer vanity, to drag down with me others who can live on in Toril and serve it as I have. I must fight this battle alone.

And fight it will be, for I shall not go down in gentle surrender. I will fight. Mind to mind, I cannot hope to stand against Nergal— for he can diminish my will in an instant by visiting physical pain on me. He is a swift, reckless, overconfident intellect—a willful child, in some ways—and cannot hope to match my store of memories or experience ... for all his long years, he has done the same things over and over and seen far less than certain old human wizards.

Yet he knows this. It is why I still live now. I am more than an idle plaything to him, more than a trophy other devils do not have, or a lure to bring rivals to where he can smash them. I am a store-house he longs to ransack, the fount of magical lore he craves—and the source of something else he refuses to admit: the memories of sensation and beautiful sights, terrible moments and acts of kindness . . . a life, all that he lacks. If I entertain, he suffers me to feed him memories he knows will not yield him mage-lore, or silver fire, or secrets of Mystra. He needs them.

I would give them freely, to make an archdevil more human, to give one being in Hell greater understanding of Toril—were it not for his mindworm, which takes what I share and strips it from my mind.

So it must be war between us. It is a war Elminster cannot win but must win. With every remembrance, Elminster is less—a little emptier, more of a mumbling sHell—and Nergal is a little more. A little more Elminster. Somehow I must fight him through the memories that go into him. I must worm my way into his mind and fight him there.

Yet, to do that, I must surrender what I have been so closely guarding. Everything. Mystra, no!

On the other hand, saith the juggler, why not? He will have it all in the end, anyway. I cannot stop him, only steer him as to what I yield, and when. My battle—and any slim chance at victory I might have—can only lie therein, in the pattern of my yielding.

Is this not what captive women have done to men who seized them, for centuries? Sought to master their captors by the manner and pacing of their yielding?

I am armed and armored in greater weakness. Well, then, I salute my foe—and the battle goes on.

I must think more on this. I need time. Let me yield another memory given me by Mystra and win some time to plot. I shall go to my tent and confer with my generals, who are all Elminster.

I hope we can agree on something.

* * * * *

Phaeldara was standing before the throne, facing the usual glitter-ing throng. Gems gleamed in her sweeping wave of purple hair. She drew herself up to her full, dignified, darkly beautiful height and said, "Lords and ladies, patience is a virtue more should cultivate. Especially in *this* palace. I—"

"How now, beloved sister of Aglarond? Are the people unaware of my tasks?" The Simbul made her voice merry, ignoring the sigh of exasperation from the far corners of the throneroom. "Or my . . . restlessness?"

With a smile of relief, Phaeldara turned to meet her and murmured as they embraced, "Hardly. I'm sure fools in red robes in Thay can feel *that*. Go and see your Old Mage for a few days, and . . . assuage your hungers."

The queen grinned. "Going delicate on me now, Phaele?"

"No," the sorceress warned her, something grim in her dark eyes. "This morn, after you brained Lorn Thorvim with that platter, I-I tried to farspeak Elminster to bid him visit you. He . . . I could not reach him."

The Simbul stiffened. Phaeldara drew carefully back as the queen's eyes went blank. The air around her slowly began to crackle. Those cracklings grew as the ruler of Aglarond poured more magical power into her questing. The little lightnings turned silver in hue.

A murmur of fear and consternation rippled through the watching courtiers. Something was very amiss.

The sword and dagger the queen was wearing began to smoke in their sheaths. The buckle that held them suddenly burst into sparks and was gone. The belt fell away with a crash—only to be whisked far across the floor by the undulating fury of the robe that followed it. The woman who ruled them stood alone, clad only in racing silver flames.

"Oh, goddess, no," they heard her gasp. Then her face tightened, and she asked pleadingly, "Oh, Mystra, may I?"

Long silver hair lashed bare shoulders as if a wild gale was blowing. A proud head was flung back to stare unseeing straight up at the vault so high above. Suddenly, the crackling arcs fell away to the floor in a fading wave of sparks, and the Simbul was moving.

"Thorneira! Evenyl, to me! Seneschal, fetched the Masked One! Phael, I'll need your gems—all of them!"

The tall sorceress immediately began running long fingers through her purple tresses, combing out handfuls of gems that all glowed with stored spells. "H-here, Lady Queen," she stammered, holding them forth.

The Simbul cupped them carefully, gliding close to kiss Phaeldara on her cheek without ceasing her hawklike glaring about the room.

"That man," she snapped, pointing. "Evenyl, slay him; he's a Thayan spy!" Without waiting to see what befell, she turned and stabbed her finger at another man. "*He* comes to make a false claim against a rival; deny him our royal intercession. Phaele, the throne is yours this time—but if Thayan envoys come in force, yield to the Masked to sit here and speak for me, while you go to Rashemen and fetch *their* envoys to come and bear witness."

"Lady Queen? You're quitting the throne?" a courtier was bold enough to ask.

The crack of his head jerking to one side was loud enough, even over the building Thayan spells and the carefully rising shields of the motherly Evenyl, to echo around the room.

The courtier's cheek blazed red, just as if he'd been slapped directly. The queen gave him a look that had death in it and said slowly and coldly, "Thorneira, Thalance, Phaeldara, Evenyl, and the Masked One speak for me at all times, and they will do so during this short absence of mine. Obey them as eagerly and as fearfully as you would me."

She did not have to add "or else" aloud; everyone in the room could hear it. Whatever reply the trembling courtier might have tried to make was lost in the booming of doors flinging themselves open, all around the chamber.

As startled guards peered into the room, objects began to sail in through those opened doors: girdles and boots, bracers and breastplates, circlets and rings, and tumbling wands, some of them winking with aroused power. The room crackled with their magic, and courtiers crept away from the end of the room where the Simbul stood.

Bare and beautiful, the queen of Aglarond spread her arms wide as her summoned arsenal of magic flashed up to clasp and clothe her.

"I go to rescue a man who's worth more than all of you," she said, her voice suddenly wavering on the edge of tears, "and far, far more than me."

With a whirling of silver flames and blue-white racing stars, she blazed up into formlessness and was gone.

* * * * *

The doors opened, and the sorceress Phaeldara strode grandly forth. Thaergar of the Doors snapped to rigid, arch-backed attention, carefully expressionless. He was astonished when she spun on one foot to face him.

"These are, I believe, yours," she said crisply, holding out his pack of cards. The little piece of cheese, a little the worse for wear and lacking its cord, was perched atop the tattooed belly—he could not help noticing—of Salambra the She-Wolf of Surthay. He kept still, unsure of what to do.

"Take them, man," she said in a low voice that had a quaver in it he'd never heard before.

Startled, Thaergar looked directly into her eyes. They were full of tears.

"Take them, and pray for our queen," she whispered, thrusting the cards forward.

Dumbly, Thaergar did so.

The sorceress broke into a run down the passage, her robes whipping out behind her like line-drying cloaks caught in a tempest.

Thaergar watched her go, and then sighed. This was turning out, it seemed, to be one of *those* days.

He stood for a moment at attention—then took two quick steps, bent down, and carefully pushed the cheese into the mouse's hole, in case he was called away to fight for Aglarond and came not back to his post. Ever.

* * * * *

WELL, WELL, WHAT HAVE WE HERE?
You seem in better humor, Lord Nergal.
I'M SEEING MAGIC AT LAST, WIZARD. BE SILENT, WHILE I PLUNGE IN AND ENJOY!
[images flaring bright]

The crawling, ever-changing flame runes of the last page challenged her, silent and yet somehow mocking.

Laeral Rythkyn, called "Laeral of Loudwater" to keep her disentangled from the Laeral who was Lady Mage of Waterdeep, had been working through the crumbling tome with her usual patience. Her excitement grew with every passing day and each new page. Patience and care had made her one of the youngest mages of power in the North. Patience and care made her methodically read, practice, master, and improve on every spell in the book.

Each page of the tome held a single spell—all of them unfamiliar, useful, and quirky in components, phrases or casting. They felt *old*.

As she'd gone through the thick book, each spell had been more powerful than the last. The last page of all was written in flame-red, spell-cloaked runes that shifted slowly when gazed upon, indecipherable and beckoning. They must hold a special spell indeed.

BEARD OF ASM—AHEM, TALONS OF TASNYA . . . AM I GOING TO BE SHOWN MAGIC AT LAST?
Hush, devil, and see sooner.
[growl] *SHOW ME. SHOW ME NOW.*

The spellbook had lain in a shattered tomb in the cellars beneath Everlund for at least an age. Laeral had found it while helping Harper friends destroy wraiths in those dark, cobwebbed ways. It had sat neglected on a table in her study all winter.

Laeral had been busy training her apprentice, Blaskyn, to master the smiting spells that made a sorcerer a power to be reckoned with. Blaskyn had done well, showing promise in devising his own incantations and adding his own twists. Soon he'd be ready to walk his own way in the Realms. Wherefore Laeral had set him the necessary tasks of practicing precision in casting and creating a new spell all his own. Meanwhile, she took up the book to further her own studies.

SO NAMES AND PLACES AT LAST—AND MAGIC, IT SEEMS, TOO. CONTINUE, WIZARD.
[images wearily unfolding]

Laeral stared at the runes for perhaps the fortieth time that day, frowning a little, teeth gnawing thoughtfully at one side of her lip. Blaskyn had said they looked like little leaping flames, these runes, and so they did—hmmm. In one long, lithe stretch, Laeral leaned over the purring cat beside her and plucked a small, battered handbook from a shelf. She sought a cantrip from her own days as an apprentice.

There it was. A simple little trick of Art, known to half a hundred wizards this side of Waterdeep. It shaped flame to form illusions or words if one had a candle, campfire, or torch to work with. Laeral hissed gently in excitement, slid a certain protective ring on her finger, and worked the cantrip, bending her will upon the page.

The runes slowed to a lazy crawl, seemed to freeze for a moment, and then flowed slowly into clear, unwavering clarity. They were in Thorass, Auld Common, with its flutings and grand swirls, and read:

> *Sit not alone*
> *On Thalon's cold throne*
> *Unless alone ye would be*
> *Unmatched master of wizardry.*
> *Sit ye there overnight*
> *And of Art gain great sight*
> *Wise beyond that of any mage*
> *In the Realms, of this age.*

Laeral's lips twisted. A labored rhyme, to say the least, one she'd come across several times before in lore books and libraries of the North. This was the oldest instance yet, though, and the only concealed one. Moreover, it had a codicil she'd never seen before: two lines of detailed directions to the throne. It was apparently in a tower in the High Forest somewhere near Alander, the Lost Peaks.

Well enough. It was high time to go adventuring again.

THIS HAD BETTER BE WORTH MY TIME, LITTLE WORM. MY PATIENCE IS AT AN END FOR DIVERSION, NO MATTER HOW ENTERTAINING.

Everything is worth your time, Lord Nergal ... or were you in a hurry to go somewhere?

[growl, slap, wry diabolic smile]

"At least tell me where you're going," Blaskyn said, showing her his easy grin. "Then I'll know where to look for you if Elminster the Mighty or some king or other comes calling."

Laeral smiled back at the eager mageling, then shrugged. Judging by his past behavior, the prettier lasses of Loudwater would have more to worry about while she was gone than she need trouble about the safety of the magic in her tower.

She smiled at herself. Save for her Art, she was one of those young local lasses. And pretty, too, if the words of some could be believed.

Well, she'd trusted Blaskyn enough these past years, and nothing ill had come of it.

"I go chasing legends, Master Blaskyn."

"As always," he said, bowing like a courtier of Silverymoon.

Laeral wrinkled her nose at him. "I seek Thalon's Throne—a stone seat said to have been fashioned by the archmage Thalon, in the days before Myth Drannor rose."

"Any wizard who sits upon the seat overnight will acquire mastery of wizardry greater than any living mage," Blaskyn quoted in a singsong voice. "I've read that in four different places in your books here alone!"

He cocked his head at her. "With all the folk who must have read about the throne down the years, you think there's still anything there?"

Laeral shrugged again. "To be a mage, one must be a seeker after knowledge." She quoted the old maxim mildly.

Blaskyn sighed. "It would seem a wizard can use that phrase to cover any amount of nose-poking into other's affairs," he said, innocently addressing the ceiling.

Laeral chuckled. "Including your own, ah, moonlit lady-walks on Wychmoon Hill?"

Blaskyn colored, looked at her silently for a moment, and grinned again. "Speaking of which," he added thoughtfully, a moment later, "doesn't the verse about the throne speak of not 'sitting alone'?"

Laeral shook her head. "No, Master Blaskyn. You're not coming. Not this time, at least." She went to a dark suit of plate armor that stood against a wall. Had it not been so covered with dust, it would have looked quite menacing.

"I need you here," Laeral said, tugging the heavy helm off the stand and turning to offer it to him. "Here, looking after my affairs in the village, and gathering news." She thrust the rather plain old war-helm into his hands. Blaskyn looked down at it and then up at her, brow raised in silent query.

"The Helm of Hiding," Laeral told him. "The rest of the armor is simply so much shaped metal." (This was not strictly true, but no mage ever surrenders all her secrets willingly.) "It hides you from searching magic, and all Art prying into the mind. At will, you can cloak yourself in shadows and escape most searching eyes. Use it if powerful foes come to call. If you value your life and Art, Blaskyn, hide—*don't* challenge! The spellbooks you've been shown are yours to use freely. The others, you will not find."

Blaskyn smiled and nodded. "Of course. I'll have things enough to try with what you've made available; you needn't fear I'll go rummaging through the tower the moment you're out the door. Or later, for that matter." He cocked his head to look at the ceiling again. "So long as I spell-lock the upper doors, may I have visitors—ones who aren't adept at Art?"

Laeral wrinkled her nose. "One at a time, I hope. And no drunken feasts—in a house of magic, the results can be fatal as well as spectacular."

Blaskyn nodded again, all traces of levity gone. "I ask again, Lady: Are you sure you should go alone?"

Laeral laughed. "I won't be alone. I'll have this." She took up the rod that lay on the cushion beside her seat. "This is the most precious of my things. It goes always with me."

Blaskyn shook his head. "It was you who told me," he reminded her, "that a mage who trusts in the magic of items trusts himself too much."

Laeral returned his gaze, and answered gently, "Trust not too much in your own magic while I'm gone, Blaskyn. Guard your words and deeds carefully, for Art alone will not carry you through all the dangers of life."

"Another maxim?" Blaskyn sighed. "You'd better go, before I fall asleep."

Laeral gave him one of her looks. She unrolled the scroll that would teleport her to a hill she knew, where the River Dessarin flowed out of the High Forest. "I don't plan to be gone long," she added.

Blaskyn grinned. "Lost is the wizard who depends on plans, for the whims of the gods twist them always awry," he chanted the old maxim at her triumphantly.

Laeral gave him another choice look just before she disappeared.

HMMPH. NOW I'M BEING FED HUMAN PHILOSOPHY. THIS HAD BETTER BE WORTH THE ATTENTION, LITTLE MAGE.

Aye.

"AYE"? IS THAT ALL YOU HAVE TO SAY? COULD THE GREAT ELMINSTER THE MIGHTY BE RUNNING OUT OF CLEVERNESS AT LAST?

As to that, we'll see.

[dark look from flaming red eyes, wary pincers stealing forth]

IF THIS IS SOME SORT OF TRICK . . .

[silence, images deftly unfolding]

In the gathering twilight, the ruined tower rose out of dark encircling trees like the black blade of an upright sword. Laeral eyed it critically and cast another spell. Once it cloaked her, she went forward to the tumbled, overgrown pillars that had once marked the gate of a courtyard.

Within, gnarled, twisted tree roots thrust aside the paving slabs. No birds sang in the branches, and the feeling of waiting death was strong. Her Art told her no magic waited close by—but if a hidden beast still guarded the keep in the traditional wizards' way, it would be about here.

The moss-covered boulder just inside the gate rose with menacing speed. Laeral used the flight spell she'd just cast to propel her away, soaring up and back to hover in midair.

As earth fell away, the rising rock opened eyes and regarded her with a look that was unsurprised but rather weary. It was a human-shaped head with beautiful female features of a green-gray hue and was as tall as she. The head swayed atop a massive serpentine body. A naga.

"So young and so pretty," it said. "Come ye here, maiden, but to die?"

"That is not my intent," Laeral replied calmly, preparing to move quickly. "Who set thee here, and what is thy purpose against me or my entry?"

"Thalon set me to guard this place and, by my powers, to slay all who cannot use Art to avoid me," the deadly guardian replied. Its eyes flickered.

The bolt that leaped from its mouth was too fast for the mage to avoid entirely. Protective Art flashed as it crackled along her flank. Laeral wasted no Art in battle but extended her aerial dodge into a twisting, darting dive toward the dark, waiting windows of the tower beyond.

Behind her, the naga hissed sadly, "Ye will not find what ye expect to, when ye reach the throne." By its tone, it seemed to like her.

The mage scarcely had time to be surprised at that. She cautiously slowed her approach to the nearest arched window but struck a solid barrier of invisible force, hard.

Had she been flying a little faster, Laeral thought as she tumbled away through the air, she'd have broken her neck. Bruised, she rose again cautiously and approached the next darkly gaping window . . . then another. Before all of them were barriers—barriers her detection spell did not show. They were there nonetheless. The lone exception flared with such a bright aura of magic that Laeral suspected the traps it held would outnumber even a handful of dispellings.

She settled cautiously to the ground and approached the lone doorway of the tower. It stood open, dark and waiting, its doors fallen. There was no magic about it that her spells could find.

Time to play the hero, Laeral told herself. Unbidden, the next line of the ballad came to mind: Time to play the fool. Sighing, she stepped forward into darkness.

Dust swirled within; dust clung to cobwebs all about. All was dark and cold and still. Laeral gently took flight again, her feet treading air inches above the dusty stones. If Tymora smiled, she'd be safer that way.

Softly glowing motes of light kept Laeral company. She floated slowly and carefully from room to room of the tower. In one lay a gigantic stone block, fallen from the ceiling. The shattered, yellowed bones of a human skeleton protruded from under one corner. Its arms reached vainly, its jaw open in an eternal silent scream. Laeral floated over it in wary silence.

A little farther, as expected, there was a pit. More skeletons lay below, twisted and broken on dust-covered spikes—the death she had expected. Warily she advanced, wondering when she'd find the traps against those who flew.

All too soon she saw a spray of quarrels, projecting like the stems of some sort of thorny plant from one side of a dark wooden archway ahead. The skeleton among them still had scraps of dark brown sinew dangling from it.

Laeral halted before the arch and unclasped her cloak. Floating in the air, she swirled it forward.

There was a dull snapping sound. A quarrel leaped from a hidden fissure and tore through its folds to join the cluster in the arch, quivering.

Laeral swung the torn cloth again, but no more quarrels came. Rolling the cloak around her forearms as a sort of shield, she darted through the arch, diving low and to the side.

The rusty blade that squealed across the top of the arch missed her entirely.

Laeral sighed again. She wondered when she'd run into the trap that would try to strip any magic items she'd brought. Unfortunately, traps one knows about kill just as effectively as the unknown sort. At least, Laeral thought wryly, I haven't run out of maxims yet.

FIRE OF NESSUS, NOR HAS SHE! LITTLE MAN, IS THIS GOING SOMEWHERE?
[silence]
[slow diabolic growl, eyes kindling into flame]

When it came, it was as blunt and effective as she'd thought it would be. The ground floor rooms had proven empty, stripped of all but skeletal corpses. Even these had mysteriously lost whatever they'd carried or worn.

The way down was flooded and choked with stone rubble, but the way up was an open stair. A skull had been placed neatly on the bottom step, grinning at her challengingly. Laeral sneered at it and flew up the stairs. Her rod rose to ward off blades and deflect quarrels.

The stair turned. The air all around her was suddenly full of springing, leaping, clutching claws—skeletal human and bestial hands that tore at her hair, face, and form, snatching and wrenching and grabbing.

Laeral swerved sharply to strike one wall with her shoulder. She rolled to run her back along the wall as she flew on, faster. Bony hands crunched unpleasantly under her spine and shoulders and fell away.

Smashing a hand out of the air with her rod, Laeral tore the throttling grasp of another from her throat. She reached up grimly to break fingers off yet another claw that was crawling down her scalp toward her eyes. Snarling, the sorceress plunged toward the steps to smash away the hands on her legs, moving like so many cold and crawling spiders.

She saw the danger just in time. Anyone on foot would have done just that, by now, and no doubt there'd be a trap waiting for them. Laeral turned her dive into a roll in midair just above the step.

The toe of one of her boots brushed the stone, and a row of iron spikes suddenly thrust upward. Laeral felt one scrape her arm coldly as she rose, leaving behind a pinioned, feebly wiggling claw.

Growling, Laeral tore another claw from her head. Handfuls of hair came too. She flung it away, twisting in midair without pause to pluck other claws from her legs. "Crawling claws," these bony hands were called. Wizards had used them as guardians for a long, long time. Laeral wondered if she'd ever feel free of the bruises this lot had left.

At least they didn't fly after her. Prying a last claw from her thigh, she punched it against the wall as she flew on. Finger bones bounced and sprayed, clattering off stone.

Another arch opened ahead. Blades snapped from both above and below this time. Laeral plunged and twisted desperately in the air, sweating now. She won past both seeking rusty steel edges—straight into a humming flight of quarrels. She arched away with furious haste and escaped with only a burning graze. One of the shafts had been swift, and she almost too slow.

Almost, aye. She flew on up the curving stairs to where they opened into a huge, dark, high-ceilinged hall. There the mage waited, floating cautiously above the last step. Motes of light stole about the room at her bidding, searching the vaulted ceiling, tapestry-hung walls, and dusty stone floor like wandering fireflies.

The room was bare save for rotting tapestries—now only strips of black, cobwebbed rags—and a simple seat carved from one massive block of stone. Half-hidden behind one of the decaying hangings was a stone shelf that held a watchful row of yellowing human skulls.

The whole thing was another trap, no doubt. Laeral let her lights wander back to her as she pondered what to do next.

Bars of faint radiance suddenly sprang into being all around her. A calm, rasping voice with an unpleasant rattle in it said from behind her, "Welcome, mageling. Who are ye, and whence hail ye?"

Laeral spun about as she dispelled the force cage. Its collapse and the end of her flight dropped her to the steps. She faced her assailant.

He was tall and thin, half-skeletal—a lich clad in a cowled black robe. Two cold white flames leaped in black pits where his eyes should have been. He smiled as his lips moved soundlessly. Bony fingers moved in gestures smooth with long practice.

Laeral sighed—was *everything* in this place to be a well-worn jest? She plucked a small token from her belt. It was shaped like a buckler of silvery hue and grew speedily to cover her hand.

She was in time. The lich's spell struck her and rebounded from the shield. It gleamed with sudden light and sang faintly.

Another spell followed. This time the shield blazed away to nothingness in her fingers, consumed by the power sent against it. The lich advanced slowly and deliberately up the stairs, ignoring the spells that crashed into him.

Laeral retreated into the room. Everything she'd faced in the tower thus far had been the tired stuff of apprentices' tales—perhaps this place was so ancient that they'd all been fresh, or the only known means, when it was built.

The rattling voice came again. "Silent, pretty maiden? A spell shield wasted on a mere sleep spell and a simple charm—and no attack on thy part? Not a word to me? How unlike a mage, not to want to talk!"

The lich raised its hand and hurled forked lightning at her. Laeral ran toward one bolt and leaped over it. Her hair danced as death crackled under her. She slammed hard into the floor and found herself fighting for air.

The lich seemed unsurprised that its attack had missed. "Have ye come just for the throne?"

Laeral saved her breath for counterspells, dispelling in turn another charm, an attempt to telekinese her farther into the room, and a spell that made her eyes water and blur ere she foiled it. She was still backing away when roaring flames enveloped her.

The odor of singed hair hung around her, but the protective shield Laeral always wore saved her from serious harm. It flickered to the verge of exhaustion. She moved quickly to one side—but even as the last of the hungry flames rolled away into nothingness, bony hands were moving again. Laeral felt the naked feeling of her magic being stripped away.

Hastily she cast another shield of cold fire around herself. This must be what a target in an archers' shooting gallery feels like!

As her foe advanced, Laeral reached to her bodice sheath and drew forth the only wand she carried. Hard-eyed, she blasted the lich with magic missiles.

They struck home, but the undead mage calmly continued its advance. Laeral fired again, her mystic bolts swarming around the black robes. Expressionlessly the lich raised a bony hand and struck back with similar missiles of its own.

Blazing agony lanced into her in five places. Laeral screamed and shuddered involuntarily at the pain, doubling over. The lich advanced.

"Thy name, she-mage?" it asked again, in dry, almost mocking tones.

Laeral made no reply. Setting her teeth, she snatched one of her daggers from its boot sheath and rose from her knees. She hissed a spell of her own devising. As the dagger spun through the air, her Art snarled around it. It grew longer, flashing and whirling as it went, becoming—a sword.

Gleaming steel whipped end-over-end through the gloom to strike the lich's shoulder. Bone crumbled amid spurting dust, and one skeletal arm fell away from the lich to the floor, collapsing there in dusty splinters.

The lich advanced as though nothing had occurred. "If this continues," it told her calmly, "I shan't be able to guard the throne—and ye'll have won."

Laeral rolled her eyes. What children's tale had all of this come from? She dodged aside desperately as the lich cast lightning at her again and snapped out a counterspell.

The lich reeled, its bony arms writhing into coiling snakes for an instant before its unlife overcame the magic. It gave her a gap-toothed grin—and lightning again.

Laeral snapped out a countering enchantment. In midair the racing bolt curved back toward its source. Bony arms moved in haste, but the undead mage was still working a spell when hungry blue-white fire found it.

The lich writhed amid smoke and fell to its knees, pointing a bony arm. "Behold—the throne!" it said hollowly and toppled into a clattering chaos of unattached bones. The flames of its eyes winked out.

Too easy, Laeral thought, scattering the remains with an unseen servant spell. Much too easy. The bones lay where she pushed them, harmless.

The mage drew forth another token. It grew into a great hammer in her hand. She used a servant spell to carry it to the bones and wield it from afar, crushing the lich's skull into shards. There came no response.

In the silence that followed, Laeral took a scroll from her belt and conjured dancing lights. By their radiance she stared all around, suspiciously. The silence waited patiently, unbroken.

She took a cautious step toward the throne. It remained empty, unadorned, and silent. She bent her will. Her floating hammer struck the empty seat, tapped it, then under her direction tapped floor-slabs all about it and ceiling stones high above. Nothing happened. She kept at it until the hammer's power faded and it dwindled away to nothingness.

Silence hung around her, waiting.

With a sigh, Laeral raised a detection spell, knowing she'd find the throne ablaze with many spells, one atop another. She frowned, took a step forward, and wondered if she dared raise her last flight spell, in case a pit trap or falling block lay waiting.

With a roar, the roof fell in anyway.

Seventeen

MUCH FIRE IN HELL

This is good fun, wizard. I would see all of it, magic or no. Proceed. As ye wish. [images glowing]

Laeral lay over stone and under stone. Great blocks from the ceiling had crashed down beside her, atop her, and all around. Dust curled slowly away.

Shrieking pain stabbed from her right leg and from low on her left side. The falling stones must have broken bones.

Echoes of the collapse died away in far, unseen corners of the hall. Her wits had left her for no more than a breath or two. Above her, a tilted stone slab was wedged against another, fallen in a peak that had saved her from crushing death—so far. Past them, by the feeble radiance of her globes of light, she could see the empty stone seat.

Laeral willed her dancing lights to grow fainter, an easy task with pain tearing her concentration to tatters. She lay silent, biting her lip. She was pinned helplessly, unable to move. It would be a long, cold death, after all.

Laeral wondered dully how much longer she'd live. One mistake, just one . . . and a swift lesson: death takes mages as easily as stable hands.

Please, Mystra: Let it be quick.

Laeral gathered her weakening will for one last sending, to tell her faraway apprentice where her secret spellbooks and treasures lay and bid him farewell. The effort cost her the last of her conjured light. She froze in the sudden darkness.

A new sound filled the dusty chamber.

Cold, familiar laughter. Radiance, conjured by another, was born and grew stronger in the room. By it she saw Blaskyn step out of the shadows, the Helm of Hiding gleaming under his arm. He chuckled again, peering toward her.

Hastily Laeral shut her eyes to slits and lay very still. From the first, he had been very good at the blasting spells.

"So ends my apprenticeship," Blaskyn said triumphantly. "The throne's 'mastery of wizardry' shall be mine!"

He strode past Laeral to the stone seat, wearing that easy grin Laeral knew so well.

Then, suddenly, Blaskyn stopped and turned. "She held the rod, her most precious magic," he muttered. His hands moved in quick, sure gestures.

Laeral closed her eyes, raging inwardly. He was far more a master of magic than he'd ever led her to believe.

Laeral felt the rocks above her deftly lift away—a telekinesis spell, no doubt. Crushing weight rose from her, gently and silently. The rocks pinning her down were gone.

With iron will, Laeral resisted the urge to shift to a position of easier rest, stilling the pain. Dead she must appear—or dead she surely soon would be.

She felt the rod twitched from her half-open fingers. "Unbroken? Good," Blaskyn's voice came, from very close above her. Laeral kept her face, twisted in pain, motionless. "Hmm . . . her rings."

She felt the rings stripped from her fingers, her ex-apprentice sighing in disgust at the blood on them.

Deft fingers wandered over her body, finding the daggers in her boots and the sheath in her bodice where the wand had been. She heard rocks grating as they were moved, and then Blaskyn's disgusted voice again.

"Broken. Well, that leaves only this." The crude, plain pendant she'd worn so long was roughly jerked from around her neck, its thong snapping. "It's some sort of magic; I know that much."

Laeral lay still as his hands wandered over her body. All the Art she had left were a few spells still in her head and a certain magical token, a lone earring hidden in her hair. He'd find it, all too soon, then leave her to die.

Probing fingers found the roughness where her leg was broken and stabbed at it, seeking hidden treasure. *The pain!* Unable to stop herself, Laeral shuddered, whimpering.

Cruel hands jerked her chin up, shaking her head until Laeral opened pain-racked eyes and stared into the cold, level gaze of her ex-apprentice.

Blaskyn smiled. "Still alive, eh? Well, you'll live long enough to tell me where all your magic lies hidden—and long enough, perhaps, for . . . other things!"

Laeral whimpered. Mockingly caressing hands shifted her leg with brutal haste. The broken ends of bone grated together. She tried to scream as he shook her, but could manage only a sob. Blaskyn chuckled at the sound and cruelly dropped her back among the stones.

Red mists of pain rose and fell before her eyes. Through them, Laeral saw Blaskyn walk to the throne, turn to salute her mockingly, and sit down with a triumphant sneer.

His face changed. It seemed to glow with white fire. His smile slid away from his lips almost immediately. Pearly radiance shone from the stone, growing stronger. In utter silence Laeral watched cold white fire race up and down his limbs.

Blaskyn's flesh sank inward, his skin withering and sagging on suddenly revealed bones. He screamed.

Her horrified gaze locked with his, Laeral saw his eyes catch fire and burn. The whites darkened and receded to become points of glowing light.

As his gums and lips shriveled, Blaskyn screamed hollowly, "Laeral! Mistress! Help *me-ee-ee!*"

Teeth sprayed from his agonized mouth. His cry died away into dry choking. His body shook and strained. He seemed unable to rise from the blazing throne.

Silence fell. What had once been her apprentice seemed to grow calmer—or less conscious. Laeral shifted herself to as comfortable a position as she could manage, wondering if Blaskyn was dead.

All at once, the slumped body on the throne began to smile. Lipless jaws worked, and then shaped words. "Ah . . . ah . . . a good body, this. Better than the wench, though she taught it but a pitiful amount of Art. It will serve."

What had been Blaskyn stood up stiffly. Her rod, daggers, and all fell to the floor with a clatter, the rings rolling slowly off into the darkness.

All too soon, the sunken face loomed up over Laeral.

HA HA! THIS IS AS GOOD AS ONE OF THOSE PLAYS NOBLES MOUNT AT THEIR REVELS IN WATERDEEP!

Aye, and all true.

OH? CAN YOU PROVE IT?

I must trust Mystra.

[scowl, snort] *WELL, ONE OF US MUST, I SUPPOSE . . . OR I'LL NEVER SEE MAGIC OUT OF YOU. PROCEED.*

Indeed.

"This fool thought to question ye before he claimed and slew ye," came a cold voice. It sounded more like the lich she had destroyed than Blaskyn. "I am Thalon and have no need to waste words trying to pry secrets and cleave through deceit. My claws will cook ye where ye lie. When they're done, and I eat thy flesh, I will know all ye know. Thy skull will join the others on the shelf—fools who accompanied the mages who lusted after mastery over wizardry. 'Sit not alone,' and all that . . ."

The gaunt face stared down at her almost approvingly. "The young and strong mages have served me as bodies, down the years. Thine is too broken and weaker than this fool's."

As he spoke, the crawling claws swarmed over Laeral. Skeletal fingers tore clothes away and raked stones aside. Dry bones scuttled over and under her bared flesh, dragging branches and twigs from somewhere painfully in underneath her.

Through all this bony violation, the burning eyes that had once been Blaskyn's looked down at her coldly and steadily.

"This fool lusted after thee, Laeral," came the hollow voice, almost jauntily, "but thy flesh is more useful to me cooked and eaten. It has been a long time . . . I hope the arundoon sauce has survived."

Thalon turned away, stopped, and picked up Laeral's pendant. He gave her a grisly smile. "The fool didn't even know what this was," he said, tying it about his own neck. "My thanks, mageling—only one globe left, but it's been years since I've worn a necklace of missiles! Not since . . . but ye need not know that." He turned and went to the stairs, walking more swiftly and smoothly with each stride.

"Don't go—I'll be back directly," the hollow voice called back to her, cold and cheerful.

Laeral shuddered and whimpered at the agony her movement had brought her.

The endless, silent crawling went on. Almost fainting with the pain, Laeral raised a numbed hand and carefully took the earring from her ear. Her last magic. Her hand closed over it and fell back amid the growing pile of wood.

A strange, horrid noise came up the stairs, growing nearer: The lich was humming. That white, sunken face smiled cruelly above her again.

Suddenly Laeral felt cold, sticky liquid falling on her. Thalon was calmly emptying the contents of a crystal decanter onto her limbs.

"Arundoon sauce," the archmage said lightly. "In splendid condition, too, thanks to the spells on the decanter. I'll just put it somewhere safe—for next time. When I come back, Laeral, we'll share a kiss; thy last, I fear, for with it I'll breathe dragon fire into ye, and ye'll burn. . . . Do minstrels still sing of kisses that burn? I gave them that phrase, though its true meaning seems to have been forgotten."

Thalon lingered above her thoughtfully. "Much about me has been forgotten in the Realms. With this fine young body and your knowledge of who works magic and where, I'll change all that. One mage will lead me to another, until I've swallowed what all of them know. I thank thee for this opportunity, Laeral. It's most kind of ye."

Laeral fought to keep her eyes open against waves of sleepy pain. He seemed disappointed. "What, no tears? No pleading? I expected some reaction, at least."

Laeral smiled at him tightly as her hand swept up. "You shall *have it!"* she hissed in answer, through fresh waves of pain, and whispered fiercely, *"Alahabad!"*

The earring twisted in the air as it flew, to become a metal hand as small as a child's. It struck Thalon in the chest, thrusting the lichmage backward with the force of its blow.

Laeral saw the lich stagger, saw the metal hand close and tighten on the last globe of the necklace that had been her most powerful magic for so many years, bent her will, and turned her head away.

HA! NOW HER REVENGE! MORE, HUMAN—SHOW ME MORE!
Of course. I've spent my life showing folk things....

Her eyes were closed, so the flash that blistered her face and side did not blind her. It shook the ceiling above her and the rubble around. Dust began to fall on her like a cloak. More pain. Tiny spears showered her side; bony splinters from what was left of Blaskyn, Laeral decided wearily.

She lay still. The shaking died away. She breathed thanks to Tymora and Mystra both. As if in reply, a thin, falling wail of rage and disappointment rose, mingled with the rolling echoes of the blast . . . and slowly died away with them.

Your turn for a little pain and disappointment, Laeral thought savagely, as black oblivion took her.

WHAT? I'M TO BE CHEATED OF THE GLOAT OVER HER FALLEN FOE? HUMANS ARE SUCH WEAK WEEDS!
Patience, Lord Nergal, and see ...
[growl, reluctant silence]

Much later, cold and pain awakened her. She looked toward the throne. It still glowed with a faint white radiance, but she saw no trace of the lich. What she sought lay at the foot of the throne.

Gritting her teeth, Laeral rolled over, her broken leg flopping uselessly. The blazing pain, as she hauled herself through stabbing branches and motionless bone claws, made her sob and shriek in turns. She crawled slowly across the floor, wondering if she'd get there in time.

WELL, IF ALL THIS WAS PASSED FROM MYSTRA TO YOU, SHE MUST HAVE SUR-
VIVED, EH?

Give the tale its time, devil. Give the tale its time. Things are more
fun that way...

FUN! [SNORT] *NOW I KNOW I'M IN THE MIND OF A HUMAN!*

Ye doubted it before?

It was long, indeed, before she reached the spot where her rod
lay. Laeral closed her hand around it carefully. Her fingers shook.
She twisted one of its end knobs until the rounded brass came free.
A small metal vial rolled out.

Tearing out the stopper with her teeth, Laeral drank the cool,
sweet potion greedily. Relief flooded through her body. She lay
back thankfully and let the healing magic bring her strength.

When she felt strong enough, she undid the rod's other end and
drank the second potion quickly. The instant the vial was empty,
she straightened her broken leg with firm hands and clenched teeth.
The pain burned and raged for only a short time, then subsided to
a dull ache.

Patiently Laeral picked up the rod again and shook it. A roll of
parchment dropped out. "My most precious magic, indeed," she
said aloud, and then added in a fierce whisper, "Blaskyn—you fool!"

She read the outermost scroll first, casting its heal spell upon herself. When she was fully recovered, she conjured up light again to
explore the tower thoroughly, gleaning from it what small, hidden
magics she could find. Not once did she touch the throne.

She found no spellbooks and suspected they were under the
throne. She looked at it once, as it sat there waiting for her, glowing silently and beckoningly, and shook her head. Only the thinnest
of smiles touched her lips.

One day it might send another foe to find her, if she did not
destroy it first. But ending the long career of Thalon was a task for
another day. Laeral unrolled the last, inner scroll—the teleport spell
that would take her home. Without bidding Thalon farewell, she
read the scroll and left that place.

AM I GOING TO SEE SOME MAGIC, HUMAN? ARE YOU GOING TO LIVE?

[silence]
BAH. SHOW ME THE REST. [growl]

Standing in her own familiar spell chamber, naked and filthy, bereft of apprentice and much magic, Laeral of Loudwater smiled wryly.

"Of Art gain great sight, wise beyond any mage," the verse had run. It had spoken truth; she'd gained great sight, indeed—of what unchecked power and fanatical mastery of Art did to archmages.

Laeral sighed and carelessly tossed her bundle (what was left of her robes, tied as a sack around the scraps of magic she'd scavenged) across the room.

Right now, the most important goal of her life lay downstairs, at the bottom of her garden: the stream where she could wash off the dust, dirt, bone splinters, and the gods-alone-knew-what-else was caked all over her, stuck to Thalon's gluelike arundoon sauce.

Laeral went down the stairs to the landing where her cloaks hung. She brushed past them to a littered desk whose pigeonholes held dusty scrolls written years before. She took out one she'd never expected to need and read it as she went slowly down another flight of stairs to the garden door.

The scroll melted away between her fingertips, and the dancing lights it conjured gave Laeral light enough to bathe by. She whispered the word that unlocked the door and went out into the night with a decanter of wine to wash away the oily sauce. Cradling it she dove headlong into the stream.

She'd have to find another apprentice tomorrow . . . where was that list Orliph of the Harpers had left her? There'd been a good dozen names on it, some of them interesting.

Oh, yes. She snapped her fingers, and out of the night sky above her a scroll arrowed down, unfolded itself gracefully above her nose, and angled itself to catch the radiance of the gently drifting globes of light around her.

Laeral scrubbed and stretched in the cool water, making small murmuring sounds of contentment as the stickiness left her. Tossing back her wet hair, she peered at the list.

Cold fear made its slow way up her spine, crawling like one of the bony claws of the archmage's tower. The list had held almost twenty names, she was sure. Now there was only one, written in flowing, darkly bold and fresh script: "Thalon."

Laeral curled her lip. Enough. That throne was going to have to go. Tomorrow.

HAH. YOU DENY ME ONCE MORE. THE PROMISE OF MAGIC, SPELLS WAVED BEFORE ME—AND THEN, NO DOING AND CRAFTING AND WIELDING.

ENOUGH OF OTHER FOLK. YOU TAUGHT MAGIC TO MANY, AND I KNOW MYSTRA WATCHED OVER YOUR DOING SO MORE THAN ONCE. LET US SEE WHAT SHE SAW. . . .

[images drifting, then flashing up and aside, flung away in the drive to go deeper . . .]

* * * * *

The abishai squatted on the sharp-spiked rocks that ringed the hollow, guarding the whorlspell. This one had not whirled and spit for long. The banners on their spears, proclaiming this hollow the territory of Great Tiamat the Many-Headed, were still new. Most of the abishai faced outward, glaring across the smoking ridges in a search for the trouble they knew would come. Only a few of the largest, eldest redhides amongst them looked inward, at the spinning chaos of the whorlspell.

The "eyes of Hell," some called them. They were, in truth, more like blindly snatching claws, scooping up creatures, gems, things of magic, water, or whatever the devil slain in the spell casting had desired most. Whorlspells grabbed things from far worlds and spewed them into Hell. They fed Avernus and gave it a constant source of entertainment—and problems. Magics unheard-of and undefended against came through all too often, and betimes creatures that could slay as easily as they were slain. . . .

This one had been sporadically spewing forth bleating, wild-eyed sheep and wet, shining fish ever since its discovery. The former were easily neck-wrung ere they could scramble away, though the guardians let the occasional one run about for a little sport. This wasn't going to be one of those whorls that spewed forth crumbling stone, all manner of strange decaying things, and lots of magic that had to be warily watched.

Some of the redhides almost desired a little danger. Even gutting sheep in ever-more cruel ways loses its delight after a while.

They were not expecting the whorl to spit a bright comet of blue-white flame into the air—still less, at the head of it, a human female with eyes like two black coals and hair like silver flame.

The Simbul knew her wands—sticks of wood, after all, amid the searing smoke and wandering fireballs of Avernus—wouldn't last long. She snatched and fired, snatched and fired, in a bright spell-web that left each weapon floating and spitting death after she'd let go of it to snatch another. Abishai exploded into shreds and gobbets before the guardians of the whorl knew what it had brought them. Their slayer was away, flying low across the trembling, rocky ground in a conjured shroud of smoke. Behind her, abishai remains began to spatter back down on the rocks amid the flaming remnants of a few banners.

El! My love, where are you?

[wordless reply, warning of being devil-ridden, diabolic awareness catching fire and sweeping around to look, contact broken]

Somewhere in that direction! Stealth was for others. Even the Simbul would find the whelmed armies of Hell a little warm for her liking. After all, she was but an ember blown from the inferno that was Mystra, and even the Lady had been forced to retreat. Strike swift and hard was both the Simbul's best road and the one that suited her.

Balls of flame flashed and arced in the distance, bright sparks against a red and starless sky. Something that might have been a dragon fluttered clumsily down behind one peak as she shot a glance in its direction.

The ground fell away into a vast, sharp-walled chasm. Into that gorge, spinagons flew as fast as their tattered wings could bear them, fleeing a hunting pack of black abishai.

Sinuous tails snaked, wings beat, and talons snatched. The Simbul crashed through the heart of them without slowing, blasting anything in her path into writhing, cartwheeling agony. The wake of seared and sizzling fiends was promptly torn apart by other devils.

The vinegar tang of abishai bodies and the sulfurous reek of devil-blood were strong around her as she stormed up and over a line of clawlike crags. Larger devils stood on a pinnacle above the tortured land—tall and terrible baatezu with their folded bat-wings arching high above them. They took wing as they saw her, grinning and hooting in anticipation. The mightiest of them surged to make the first and most satisfying strike against her.

The Witch-Queen never slowed, racing on as the pit fiend soared to meet her. Its great wings blotted out the sky ahead. Its mighty arms spread, and its fangs bared in delighted laughter. She hurled a spell in front of her—a bright burst of lightning that raked its chest like the tails of a whip—and let it bellow mirth at her feeble magic.

It was still laughing when the claws of her will tore it apart, flinging its jawbone into the face of one startled cornugon and its skull into the snarling maw of another.

"I'd love to stay," the Simbul snarled to the winds as she plunged on, the hot blood of her foe settling on her in a stinging cloud, "but I'm busy just now. Perhaps another time . . . soon."

She sent forth another mind-touch . . . and found both her beloved and the dark fury of an archdevil awaiting her. She broke the contact before his mind bolt could do more than leap toward her. Twisting in the air, the Simbul flung herself over on her back in a sharp turn that would bring her to where Elminster was being held.

If she tore through the smoking stink of Hell just a little faster, she might even reach him in time. . . .

* * * * *

NOT GOOD!

Nergal broke his hold on Elminster's mind, leaving his captive to blink and whimper in the sudden din and reek of Avernus. He lifted his head to peer across the blood-red sky.

"She comes," he snarled, "and Orochal didn't even slow her. What manner of woman d'you lie with, wizard, that she can tear apart pit fiends without even slowing?"

The wormlike thing that was Elminster made no reply but a wet, bubbling moan. Nergal glared down at it for a moment, and then back up at a small darkness that was streaking across the sky, racing nearer . . . and nearer. . . .

Cursing, Nergal lifted taloned hands and wove a spell mighty enough to leave him trembling—or rather, several spells spun together. It cost him a lot of his strength and something precious that he'd been saving for a long time—a sphere of fused rock crystal that held a drop of blood from a certain other devil.

Yet Nergal was smiling through the brimstone burst. His magic snatched him away to another corner of Avernus. At the same time it plucked Elminster Aumar elsewhere, into the very lap of the devil whose blood he'd been keeping safe.

Two breaths later, the Simbul came down through the sky like an Avernan fireball, spitting lightning before her onto the bare rocks where her foe had been.

They triggered a blast that should have slain her—and did hurl her back across the sky.

She smiled grimly through that battering. She knew El's captor had hurled her beloved in one direction while taking himself to safety in another. She little cared. The scaly skin of this archdevil or that was of no interest to her. Avenging torment was a task for another day. She was here to bring the Old Mage home.

Her mind seeking was fleeting, this time—he was over *there*. Powering herself out of her tumble, heedless of the magic she spent in doing so, the Witch-Queen of Aglarond turned in the air and raced off in another direction.

All over Avernus, devils dropped whatever they were doing and scrambled to get a look at this new entertainment.

*   *   *   *   *

Tasnya arched over her bed of blood. She was a dark and sinuous thing of many spine-studded breasts. The abishai that wrestled her screamed as her long, curving spines transfixed them. The sound rose in a keening music that made drinking their blood all the more pleasant.

"Well, well," Tasnya purred, "what have we here?"

The helpless thing that Nergal had been amusing himself with arrived suddenly. It was but a passing distraction. She spell-swept it aside to smash bloodily against distant rocks. Nergal no doubt had laid spying or explosive magic on the thing.

Moments later, a bolt of otherworldly fire with a furious archmage in it streaked across the sky.

Tasnya of the Torments rolled over. Writhing, screaming abishai covered her like a grotesque, blood-dripping cloak. She lifted a lazy hand to trace a spell that called on the blood around her, sending forth bloodfire in a hungry arm.

It swept up to snatch the onrushing human—and it tightened into a coiling, shrinking spiral.

The Simbul swerved to avoid it—and then swerved again.

Tasnya smiled like a hungry wolf and sent a careful spell right at the intruder's face.

It met and shocked back from a spell coming the other way. Lightning clawed. The ground shook. Bloodfire lances flew in all directions, impaling abishai and Nergal's pet.

Tasnya lifted an eyebrow and sat up smoothly in the gore. She awaited her foe with lengthening, spearlike spines. No spell could get through her own curtain of magic. The bloodfire wrapped her foe in a shrinking cone that would keep her from getting away. As their spells wrestled, it would be Tasnya's Hell-spawned body against the frail, onrushing human.

"Breast to breast, bite to bite, claw to claw," she murmured eagerly, anticipating much amusement—and a lot of magic—soon to come.

The very air roared as the Simbul of Aglarond came racing down at the waiting, gloating archdevil. Spell after spell snarled and contended around her, caught up in the archdevil's own awakening magic. Flames of wet, glistening blood roared around her, rising into a tunnel, forcing her down, down toward waiting spines. . . .

Whispering frantically, the furious sorceress did the only thing she could. Heedless of torn nails and bleeding fingers, she unbuckled and unsnapped and tore off armor for all she was worth. Metal sang and shrieked off metal as she spell-thrust greaves and plates and all in front of her, into a shifting shield. A grinding chaos of curved metal hurtled toward waiting spines, glowing with the spells the Simbul was still hissing when the crash came.

The sorceress screamed. A spine as thick as she burst up through the crashing steel and laid open her side. Nude and blood-drenched, she crashed into rock after hard rock after harder boulder. She bounced and rolled with clenched teeth. The last of her spells collapsed, and the burning blood sent by her foe ate its sizzling way into the rocks all around her.

Behind her, the archdevil had stopped screaming. There was nothing left of it but flames in a pool of scorched gore. The sticky, blackened hollow of bone and stone was still being hacked at by the pieces of armor she'd animated into a score of slicing, chopping, stabbing blades. Vicious steel rang tirelessly on unfeeling stone.

"Gone elsewhere to rise again, if it knew spellcraft that strong," the Simbul muttered, ignoring the pain of her burns. Elminster would doubtless need the amulets at her throat and beneath her breasts far more than she did, if he—

—was anywhere to be seen. There was nothing on the rocks where he'd been but a dark splash of blood. Maggots squirmed eagerly to roll in it.

The Simbul sighed. "See Hell in an afternoon, and make sure lots of folk remember your visit."

Wearily, the boldest flying devils began to circle in the distance where they could see the battlefield.

The Simbul spun a spell that would bring her armor of tirelessly hacking blades back to her. Perhaps she could hang them around her, in a forest of moving, hostile steel, and fly on awaiting *her* turn to embrace foes.

On the other hand, she was in no hurry to end up as a blackened pool of blood enlivened by a few flames. The Simbul looked around at the harsh peaks and the bat-winged devils perching in long lines atop them.

"Asmodeus," she told the empty air, "perhaps we could bargain. You give me the man I came for—alive, untainted, and unharmed—and I'll slaughter whichever dozen archdevils you'd like removed from the scene. Have we a deal?"

The sound that raced through the rocks under her bare and bloody feet seemed a thunderous snort of amusement. When it reached the peaks around her, the hundreds of devils took wing in frightened unison, flapping frantically away in all directions.

Alone in Hell, the Simbul gathered her magic and her garments once more about her. "Well," she muttered with a shrug, as she knelt to pick up a twisted shard of armor plate, "if you should change your mind . . ."

* * * * * *

HO! HO! QUITE A LADY LOVER YOU'VE GOT THERE, LITTLE WORM. I'LL GIVE YOU TO ANOTHER UNFRIEND OF MINE SOON . . . JUST AS SOON AS I GET WELL DOWN INTO THESE JUICY MEMORIES HERE. . . .

[scream]

HAH! NOT SO MUCH FUN TAUNTING ME NOW, EH? AM I FINALLY GETTING CLOSE TO SOMETHING YOU'D RATHER I NOT HAVE? DEAR, DEAR . . .

[roaring bellows of diabolic laughter]

Eighteen

HELL RISING

The spinagon toppled off the ridge, its head an empty, burnt husk. Smoke streamed from the sockets that had held its eyes. Nergal wanted no trail left back to him, and the work of his coerced spy was done.

It had watched the pit fiend that was not a pit fiend race past like a dark fireball—wings folded behind it, unused. The Simbul cared about hiding her armor of whirling blades but did not care that there was something odd about the shape she'd assumed. If wandering abishai drew back from attacking the pit fiend that was somehow *not* a pit fiend, that was enough.

She was on her way to strike at the outcast devil Harhoring—who had unwittingly received the unwilling bundle that was Elminster. Nergal had forced his mind-captive into the shape of an old, scorched devil's thighbone, to better hide the wizard in the huge bone pit that Harhoring called home. The future Lord of All Hell hadn't wanted the Lord of Bones noticing the gift while he was still linked to Elminster's mind.

Snarling, Nergal wondered not for the first time just why he was wasting his time trying to glean useful memories from the wizard. *Again* he'd been shown useless kindnesses to nobodies, not the secrets of wielding great magic. Did the human have an endless supply of useless remembrances?

Just how long could one mortal keep a devil dancing?

Thrice, now, Nergal had tried to drive hard toward a memory—*any* memory—of Elminster actually casting a spell, teaching or being taught magic, or storing or hiding anything enchanted. The human's mind had crumbled, yes, collapsing as it should before his fury . . . and yet, somehow, when he ceased charging, confident he'd finally seized on something—he found himself empty-handed once more. How did the human do it? He was puny in body, had no hidden magic except the silver fire lurking somewhere inside him, had been torn apart and healed any number of times now, and involuntarily transformed even more often. . . . Still he fought, subtly, deep in the very mind that Nergal was tramping around. Every memory yielded was lost to the man—yet he joked, he made sarcastic comments . . . he was still sane.

Sane at least as far as an archdevil could tell about a human. . . .

Fires take all, he was *not* going to give up. After all this work, to end up with nothing. He was going to take this Elminster's mind apart memory by memory, for all the wearying years this old wizard had managed to live, and he was going to find that magic. Magic to make Nergal a lord of Hell at last.

Let the Simbul slay his rivals, one after another, while a fresh mind-worm burrowed into her beloved. She'd be going to a lot of work to rescue a drooling husk.

Nergal cast the spell carefully, letting the old one crumble only an instant before he began. He must unerringly find Elminster again without alerting either the human sorceress or Harhoring.

He drew in a deep sigh of relief when the familiar vaulted darkness loomed in his mind once more. He was back inside Elminster's mind . . . and never noticed that his host had used silver fire in a wild frenzy of healing, in the brief time he'd not been riding the wizard's mind. At least physically, El was whole—if weak and weary—once more.

HAIL ELMINSTER, ARCHMAGE OF SHADOWDALE, he thought mockingly.

Hail Nergal, Lord of Hell, came the mocking reply.

Rage flared like bright fire in the tentacled archdevil, but he wrestled it grimly down and slipped deeper into the human's mind as gently as if he was a lover come to caress, and not a ravager come to seize and destroy.

LET US BEGIN AGAIN, LITTLE PIG OF A HUMAN.

[mind lash, pain, savage diabolic grin, rending bright images, hurling, burrowing, clawing aside more]

AHA! WHAT HAVE WE HERE?

[images surging]

The chancellor's eyes were black and glittering. He might have been one of the ravens of the battlements as he turned on her.

"We've heard lies to spare from you lips, my lady," he said coldly. "Speak truth to me, and soon, or I may just decide to waste no time on you ever again."

Suddenly his fingers were in her hair, tearing, hauling Silaril roughly to her knees. His rings were cold against her cheek as his sword grated from its scabbard.

"I have had *enough* of your twisted words, 'Lady.' I have been patient too long."

Steel stung Silaril's throat. She forced herself to remain silent, her face still—but she could not stop her chest heaving, brushing the arm that held her captive.

The chancellor knew her fear and smiled slowly and coldly. "I will now hear truth from your pretty lips. If you refuse, or speak falsely, your body will taste some truth from this sword. My patience is at an end."

NOW, WHAT WAS THAT, I WONDER? PITY THE REST IS GONE. WE ARCHDEVILS ARE SO MIGHTY, YOU KNOW, THAT EVEN WHEN WE'RE TRYING TO BE OH-SO-CAREFUL, SOMETIMES THINGS JUST GET . . . BROKEN. CLEVER HUMAN WIZARDS, FOR INSTANCE.

I understood thy heavy-handed point, Nergal. Have ye something particular in mind for thy viewing pleasure?

NO, MAGE, I LET YOU LEAD ME LONG ENOUGH—AND A FINE, LONG, AND WASTED ROAD YOU LED ME ON, TOO. I BELIEVE I'LL LOOK WHERE I WILL, WITHOUT YOUR GUIDANCE—AND JUST MIGHT THEREBY FIND WHAT I'M SEEKING WITHOUT A LOT OF CLEVER BACKTALK FROM A HUMAN WHOSE LIFE HANGS BY THE THINNEST OF THREADS.

[silence]
[diabolic chuckle]
[images swirling]

Somewhere in the Stonelands, Manshoon raised his head and looked back the way he'd come, coldly and calmly. The reek of rotting flesh was strong around him. His nostrils twitched at the sharp stench. For a moment he remembered his first fearful experimentation with zombies, in a crypt far away and long ago. . . . One never forgot the smell.

[diabolic sigh, more images flung side, others torn apart]
ALL RIGHT . . . THIS ONE!

The skull watched all of this, nodding knowingly from time to time.

BAH! NOTHING LEFT . . .
[more images shining proudly]

The other beholder turned an eyestalk or two to gaze at its fellow. "Can we defeat Manshoon, were he to gain spellfire?"

The first eye tyrant bobbed slightly in the air. If it had possessed shoulders, the movement might have been a shrug. "See how easily he's swayed to our bidding now," it said, in tones cold with scorn. "A mighty tyrant and mage as humans reckon such things, to be sure—but blinded with lusts and mistrusts and paranoias, need for power, hunger for triumph. He's a stunted, twisted thing. Spellfire could not right all that."

The second beholder blinked. "Agreed."

AMUSING, ELMINSTER. A WARNING FOR ME, I SUPPOSE? OH, SO AMUSING. WELL, IF YOU'RE GOING TO PERSIST IN TRYING TO MEDDLE IN MY SEARCHING, SHOW ME ONE OF THE SEVEN RIGHT NOW! SHOW ME—STORM!

[pincers like claws of steel gripping fiercely; dark will set afire with rage bearing down hard]
[pain]

[satisfied snarl]
[pain]
SHOW ME, WIZARD!

Moonlight traced the magnificence of a bare shoulder as Storm Silverhand rose on one elbow and put a firm hand over Elminster's mouth. "Stop dispensing twaddle and go to sleep," she told him, not unkindly, and moved her hand to his chest, thrusting him back flat on the bed.

He drew breath to protest as to the importance of what he'd been trying to say.

She put her mouth down where her hand had been, thrust her tongue into his mouth, and said along its thrilling length, "Go to *sleep*, I said. Despite my provocations to the contrary."

That seemed like a good idea to Elminster, drifting numb and wearily in floods of chaos that no longer brought pain to his bruised and battered wits. He found a dark cavern that was undisturbed as yet, where the memories were covered with the dust and cobwebs of long neglect, curled up therein, and let Avernus fade away from him as Toril was beginning to do.

NO, DON'T GO TO SLEEP ON ME! I AM NOT PLEASED.

ARE YOU GOING TO SHOW ME EVERY LAST KISS YOU'VE RECEIVED IN YOUR OVERLONG, MISERABLE LIFE, HUMAN? YOU TRY MY PATIENCE TOO FAR!

[searing mind lash, bright bursts of pain, shredded memories tumbling]

WELL, WIZARD? SPEAK TO ME!

[pain, writhing, gasping struggle to mind speak]

Every memory shown ye, devil, is one lost forever to me. To show ye every last thing, and lose it all, would not be the act of a sane man.

AND ARE YOU A SANE MAN?

[silence]

WELL?

[grim silence]

[diabolical laughter, booming and rolling through every dark corner of a shuddering mind]

"This is *ridiculous!*" Rathan cursed as they hurried down the stairs, leather creaking and mail jangling. "Up tower and down! Why can't all these craven fools march up to the gate and declare themselves, like in the children's tales? 'Twould be far easier on my aching feet!"

"I'll try to remember to tell them that," Torm called back merrily. "I'm sure this is all just a misunderstanding and that anxious regard for your bunions is and will be the first and overriding concern of all armed Zhent war parties who show up in the dale a-raiding!"

Rathan's reply was a heartfelt roar of anger. He felt for the flask of firewine at his belt as he ran down the steps, bouncing and lurching. Three turns farther, he got it unstopped and up to his lips—which was about the time his elbow had a brief but painful meeting with a protruding block in the stone wall.

Firewine stings when dashed into the eyes, and overweight priests of the goddess of good fortune throw all caution to the winds when pursuing holy business. So it was that Rathan was off balance and moving far too fast. Momentarily blinded and fumbling with his flask stopper when he should have spared a hand for the rail, he launched himself where he imagined the curve of the stairs to go.

He was regrettably mistaken.

The wall was unforgivingly hard, almost triumphant in its bruising resistance, and it was curved. The stairs were similarly hard, worn smooth by years of many feet, and pitched in a steep descent. Rathan was large, round, and loud in bellows and roars of pain. He bounced off the wall once, twice, thrice, ricocheted from the central pillar, tumbled down over the edges of three very sharp steps, and struck the curving outer wall again, liberally doused with lubricating firewine this time and driven into a more or less helpless ball.

Tymora encourages her faithful to take chances, but Rathan Thentraver was neither a slender nor energetic man. His armor was more impressive to the eye than it was to the sword—or to immovable stones.

His precipitous descent down the stairs began with a startled shout and a clatter and commenced to acquire the full-throated thunder of crumpling armor and a hurtling, heavy body that is embracing its fate with holy rage rather than the silence of acceptance or insensibility.

Torm was not slow of wit or foot, but he could jump only so high before negotiating his own inevitable meeting with stone walls, steps, or ceiling. His frantic leap to avoid his bouncing, rolling friend failed. He rebounded from the ceiling down onto the whirling armored ball. With a stream of colorful curses all his own, Torm was swept down the stairs in similar rolling tumult.

The smile of Tymora brought a Zhentilar guard captain striding into the antechamber. The crossbows of his men had cleared the tower entrance of guards and driven the few defenders into flight out through the kitchens. His duty was clear. "Open yon door," he snapped, through the din of shrieks, laughing men, and horses thundering past outside.

Obligingly, his men did so, blades and bows at the ready. A spiral stair awaited—thankfully without guards or any traps. The boldest guard took a cautious step forward and peered up into the gloom.

"Well?" the guard captain snapped.

"There's something," the soldier replied, with a frown. "A sort of crashing . . ."

The officer snorted. "A 'sort of crashing'? *What* sort of crashing?"

Rathan's hurtling form rattled around the last bend, bounded off the edge of a particularly hard step, and sailed down into the antechamber like a large, jagged armored juggernaut. He smashed the guard captain to the floor like an angry cook dashing an egg. Zhents scattered as a raw groan arose from the wreckage. A ribbon of blood slowly followed, and the soldier at the doors turned and snarled, "*That* sort of crashing. Sir." Crossbow leveled, he grimly approached the chaos of armor plates and heaving flesh.

The smaller, much quieter ball of Torm hurtled out of the doorway and struck his legs. With a crack, the crossbow fired its bolt into the nearest Zhent. The bowman's head cracked almost as loudly against the floor.

Torm fetched up against Rathan in a cursing, panting tangle. "So how *are* your bunions, Old Barrelhead?"

Rathan's reply was long and loud and extremely colorful. Tymora was not visibly present to wince and cringe, so Torm did it for her.

WELL, THAT WAS IMPRESSIVE. NOT USEFUL, BUT AT LEAST IMPRESSIVE.

[images plunging]

"It is my hope, Lord, that you never find out," Tessaril replied, her eyes grave. As she spoke, there was a sudden crash, inside.

ANOTHER CRASH? HMMM. THE REST IS LOST. ANOTHER HUMAN WENCH, THIS ONE WITH EYES LIKE SMOKE. NOTHING BUT A SNIPPET LEFT . . . BUT IS THIS NOT HER FACE AGAIN, OVER HERE?

"Now," Tessaril said, "we wait. Would anyone like something to eat, before conquering Zhentil Keep?"

BAH! A SNIPPET ONLY, AGAIN—I COULD HAVE SWORN THERE WAS MORE . . .
If ye handled my remembrances more gently, devil, ye might see more. There was more to that . . . but "was" is the right of it, now; ye destroyed it!
DON'T TELL ME WHAT TO DO, LITTLE MAN! NERGAL WILL RUMMAGE AS HE PLEASES!
[mind lash, pain, frenzied rushing images]

They chuckled, and then the Royal Magician of Cormyr lifted an eyebrow and asked disbelievingly, "This little maid called Shandril?"
"Aye, Shandril. She didn't know that no one dares attack Manshoon in his lair—so she went ahead and attacked him."

AGAIN THE LITTLE MAID OF SPELLFIRE. YOU HAVE SPELLFIRE TOO, DO YOU NOT?
[silence]
ELMINSTER! ELMINSTER!
Sorry, devil, I was in too much pain to hear thee. . . .
CUTE PLOY, HUMAN. CUTE. NEVER MIND—I'LL SEARCH WITHOUT YOUR HELP OR CLEVER COMMENTS.
[images spinning]
BAH! I WANT TO SEE ANOTHER OF YOUR REAL MEMORIES, SOMETHING CLEAR AND LENGTHY AND USEFUL TO ME . . . SOMETHING VIVID AND RELEVANT ABOUT ONE OF THE SEVEN SISTERS COMING INTO HER POWER. GIVE SUCH A MEMORY TO ME, AND GIVE IT NOW.

STORM SEEMED TO WORK LAST TIME. SHE'S BEEN YOUR LOVER A TIME OR TWO, HASN'T SHE? GIVE ME STORM—AND THEN ANOTHER OF THE SEVEN.

Nearby, a heap of twisted Zhentarim bodies heaved, shifted, and convulsed. Out from under it emerged a bloody, panting, wounded Storm.

AHA! MORE, AND NOT DESTROYED! I CAN DO IT!

Silence fell over the field of the fallen.

[growl] *WELL, I DESTROYED ONLY PART OF IT. THERE'S N— BUT WHAT'S THIS? THE SHANDRIL WENCH AGAIN?*

"Ye must join the Harpers, lass," Elminster said gravely.

Shandril looked up at him with something like spellfire glinting in her eyes and replied, "I 'must'? Why?"

The Old Mage shrugged. "Somehow," he said in a dry voice, waving a hand at the smoking destruction around them, "ye must learn when *not* to start something like this."

BAH! YOU TEACHING, YES, BUT WHAT USE CAN I MAKE OF IT?
[images clawed aside, whirling]

"I can't be bothered wasting spells on them. Hang them, for the citizens to watch."

"You'll watch from the balcony as usual, Lord?"

"No. I have work to do, and one death upon order is very much like another. There are things in life that give me greater pleasure . . . and *far* greater amusement."

WHO WAS THAT?

Manshoon, a mage cleverer than some give him credit for, playing the sinister ruler of Zhentil Keep, some time ago.

AND WHO ARE THESE BUFFOONS, HERE? I'VE SEEN THEM IN YOUR MIND BEFORE. . . .

Adventurers. The Knights of Myth Drannor.

MIGHT THEY BE TALKING OF MAGIC?

Those two talk only of drink, riches, women, brawling, and magic, so ye've a one in five chance....

HMMPH. BETTER ODDS THAN SOME YOU'VE GIVEN ME.

[chosen image rushing up large and bright]

Torm coughed. "Ahem," he began, artlessly. "By all the good watching gods, lords and ladies gentle, be of good cheer! 'Tis a mighty day, to be sure. Rathan the Mighty rides again, and I with him. Full five score times ago did I first sally forth, blade in hand (leaden rapier though it's oft proved to be), to inflict this priest upon thee. Thou hast stood up to his sermons both manfully and woman-fully, as thy styles most rich and various bid. Certes, this heartens me, wherefore I bid ye: once more into the hungry, grim-a-visaged fray, b'yr deity whatsoever—once more!"

"Belay that knightly speech," Rathan replied crisply. "*I'm* the clever-tongued orator here!"

"Not with a flagon that small, you aren't," Torm replied slyly, from just out of reach.

[diabolic snort] *DROLL. VERY DROLL. IS THERE MORE OF THESE TWO?*

[silence, image spinning to the fore]

"Furies and gargoyles be damned, man," Torm said in mock fury. "I ordered the bridal bed, and paid you well! You said noth-ing at all about my having to provide my own bride! Why, in Waterdeep, six gold buys you the warm company of a lass betrothed to you for the night!"

Rathan sent a discreet cough over the shoulder of the glowering innkeeper, and to it added the murmured words, "Bold blade of my heart, ye forget something: We are *in* Waterdeep. Thy claim rings a mite false."

The innkeeper rounded on him, still furious, and growled, "Unless you pay for a bed, sir, *you'd* best be his bride and share!"

Rathan raised his eyebrows and shot Torm a querying look that widened into astonishment. "Nay!" He exclaimed. "Not *that!*"

The innkeeper wheeled around again to see what had caused this reaction. Rathan coolly raised the hilt of his mace to his shoulder—and brought it deftly down across the back of the innkeeper's skull. The man crashed to the floor like a sack of potatoes, leaving Rathan standing innocently over the wreckage.

"If we carry him out to the stables," he told Torm. "I can have your bed—and you can have his and get a bride after all!"

"Oh, no," Torm said warningly. "No chance! I've seen his wife—*she* should be in the stables!" He frowned at his friend's sudden frantic gesticulations and asked irritably, "What?"

The skillet that felled him made Rathan wince. In the few seconds before the stout priest of Tymora whirled and broke into puffing flight, he reflected on how anger can make even four-hundred-pound, wart-studded women attractive. Being about a dozen pounds lighter, he managed to stay just ahead of the innkeeper's wife all the way out to the horse-trough—where, unfortunately, he slipped in something.

HAH! HAH! THESE TWO IDIOTS ARE A DELIGHT TO WATCH! HAVE YOU MORE?
Elsewhere, Lord Nergal—over among my memories of Shadow-dale. Just—
OH, NO.
No.
AMUSEMENTS CAN WAIT. I'M NOT LETTING YOU LEAD ME ABOUT THROUGH EVERY BACK ALLEY OF YOUR MIND. YOU ALMOST TRICKED ME, HUMAN—BUT ONLY ALMOST. BE STILL AND SILENT. I'LL GO RUMMAGING AGAIN.

[A cloud of whirling images bursts into shimmering falls and fades—and out of it, one image is seized upon and rises brightly.]

The King of Cormyr stood on the battlefield and shook his head ever so slightly, his lips pursed and his face grim. "My path lies clear before me," he said to the man at his shoulder. "That straight and narrow road to the waiting grave."

The Royal Magician of Cormyr coughed discreetly and observed, "My king, the path you see is every man's path. Kings simply have a way of not noticing their route for longer than most can ignore it. Something to do with the distractions of more engaging scenery."

"Ah," Azoun said, hefting his sword, "I see. Invading armies, dragons tearing the roofs off fortresses, death spells dropping out of the skies with sharp talons—that sort of 'engaging scenery'?"

Vangerdahast nodded. "That, and the paintings on many a boudoir ceiling," he told the backs of his fingernails innocently.

If the look Azoun gave him had been just a little sharper, the Royal Magician's life might have ended right then.

But then, the wizard reflected, as their eyes met, Elminster would have considered that he'd taken the coward's way out.

YOU TUTORED HIM, DIDN'T YOU? I WONDER WHO—ASIDE FROM YOUR PET GOD-DESS, OF COURSE—TAUGHT YOU MAGIC? CARE TO SHARE ANY OF THOSE MEMORIES?

If ye insist, why of course—

NO! NO, WIZARD! JUST SIT QUIET, AND I'LL FIND MY OWN WAY. IT'LL SAVE MY TEMPER AND SAVE YOU MUCH PAIN. HEAR ME?

As ye desire, devil.

[diabolic satisfaction, images flashing up in disarray, then spinning past]

"Life," as the archwizard said, "is like a squirming maggot—isn't it?"

[bewilderment] IS THAT ALL THERE IS OF THAT? WHO WAS THAT? ELMINSTER?

Nay, Nergal, it was another *arrogant old mage, not me.*

I KNOW THAT, YOU FOOL! I WAS BIDDING YOU ANSWER ME!

Ah. Well, I was just sitting quiet, letting ye find thy own way.

[raging growl] I'LL BREAK YOU, PUNY HUMAN!

Ye did that already, and don't seem pleased with the result. With such wavering resolve, Nergal, how are ye ever *going to rise to rule Hell?*

DON'T MOCK ME, ELMINSTER—UNLESS YOU WANT TO SPEND AN ETERNITY IN TORMENT.

In many ways, devil, I already have. Think on that, and bluster less.

[snarl, mind lash, bursting mind bolts, raw screams of agony, diabolic satisfaction, images whirling past like bright embers flung from a roaring fire]

"Holy . . . dancing . . . hobgoblins," Asper said slowly, her voice unsteady.

AND WHO OR WHAT WAS THAT? EL—OH, NEVER MIND.
I WILL MAKE YOU PAY FOR THIS, HUMAN. I SWEAR BY THE—
OHO! IT BEGINS!

* * * * *

Horns as tall as men thrust into the blood-red sky. Their cruel tips, curved slightly toward each other, were adorned with rows of charred spinagon skulls. The head beneath those horns might have belonged to a giant goat, and its large, sharp glistening black eyes bespoke fell, alert intelligence. It was a pity Harhoring's face was also permanently lined with the pain given him by the Curse of Asmodeus.

It was not a rare distinction in Hell to have earned the displeasure of the Lord Most Deep, but few wore the sign of it as a constant, active torment. The Horned One was the only one of those victims free to move about and pretend to even the tiniest shred of freedom. It was freedom laced with pain, the constant reminder Asmodeus desired it to be.

Worms Harhoring could not slay—for they were made of his own living guts—gnawed at him endlessly, burrowing in and out of his bulging belly. Streams of blood and foul fluids dripped ceaselessly from the wounds they made. Harhoring's own talons and spells passed like smoke through the curseworms.

Only commanded devils and captured beasts could strike the worms and slow the gnawing that daily weakened Harhoring. As it was, only prodigious feeding and frantic seizing of magic by the goat-devil kept him alive. He knew Asmodeus watched him and gloated— wherefore his mood was seldom less than savage.

Harhoring was enjoying one of those "seldom" moments right now. He squatted atop a pinnacle slick with his own gore, tearing hungrily at the ribs of a dragon he'd spell-fooled into flying at full speed into the mountainside above. Thrice he'd had to fight off pit fiends seeking to claim its heart or brain—and he'd given up chasing away spinagons and abishai from spattered gobbets of dragon flesh and errant scales.

This was the first large feast he'd had in days, and the Horned One was anticipating a serious interruption soon. The immobility of the dragon's huge carcass kept him in one spot to dine on it . . . and that meant foes could find him easily. Harhoring had prepared a few magics and was watching warily as he ate. In Hell, mistakes are luxuries one rarely survives.

There! Something coming fast, rushing up without any attempt at stealth or subtlety, hurtling across Avernus like a dark, silent bolt of devil-flesh . . .

Harhoring had keen eyes, and he used them now. This was an unfamiliar foe, or an old one wearing a guise he'd never seen before. Like a pit fiend, it seemed, but flew with its wings folded and drawn in behind it, as if it was an arrow shot from a bow. There was something strange about its body, too, as if it had many tiny legs, all constantly a-whirl around it. . . .

Harhoring favored the arriving foe with a toothy smile liberally adorned with raw, bloody dragon—and unleashed his first spell.

Talons of acid sliced the air. The dripping latticework of death sizzled and spat as the foe struck it. A few scraps of armor, it seemed, caught the energy. They dwindled and tumbled as the acid ate through them.

The onrushing foe seemed a human woman, clad more in her own hair than in anything else. That hair was long, as willful as the tentacles of a hunting squid. Those tresses held wands and rings and other items of magic . . . and even aimed them!

Harhoring's second magic slammed into her. The spell created stars of long thorns bristling in all directions, then caused them to explode, hurling their deadly shrapnel. The nearly bare woman writhed in her own blood, studded with dozens of javelinlike thorns, and fell through the air. . . .

Fires of the Pit! She was going to plunge into the still-steaming guts of the dragon! What if she lived and fought on—what would survive of Harhoring's meal?

With some alarm, but also with savage glee, the Horned One cast a bloodhook spell and pulled hard. The spell would snatch the human female—torn open and writhing in her death-agonies—to his feet.

The hook plunged home. The woman threw back her head. Cords of straining flesh stood out in her throat. She screamed her pain at the blood-red sky. Then she seemed to *leap* across the space between them. Somewhere along the way, her helpless parabola became a pounce. Her face grew a grin to match Harhoring's own.

Magic flashed and flowed around the human sorceress as the two damned creatures came together. In sudden alarm, the Horned One belatedly conjured burning talons to augment the razor sharpness of his own.

They were just swirling into existence as the foe smashed into his chest, her own hands glowing fiercely.

Harhoring knew worse pain than anything he'd felt since the hand of Asmodeus himself. Red, shrieking agony! The Lord of Bones roared as his foe pierced him, and helplessly, convulsively, shoved her away to free himself—thereby winning greater pain.

The woman's spell had briefly turned her hands into metal fauchard forks, each with a long point that stabbed deep into the goat-devil. A cruel hook below tore the gash wider. Her points drove deep—one piercing right through the devil's body.

Shuddering and flailing, Harhoring spat flaming blood on her and wept more flames as he thrust her away. He pulled himself off her blades with frenzied, convulsive strength.

Coolly she caught both hooks around his exposed intestines as she went. She fell away to one side, and the fury of his shove carried her on past the screaming devil. Her hold on her foe's guts jerked Harhoring sharply around.

Squalling, the horned devil fell from the pinnacle, sprawling onto sharp rocks. Steaming innards tore themselves out of him in the fall. The curseworms reared and writhed in hungry agitation around his midriff.

Thrashing on the rocks in arching, broken agony, the Horned One cursed the hand of Asmodeus, which prevented outcasts from summoning any devil to them and their service. By all the blood in Avernus, he needed aid now!

With twin shimmerings, the woman's hands dwindled back to human form. She wrapped a loop of glistening devil guts around one forearm and began weaving another spell with her free hand.

Harhoring wallowed on the rocks, trying to get upright despite the burning pain of broken bones. He needed to spin a desperate magic of his own.

HARHORING OFFERS LITTLE CHALLENGE, IT SEEMS. HMMM. I'D THOUGHT HIM ONE OF THE STRONGEST AMONG US OUTCASTS.

COME, LITTLE WIZARD: IT'S TIME FOR YOU TO SEE ANOTHER CORNER OF AVERNUS.

[mindworm fades to quiescence, casting commences, magic rising dark and strong]

Blue-white fire raced along the goat-devil's guts, snarling on its swift journey from the grim and trembling human sorceress to the fallen, thrashing devil.

"Where is he, devil?" the Simbul snapped. Death reached for the Lord of Bones. *"What have you done with my man?"*

Puzzlement joined rage in the horned devil's eyes. It leveled a shuddering arm to point at her and unleash a last, desperate magic. The harsh word it said next was the beginning of an incantation, not an answer . . . but then her blood spell reached Harhoring.

The explosion tore the horned devil apart, huge shoulders and all, drenching rocks all around. The Simbul stood, coated in dark ichor. Gore spattered down in a grisly rain that drowned out the sound of her sigh. The trace had faded. She was alone once more. Elminster was gone again, snatched away elsewhere in Avernus.

"Someone wants a lot of devils slain," she said aloud, wearily. "Surely there are more efficient ways of doing that than throwing a lone human mage at them. Even this one."

She looked down at her blood-drenched limbs. A few tiny fragments of armor were still whirling around them. The Simbul shook her head. With a careful spell she transformed the shards into dark wings. The slower way would have to suffice for the rest of this manhunt if her dwindling magic was to see her through another fray.

"Time for Hell to tremble a little more," she murmured and leaped into the blood-red sky.

* * * * *

Fiery eyes narrowed. "Saw you that?" a harsh voice rumbled.

"Aye," the nearest pit fiend said. "Another incursion that's more than it seems. No human sorceress should have been able to slay Orochal, let alone Tasnya the wanton and as deadly a hunter as Harhoring. Three gone to the flames where none should have fallen."

"Indeed. Whelm our troops. Let there be fire in Avernus—and this human intruder writhing and pleading on my cooking-spit in its midst."

"At your dread command," the pit fiend said, bowing its head. It took wing in ungainly, flapping haste. Good sport was not so common in Hell as to be willingly missed.

* * * * *

A ball of flames gouted up from a brazier, with a roar as sudden and sharp as a gong. Horned heads turned.

"Saw you?" asked a deep voice that made the floor tremble with its force, and the listeners with their fear.

"Aye, Dread Lord," they hissed, more or less in chorus, reluctant and anxious.

"To arms," the voice said simply. "Fail me not."

Flames rolled up from the brazier more fiercely than ever before. There was a sudden tumult as devils scrambled to leave that trembling place.

* * * * *

WELL, WELL. YOUR WITCH-QUEEN HAS SNARED MORE THAN A LITTLE ATTENTION IN HELL AMONG THE DEEP AND POWERFUL. HOSTS WHELMED, MIGHTY MAGIC TAKEN OUT OF HIDING, NERGAL HAPPY . . .

Pet humans once more of service, hmm?

CLEVERNESS, CLEVERNESS! ALWAYS I'M TREATED TO ELMINSTER BEING WITTY,

ELMINSTER MAKING MOCKING PRONOUNCEMENTS, ELMINSTER SAVING THE DAY WITH A SNEER FOR THE DOLTS HE DEALS WITH! I COULD WRENCH YOU TO BLOODY PULP IN AN INSTANT, FLAMES TAKE YOU!

And yet ye don't. Why?

BECAUSE NO OTHER DEVIL IN HELL HAS A HUMAN IN HIS HANDS WHO PER- SONALLY SERVES A GODDESS AND HOLDS ANY TRIFLING MEASURE OF HER POWER. SOME DEVILS CAJOLE OR THREATEN OR INFLUENCE MORALS OUTSIDE HELL, BUT YOU'RE MINE, BODY AND MIND. OBVIOUSLY POWERFUL AND WISE, AND POTEN- TIALLY VERY USEFUL.

AND YET I CAN'T MANAGE TO LEARN ANYTHING USEFUL FROM YOU. YET.

And—?

AND I WON'T WAIT MUCH LONGER. YOU WILL YIELD TO ME, OR DIE AS HORRI- BLY AS I CAN CONTRIVE.

THAT IS, IF MALACHLABRA DOESN'T GET YOU FIRST.

[unvoiced human query, mental eyebrow raised]

OH, YES. SHE SURVIVED OUR LITTLE BATTLE OVER YOU, IT SEEMS, BUT HAS GOING INTO HIDING FOR FEAR OF NERGAL THE MIGHTY . . . SO IT'S ONLY FIT- TING THAT I GO TO HER. OR RATHER, SEND HER TWO LITTLE GIFTS. YOU AND YOUR AVENGING LADY LOVE.

[rising bellow of diabolic laughter]

Nineteen

RAGE IN HELL

The chaos of stagnant pools and jagged rocks around the pool of blood was alive with crawling maggots. Those rocks were also home to something else, something broken and shapeless, scorched dark, something that might have answered to the name Elminster if it had possessed a jaw to do so. He dared heal himself only *very* slowly. Maggots sucked and gnawed at him hungrily where he lay, motionless in the deep shadows.

The dark thing splashing in the pool hadn't noticed Elminster's arrival. She was too busy spinning a spell of her own.

It was a hovering sphere of bright, shifting glows and little chimings. In its depths, dark shapes quavered and broke, roiling like smoke.

Its crafter hissed in annoyance. She frowned, feeding it more power through her long, hooked talons. "Work for Malachlabra," she breathed fiercely, peering into the depths. "Show me the human wizard—not my own cavern!"

A rumbling sound echoed down stony passages to the pool. Anger kindled like red flames in ale-brown eyes. Malachlabra lifted her head and stared hard down the passage she'd used to reach this secret place. . . . The passage was strewn with the gnawed bones of the dragon who'd dared to think it owned a fine lair here.

The sound faded and came not again. With a growl the daughter of Dispater rolled over in the smoking blood of the pool and reclined on her belly, idly slapping the gore into little waves with her three serpent tails. She stared even more intently into the depths of her spell-spun sphere.

Shadows swirled in the heart of the sphere. Once more it shaped jagged rocks and steaming blood-water, with a long, sinuous obsidian form lying at ease in the pool, peering into—

The magic burst in a shower of sparks, as all such weavings do when turned to look directly upon themselves. Malachlabra, Duchess of Hell and daughter of Dispater, reared back with a snarl.

"Are my spells so feeble? Or is there something here, twisting my magic? The sphere of seeing has always worked before!"

Bat wings flared once as she stretched restlessly. Sleek obsidian flesh reared up from the hot blood of the pool. The thick red liquid dripped from high breasts, and ran down the curves where serpent-tails met in a wide pelvis. Malachlabra had the body of a lush human female, though for a woman, her snakelike, undulating neck would have been grotesquely long. The two horns curving up from her temples looked anything but human. Her forked tongue flickered thoughtfully between her lips, darting forth to taste the air, as she thought about how to get back at Nergal.

Nergal the brute, stupid and always trusting overmuch in his power and cleverness. Nergal the spy, always slyly watching the doings of others, so as to pounce on this and manipulate that, thinking himself the rightful successor to Dread Asmodeus himself! Well, she'd—

The thing that came rushing at Malachlabra out of the mouth of the passage gave no warning. It was barely a tail length away when it flared into a dozen bright blue bolts of ravening magic.

The serpent devil had no time to try to see what had cast those bolts. They shocked into her, spreading their own cold, cutting pain. Spell-plucked rocks smashed into her from behind, driving her down into the pool and drowning her sight.

Desperately she lashed the air with all her tails, slapping hard at unseen nothing, and was rewarded with a heavy, thudding impact.

Fires of Nessus, but the pain was intense! Shaking, Malachlabra surfaced with talons at the ready, seeking—

Anything but what she saw: a human sorceress with crude bat wings crumpled around her, standing amid the bloody rocks. Her hands racing in intricate gestures. "I *feel* him!" the woman hissed, her eyes blazing. "What have you done with him, devil?"

This intruder did not wait for a reply. The spell she'd spun burst into another volley of blue bolts that sprang into the she-devil.

Screaming amid white fire, Malachlabra twisted and arched. She fought to weave magic of her own and sobbed with unaccustomed pain by the time it worked—snatching her elsewhere.

In midgasp she was back on the smoking, spinagon-swarming surface of Avernus, not far from the cavern she'd just fled. Shuddering, she thrust aside hate and pain and tried to think how best to smite this astonishing foe. How had a human even *reached* her—?

The third volley of magic missiles left the serpent-devil on her face on the rocks, clinging to life and awareness through a red haze.

"We weren't done yet, devil," she heard the human say angrily from behind her. "Or at least *I* wasn't."

The blade that pierced the base of Malachlabra's skull was very cold and hard. It slid through her and out her nose before she could even shriek, pinning her jaws half-open, and struck a spark off a stone in front of her.

Summoning all her will and power, the devil threw her awareness into that spark and rode it away. . . .

"Die, devil!" Alassra Silverhand hissed.

The Simbul's spell sword melted out of her hands, leaving its own fiery pain behind. She flung herself back as flames roared up in a thunderous column, shaking the stony ground. Heat forced the Simbul a few hasty paces farther away.

The serpent-devil's limp body withered and writhed at its heart. It shrank and faded away.

Another column of fire burst into being behind her, melting the tip of one of her wings. The Simbul gasped at the pain. She whirled to face this new peril and hastily murmured the words that would make her wings pass out of existence.

"Look up, human, before you die," came a cold command.

For once, the queen of Aglarond obeyed.

A pit fiend larger than any she'd ever seen before hung in the red air high above her, flanked by two others. In the distance, flights of erinyes were flapping nearer. A series of smoking explosions occurred on rocks all around as summoned barbed devils appeared. They strode, grinning cruelty at her as they advanced. One of them seemed in distress, convulsing and growing as it came. Its legs lengthened into three serpent tails. Its body became taller and more shapely. . . .

Another column of flame burst into being and roared skyward, ringing the Simbul. Over the lip of the dell in which she stood, a pale, glistening army appeared: a moaning wave of goggle-eyed, shapeless fleshy things. Lemures, the mindless, maggot-like living refuse of Hell. Terror was written on their empty faces, but their eyes held only darkness. They reached with misshapen arms toward her. Whips cracked over them, and abishai overseers peered eagerly at the lone human in the midst of the flames.

Slowly, the Simbul's wings sighed into nothingness. She went to her knees on the hard rocks, crossing her wrists in the gesture of surrender into slavery.

"Well, well," the pit fiend said softly, "this is going to be easier than I'd thought. Stay just as you are, human, while I chain you."

Minute sparks burst into being between the Simbul's wrists, where the metal scales embedded in her skin touched. She'd transformed her bracers into them after destroying Tasnya, and thrust the last few powers of her scorched garments into them. Now it was time to call on their true powers, one of the mightiest magics she'd ever crafted.

The eyes of the queen of Aglarond narrowed. Her magic was dwindling fast, and there were too many foes here to fight. It was time to use the Blood Ring.

She shuddered, her eyes locked pleadingly on the gloating gaze of the pit fiend that descended to her. It lazily shook out the links of a barbed chain crusted in old blood. The Simbul's will bore down on distant creatures . . . and her magic took them.

There was suddenly something in the air in front of the pit fiend. Something spherical and floating that sported a wide, smiling, many-toothed maw, a central eye that was wide with rage and fear, and above this, like a wriggling crown, a writhing forest of eyestalks. The pit fiend stared in amazement, then sneered at what had to be a desperate illusion. No beholders roam free for long in Hell. Many eyes trained their gazes on the winged fiend.

"Very clever, human!" it jeered—just before the eye tyrant's magics reached it. The pit fiend struggled in midair for a moment, caught in those gazes. It stiffened, turning dark . . . and began the slow, stony fall to a shattered death on the rocks below.

It had been only one of many foes. Lemures tumbled and slithered down into the dell. Hamatula stalked to the gaps in the flames. Fiends filled the air.

Other creatures suddenly appeared beside the kneeling sorceress. Two human mages looked around in astonishment and mounting terror and snatched wands from their belts. Neither seemed to see each other or the Simbul, only devils, devils everywhere.

In their midst, the sorceress closed her eyes and bade the beholder strike at the other two pit fiends before she bent all her will to calling one other creatures. Yes: the dragon . . .

It had taken decades of daring and careful acting and pain to craft the Blood Ring. Every creature linked to it had to have some of her blood within it, lingering in some cyst or scar tissue or body fat, thrust there by the Simbul during bloody battle. If she survived this foray into Hell, it might take her centuries to rebuild the ring. Of course, that was a large "if" just now. . . .

Erinyes swooped down thickly. Ravaedrin of the Zhentarim whimpered aloud at the sight. Desperately he shouted a spell that made one of the columns of flame into a geyser of acid. It sprayed in a great plume, dying in a single burst that hissed deafeningly down onto screaming devils.

On the other side of the Simbul, Kaladras Yarlamm of the Red Wizards saw the effects, though not who'd caused them. He abandoned the lightning that he was lashing a fiend with, to do the same to the flames nearest him. Some of the hamatula were only a few strides away, and he'd have to—

Die, screaming, as pit fiend magic sent him staggering into the reach of a barbed devil. It casually tore out his throat and face with one sweep of its talons.

A moment later, a pit fiend burst apart overhead under the magic of the beholder whose eyestalks it was savaging. It vanished too in a swirling cloud of gore and stabbing daggers and shrill shrieks.

The last pit fiend, still writhing from the lightning the Red Wizard had fed it, wheeled in the air and fixed its baleful gaze on the woman kneeling at the heart of the battle. She was the cause of all this tumult in Hell. She was the one they'd been commanded to bring back in chains—or as bloody, dripping fragments. The pit fiend Garauder favored the latter. He sent himself into a dive that would end at her throat.

He never saw the dragon that appeared in the air behind him. It spread jaws and clamped down, sharp fangs shearing away all of Garauder's hates and schemes in blood-drenched oblivion.

Gasping wearily, the Simbul rode the dragon with her will. She bade it smash through the erinyes thrice, then land and roll crushingly over the wounded, shrieking survivors. A hamatula staggered sightlessly past. Lemures squelched and died under the rolling dragon.

The Witch-Queen of Aglarond took stock of her tattered remnants of magic. She was too weak to fight on and survive.

Mystra defend thee, El.

There was no reply to her thought but a pain-laced, feeble flickering—flashing out, just for a moment, from behind a dark, fell awareness. She knew that mind-touch.

Despite herself, tears rose and broke over Alassra Silverhand's iron will.

"Elminster!" she shouted through tears of pain and rage. "Hold on, love! I'll be back!"

The spell that would spin her back out of Avernus took hold. Mystra's strength cleft a road where the spells of mere mages could not.

With her last magic, the Simbul snatched the dragon and the surviving wizard back out of Hell. She returned them whence she'd brought them. They did not deserve to die here, trapped and in torment. They did not deserve Elminster's fate.

HAH! SO MUCH FOR HER LOYALTY—AND YOUR HOPE! YOUR LITTLE BITCH-QUEEN'S GONE, FLED AWAY BACK TO THE LANDS OF BRIGHT DAY, LEAVING HER LITTLE ELMINSTER HERE IN TORMENT.

YOU'RE GOING TO BREAK, MAGE.

YOU'RE GOING TO SHOW ME EVERYTHING YOU KNOW AND REMEMBER, AND BEG ME FOR THE RELEASE OF DEATH. YOU'RE GOING TO PLEAD FOR MY MERCY, PLEAD IN VAIN, KNOWING ALWAYS THAT NEGAL IS YOUR DOOM!

[wild, diabolic laughter]

IN THE MEANTIME, HUMAN, SHOW ME SOME MAGIC—SOMETHING WORTH-WHILE—OR I'LL EAT A LIMB OR TWO OFF YOU RIGHT NOW, KEEPING YOU AWARE AND IN FULL PAIN THROUGHOUT! SHOW ME!

Aye, but this will be a long showing. Ye must be patient and see all, so as to understand what ye're seeing....

YES, YES. I UNDERSTAND ALL TOO WELL THAT AGAIN AND AGAIN YOU'VE TRICKED AND CHEATED ME, PROMISING GREAT REVELATIONS OF WHERE MAGIC IS HIDDEN AND HOW TO CAST THIS OR UNLEASH THAT ... ONLY TO SHOW ME ALL SORTS OF ROMANCE AND MORAL PREACHING AND OTHER USE-LESS DROSS. GIVE ME MAGIC, AND LIVE—CHEAT ME AGAIN, AND DIE. SIMPLE ENOUGH?

Indeed. Let us begin, then, when night comes to Tamaeril.

WHENEVER. JUST CHOOSE THE RIGHT ROAD FOR ONCE, MAGE: YOUR MOST RECENT MEANINGFUL MEETING WITH MYSTRA, REMEMBER. IT'S YOUR LAST CHANCE.

[images spiraling, flashing up to spread glory before the mind's eye]

The little pattern of twinkling lights shifted to hang beside his right cheek. "I confess you make me more than a little uncomfortable, Elminster," Mystra said.

"I can tell," the Old Mage said, not slowing in his magical flight. "Please, Lady, set aside all hesitancy. Have no worry for my emotions—speak freely. Ye cannot offend me."

The rushing lights drifted a little nearer and seemed to sigh. "Well, then. You are the lover of she who held this name and power before me. She intended you to be my guide and teacher, and you have been. Admirably. The proud, willful, and empty-headed Midnight is no more."

The lights were all around his head now, brushing his skin with what felt like dozens of soft, swift caresses. "Yet—you trouble me, awe me . . . frighten me. Repel me, a little. I've little desire to shape a body and join with you, as she often did. I've done it, yes, but behind the thrill is the feeling of her watching me and judging. *Your* watching me and judging. Elminster, old and wise in her service and with her memories.

"The old ways awaken a restlessness in me. The Weave stirs, and other magic crawls around and within Toril. I am not the old Mystra. I am . . . humbled by what you have done for me and for she who came before me—and when you seem in danger, she awakes within me, and I desire you and rush to protect you and hold you more precious than all others. I want you always to be my trusted servant—more than that, my friend. Yet I can see how twisted you've become in the service of Mystra, down the centuries. Trust in you comes hard to me. It would be easier, I think, if I stripped away all of the great secrets you hold, all the memories of my power. No one else could learn them from you in time to come, and I'd not feel you were judging me disapprovingly. I—I must do this."

There was silence for a moment, but for the wind whistling past. She spoke again, as anxious as a mother who knows her words wound a favored child. "How does hearing this make you feel?"

Elminster stared into the night sky ahead of him and said, "A little sad. Relieved more than that. Not angry, nor unwilling. I swore to serve Mystra long, long ago when I could have become king in Athalantar. I am nothing if I break my oath. I have had centuries more to taste and smell and see and do than most humans, and regret none of it. If your need or even whim snuffs out my existence in a moment, or changes me to a stone to spend the centuries to come, I am content. If taking memories gladdens you, it pleases me to yield them. I will do whatever you desire, eagerly, and with love."

He smiled. "So do your best to me, Lady. You always have."

He'd never heard a swarm of enchanted motes of light weep before, but then, most wizards never do.

Twenty

PRAYERS AND PLOTS

Nergal the Mighty was not happy. He restlessly prowled the shadows under his favorite overhang, wondering what fancy-dance his human mind-slave was leading him on *this* time. The goddess told him she would pillage his mind of everything useful to greedy archdevils? What good was that?

But then, what good were wrinkled old noblewomen being stabbed in the human city of Waterdeep? How much useful magic had he gained?

A good distance across Avernus, he'd spell-snatched the wizard away from that cavern. He didn't want an army to find him—or even Malachlabra, who'd escaped by the very graze of a horn.

Elminster was free again, to stumble where he willed—which seemed, right now, to be down some steep, rocky hillside. He seemed to be healing himself again, and Nergal was keeping a sharp watch over him. For all his pretended weakness and helplessness, the human was calling on his silver fire in some way Nergal couldn't catch him at.

Two abishai sprang up from a rift, snatched a passing spinagon out of his flapping flight, and tore him apart. With a yawn, the outcast turned away to stride along the overhang one more time.

The maddening little mage was leading Nergal on another lengthy mind chase. Useful magic, my left smoking buttock! This time, however, he'd follow the trail of memories to the end as doggedly as any Hell hound, surprising the Old Mage and perhaps, just perhaps, breaking the human's mind at last. He might as well; his attempts to search the wizard's mind without Elminster as a guide had failed utterly. Humans had minds like cesspits.

*   *   *   *   *

Stars twinkled softly and endlessly on the ceiling above her; his creations, of course. Another spell she'd meant to ask him about, and never remembered to. Another magic and secret that'd be lost forever with him if he perished.

Lying alone on the round bed in the topmost room of Elminster's Tower in Shadowdale, the Simbul stared unhappily up at the stars so close above her until they melted and glimmered in a fresh flood of tears.

"Mystra," she whispered into the darkness, "preserve him! Oh, goddess, if you love me—!"

Somehow she'd moved from the table to her knees on the hard floor beside it, worn fur rugs thrust out of the way against the wall. Two old, thick candle stubs stood here, stuck to the floor by their own melted, puddled wax . . . evidence of a long-ago prayer to Mystra. Elminster must have knelt naked between them just as she was doing now to make his plea to the goddess.

Sobbing, Alassra Silverhand made fresh use of the candles. She lit them by the smallest of cantrips and by the fire of her will. As their flames rose up, she held herself so that her tears dripped into each flame, and then said fiercely, "Mother Mystra, Lady over and of all who work magic, hear my prayer, I beg of you. I will do anything you command—anything, yielding my life, my magic, my realm, my health or looks or wits, *anything*, if you'll give me magic enough now to rescue my Elminster. Oh, Mystra, hear me!"

Suddenly, without a sound or a trace of smoke, the candles both went out. The fine hair all over the Simbul's body stood on end as sudden power awakened within her and flowed through her. The only light in the darkness was a flickering blue flame—coming from her own mouth. Her breath was afire.

Warrior of the Seven, the voice of Mystra said out of the darkness all around her, *I am here, and heed your cry. Hearken to what we both must do. . . .*

*   *   *   *   *

Something moved ahead, among rocks and stunted trees. Their boughs had been broken off repeatedly by passing devils for moments of sport, and they bristled with thorns.

Elminster was whole again, though he took care to shuffle along slowly, hunched over, and slump into motionlessness whenever a devil flew past. He was somewhere on Avernus, he knew not where—but it was far from any of the gates out of Hell he knew of. Almost all of them were in large, closely guarded fortresses. Of the two out in the desolation of Avernus, one was behind a bloodfall—a waterfall of blood, somewhere in Arlkan's Rift—and the other was atop Tabira's Spire, where of old an erinyes had been impaled for disobedience and died pleading for mercy. Her bones still clung to the shunned rock, and the gate out worked only for someone touching one of them and saying the right words.

At least he remembered *those.* Now all he had to do, naked and bereft of spells, was find the bloodfall or the spire, elude whatever guardians or malicious wandering devils saw him, and—

Something moved again in the rocks ahead. It might have been a woman—if human women had been twelve feet tall, ruby-skinned, and had horses' heads instead of breasts. Those strange-looking appendages snapped their teeth at him as their owner stepped out to block his way. Her shapely legs ended in cloven hooves, a slender barbed tail curling in her wake. Her bat wings folded into a huge single sail of flesh rising high above her head. That head looked human except for the delicate fangs and pupilless eyes like two white flames.

Her voice was low and husky as she raised her arms in warning— arms that sported rows of cruel barbs—and asked sharply, "Who—no, *what* are you?"

"What I appear to be," El answered her. "A human."

An eyebrow lifted, and a slender, barbed tongue licked those dainty fangs eloquently.

"No," the Old Mage told her, gathering silver fire within him in case he'd need it very soon and very swiftly, "ye don't want to do that. I am—I belong to Nergal, and any attack on me will draw him to this place. That's not worth a few mouthfuls of raw, tasteless human."

His captor's name had evoked a hiss. The she-devil drew back between the rocks once more.

El went on down the hillside and was two steps past the rocks when the outcast devil's voice came again. "You have no magic?"

Elminster turned around slowly, and spread his empty arms. "No. Do I look as if I do?"

"I am *so* hungry," the voice came back plaintively. "Nergal will just have to get over your loss."

And the devil sprang.

El sat down abruptly, feet together, then sprang off to one side in a frog-like hop. The pouncing devil crashed onto the rocks beyond and skidded to a spitting, snarling halt.

The hillside was steep and bare. The only cover was the cluster of rocks and thorn-trees where the devil had been. Grimly El leaped and trotted toward it. Wings clapped behind him, and he sprang to one side again, dodging around a sparlike boulder.

The she-devil hissed close by his ear as she passed by again, missing with her reaching hands. "Stay still, human, and I'll make your death less painful!"

"Now *that's* an enticing offer," Elminster replied mockingly, spinning away from another grab. "Almost had me with that one!"

Snarling, the she-devil bounded into the air and glided after him. He ducked into the devil's lair—a dark cleft between the rocks where the floor was littered with old, gnawed bones. Tumbled rocks formed a roof of sorts. Once he was inside, and she followed, there'd doubtless be no way out that her body wasn't blocking.

On he went, into stinking darkness.

With a little laugh of triumph the outcast devil folded her wings and followed. "Now you're mine," she breathed.

El had backed as far in as the narrowing rocks would let him. The only light came from the white flames of her eyes. The horse heads of her bosom snapped at him as she advanced, arms spread wide to prevent his escape.

"To raise a very original question," El said calmly, "Who and what are *ye?*"

"Marane is my name," she said, drawing closer. "Marane the Hungry!"

Elminster tensed, bending low. He had to unleash silver fire fleetingly, when a spell-scrying Nergal wouldn't be able to get a good look at what he was doing, so their bodies had to be pressed almost together. Somehow he had to avoid those fangs above, and those snapping jaws lower down. A stone rolled under his foot, and he stumbled and almost fell.

Marane hissed again, but no jaws closed on him.

El looked up—and saw faint glows above and behind him. They illuminated the body of the outcast devil, as she arched over him to reach the stone and set it back in place.

"What're those lights?" he asked, feigning wonder, as he ducked low and turned so his shoulder brushed against a shapely devil leg.

"Things of magic," she snapped, "seized from other prey down the years. A pity you carry nothing to add to it. But *enough*."

Marane turned then, extending a long-nailed hand like a claw right at his eyes—

El thrust his hand up along her leg and gave her silver fire.

"Quite so," he agreed coolly, as her entire body convulsed and sprang upward, smashing her head on the rocks overhead.

Smoke curled out of Marane's mouth. She tumbled limply to the floor, and her eyes went dull. Something moved in Elminster's mind, and he kept the image of Marane's reaching talons vivid in his thoughts. Trying not to think or look at what he was doing, he clawed blindly at the stone until he felt it roll. He thrust his hand in amid the cold glows beyond.

Something among them felt like a wand. He snatched it, let its fading enchantment tell him its triggering word and nature—a lightning-wand, thank Mystra and Tymora both—thrust it into Marane's gaping mouth, gathered silver fire to keep himself alive if need be, and activated it.

Blue-white fire howled around the tiny lair. Diabolic limbs flailed bruisingly as the reek of cooked devil-flesh rose strongly to take hold of his throat. Marane slumped and began to shrivel.

HO, HO! MAGIC! MUST HAVE IT!

Nergal's mind bellow was almost deafening. El smiled grimly and raked through the magic with both hands, letting the chaos of command words and purposes and powers wash over him as he sought something—anything—useful.

Rings that spat fire, wands that melted flesh, bracers that—wait! *This!*

With shaking hands El plucked it forth and held it, just for a moment. He set up a snarl of silver fire in his mind so that Nergal wouldn't be able to read his thoughts. Yes, this would do admirably—a scepter only as long as his hand, dark and finely made. Netherese—crafted, in fact, by Shadow Master Telamont Tanthul long, long ago. It could make two hands, or three, or six, out of one. Three hands, or three hearts, or three legs, as desired, but only bone and blood and flesh. A way of whelming armies or healing the maimed . . .

Hurriedly he raced out of the lair, keeping his mind full of fire, and hid the tiny scepter under a stone near a certain tree. Then he retreated to the lair, stumbling dazedly around amid the magic and staring at Marane's dainty fangs.

With an excited growl, Nergal crashed to the ground outside.

El let the fire fall and sent forth his thoughts in a feigned fury of excitement. *These should be enough! Just let old Nergal set foot in here, and I'll blast him to ashes! Why, there's not a devil in Avernus that can stand against these, now that I've poured all my silver fire into them! I can—oh, gods!*

Tall and terrible, Nergal loomed in the cleft and sent a forest of flailing tentacles stabbing into the darkness. In a trice Elminster was battered against stone, shoved along it, slapped nearly senseless, and then snatched out into the light again, blinded and strangling in the grip of a tight-clenched tentacle, while clinks and rattles told him Nergal was gathering magic in a frenzy.

I COULD CRUSH YOUR SKULL LIKE A ROTTEN FRUIT, MAN. GIVE ME ONE GOOD REASON WHY I SHOULD NOT.

The silver fire will explode out of me and slay thee too.

DON'T Y—EH? IT WOULD?

Aye. Best leave my head and neck alone.

So I SHALL, Nergal agreed savagely, twisting and wrenching.

Only silver fire kept Elminster from fainting at the sickening pain. Dimly he was aware that the devil had torn away both of his arms at his elbows, leaving jagged, dripping stumps of broken bone.

He called on the fire to give him strength, and feigned a mad frenzy, keening as he rose and kicked out and flailed away with his arms. He leaked enough silver fire that Nergal hissed in pain and flinched away. El grimly thrust the stumps of his arms into the outcast devil's wounds, like a child stabbing with a stick in blind rage and utter futility.

After a moment, Nergal chuckled harshly and dealt Elminster a blow that sent him spinning away to crash down on distant rocks. Pain made him bound up again in shrieking spasms. "Stupid wizard."

Behind silver fire, El thought, *Stupid devil. I thrust my broken arms deep into you, and left bone chips behind. Deep inside, beneath thy healings. It may not be Alassra's Blood Ring, but 'twill do. Ye'll see.* He let the fire fade again—and was almost deafened by Nergal's mind-voice, crashing in.

AGAIN YOU WHISPER TO YOURSELF OF YOUR OWN CLEVERNESS! ENOUGH! THIS MEMORY OF YOURS, AND THIS, AND THIS ONE, TOO, SHOW ME WHAT TO CAST, TO KEEP YOU ALIVE—HAH! THUS!—SO I CAN DO THIS!

[tentacles stabbing out, slapping around arching torso, and then wrenching . . . flesh tearing wetly . . .]

[scream, ripping agony *No devil no devil agghh gods please* no!] *THAT'S RIGHT, PLEAD! GO ON! PLEAD, AND I'LL IGNORE YOU! HAHAHAA!*

[diabolic laughter, roars of rage and glee, tentacles shredding and flailing, pulping what little is left]

A tall devil that once more wore the shape of a pit fiend stood glowering down at the seared, feebly crawling pieces of what had once been a man. With a reluctant snarl, Nergal sent forth tentacles to gather up quivering flesh and heal, knitting it to neighboring flesh. He slowly reassembled a limp, broken body.

LIVE AGAIN, FOOLISH WIZARD. ALMOST I TORE YOU APART FOR GOOD—BUT YOU ARE A TOY I HAVE, AND OTHER DEVILS DO NOT. MOREOVER, YOU ARE AT LEAST . . . INTERESTING.

I KNOW WHAT YOU'RE DOING. TIME AND AGAIN, TURNING ME SKILLFULLY ASIDE AMID YOUR SHADOWS, REVEALING WHAT IS UNIMPORTANT AND HIDING FROM ME WHAT I SEEK.

THAT'S OVER NOW. I SHALL BEAR DOWN AND SHRED YOUR MIND WHENEVER YOU TRY TO DO THAT TO ME AGAIN. I HAVE MOST OF YOUR SPELLS NOW—YOU CANNOT RESIST ME. THIS TIME I SEEK MEMORIES OF YOUR USING POWER OVER IMPORTANT FOLK OF YOUR REALMS—NOT MAGES THIS TIME, BUT THOSE WHO RULE AND WHO ARE HEARD WHEN THEY SPEAK. [snort] *UNLIKE ME.*

[mindworm, spiraling down, down, down . . .]

"Interesting," the Srinshee said gently, her fingertips tracing the line of his chin. "Most of my Cormanthan kin fear the ridicule of their peers more than anything else, and loss of wealth and magical power after that. You fear failing your friends and losing them to death. You are both older in your wisdom than most elves of this city and more tragic. You've already lost more friends and kin than the younglings of Cormanthor; only we elders have known the weight of tears you bear. Yet there is something more in you—a backbone of power, always there, always warming you against the storms of life."

Her hand went to the crotch of the elaborate filigreed gown she wore, and drew a tiny dagger from a sheath there. Eyes on his, she murmured, "Forgive me. This is no attack, but I must know." Choosing a spot on the outside of his forearm, she gently drew the gleaming knife along his skin. Blood welled forth, and then—a few sparks.

The Srinshee breathed something, reaching with a finger. The silver radiance that burst from him sent her staggering back with a little cry, wreathed in flames.

Elminster spun away, clapping his hand over the wound she'd made and stammering apologies.

Weakly, from among rising tendrils of smoke and the ruins of her garments, the Srinshee replied, "Nay, man, the fault was mine. I worked the spell that tried to steal silver fire from the wound I'd made in you. Mystra is even stronger in you than I'd thought."

THAT'S ALL? AND YOU WHIRL IT AWAY FROM ME LIKE THAT? WHAT IF I JUST SNATCH SOMETHING OUT OF YOUR MEMORIES THUS? NO, DON'T SCREAM. YOU BROUGHT THIS ON YOURSELF! LET'S SEE WHAT WE HAVE HERE. . . .

Elminster looked up from his book, frowning. What befell—?

A mote of light grew in the air. . . .

He sprang up, tossing his tome aside and snatching his newest, most powerful warding wand.

The light was almost his own height now, and blinding bright. Golden, it was, and somehow come out of nothingness right through his defenses! What could—

The light was coming from a blade. Slender, beautiful—an enchanted elf blade, held aloft in a slender arm . . . the Srinshee!

"Auluua!" Elminster cried, his wand crackling in his hand—just in case. "Is it you?"

The tiny elf-maid smiled at him, though her face was sad and shadowed. "Only you call me that, El. Ah, but 'tis good to hear it again!"

She let go the sword and ran to him, leaving it floating upright in the air behind her. Golden radiance curled down like smoke from its point.

El frowned at it. "Is that the Ruling Blade?"

And then she was in his arms, looking up at him with unshed tears glimmering in her eyes, and he forgot all about swords and magic. "Hold me," she said, her voice teetering on the edge of tears, "and—kiss me! Kiss me, damn you and Mystra and all proud elves and doom, doom everywhere!"

She was weeping when he bent down and put his lips to hers, and as he lifted her in his arms her mouth was fierce and demanding, and her tiny hands as tight as claws on his arms and shoulders. Their minds met, hers like a dark sea lashed by storms, all despair and need, and his wondering and warming and wanting to soothe. . . .

There was blood in his mouth from where she'd bitten him. The Srinshee threw back her head, shuddering, and hissed, "Listen to me. Listen, for haste rides me and goddesses other than yours. Fell magic may well follow swift at my back!"

El grinned. "Ye always did lead an interesting life of plots and secrets. I hear. Speak!"

With a wild smile, she dealt him a slap. Her dark mood broken, she murmured into his ear, "I must disappear for a time—perhaps a very long time. You will probably never see me again, or hold me thus. Know this: Mystra has granted me a boon. I'll always be able to speak to you through the silver fire. Listen when it sings, and call to me, and I'll be there. Now kiss me again, damn you! It may be the last kiss I'll ever—"

[slap]

[confused chaos of images dying away, mirror-shattered and going dim]

SO THIS IS THE LITTLE SECRET YOU'VE BEEN HIDING FROM ME! YOU'VE BEEN TALKING TO HER ALL ALONG, HAVEN'T YOU? CALLING YOUR FRIENDS TO HELL AGAINST ME, SOME DOUBTLESS WORKING SLY SCHEMES WHILE THE MOST RASH AND STUPID TRIED TO CHARGE THROUGH ALL AVERNUS TO GET TO ME! THEY'RE AT WORK RIGHT NOW, AREN'T THEY? HUMAN WORM!

No, Lord Nergal! Hear me: I can no longer speak to the Srinshee!

[suspicious glare]

Look, here. Truth, see?

OH. SHE DIED, EH?

I know not. We did speak, back and forth, when each of us very lonely, for years ... centuries. Until the Godsfall, when Mystra thrust her power upon me. A lot of things were burnt out inside me, then ... and this was one of them. Unless the Srinshee comes to me, and works some magic beyond my skills, I've no way of speaking to her again.

ALMOST I PITY YOU, HUMAN. ALMOST.

[bewilderment, flare of anger ... giving way to utter puzzlement]

NOW, WHY DID I SAY THAT? WHY DID I FEEL THAT?

[smiling silence]

NO, ELMINSTER, I'M NOT BECOMING WEAK AND SENTIMENTAL. KISS SOMEONE ELSE. IT'S MAGE-LORE I'M AFTER. THOUGHTS AND MEMORIES I CAN USE IN HELL, AND YOU KNOW IT. SHOW ME MORE!

Of course. That's just what I've been doing: showing ye magic, its uses and effects.

BAH! YOU SPLIT HAIRS EVEN MORE FINELY THAN AMNIZU! HUMAN, YOU DISGUST ME!

Another achievement to be proud of. I'm collecting them.

*WHAT PRICE YOUR COLLECTION, SMART-TONGUED MORTAL, IF YOU CAN REMEM-
BER NOTHING OF SUCH ACHIEVEMENTS—OR ANYTHING AT ALL? I'LL HAVE EVERY-
THING SOON ENOUGH ... LEAVING MIGHTY ELMINSTER TO DROOL AT NOTHING ALL
THE REST OF HIS DAYS.*

Threats. [mental sigh] *That reminds me of something. . . .*

[mental shimmering, memories flashing past to a certain moment,
glow found and chosen]

"Halueve Starym," the man in black snapped crisply, "is this wise?"

The elf with three crackling braziers floating in midair before him
turned, eyes flashing with anger, and sneered, "Ah! The human who
doomed fair Cormanthor! Speak not to me of wisdom, Slayer of the Fair!"

"Well, then," Elminster Aumar said mildly, striding forward, "let
me speak of folly—yours. Anyone is a fool who thinks to enspell
devils to do his bidding . . . and truly be their master."

CALLING UP THE FIRES OF HELL, HMMM? IT'S BEEN DONE BEFORE, YOU KNOW.

Aye. And since.

ON, WIZARD!

Halueve Starym's sneer broadened into a snarl. "Speak not to me
of folly, human!" he spat. "Get you gone while you still have legs to
carry you! I can send devils to your bed to peel the skin right off
you, a limb at a time!" He acquired a soft, evil smile, and added
tauntingly, "And you have to sleep, you know . . . weak, puny, meddling human." Although he'd not appeared to lift a finger in spell
weaving, a line of leaping flames raced between the two wizards,
circling Halueve Starym. "Begone, Elminster. You are so weak in
your Art that I can smash you at will—and if you annoy me further,
I'll shatter you now. Go, while still I show mercy!"

Power roiled unbidden within Elminster, and silver sparks danced
briefly before his eyes. He stiffened.

*Flee not, El. He's released a ready magic that seeks to feed on you,
eating flesh and blood and mind together. Simply stand and do
nothing but defend yourself with your own spells . . . and the silver
fire will be his undoing. 'Ware you the right-most brazier; it is a
watching devil.*

Auluua! Elminster's heart leaped. *Are you still there?*

Barely. [smile] *Have this kiss, ere I fade. . . .*

Warmth surged through him, and a feeling as of sweet water and a gentle breeze, summer sunlight, and caresses of spell power. . . .

The slaying spell that struck him jolted him out of pleasantness. It washed over his shielding magic, tearing it to shreds.

El gave the Starym mage a wintry smile. "My, my, my," he said mockingly. "Fling flang floom, and I'm still here. I guess thy spells aren't quite as puissant as all that. Perhaps ye deceive Halueve Starym even more than ye do Elminster Aumar. Drained enough from me yet?"

The elf shrieked in fury and raised his hands like claws, hurling forth a spell whose use was foolish even when spell-armored for battle. The room cracked and rocked even before Elminster's blood was drawn.

Silver fire flared forth to bring real doom to Halueve Starym. Elminster made sure the first bolt he could shape destroyed the right-most brazier, and was rewarded, as the keep began to fall apart around him, with a long, harsh, and despairing cry. . . .

NOW, THIS, LITTLE, MAN, AT LEAST TAKES ME TO YOUR YOUTH AND BRUSHES WITH MAGIC . . . AND I THINK I SEE, CLOSE TO MYSTRA. YOU'RE NOT AFRAID TO SLAY DEVILS, I SEE.

After my first few centuries, Lord Nergal, I used up most of my fear. These days, I have almost none of it left.

WE'LL SEE ABOUT THAT, HUMAN. OH, YES, WE'LL CERTAINLY SEE ABOUT THAT.

Twenty-One

REVENGE EATEN HOT

It so happened that a band of adventurers entered the dark, echoing chamber deep in Undermountain before the madness passed. They took one good torchlit look at the man barking and whimpering alone in the middle of that vast, bare stone floor and fled, as swiftly and as silently as they knew how.

Halaster had called on all of Mystra's vested power to heal the great wound that should have slain him. That terrible, impaling bone spike had pierced and crushed all of his innards. Worse, Nergal had laced his spells with a curse. The lord of Undermountain lived, but had no magic to gainsay Nergal's cruelty. A day, perhaps, or more, had passed as he wallowed on the cold, dusty stone, helpless to stop the sickening rise and fall of the changes that passed over his body. Bat wings, scales, tails and talons sprouted and faded, receded and flowed, unchastened by the cries and curses of the writhing mage.

Spines and horns and breasts thrust forth, curled, and then cruised along his body like ripples across water. In the heart of the agonizing chaos Halaster vowed to return to the Nine Hells. He would visit torment on the devil Nergal even if he died in trying, Elminster or no Elminster.

At long last it ended. Halaster Blackcloak lay panting and drenched with sweat. He stared up into dusty darkness. The rags of his shredded robes clung to him.

"Revenge," he announced calmly, as he forced his last shudders into oblivion, "will now commence."

He did not, however, move for a long time, even when the cold made him shiver. He lay still, remembering every last detail of Nergal's movements, words, and reactions, the archdevil's precise appearance . . . and what spells would make the best weapons against such a one.

Just as patiently, he recalled the drawbacks and precise effects of each suitable spell and his best tactics for using them in Avernus. At length, he smiled coldly and told the darkness, "It seems Halaster Blackcloak would make a good devil himself."

The smile slowly faded from his face, and he said more gently, "Lady Mystra, I have need of your aid. This task I would do for you has proven beyond my present mastery. May we speak?"

The stone floor beneath him grew warm. A tingling arose within him. He was suddenly no longer sweating or soiled, but whole and strong and alert. It felt almost as if warm, motherly arms wrapped around him.

Halaster Blackcloak did something he'd not done for centuries: He purred, shifted contentedly onto his side in a curled-up position, and drifted off to sleep.

In the warm, forgotten time thereafter, he dreamed that he suckled a motherly breast, that he explained his needs and revealed his thinking. He received in return the spells he needed and the wise advice of a battle master among wizards. . . . At one point he floated on his back through an endless array of lit candles that sprouted out of nothingness. Their flames warmed him but did not burn . . .

Halaster Blackcloak suddenly found himself standing in a room he rarely visited, deep in Undermountain: a chapel consecrated to Mystra. He was awake and alone. The flames of two candles burned above the bare stone altar he faced. No candles fueled those wisps of fire. He felt strong. Magic moved like raging fire within him, more than he'd ever felt before. All the spells he'd thought about were ready in his mind, and more besides, some completely unfamiliar and fascinating. He wore simple robes of black, and boots and a belt to match. All of them were unadorned, yet of the finest make and perfect fit. His flesh was bare of all rings and markings and adornments. Someone had trimmed his beard.

"Lady," he told the altar, "have my thanks. Thy will be done."

He turned from the altar and took nine paces. He reached a place beyond the consecration, intending to weave a spell flight to Hell.

The moment he thought of his destination in Avernus, his spell yet uncast, the world became blue-white around Halaster. He felt as if he were falling endlessly, though he could see nothing around him to show him for sure. When the blue mist fell away, he was standing on empty air a hand's width above rough black stone, in a place of tortured rock and squalling spinagons, beneath a blood-red sky. He stepped down into Avernus, and never saw or heard the ghostlike wisp that had come from the altar flames to Hell with him.

It wavered a little, as yet invisible, holding far more rage than he. The Witch-Queen of Aglarond had gone to Hell again.

* * * * *

A broken man wandered aimlessly amid the stone fields of Avernus. Gore dripped from the shattered stumps of his arms. He stumbled from time to time—and during those moments, black and red flames gouted from his eyes. Spinagons and abishai alike shrank from him and flew away. Even the slithering lemures and maggots hesitated to approach.

Sometimes his lips fell open, and he muttered echoes of the great mind-voice crashing in his head. Other times he grunted and squealed like a hog or made little birdlike trills. The lesser and least devils kept well clear. They had no wish to share in the torment of another.

The trudging husk of Elminster returned to a place of rocks and trees where Nergal had gnawed the dripping bones of Marane and dashed his mind-slave repeatedly against rocks. Slowly and with infinite subtlety, the silver fire within him rose, clouding, making memories swirl like dry fallen leaves spun by a breeze. The devil riding him plunged into those memories with roars of excitement . . . and never saw the moment when Elminster lifted a stone, plucked out what was waiting beneath it—and thrust it through the long, matted hair above his left ear.

Its weight rode there, solid and reassuring. Again he rose, wandering in apparent aimlessness, having regained the magic item he'd hidden earlier. Netherese, the work of the Shadow Master Telamont Tanthul, able to unleash a multiple clone spell to "grow" bodies simultaneously from one body part or relic—and so whelm armies.

Elminster put those thoughts firmly away again before a cloak of silver fire and let Nergal gloat at the length and vivid depths of the memory trail he'd been following through Elminster's mind.

AH, LITTLE HUMAN, BUT WE MUST BE CLOSE TO SOMETHING WORTHWHILE AT LAST. I CAN FEEL IT, AS IF YOUR PRECIOUS SILVER FIRE IS SURGING IN YOU! YES! ONWARD—SHOW ME MORE!

* * * * *

"Dread Lord Geryon," the youngest and most ambitious of his pit fiends murmured, pointing at a shimmer on a distant, rock-studded hillside, "there."

The Overduke smiled, though the dark helm he wore showed the company of devils only the tiniest curve of his lips. "Thank you, Albitur. The first assault is yours." A massive barbed tail twitched.

Some of the gathered pit fiends drew back half a stealthy pace. Geryon was excited or angry—and for those desiring to survive, it didn't really matter which.

At least the orders the Lord of Nessus had given them hadn't meant a wait of years . . . or an eternity. Great Asmodeus had said this Halaster would return soon, armed with power enough from his goddess to be a threat to Hell. As always, but more so this time than most, the Lord Asmodeus had been right.

Albitur took wing like a dark storm, gathering the cornugons and pit fiends of his command as he went. Across a deep cavern of poisonous smoke they flew, to sweep over a ridge where rock pinnacles stood like fangs. They glided down in a deadly dive at the lone human figure, silent but for the wind whistling through their wings.

Forty devils and more against one, but no one standing with Geryon laughed or made wagers. How many, in the measure of fiends, is the aid of a goddess?

The human saw death coming. He lifted his hands to trace gestures in the air.

Devils swept down, and bolts of lightning stabbed forth from them. On the rocks around the lone wizard, flames roared. Devils conjured walls of fire.

The air above the pit fiends was suddenly full of head-sized, plummeting rocks. The rain of stone battered the devils to crash brokenly below. A stone crushed the skull of a hapless cornugon, leaving nothing but a smudge of blood atop its neck.

Halaster swayed in the heart of the devil-hurled lightning. The spasms seemed to invigorate rather than harm him.

Devils swept down with barbed whips snapping and flailing. They flew into a cloud of little silver hands that snatched and gouged and choked and punched, searing diabolic flesh.

Blinded pit fiends fell screaming to the stones. They rolled and thrashed in agony, arousing maggots to swarm over the rocks.

Fires leaped up all around the wizard. One eruption tumbled Halaster onto his face. Through the flames swept rippling-muscled pit fiends and cornugons, plying their whips so vigorously that more than once they entangled each other and were forced to break from the tightening fray. Punching and raking and kicking, they swarmed the wizard. Red and black flesh hiding him from view.

"They must be almost done tearing him apart," muttered a pit fiend beside Lord Geryon.

Even before the Wild Beast's hairy hand swept up in a rebuking gesture, there was a flash of blinding silver light from the struggling knot below. Those few devils who weren't hurled shrieking across the sky toppled on their backs, ashen husks silent forever.

"Qarlegon," the Overduke said calmly.

The named pit fiend bounded into the sky like a hound off its leash. His cornugons sprung up from the rocks around to follow.

More than sixty strong was this second force. It swept down on Halaster from all sides, in a slowly settling net. Its commander hovered, gesturing this way and that.

Halaster looked up at the fiends approaching so carefully—and unleashed chain lightning among them. It fizzled and died, failing before the magic-quelling nature of the fiends.

Qarlegon's hand swept down, and in unison the fiends dropped.

The human wizard frantically worked spells as the devils descended, but Geryon and all the pit fiends winced long before Halaster could have unleashed anything. The very air around them trembled momentarily. Their horns and ears and fingertips tingled.

"What was *that?*" a devil exclaimed, shuddering his way back onto his rocky perch.

"Truly mighty magic," an old, scarred pit fiend said unnecessarily. "Belike the hand of Lord Asmodeus himself."

Some of the more junior devils bowed their heads and made warding signs at the utterance of that name. Most stared narrowly down at the human wizard and frowned.

"Not from him," one of them muttered, and others nodded.

The pounce this time was a single, united thrust of flailing and jabbing. Then all drew back to leave Halaster bloodied and staggering. They converged again, so he could not help but be overwhelmed.

When the devils drew back again, the human swayed, one arm dangling torn and useless from its shoulder. There were chuckles at his sudden barks and capering.

The third charge provoked a burst of silver fire. It was more feeble this time. Only half a dozen devils fell headless and dead. Twice that number were hurled away or fled shrieking. The fourth charge closed over Halaster, and he did not rise again.

The fiends standing with Geryon were just beginning to relax when a sudden flood of blue-white lightning washed over the melee. Devils erupted in struggling agony. They took wing in a flurry of agonized flaps, roars, and groans—only to be transfixed by bolt after bolt of leaping lightning. In seconds, two dozen devils fell.

"Who—?" a pit fiend gasped.

"Find out," Geryon snapped. "Perstur, Agamur!"

Obediently, those pit fiends surged into the sky. They flew with swift swoops rather than a straight run toward this new, half-seen foe. A lightning cloud hid whomever it was from view. The cloud reached forth crackling fingers to lift the arching, howling, broken body of the human mage tenderly into the air. White light blossomed around Halaster Blackcloak, flaring to a brilliance that made all of them turn their heads away. When it faded, the floating wizard was gone.

"Could it be that goddess again?" one of the pit fiends rumbled disbelievingly.

The lightning cloud retreated a little, and Qarlegon's force advanced warily to encircle it. Whoever or whatever this newcomer was, it was now cloaked in an upright oval of blue fire. It didn't seem to want to be encircled.

"That's a shape I've seen Mystra of Toril use," the old, scarred pit fiend growled.

Thrice the nimbus winked or leaped backward, out of the forming ring of devils. Thrice they inexorably moved to encircle it again, backing it up the hillside to where pinnacles swept up like blades into the blood-red sky and a little gorge ran up to a cave mouth.

"That's the lair that used to be Barbathra's, yes?" a pit fiend asked. The old, scarred fiend and Geryon nodded in unison. It was the Wild Beast who added, "Yarsabras uses it now."

As if the Overduke's words had been a cue, the hound-headed outcast devil he'd named burst from the cave with his many claws extended. His talons formed a wall of glittering blades.

The mysterious intruder ducked suddenly, with a smooth grace that reminded the watching fiends of elven dancers.

Yarsabras sailed on helplessly into the line of advancing devils, to crash and flail and be flailed. At the best of times, loyal hornheads had little love for outcasts—and this was assuredly not the best of times. The fire-shrouded intruder bobbed upright again to send lightning crackling and spitting among the advancing devils.

"That's a she," the old pit fiend said suddenly, catching a glimpse of hands raised to weave a spell.

Geryon nodded. "Your eyes were ever keen, Grimvold," he said approvingly. "Goddess or mortal?"

The scarred old pit fiend frowned. "Mortal, I think. She stays low, where the divine tend to tower high and look down."

The Wild Beast nodded again.

"Strange," another of the pit fiends watching from the height said suddenly. "Earlier she struck to slay—bolts that transfixed individual loyals, of her choosing. Now she tries to hold Qarlegon's flight at bay. Why?"

There were puzzled nods and frowns.

Someone asked, "Could she be opening a gate?"

"That's why we're here," Geryon told them calmly. "If I give the order, we're all to call in all we can, and whelm a host, to seize and destroy any such portal."

"No!" Grimvold snarled suddenly. He wove a spell right at the Overduke's elbow.

Several pit fiends shrank away, expecting Geryon to lash out with deadly force to punish this impertinence. The Wild Beast did nothing. The scarred old fiend shouted, his farspeaking spell making his voice oddly echoing and distant, "Qarlegon! Move your loyals! Move toward the gorge—now! Move or *die!*"

"What by all the fires of Nessus—?" one pit fiend cried angrily. "Who do you think you are, Old Scarred-Horns?"

"Why?" another asked simply, as the pit fiends below looked up in bewilderment. Qarlegon rose over them, peering quizzically.

"Look you all," Grimvold said grimly, jerking a talon at the horizon. "That."

They scarce had time to look before it whirled out of the sky at them—or rather, at the devils massed on the hillside.

It was huge, tumbling up from far across Avernus. Large and dark, the fist of stone had been a crag or mountaintop torn from its roots. The gigantic boulder turned slightly as it rushed at the hillside.

"Fires above," one of the pit fiends gasped in awe. "It's going to—"

"*That* was the magic we felt earlier," Geryon said quietly. He put one huge, hairy hand on Grimvold's shoulder. "You warned them," he added with a sigh.

The crash of the great stone shook Avernus so badly that they were all flung off their feet. The roaring boom was deafeningly loud. The crag struck, bounced, struck again, ground along for a moment, rolled, and started to break up. Three of its shards struck the pinnacles crowning the hillside, then toppled onto whatever was left of Qarlegon's force.

"Well," a particularly stupid cornugon said from somewhere near the height, "at least it struck down the intruder, too! Nothing could have s—"

He was one of the ones crushed to nothingness, a moment later, when blue fire brought a castle-sized fragment of the great stone out of empty air to crash down on the height, smearing most of Geryon's force to smoking ichor in an instant.

The Overduke and Grimvold exchanged glances, but neither moved from where they stood. "She's gone," the old pit fiend said grimly. "That was a last thrust."

Geryon nodded, folding his massive arms across his chest. "Gone to seek Nergal and his captive human, or I miss my guess."

Grimvold sighed. "Do we whelm an army?"

The Wild Beast smiled coldly. "No. Let Nergal, rightful Prince of Hell that he is, do a little mustering and commanding. Avernus welcomes all."

The scarred pit fiend smiled slowly at the old saying. The two old devils stood together on the hilltop as a breeze whipped around them, bringing the scent of death. Both breathed deeply, remembering good old days of blood and battle and torment.

* * * * *

The Simbul stood alone atop a dark needle of rock somewhere in Avernus. Her long silver hair lashed the blood-red air as she caught her breath. She was still weak from boosting a mountaintop across half a Hell to crush her foes, a bare breath or three after whisking poor howling-insane Halaster back to Toril. Still, even slaughtering a thousand devils instead of a paltry hundred meant nothing, if she missed the one called Nergal. Even now her magics were drifting out to sniff the tortured gorges and ridges of Avernus for any trace of—there!

She unleashed the bolt without a moment's hesitation, sending blue fire streaking across Avernus. Hello, devil. Welcome to a life truly in Hell, brought to you by the queen of Aglarond, dainty human hide and all . . .

* * * * *

Blue fire crashed and roared. Nergal tumbled through the air, his body aflame. *AARRGH! PAIN!* he roared, with both mind and voice. He worked frantic magic even before he smashed to ground.

Snatching magics. He and Elminster were abruptly elsewhere. Somewhere dark and private and dripping, a cavern that had none of the tumult of Avernan hillsides.

[claws grimly clinging]

WIZARD, SHOW ME MORE VIVID MEMORIES, OMITTING NOTHING. WHATEVER WAS TRYING TO SLAY US, IT CAN'T REACH HERE.

Oh? Ye'd bet on that?

I WOULD AND HAVE, HUMAN. WITH BOTH OF OUR LIVES, OF COURSE.

[equal parts respect and reproach, images silently proffered]

Elminster looked up from pages that glowed with glyphs of deep blue and gleaming copper hue. Though his expression was mild, the glint in his eye matched the metal of the symbols. "The hour is late . . . the lamps burn low. Thy ever-borrowed wit grows harsh on these old ears. Unburden thyself without delay."

Torm nodded, smiled sweetly, and swung himself up to perch atop a precarious pile of parchments. Dust rose about him in a shadowy cloak. He matched Elminster's long-suffering look with one of his own, set his chin in his hand, and echoed the Old Mage's own tones. "I've a few words to impart, old friend; let us discourse together awhile."

I'M SUPPOSED TO BE IMPRESSED AND LEARN MY LESSON? THAT I AM ACTING THE PART YOU PLAY IN THIS REMEMBRANCE, AND YOU NOW MOCK ME AS THIS TORM DID YOU? WELL, YOUR PLOY HAS WORKED, LITTLE MAN: I AM IMPRESSED.

YOU MAY HAVE LITTLE LIKING, I FEAR, FOR THE RESULT.

I CAUGHT SIGHT OF A FEW MEMORIES, SOME WHILE BACK, THAT TOLD ME YOUR MYSTRA SET YOU THE TASK OF TRAINING THE SEVEN SISTERS. I'M GOING TO WATCH THAT TEACHING—OR WHAT YOU STILL RECALL OF IT—AND SEE HOW THEY, THROUGH YOU, LEARNED THEIR POWERS.

[bright images flying]

NO. NO, DON'T SHOW ME. THIS TIME I'LL DIG AND FIND WHAT I FIND—NOT WHAT YOU WANT TO SHOW ME.

IF THE JOURNEY PAINS YOU, REMEMBER WHOM YOU HAVE TO THANK FOR ITS NECESSITY, OVERCLEVER LITTLE STRUTTING THING.

Not a wise idea, devil, but I suppose ye'll have to learn that the hard way. . . .

I THANK YOU FOR YOUR KIND CONCERN, MIND-SLAVE. MAKE SURE TO GROVEL AS WE GO!

[mind bolt, wince and stagger, tentacles drumming impatiently as their owner strides on, and in, and down . . .]

I have so little left. I can't think . . . no, can't remember. Much of anything. I am empty, almost empty, all poured out into this devil. I am . . . almost nothing. Down to the last, now, all my spell lore gone to him while I noticed nothing, all the years of faces and names—even the shames I hide from myself, most days. Down to the last things, long buried and forgotten. My last little secrets. Gods, so many wearying years, and I'm still not ready to let it all go and drift away into the darkness. . . .

El, ye always were a selfish bastard.

Mystra, forsake me not. Preserve me. Please.

[images flaring up]

Elminster's mouth was suddenly very dry. "Gods, but she's beautiful," he said involuntarily.

His scrying-stone showed him a tall, slender lady in black leather and purple silk striding along the path. Her glossy cascade of midnight-black hair gleamed in the sun. Her skin was white and smooth, her face . . . words failed him. Hope stirred in him, just a little, and he let it dance near his heart. He had been so lonely for so long.

His blood boiled. *Love her, of course, but don't lose yourself in her. This one* will *betray you.*

The Srinshee spoke to him seldom these days, and there was so much he wanted to say, to talk over, but—

Elminster's hands tightened on his staff. "She will?" he muttered. "Then why not—?"

No. No, El. You must give her the chance. Mystra lays it upon you, and I think it best. Love her, teach her, but don't lose your heart to her. Make her admire you, and it may give you some guidance over her when she casts you aside to make her own way in the world.

"But how do ye *know* this?" Elminster burst out. He brought his fist down hard on the edge of the polished table. The horned skull on it clattered and the floating shards that had once been a crown jangled eerily.

Later, El. Your lady has arrived.

"I—by the Nine Hells Nergal Desires—"

HAH! YOU DID *READ THOSE BOOKS OF YOURS, DIDN'T YOU?*

"—blast and *damn* all swift-striding would-be apprentices! I—"

The raven-haired woman calmly pushed open the door before he could wipe her image from the floating crystal sphere. She gave it a sidelong glance and a little smile as she strode up to him. Crossing her arms across a magnificent bosom, she stared into his eyes with a look of dark promise. "I understand you're looking for an apprentice." Her voice was a musical purr.

Elminster stroked his beard and tried to look puzzled. "Oh? And how did such a wild understanding come to thee?"

"Mystra told me," the beauty said simply. "Out of the altar I knelt at, last night."

Elminster allowed himself a slow smile. "Well then, of course, I must be. I was thinking more of a small, gruff, very male dwarf this time, instead of—" He sighed. "—*another* young and beautiful human female, but . . . I *suppose* . . . what's thy name, lass?"

"Symgharyl Maruel." She hesitated a moment, coloring a little, and then threw back her head and announced proudly, "At mage fairs I call myself the Shadowsil. I saw your crown of fireballs at the last one, Lord Elminster; *very* impressive."

" 'Lord Elminster'? I hope not. 'Old Mage' sits better on the tongue, or 'El' or even, 'Ho, Longbeard!' So, Lansharra, how would ye like *me* to address *thee*—if, say, we were to dwell together, as master and apprentice, for some ten or twelve summers at least?"

All the color drained out of her face. She swallowed, ducked her head, and asked very carefully, "How is it that you know my true, secret name?"

Elminster gave her a smile that held only kindness, shrugged, and spread his hands in a gesture of innocence. "Mystra speaks to me, too."

DO YOU NEVER STOP? WOMEN, WOMEN, WOMEN—IF YOU HADN'T BEEN ONE FOR A BIT, I'D THINK YOU WERE UTTERLY ADDLED OVER THEM.

I'M NOT SEEING MAGIC, WIZARD! YOU'RE NOT DELUDING YOURSELF INTO THINKING MY PATIENCE IS GROWING, ARE YOU?

On Toril, Mystra is magic.

YES, YE—MEANING? OH. OHO. SHOW ME, WIZARD!

Of course.

Twenty-Two

THE EMPTYING OF ELMINSTER

The voice he loved so well seemed to come curling huskily up out of the fire. "Why Aglarond? Are you growing tired of scouring the same old places, O Sword of Mystra?"

The bearded man in black abruptly stopped his pacing to peer into the crackling flames. "Auluua?" he cried. "Teacher?"

"The same." Flame crackled up in leaping tongues. "I am a little lonely, Prince of Athalantar. The years pass, and I sit waiting of nights . . . and you never call."

Elminster almost ran into the fire, arms outstretched to embrace—nothing. Firelight danced across his face as he swayed above the hearth, sudden tears hissing down into the blaze at his feet.

"Your boots will scorch, El," the Srinshee said, her voice softer now, and less playful. "Stand you back, and leave off weeping, or you'll have me sobbing too."

Almost reluctantly Elminster did as he was bid, staring into the flames. "How is it that ye come to me?" he asked in wonder.

"You called on me—just now, in your muttering. When you said 'This mage murderess must be the Srinshee's peer at hurling deadly spells.' My peer, indeed!"

El grinned and strode across the chamber, waving his hands. "Well, she must be. Look ye: emissaries battle with spells in the palace of Aglarond, and this seneschal-'prentice, the Simbul, who's not been heard from before, hurls them all down with her spells—*thrice!*"

He ran out of room to pace across, and whirled around to stride back. " 'Tis not easy work, impressing Red Wizards, but this mysterious wench has done so mightily. Instead of signing her realm's surrender, Great Queen Ilione signs a *treaty* with Thay that makes them nearly allies! Everywhere among mages I hear talk of this wild-tempered woman and her slaying spells, and they tell of Ilbrul the Ramshorn, who claimed to hail from Netheril, and Englezaer the Enchanter, and the spell hunters Ammarask and Brastimeir the Bold *all* going down in battle against her! Aglarond grows too strong, I say—and this Simbul must be stopped!"

"That roster of the fallen is true, every one . . . and yet, bold lion, there was a time when you *admired* strong she-wizards! Or does your memory of fair Cormanthor and the glorious time of Myth Drannor fade?"

"Nay, but Mystra bids me nurture magic, not stand idly by whilst one ambitious mage, man or maid, cuts down wizard after wizard, snuffing out so much learning in moments!"

"So why have you not long since cloaked yourself in wrath and mighty weavings and lain waste to Aglarond, trampling down this Simbul at its heart? Are you afraid?"

Elminster snorted. "Foolish I may be, but afraid? Only of doing the wrong thing, if I may flatter myself thus far. Nay, whenever I resolve to challenge this Simbul, I hear Mystra whispering, 'Look well, first.' "

"And so?"

"I've been too busy with other matters of magical import and service to Mystra. Yet too much time has passed, and 'tis more than fitting that I now cast down this Simbul . . . after looking at her deeds and manner as Mystra bids, of course."

"You seem to have already made up your mind she must die, Sword of Mystra. Yet it might not prove so simple as all that; do you not fear defeat and death at the hands of this obviously mighty mageslayer? She *is* dangerous . . . she could kill you."

Elminster spread his hands. "I could be overwhelmed and slain at any time, and what will the measure of my life be then? I am nothing but some small part of the service I have done to others."

The flames seemed to shape a smile for him; a smile he knew so well that tears welled up again almost to choke him.

"I fade, El, so heed me now: If you go to Aglarond, go armed for the worst spell battle of your life. Go also with an open mind and prepare to be surprised."

There was a great puff of spark and ash, and the fire went out, plunging the room into darkness.

AHHH, AND YOU WERE SURPRISED. YOU CERTAINLY DID YOUR PART TO MAKE FAIR FAERÛN AN EXCITING PLACE FOR MAGES—BUT I'M STILL NOT SEEING THE SECRET MAGIC I SEEK, AM I?

[bright images flying]

"Rumor, Lord Elminster, runs like a yapping dog; the truth creeps like a silent snail in its wake."

Elminster sighed and nodded. "A nice phrase, Thauntar. Yet the wizards *are* dead—and an impressive heap of them, too."

The one-eyed warrior shrugged in his mismatched old armor and replied, "I try to see truth, as the Lady we both serve taught me to, and I apprehend you may have heard far more than what is true. The treaty is not a war alliance, but a non-aggression pact. Aglarond achieves its own survival—for a few years, at least—and Thay wins an unopposed chance to infiltrate and influence. . . . In the longer term, they will absorb Ilione's realm with a minimum of cost and effort."

Elminster shrugged.

Thauntar raised one rusty gauntlet and added, "Moreover, this agreement was won only after the one called the Simbul slaughtered three sets of visiting Thayan emissaries."

"Aye, and why would she do that? Were they all rude to her?"

"What Thayan isn't rude to nigh everyone outside Thay? But there's more, Lord: All of those envoys turned out to be wizards eager to spell-slay everyone in the palace, once they were settled inside it."

"I heard this Simbul blasts almost every mage she meets with—and yet I can scarce believe the sum of her harvest, in so short a time!"

"*The* Simbul, Lord . . . and mark my words: she destroys only those who strike against Aglarond."

"Oh, come—mages from *Cormyr?*"

"An embassy arrives from a city in Chessenta this very night, Lord. Yet Thayan agents lurk within its ranks. So, too, did Cormyr unwittingly harbor serpents of Thay."

Elminster frowned. "I thank thee for thy counsel, wise Thauntar. I will go and see this Thay-slayer for myself."

"That's always best," the warrior agreed. They nodded and then embraced, clapping each other's shoulders. Waving their hands in salutes, they parted—the one in a whirl of spell sparks, and the other trudging on up over the hill in worn boots.

I suppose you loved him *too, this brawny warrior?*

No, but Mystra did.

And?

And nothing. He died.

Hah! Her time and attention wasted!

Not so. She does not regard humans as tools, to be measured by their usefulness to her ends of the moment, but rather as flowers to be nurtured in a garden. Each passing year holds a better display, and affords grander possibilities.

[diabolic snort, clawing aside of memories like cobweb curtains, pain visited on gasping wizard]

Stop wasting my time, Elminster.

The Mouth of Moreyeus shuddered in open fear as the slender, wild-haired woman in the simple mauve gown languidly made the hand sign for peaceful parley. Her waist was girt about with a sash, not a belt, and she bore no weapon. Even her feet were bare on the grass of the courtyard.

"Aglarond bids you welcome," she said with a smile that held sly amusement. Her hair was a fall of white splendor, but her eyes were dark mysteries. "All who would be our true friends are welcome here."

Behind the gold-bedecked, many-ringed Mouth, in his gold-woven garments and spade beard, the other envoys and factors regarded her in silence. Some trembled openly. Others clenched white hands on weapons or talismans. Not a few were drenched with sweat.

She gave them all a warm, almost motherly smile and turned to lead them up the last bends of the path. Gracious and regal she seemed, more a ruler than an apprentice. Only a few stray motes of light, drifting like restless stars in her wake, revealed the might of her risen Art—a spell shield that would turn any treachery striking at her back. Not a man present thought that those little stars were visible by accident. 'Twas said that leaves did not dare drop in Aglarond without the Simbul's expressly granted will.

The path wound amid pools of lily pads. Tiny bright fish called sunsilver leaped to snatch gnats from the air. The trail led up across shaded garden slopes to a side entrance of the palace. Warmed by the Simbul's smile as she ushered them across the threshold, the embassy filed within. The seneschal stepped into their wake—and casually blasted certain of the men ahead of her to ash with a bright arc of ravening spells.

The untouched survivors screamed.

Behind a nearby tree, Elminster snarled a soft incantation. It spun an image of himself and set it in midair outside the door.

"Murderess!" he snapped. "Turn and behold thy doom! Thy slaughter has gone on long enough! I challenge thee!"

The bright silver lance of the spell that would have blasted him, had he been a living man, lashed out even before she spun around, eyes flashing. "Begone, minion of Thay."

"I am no friend to Thay," the bearded, floating man in black told her.

"If you do their work, you are a Thayan to me. All enemies of Aglarond are Thayans at heart, whatever allegiance they profess," she snapped back.

Elminster raised an eyebrow. "Come forth and fight," he said softly, "Slayer-from-behind."

"I invited possible spies and vipers into this, the palace of the great queen," the Simbul replied, darting a look behind her at coughing, staggering men. Lost in the smoke of her spells, they were blindly swinging swords. "They are thus my responsibility. I choose when and where to fight, man—and have no interest in petty duels. Get you gone."

Elminster gave her a crooked smile in reply. He turned, eyes never leaving hers, and aimed his arm like crossbow. Bright bolts lashed out from his fingers. A palace turret flew apart and collapsed into the gardens with a roar.

That made her mouth gape open. His smile tightening, Elminster lifted his other hand and toppled a slender trio of spires.

Eyes blazing, the Simbul raised both hands over her head. From linked fingers, she smote him with a hungry flood of lightning.

The titanic bolt roared forth, shredding his spell-spun image in an instant. It bounced and screamed its way through the gardens and out of sight, quite drowning out Elminster's brief gasp of pain as he shuddered behind his tree.

"Ha!" the Simbul cried in triumph.

In reply, the turret beside the doorway where she stood blazed from top to bottom with sudden ruby flames—slumped into a hot river of rock.

"Fight me, or lose your palace," a door gong beside her explained calmly. With a shriek of rage the Simbul turned and blasted it.

Another turret crashed down, and a sentry's helm rolled out of its ruin past the Simbul's feet. "Oh, is this a race to bury Ilione's throne?" it asked.

The Simbul's eyes burst into flames. Her hair writhed around her in a tempest as she rose into the air, arms as swift as speeding arrows. "Reveal my foe!" she howled. The air around her crackled with gathered power. *"Show me this snake!"*

Abruptly the sky filled with curving trails of force, a great web of crisscrossing paths . . . and *there*, behind a tree, a man who even now was weaving another spell.

The Simbul hurled tears of death at him, a magic whose slowly descending curtains of force would block any translocation. She snapped the word that would bring her girdle of sceptors from her chambers to her.

Even as she buckled it around her waist, bright blades of force sheared away her deadly curtains, sending their energies spinning through the air. One whirling fragment became a snarling ball of flame and crashed among cottages downhill. It shook the ground, and fires rose there with greedy speed.

The Simbul turned from that destruction and tearfully screamed out her rage. Two of her scepters tore open the ground under her foe's feet, spilling him end over end down the garden.

Few wizards would have dared to use both of those wands together. The magic snarling out of them seared the Simbul's hands. Rampant energy clawed its way up and down her body, almost choking her. She bounded barefoot forward through the air and screamed, "Take this fray elsewhere, man, or so help me, I'll bind us together with spells and hurl myself into the heart of Water-deep—or an inner chamber of Candlekeep!"

Needles of force that were curling around her like gigantic pincers slowed to a stop. Her challenger's voice came back to her: "Where, then?"

"Crommor's Fang," she spat. "Know it?"

"See ye there, murderess," came the level reply—an instant before bolts of force raced down to strike her mantle. The Simbul's world became a deafening inferno of numbing, dancing white fire.

A few familiar words snatched her out of raging doom and hurled her across half the Sea of Fallen Stars to the Fang. She was wont to hurl her wildest magics on it, or lie alone on its rocky height to look up at the stars. This time the Simbul was not kissed by the cool breezes of sunset, but rather muffled, warmed, and slowed in the heart of a bright, shimmering dome of magic.

Mystra, but this man was fast! A dueling ward of old Myth Drannor! She'd seen only one other, and that—

The ground beneath her grew stabbing spears of stone. They thrust up in energetic, many-pointed fury. The Simbul snarled an incantation that would turn them back on their source. One of two of the dissolving razors laid open her legs. She fell hard on unforgiving stone amid ribbons of her own blood.

The stones rocked under her with the fury of a distant explosion. Her challenger had no greater like for his spears than she did. The Simbul smiled grimly and used her trickling blood in a spell that snatched her across the Fang to where another human was bleeding. As the world whirled, she thumbed a locket at her belt and broke a tiny crystal therein.

Magic thrummed like a releasing bow. It rushed out around her, spinning a cage. Nose to nose in its crackling heart—a place where no spells could kindle—the Simbul and her challenger stared at each other. Her magic had happened to capture one of the few trees on the Fang, and its thorny branches groaned as the cage tightened around them. The air would be full of hard-driven splinters in a moment—

A scepter became a knife in her hand and thrust up at his ribs. It bit home. Her hawk-nosed, bearded foe kicked her hard in the crotch, hurling her upward. The knife trailed his blood through the air. Her hand struck a tree branch with numbing force and the knife tumbled away.

The man palmed it out of the air like a juggler. She bounced on the ground, losing her breath in a helpless groan. He pounced, crashing down atop her.

They rolled together. Her tightening magic sang around them. The Simbul saw the knife sweep back for the slash that would lay open her throat.

Desperately she flung up her hand to guard herself. Bright steel burst through it, the wet point jutting out of the back of her hand.

Mystra, such *pain!*

Sobbing uncontrollably, the Simbul thrashed on the ground, seeking to hurl her foe off and away, so she could snatch the fang of her torment *out*, and—

The weight atop her was suddenly gone. A searing chill flowed out of her, and the blade of her dagger melted away like smoke.

Elminster stared down at the silver fire cascading over the Simbul's fingers. Her wound closed, and she winced, shaking her hand as if she could wave away the pain.

"Ye—ye serve Mystra!" he gasped, at last.

She looked up at him from under tresses of suddenly silver hair that curled and writhed like snakes. "Of course," she replied calmly. "Doesn't everyone?"

Twenty-Three

FIRE IN HELL

Echoing darkness, the labyrinth empty . . .

I am afraid. I . . . cannot think. Where are my wits . . . where are my memories? Where am—I? There is nothing left. Nothing but fear. I am afraid. I am so alone. Dark, drifting . . . cold, all the brightness fled away. I am afraid.

AHA! SILVER FIRE AT LAST! BUT IS THIS ALL? HAS YOUR GODDESS SNATCHED AWAY FROM YOU EVERY . . . LAST . . . LITTLE SECRET I CRAVED? I'LL SMASH YOU INTO BONE SHARDS AND POWDER! I'LL MAKE YOU SCREAM FOR AN EON, KEPT ALIVE IN TORMENT, BLIND AND WRITHING, AS LEMURES FEED ON YOU AND THEN VOMIT YOU FORTH FOR THE NEXT TO GNAW ON! I'LL—GAAHH! HUMANS!

Here I am. Over here, in Nergal. Back in my bones, nothing is left. Nothing at all. He has won.

INDEED, PUNY HUMAN WIZARD, HOW COULD IT BE OTHERWISE? [gloating] *YOUR MEDDLING GODDESS MAY HAVE STOLEN HER SILVER FIRE FROM ME, AND HER TRUE SECRETS, TOO, BUT I HAVE YOUR MEMORIES—CENTURIES AND CENTURIES OF WHERE THIS ENCHANTMENT IS HIDDEN AND HOW TO AWAKEN THAT MAGIC, AND ALL THOSE GATES, TOO. . . .*

I DARE NOT STRIDE INTO FAERÛN AND AMUSE MYSELF PROPERLY—BUT OH, HOW MANY DUPES I CAN COMMAND AMONG YOUR CRINGING HUMANS, ARMED

WITH WHAT YOU KNOW AND THE FAVORS OWED YOU TO RAID YOUR TORIL AT WILL AND BRING BACK EVER MORE MAGIC TO ME.... AH, BUT HELL WILL TREMBLE AT LAST!

[whirling images of Avernus, awareness flung far]

AND LET IT BEGIN NOW, WITH THE SMASHING AND HUMBLING OF YOUR LITTLE PLAYTHING, COME CALLING TO SAVE HER ELMINSTER!

[magic rushing out of Nergal like a mad torrent, rolling diabolic laughter, rock pinnacles topple onto a lone human figure]

HAHA!

[Head snaps up. Silver hair writhes. Lightning crackles, bursting rock into dust and rubble, hurled far away. Two eyes glow like flames within the tumult of roiling dust. A low, soft hiss somehow comes across half Avernus to their ears.]

"So, devil. *There* you are. Taste you now what I give to Thay."

[Art rushes, so quick and bright that Nergal grunts in amazement. His bat wings beat in sudden urgency, arching and twisting and—Hell explodes in bright fury. The archdevil spins helpless through shrieking air, a broken human in one fist.]

FIRES OF THE PIT, BUT SHE'S STRONG! WELL, WE'LL JUST HAVE TO ...

Gaze upon her longer. Such grace, even in fury. Fascinating ...

AYE, AYE, SUCH— WHAT ARE YOU DOING, HUMAN? WHISPERING IN MY HEAD WHEN I SHOULD BE—

[bright inferno, roar of diabolic pain, bodies hurled helpless once more, two blazing eyes following amid silver flame]

ENOUGH! ELSEWHERE, AND LET HER FIGHT ACROSS HALF HELL TO FIND US!

Red lightning wreathed them. It died, leaving them elsewhere in Avernus. Nergal's taloned hand came down on Elminster's shoulder and spun a chain and collar out of nothing.

Red lightning came again.

"Right behind us," Nergal growled, "blasting everything that stands against her. From lair to lair of my rivals we go, and let Avernus be laid waste!"

He roared with laughter—and they were elsewhere again. Red smoke and lightning rolled around their feet.

The outcast devil looked back and shook his head in what might have been admiration—or might have been fear.

"Devils tumbling down broken out of the skies," he murmured. "It won't be long before He of Nessus is alerted. I'd not want to be your little lady-love then!"

Lightning again, and darkness. A pit of offal, Elminster chin-deep and strangling on his collar as the firm-held chain kept him from drowning. . . .

COMFORTABLE AGAIN AT LAST. NOW, WHERE WERE WE?

HO. YES. FROM ONE SPELL DUEL TO ANOTHER. STILL, 'TIS BETTER THAN THE LAST MEMORY WE SHARED: SEDUCING APPRENTICES SEEMS A MITE HOLLOW AFTER HELL-HARROWING AT THE HANDS OF PERSISTENT GODDESSES.

Hmm. I fear ye require more refined judgment than ye presently possess.

[snort of dismissal, single mind lash] CLEVERNESS LATER, WIZARD. SHOW TIME NOW.

[image proffered]

WHY, THAT'S STIRRING IN ME! WHERE ARE YOUR—

Deep within ye, devil. Ye have it all, now. Elminster in thy head.

I—I—

See her, devil. Such magnificence, as she throws back her head and glares fearlessly around Hell, seeking us. See her as I do. How can one break or bend such a bright blade? She could be everything to ye! She could be thy warrior-scourge of Hell, smiting all who stand against thee, loving thee as fiercely and hungrily as she now slays. . . .

TONGUE OF ASMODEUS, HUMAN! YOU ALMOST MAKE ME WANT TO—

Remember her lips, her silver hair lashing and then caressing . . .

YES. OHHH, YES.

Recall her embrace, her murmured promises, her—

YES. YES! THIS IS THE ONE FOR ME!

Aye, see that memory again, as we—

Are hurled back again, Hell crashing and quaking around us, as the scepters that the Simbul had plunged into her own flesh like daggers boil away with the last of their power exhausted and are gone. She shudders, going to her knees amid the flames of strewn devil-corpses and shattered stone citadels, and we want to reach out to her, to draw her close and comfort her, to heal. . . .

Eyes look up and catch flame once more. "*You!*" Her growl rises into a scream that spits raw, snarling power out of her.

Nergal knows pain.

AARGHH! NESSUS TWIST YOU, BITCH! I—I—

Love thee. Love thee more than all the fires of Hell.

YES! [slaying bolt hurled wide] *YE—NO! FANGS, HUMAN, WHAT ARE YOU DOING TO ME? GET OUT OF MY HEAD!*

The Simbul's next spell rains bright knives of flame down in a hissing cascade of death upon rippling diabolic thews. She spins like a dancer to send the same fury down the throats of the devils now converging on her across the broken rocks of Avernus.

Black and red flesh convulses. Screams rise in a ragged chorus of woe.

Nergal shudders and catches hold of a nearby horn of rock to steady himself, gasping at the pain.

I CANNOT SMITE HER! SHE'S SO BRIGHT, SO BEAUTIFUL! I MUST HAVE HER, I MUST—ALASSRA, HERE I AM! HERE!

The Lord to Come of All Deep Hell bounds into the air, tentacles become mighty wings, arms spread in welcome.

QUEEN OF ME, HERE I—

The bolt that shocks out of the Simbul is so fierce that it plucks her from her feet and hurls her backward. As she falls, she sends her will riding along the beam, to pierce the mind of her foe even as the bright lance of her silver fire stabs him.

[In a brief glimpse across Avernus, a lone human female rises into the air like a beacon, her hair a halo of flame around her. Devils everywhere wince and roar and cringe. Distant mountains erupt in smoke and flame.]

Silver fire crashes into hot darkness, roiling . . .

El, I am come.

I live, and love thee. I am in this devil, all of me. Mystra, but ye are magnificent!

[amusement] *But of course.*

Nergal, roaring in torment at the fire raging in him, the Simbul ruthless in her scorching and searing, leaving him a broken sHell that lives only because her Elminster is trapped within it, only to fade as her fire does, fade away . . .

No, leave me not!

NO, LEAVE ME NOT! FADE NOT FROM— WHAT AM I SAYING?

OUT, HUMAN WORM. OUT OF MY MIND! YOU INFECT ME, YOU—GET YOU GONE!

[Nergal summons all of his power, a black-and-red wave, dark and swift enough to shatter even the Simbul's fury. He *thrusts.* Images whirl in insane chaos, brightness like shards of shattering glass, memories and tears and laughter all together, into the thing in the offal pit. A naked human retches and squirms as Hell is torn apart around him.]

NOW, WITCH, IT'S YOUR TURN!

[Red-and-black bolts howl out of the great winged devil, cleaving the blood-red sky like reaching fingers.]

Crash, stagger, bright beauty still standing . . .

Bloody lips twist. "Is that the best you can do, devil?" Slender fingers point, and fire surges forth, a little wearily now . . .

Burst of blue-white fire, Nergal screaming . . .

[frantic red lightning, and flight]

THIS HAS GOTTEN OUT OF HAND! WHERE IS ASMODEUS? WHERE ARE THE HOSTS OF HELL? IS SHE GOING TO BE ALLOWED TO KILL US ALL?

FIRES OF THE PIT, SHE CAN STRIKE AT ME THROUGH YOU!

[mind bolt, dark and huge, sent to slay, roaring through the vaults . . .]

[. . . and rebounding back through the darkness to slap down Nergal]

* * * * *

Sobbing and convulsing, the tentacled devil rolled in darkness, his chain melting away.

"Sorry," said the naked, filthy man beside him. He waved stumps that were his arms. "We're too closely linked now, devil, for *that* to work."

With a sudden, furtive movement, Elminster raised one arm to touch what was tangled in his hair. He said in his mind, cold and crisp and hard, *By the will of Tanthul and my need, let it be my bone shards, yonder—and let it be* now.

Nergal had just time to dart a look at his mind-slave before the bone fragments in him expanded into duplicates of the larger bones they'd been a part of—and the archdevil's body burst apart with a deep, wet roar.

[song, mad music wild and screaming, red fire and staring, disbelieving diabolic eyes, fading to darkness . . . oblivion]

Alone and maimed in a cavern deep in Avernus, Elminster went to his knees and sobbed bitterly. The mind that had ridden his for a seeming eternity was stilled and gone. . . .

It's a dark thing to lose any being one knows so well.

*   *   *   *   *

[red, writhing pain, drifting back so slowly through torment, at last to the light . . .]

"Fires take all," Nergal muttered, as weak and sick as he always was when coalescing back from tattered smoke and essence to solidity once more. He glared around blearily at the offal-choked cavern and the small, round black stone that was always there when he cheated death. More mighty contingency magic spent, wasted because of carelessness.

"That was a near one," he whispered, not yet strong enough to growl. "I'll never reign in Hell if I go on underestimating humans."

"Too true," a voice said sweetly, from behind him.

Nergal, rightful Prince of Hell, whirled around as quickly as he could on rubbery limbs. He stared into the smiling face of the Witch-Queen of Aglarond, who floated less than an arm's-reach away.

Her smile was as wide as that of a wolf, and her eyes were two dark flames.

"Go down forever, devil," she hissed—and spread her hands. Holy water that was afire with blue-white and silver flames burst over him in a torrent. The last thing Nergal ever heard was the Simbul snarling, "For what you did to the one I love, I just wish I could slay you again and again!"

*   *   *   *   *

A dark, scaled hand set down a goblet that smoked and bubbled green in the gloom. "How amusing," Asmodeus observed from his throne of linked, living she-devils, and meant it.

Idly the Lord of Nessus reached out. Slaying magic built and snarled darkly up his arm and filled his cupped hand. When his palm was full, he'd flick his wrist and sent it to Avernus. There it would slay the exhausted, sobbing human sorceress whose image floated above him. She even now embraced the ruined, armless body of a man in a hidden cavern, all her attention bent to pouring her vitality into him.

Asmodeus started to smile. Ah, sweet irony . . .

* * * * *

In a void of drifting stars, Mystra drew the howling man from her breast. She held Halaster out to face a whirling vision—the greatest devil of all smiling as dark fire filled his hand. She whispered urgently, "Now!"

Halaster Blackcloak broke off a slobbering sound that was half-howl and half-giggle, drew himself up with dark eyes blazing, and snapped, "Asmodeus! Bow *down!*"

The Lord of Hell turned his head in astonishment—and across the voids and spheres and drifting chaos, their eyes met.

With a crooked smile Halaster Blackcloak said the word of the spell Mystra had taught him. All his raving madness roared out into Asmodeus, jolting that elegant body.

Those amused and sinister eyes rolled up and leaked golden fire. That quirked mouth parted in a cry of astonished agony. The fire of that titanic spell raged through the devil's mind.

As Mystra firmly closed the link between void and Nessus, Asmodeus blinked at the gloom all around and took another sip from his goblet. Now, what was it he'd been going to do? Something amusing . . .

* * * * *

Mystra laid down the black-robed wizard like a little doll on his own bed deep in Undermountain, patted the heads of his guardian deep dragons, and turned back to the void and the waiting arms of Azuth.

As they floated together, she sighed, smiled, and said, "I *do* love happy endings."

Before he kissed her, Azuth frowned and said gently, "That might well prove a problem in the future."

* * * * *

In Avernus, the black flames that had been Nergal died down. A lemure sniffed and flowed hungrily toward the smell. The fury that had blazed here, scorching rocks that had been scorched so many times before, was spent. For now.

Twenty-Four

BRIEF EXCITEMENT IN AGLAROND

"May I present," the Masked One said in amused tones, handing the lovely gowned lady forward with a flourish, "Thorneira Thalance, now Acting Crown Regal of Aglarond."

Phaeldara looked up from the throne. "Not for another three breaths, she isn't. And didn't the Crowned Fury say to just call ourselves regent now, and abandon all these titles that give envoys and heralds such fits?"

"That's why I do it," the Masked One replied with a chuckle. "Three breaths, my right haunch! You should have been up off there at least two breaths ago!"

The courtiers and envoys ranged along the walls leaned closer so as not to miss a moment or nuance of merriment.

Phaeldara rose, tall and elegant, and said plaintively to Evenyl, who sat on a lounge floating nearby, "Was *ever* a woman so wronged?"

The fourth sometime-regent looked up with an innocent smile and held up her hand with fingers spread to use for counting items off. "Oh, let me think. There was—"

A flash and rumble shook the throne room. The regals whirled around as courtiers gasped and murmured along the walls. They all fell silent at what they saw.

The Witch-Queen of Aglarond stood in the center of the chamber, as naked as the day she was born—naked, battered, and entwined.

Her hair swirled and writhed around her shoulders as if it were alive as she glared around the room. Her eyes were two dark and deadly stars. If wearing nothing but smears of soot and dung and blood bothered her, she showed no sign of it.

Her arms were around the waist of a bony, bearded, filth-covered old man with stumps where his forearms should have been. He was sagging, bent over limply like a child's broken doll; it was clear only her grip kept him from falling. Firmly she caught hold of his hair and laid his head back over her shoulder. Then she smiled down the room into the astonished faces of the regals.

"To coin a phrase," the Witch-Queen of Aglarond said dryly, "We're back."

As if in reply, explosions of black-tinged fire burst into roiling existence behind her, amid shrieks from the watching courtiers. A brimstone reek filled the room. Grinning devils strode forth from the flames, long-horned and bat-winged, tusked and terrible. Their talons stretched out to snatch the Simbul and the man in her arms.

"Geryon, Overduke of Hell, sends us," one of them said smugly, "to fetch you back to your deaths—in long, long torment!"

The Simbul whispered a word. Lightning raged from the tiles under the devils' hooves to the ceiling high above and back again. There were faint cries—then nothing but empty tiles and the oily smoke of diabolic bodies collapsing.

The Witch-Queen smiled through those remnants.

Another rank of devils emerged from the flames. They wore rather smaller smiles.

"Did you really believe seizing me in my own lair was going to be easy? Here I stand not alone."

A tongue of blue-white flame leaped up from her empty hand. Behind her the regals, with set, determined faces, held out their own hands to cup more feeble blue flames.

"Neither, witch," said a courtier loudly, lifting his own hand and letting swirling magic fill it, "do they!"

"Aye," said another, farther down the hall, throwing aside his cloak. "For Thay!"

"Yes," came a third voice, hard and cold. "Let the queen and Aglarond fall together, for the greater glory of Thay!"

Eyes blazing, an old courtier snatched a dagger from his belt and thrust it into the throat of the revealed Red Wizard beside him. The room erupted in shouts and spells.

The doors by the throne burst open. Thaergar of the Doors strode in with a bright new sword drawn. He stared open-mouthed at the tumult, then snatched and hurled a dagger from his belt—straight back out the door at the alarm gong.

He charged forward, raising his blade. Red flames burst out of the air in front of him, hurling him to the floor. He glared up at that dark magic in time to see a huge, ruby-red devil stride out of it, fork in one hand and barbed whip in the other, to loom over Phaeldara, foremost of the regals.

"Pretty meat," it gloated, reaching for her.

Thaergar of the Doors and Phaeldara stared at the pit fiend, the Red Wizards and charging devils beyond, and deadly magics singing and snarling everywhere.

"Oh, *dung*," they gasped in unintentional unison.

* * * * *

The air above a table commenced to shimmer. Tiny silver and blue sparks whirled out of thin air to race around each other in a small, tight sphere.

Their radiance made a head snap up, and two eyes glared at them in astonishment and alarm.

A moment later, a chair went over with a crash. The man who'd been sitting in it crossed the room with surprising speed for someone of his age. He snatched down two crossed, rusty daggers from beneath a shield on the wall. In his hands they twisted and became a wand and a scepter. Pointing them both at the whirling lights, the Royal Magician of Cormyr snarled, "How, by all the whims of Holy Mystra, did that get through the wards? And what *is* it?"

In obliging answer, the whirling lights sank a little and unfolded themselves downward to the floor in a cascade of silver. They formed a wraithlike figure: a female elf of tiny, nigh-perfect beauty, who looked perhaps nine years old—except for her eyes, which were as old and wise as those of a goddess . . . or at least a Chosen who has seen many centuries.

Vangerdahast lowered his wand and scepter. "Who . . . are you?" he asked hoarsely.

"Most call me the Srinshee," she replied. "You and I are both needed, right now, in the throneroom of Aglarond."

"Aglarond? *Why?*"

"Elminster is there, embattled and in urgent need of us both—and Mystra bids us come," she said simply, and held out her hand.

Vangerdahast stared at her for a moment. An almost fierce joy flashed across his face. He ran across the room like an eager young man. "Yes!" he snarled, eyes bright. "Oh, *yes!*"

*   *   *   *   *

Men shouted, ran, and snatched out swords in the throneroom of Aglarond. Spells crashed and devils pounced. They also reeled, screamed, and died.

Blistering fire burst among shrieking courtiers. Men who'd been enthusiastically plunging daggers into a Red Wizard vanished into crackling columns of ash.

Among the terrified sprinting and shoving, a serving-maid let fall her silver tray with a crash as a devil's talons clawed at her bodice. Thrusting a slender arm, she drove her hand right through the grinning pit fiend. It vanished with a roar of blue flames and a terrified shriek.

A Red Wizard stared at the maid in astonishment as she reached for the next nearest devil, her eyes aglow, and snapped, "This is quite *enough.*"

There was a double flash this time. Maid and devil vanished together . . . but where Mystra had been, nine silver stars floated, tracing an upright circle around a blue flame.

There was barely time for all the color to drain out of the Red Wizard's face before that flame died and the stars rushed to the floor and vanished. Where each touched the tiles, a startled being suddenly stood, staring around at the raging battle.

"Khelben Blackstaff," the Red Wizard gasped, eyes bulging, "and—the *Seven!* All of them!" He was to be forgiven for not announcing the arrival of the mages Vangerdahast and a wraithlike lady elf, where the last two stars touched down. . . .

A moment later Khelben lashed three devils with howling bolts of lightning. A certain Red Wizard, caught in the wrong place, ceased to care about anything ever again.

Rage blazed on the face of the Lord Mage of Waterdeep. With a growl, he tossed his black staff into the air. It hung there, motionless and horizontal, crackling with magic. Many of the beams and bolts snarling across the room veered to it and blazed in harmless spell chaos.

That left the air clear enough for everyone to see the Simbul, on her knees shielding Elminster. She thrust up her hand to send silver fire out to all of her sisters. In turn from each of them a beam spat forth, vaporizing any devil it touched.

"Sister," Dove gasped, "what're you *doing?* Mystra forbids—"

"Not now she doesn't," the Witch-Queen of Aglarond snapped grimly. "Behold!"

Her hand this time pointed to the shimmering air above Khelben's staff.

The trapped, roiling spells were rapidly being transformed into a shining spider web of magic. Glowing, ever-shifting lines of power rapidly filled the air. The ghostly form of the Srinshee raced along and among them. The web winked as it swiftly grew, and was already almost too bright to look at.

"The Weave!" the Simbul snapped. She swung her arm around to point to the entry arch, where shadows gathered. "And our foe!"

No, not shadows—a web of dark lines that mirrored the Weave. Strangers were entering through the archway below it: mages wielding wands and staves, who chanted, "Shar! Shar!"

"An anti-Weave?" one of the older courtiers gasped. "Can there be such a thing?"

A dark-robed courtier beside him gave the gaping man a snakelike smile—and slapped a tentacle around the elder man's neck, snapping it with casual ease. "Indeed there can," he remarked almost merrily to the toppling corpse. "And some of us who walk in shadows see our bright future in it!"

All down the chamber men and women and devils were dying as spell wrestled with spell. Magic slew with terrifying speed. Three devils pounced on the Simbul, trying to wrench her head off. One frantically thrust talons into her mouth to stop her shouting spells.

The dirty, trembling man she'd been torn away from lay forgotten on the tiles. A titanic crash nearby roused him to wakefulness. He peered around at the spell battle, shook his head in disgust or despair . . . and started to crawl forward. He passed among sprawled bodies and the rubble falling from the ceiling. The walls of the room were rippling, goaded by wild, clashing magic.

The Simbul struggled against determined devils. Bolts of dark magic spat from the Shar-worshipers and smote the tiles around the crawling man, showering him with stone shards.

He seemed not to notice, but struggled on, slithering across the room in a manner not all that different from the maggots of Avernus.

"Who—?" shouted a Sharran mage, as he caught sight of the crawling man. "Stop him!"

That cry came too late for those who trust in dark dreams. Elminster Aumar, who long ago had herded sheep in the forgotten land of Athalantar, fell forward. His battered, pain-racked face touched the silver tray that had fallen from the hands of Mystra.

A roar echoed around the throne room. Everyone stopped and turned. Even spell blasts and the screams of the dying hushed. It was the roar of massive magic unleashed, Mystra's power left behind for her Chosen.

In its blue, raging heart stood a man, a wizard made whole again, a figure of white fire tinged with blue around its edges.

He strode from where the tray had been, swaying in the throes of power that made the very air throb.

Beams lanced out from Elminster's trembling fingers and glaring eyes—to smite devil and Red Wizard, Malaugrym and Sharran alike, consuming them in sighing instants until none were left in the throneroom.

The Old Mage leveled both his hands to point at the shadowy web filling the end of the room. Blinding flames of blue-white and silver roared forth from his palms.

The explosion that followed left only bright sky and crumbling ashes in that end of the palace. Elminster blinked at the destruction with the same awe felt by the others still alive in the throneroom. In the ringing silence that followed, the shattered roof above them groaned loudly and started to fall.

Blocks of stone rained down, ponderous and deadly. If it hadn't been for bright bolts fired so frantically by the crouching Seven and the blasts emitted by the Blackstaff, the roof might have claimed the lives of everyone in that place.

Instead, dust rained down, thick and choking, bringing with it an almost ominous quiet.

*　*　*　*　*　*

The sky was darkening into purple dusk before true peace came to the dust-shrouded throne of Aglarond. Gone were the courtiers, corpses, and those sent by Mystra. The throne room stood open to the sky. Fallen stone blocks lay strewn here and there beneath the winking stars.

Elminster and the Simbul stood together in each other's arms. Three regals knelt a little distance away, awaiting their queen's command. The fourth regal was missing, but they kept their thoughts away from her face and name. There would be time enough for grieving yet.

"Oh, my love," the Simbul said fiercely, "When I thought I'd lost you ..."

"Gently," Elminster murmured, kissing her nose and brow and ears. " 'Tis done—and hear this, lady of my heart: I vow henceforth to spend more time with thee and let Faerûn run more of its own affairs without my meddling."

"That shall be my vow, too," the Queen of Aglarond said in a trembling voice. She reached for his lips with her own.

"Well said," hissed a voice from rubble nearby.

Phaeldara lay trapped with Thaergar of the Doors, pinned under a slab of roof thrice their combined size. It had been prevented from crushing them outright only by the twisted ruin of his sword and a shield he'd snatched from the wall in the heart of the fray. Even so, the weight upon them prevented their calling out. "Let this ... be a vow both of you ... keep!"

"Aye," Thaergar gasped, wincing as Phaeldara squirmed beside his shattered arm. "I cleave . . . most heartily . . . to the same view!"

The three kneeling regals heard them and shrieked—cries that brought Elminster and the Simbul running.

As the spells that would free them were hastily chanted, the fainting man and the woman under the fallen stone thought they heard something else.

A strange echoing mirth that just might have been a god and goddess of magic chuckling, not so far away . . .